Dedica

To Adam M, with thanks.

Author Note

This book is a work of fiction, intended as entertainment, and should not be construed as an attempt to accurately depict the places, events or culture of any real historical period. I have included a number of deliberate anachronisms in my fantasy version of 9th Century Arabia.

Janine Ashbless

Praise for Janine Ashbless's
Heart of Flame

"A fantastic read for any genre lover. *Heart of Flame* gets better and better as the tension builds page after page."
~ *Sizzling Hot Book Reviews*

Heart of Flame

Janine Ashbless

To Lisa

— Thank you so much
for getting me naked!
xxx
Janine

SAMHAIN
PUBLISHING

Samhain Publishing, Ltd.
11821 Mason Montgomery Road, 4B
Cincinnati, OH 45249
www.samhainpublishing.com

Heart of Flame
Copyright © 2012 by Janine Ashbless
Print ISBN: 978-1-60928-819-8
Digital ISBN: 978-1-60928-752-8

Editing by Sue Ellen Gower
Cover by Angela Waters

First Samhain Publishing, Ltd. electronic publication: December 2011
First Samhain Publishing, Ltd. print publication: November 2012

Chapter One

In which snow melts in the High Atlas.

Not all the world belongs to Man.

In the thin air over the mountain range something moved, high above the stony wastes of the middle slopes and the upper line of the pines. Something pale against the deep sky and dark against the snowfields. An observer, if there had been one, might have seen that it was eggshell blue in color, rippled with subtle shades like shadows on ice. A long strip of silk, sheer and delicate, it undulated like a live thing as it hung in midair, snakelike where no snake had any right to be. And it moved against the wind, not with it.

Scudding over the glacial slopes, the silken banner closed upon a shoulder of the mountainside from behind which steam was rising. Cresting the saddle, it paused momentarily, describing a loose-woven knot. The rise concealed from below a sheltered bowl of rock that had, until recently, been full of snow. Now meltwater was trickling over boulders and tunneling into the snowdrifts below. The source of the heat was a rent in the hillside, a pool filled with the sullen glow of heaving lava. On a spit of rock jutting out over the magma knelt a man.

It would not have been possible to mistake him for human. No human man could have crouched there in that heat without his lungs being scorched and blistered at the first breath. Besides, he was taller than most men—and broadly muscular too, though his height made him look sinewy—and all over the ash-colored skin of his bare torso and arms and scalp were tattooed lines of a script that seemed to crawl and flow in the heat ripple. He was staring into the air that danced directly over the centre of the magma.

The silken veil descended to the shoreline and coiled about itself as if encompassing an unseen column. As the coils tightened, the shape described beneath took on feminine curves, and then suddenly there wasn't a wisp of silk there at all, but a slim young woman with feathery white hair. She was naked except for a broad belt of spun silver that draped her loins and hung down to her perfect ankles, and her nipples were pale blue, like ancient ice. She stared at the rippled muscles of the man's back.

"Yazid!" she said in a silvery voice. "Here again?"

The man glanced over his shoulder. Black arched brows were the only hairs that ornamented his head. His irises were as colorless as ice and his mouth downturned with displeasure. With a grunt he reached into the lava at his feet and scooped a handful out, flinging it in her direction. She held out her hand and the molten glob of rock flew apart into a scatter of glowing pebbles that spun round her before shrinking, losing their color and becoming a hanging veil of uncut crystals, a diamond halo. He showed no particular sign of surprise.

"Isn't there any place I may call my own, Zubaida?"

She ignored his protest. "Is she so beautiful that you have to watch her night and day?"

"Judge for yourself." With a hand that had been plunged unscathed into molten rock but looked quite ordinary, except that the nails were black and curved to points like the talons of a bird of prey, he indicated a mirage that hung in the heat shimmer—the figure of a woman in an embroidered robe of peacock blue. Zubaida strolled forward along the edge of the magma pool for a clearer look.

"She is beautiful," she admitted. "For a mortal."

The visionary woman was sitting alone by a pool of water, one knee folded up, one hand playing idly with the strings of pearls looped about her throat. Her face was still and pensive. The object of her gaze was a small book whose open pages revealed elaborately written text. Her youthful skin had none of the pallid tone of her two observers and her long hair fell in dark curls, netted by a glinting filigree of sapphires and gold thread.

"The most beautiful woman in all the lands of Al-Sham and of Persia."

"But still," Zubaida said, "only mortal."

"Only? Ahleme is of the bloodline of Solomon and Bilqis, though she doesn't know it. Don't you see the resemblance?"

"She looks...somewhat like the queen used to, I suppose."

"A perfect scion, after all these centuries."

Zubaida's delicate features rearranged themselves in an expression of restrained dismay. "What are you planning, Yazid?"

"I'm thinking that she would look well in my bed."

"Is that your idea of vengeance?"

"And that if she were to bear me a child..."

"A child?"

"Heh. I thought that might discomfort you."

"That's...unthinkable."

"Yet I have thought it. And it seems good to me."

"She's a Daughter of Earth! Toy with her if you like, but—a child?"

"A son of the blood of Solomon and Bilqis, and of our blood. Don't you see? He would have the power of our people—and he would have the authority to erase that which his forebears wrote."

For a long moment Zubaida stared, her eyes diamond pale like his—and diamond hard. "If you were not my brother, then I'd denounce you before the Court of Angels."

Yazid smiled, not pleasantly. "If you were not my sister, then I'd kill you first."

She drew herself up taller. "Besides, you cannot remove her against her will. It is written. You know that."

"But she will come with me willingly. Already I have sent dreams to woo her."

"You'd dishonor all our tribe for the sake of a half-breed

child?"

He rose, a fire in his pale eyes. "I will risk dishonor, Zubaida, so that once more we might all be *free.*"

Chapter Two

In which a wanderer and a sorceress meet,
and it is shown that it is not always easy to act like a man.

The streets of Dimashq-al-Sham, accounted by its inhabitants the oldest inhabited city and Mother of the World, were crooked and crowded and no place for a woman to walk unaccompanied. Even veiled and in company there were places a woman couldn't decently be seen in and conversations she wouldn't be allowed to hear, so the sorceress Taqla bint-Yusef chose to venture out in male appearance that day. Because she liked to feel the sun on her face when the narrow lanes opened up into little squares, and the air on her skin when the parched breeze of summer moved down the sticky alleyways, she went as a humble man clothed only in loose trousers and a little sleeveless jacket open at the front. And because she didn't wish to attract attention, she went in the masculine guise she wore most often—a youngish man with a broken nose and pleasantly ugly features. He was known, by those few who remembered him passing through their lives, as Zahir of the household of Umar, in the Souk of Glass.

Umar, of course, did not exist any more than Zahir did. Both were masks Taqla wore at her convenience.

She loved going out in public this way. Her own house was secluded by its high walls, and the hubbub of the streets rarely disturbed the calm within. To have that sanctuary, and then to be able to emerge from it into the clutter and color and noise outside, filled her with delight. She loved the glint of light on copperware and the smell of roasted mutton and the banter between buyers and sellers. She revelled in the sunbeams that rode the dust between the awnings and the sizzle and pop of roasting nuts on the charcoal braziers at street corners.

In Zahir's guise, Taqla wandered up Straight Street, which was indeed a lot straighter and a great deal broader than the other thoroughfares of Dimashq, and idled through the bazaars that lined it, each twisted passageway a souk specialising in a particular trade—woodwork or perfume, textiles or spices, sweets or soap. It was said that in Dimashq one could buy anything—cosmetics and slaves, silver and brassware, carpets, musical instruments, shoes, olive oil, incense and water pipes. Fruits of all kinds were grown in the city's famous orchards and the finest meats came from the flocks grazed on the slopes of the mountains to the north and west, or along the banks of the river that headed out to die in the desert to the east. The illiterate could have a scribe write or read a letter for them, the sick could seek the refuge-hospitals set up to give them succor, the begrimed could cleanse themselves in the many public bathhouses. The only problem, Taqla often thought, was that you couldn't be in a hurry for any of these things because nothing in Dimashq was found quickly or accomplished urgently. "Patience is the key to the house of happiness," ran the local proverb.

So she rested awhile in a coffeehouse and played three games of backgammon with the local champion, graciously losing two. She listened to the blind storyteller who held court behind the Great Mosque of Caliph Al-Walid and gave him a silver dirham for his story. She haggled for a length of silk rope, which was in theory the goal of her perambulation that day, and struck a reasonable bargain but not so much as to be remembered for it. With the coil of rope worn across her chest, she bought a white dove in the Street of Birds and released it at the foot of the Citadel, in memory of her great-grandfather who had been executed there in the days of the Umayyads, when the practice of sorcery was less tolerated.

These days, now that Dimashq was diminished in greatness and no longer the seat of the caliphate, there was far less danger for those who studied the Art of Solomon, though perhaps not so much because of moral laxity as the fact that the city's rulers now lacked the power and the will to force the issue.

Above all, Taqla gathered news. She heard that Ahleme, eldest daughter of the amir and commonly accounted the most beautiful woman in Dimashq or even all Al-Sham, had, with her entourage, visited a holy shrine up the Barada river and that, although nobody had been permitted to look up from the ground as she passed on camelback, lilies had sprung up along the banks in her wake. Taqla smirked privately at this. She heard that a flock of birds with bronze plumage had been seen near Halba and had laid waste to a village before being driven off by soldiers banging copper pots. That the amir had appointed a Nasrani as his personal doctor. That the price of bread was rising again. That a stone had fallen from the crumbling north wall of the Citadel and killed a goat but narrowly missed a child, by the grace of God. And that Rafiq the Traveller was back in the city.

This last interested her most immediately. There were several merchant-masters in Dimashq who were wealthy enough to equip whole caravans east to Samarqand or south to the coast where the trade vessels from India and Africa docked, but Rafiq was the only one young and restless enough to make the journey with his men. It was always possible he had come into possession of something on his travels that might be of interest to her, so Taqla amended her ambling path through the quarter to take her to the Caravanserai Al-Jurraia, the warehouse that Rafiq's family owned and where he rented rooms to lesser merchants. She was reasonably certain that he would be somewhere in the vicinity if he had recently got back, or that someone there would have his goods list.

Two streets from the caravanserai, she was passing a barber's shop when she happened to glance under the awning and saw a small crowd of men all squatting on the ground. They listened raptly to the customer on the stool, who was having his beard trimmed and his throat shaved and yet was talking calmly while the knife swept up his skin. Taqla paused, wincing inwardly. How did men do that—let a stranger hold a blade to their necks? She was glad that as Zahir she had no need to submit to a shaving. She simply re-imagined him anew, every time she cast the spell.

"...and in the city of Shibam the houses stand eleven stories high, as high as our Citadel tower, even though they are only made of mud-brick," he was saying, his chin lifted and his eyes on the roofline, "and on the tops of these towers stand hollow statues of lions that roar when the wind blows through them." The barber flicked his blade under the man's jaw.

Taqla's eyes narrowed. The client was a reasonably young man, his small beard unmarked by gray hair. He was plainly dressed, but he did carry a scimitar sheathed at his hip. She dropped to her haunches at the back of the audience and whispered, "Friend, who is that man?"

Only half a glance was cast in her direction. "That's Rafiq the Traveller. He's been south to the land of Saba, from where Queen Bilqis came to visit King Solomon the Wise. He's about to seek audience with the amir."

Taqla allowed herself a mental pat of approval. The instinct of a sorcerer is a thing to be cultivated and in the most acute of cases allows them to see the paths of Fate. She had found by chance the man she sought.

"And from Saba comes frankincense and dragon's blood, which is a medicine most difficult to get hold of and most expensive for that reason. The dragons live upon an island off the coast and are slow-moving beasts that feed upon the leaves of certain palm trees. With my own eyes I saw them. They're gray and scaled and larger than a camel, and to draw their blood a man must run in with an awl and drive it between the scales behind the forelegs. When the blood runs out it dries in droplets upon the scales, and when the beasts sleep it can be scraped off. But the men must take great care, because should one drive the awl too deep and cause it pain, it would turn its head from the palm crown and look down, and these beasts are so venomous that a single glance is enough to kill. From Saba I bring a bowl of dried dragon's blood for our amir, and the bowl is of ivory carved in the shape of a sailing ship, the sails and even the rigging carved from ivory too, and the hull set with green emeralds and black pearls."

Taqla felt a stab of interest.

Rafiq carried on talking, encouraged by questions from his audience and barely interrupted by the barber's ministrations as he was shaved and rinsed and a flame was patted to his cheeks to scorch off any stray hairs, then had perfumed oil massaged into his scalp to finish off with. Taqla waited patiently as he wound up his stories, stretched, paid the barber, distributed a few coins to the inevitable beggars who pressed forward, and then took his leave from the company. Only then did she approach him and bow. "Peace be upon you."

"And upon you."

Close up, she found him a handsome, vigorous man, dressed plainly but in finely woven fabrics. His thick black hair was tousled by the massage and he had rather a strong nose. His dark eyes held a good-humored glint—when he took in her appearance, he didn't assume an air of irritated superiority as so many merchants would. But when she reached out with her sorcerous instincts, she thought, *That affability is a mask.* There was something else underneath. She cleared her throat.

"You've recently returned to our city, friend. I trust you are well after your travels." It would be astonishingly rude to launch straight into business talk, so for a few moments they exchanged the usual pleasantries. Then Rafiq spread his hands.

"You must forgive me, my friend, but today I'm truly busy. I must get changed and go seek audience with the amir this afternoon to report upon my caravan's fortunes, and you know that one can be kept waiting for hours in the outer courts..."

"Might I have a moment of your time to walk with you and talk of purchases to be made? I'm Zahir abd-Umar, whose house is in the Souk of Glass."

"And what does your master Umar wish to buy?" Rafiq gestured for Taqla to fall into step beside him as he walked.

"You spoke today of black pearls."

Rafiq shrugged. "I did."

15

"They're not black but gray, with a great lustre and a dimpled surface?"

"That's them. They're very rare, being taken from shells that grow at great depth."

"But not so desirable as the ordinary ones in the eyes of most. Not so pleasing to look upon."

Rafiq smiled. "Yet your master would have an interest in them?"

"Have you any for sale?"

"Some handful, of different sizes."

"Then my master might, if they were of good quality."

"Is he a sorcerer?"

Taqla nearly stumbled. She shot him a hard, unguarded glance and he gave her a crooked smile in return. "What makes you say that?" she blustered.

"I've heard that a string of one hundred thousand black pearls will make one invisible to the Djinn."

Some people hear too much, she thought. "Perhaps it's true," she admitted. "I wouldn't know. I'm sure my master wouldn't either."

"Maybe he's just a collector of rare pearls," Rafiq suggested dryly, and she was so busy trying to read his expression as she walked that she didn't see the man coming in the opposite direction until his shoulder clipped hers, hard. She opened her mouth to protest, just as the man's foot swept her ankle from under her and she went flat on the alley floor, hands in the dust and face inches from a heap of donkey droppings.

Her first sensation was a wave of humiliation and hurt, and at that she felt the spell that held her in male shape fracture. She took a sharp breath and shut her eyes, seizing the enchantment with her will, concentrating on the rush of anger that swept through her blood while the spell, as fragile as all shapings were, shifted momentarily in her grip like a pot riddled with hairline cracks. The spell settled back into place. Only then did Taqla open her eyes and try to gauge her surroundings.

Her first suspicion, that the assault had been instigated by some crony of Rafiq's, turned out to be very wrong. The merchant-master had backed up a few paces now and wasn't even looking at her; his concentration was fixed on the two men who had stepped between him and her. They were dressed in robes of the same striped cloth as each other and were holding knives. Rafiq put his hand on his sheathed scimitar and they laughed, shifting forward.

"Son of a dog," sneered one.

He grimaced, but did not draw. "You know, that is the last time I do business with your family," he said through bared teeth.

"It's the last time you'll do business with anyone," said the other, and spat.

Taqla understood Rafiq's problem—to keep the civil peace the amir's law said that although swords could be carried in the city, drawing one against someone was a capital offense. And they were surrounded by witnesses here, where the narrow street was lined with the shops of furniture makers. Already people were turning to stare, watching even as they edged away to a safe distance. Rafiq stood little chance against two knifemen, she thought. She cast about for options and saw at the side of the alley, within arm's reach, a broken wooden strut protruding from a drift of wood shavings and sawdust.

Grabbing the splintered end, she hauled it out and without even trying to stand, whipped it round into the backs of one of the strangers' knees. The man crumpled with a cry, landing on top of her. As his companion turned to see what had happened, Rafiq took his chance and kicked his second assailant hard in the guts, punching him in the face as he doubled up.

The first man had fallen partially over Taqla's legs, pinning her. As he rolled, lifting his knife, she tried to swing the length of wood again but it was unwieldy and he managed to get his knife arm up to parry the blow. She was quite surprised when the knife flew from his cracked hand—she never quite got used to how strong she was as Zahir. He grunted with pain and grabbed her by the ear, hauling her to within an inch of his face.

"Not your fight, you pizzle of a goat!" he roared.

The grip on her ear was horribly painful, but he was trying to stop her pulling away from him. He was taken entirely by surprise when she lunged forward and clamped her teeth as hard as she could on his nose, grinding into the gristle. This time he screamed. She felt a punch glance off her head and then the stranger pulled away, his face streaming with blood, and gave her enough room to kick him in the crotch with all her strength. He went down and lay there retching.

Taqla looked up to see Rafiq staring at her. "You bit him?" he blurted. But then his gaze was wrenched away. "Get up," he snapped. "Hurry."

A glance showed her what was worrying him—other men in similar robes were pushing up the souk in their direction. Taqla scrambled to her feet and followed as Rafiq dived into one of the shops, spitting to clear her mouth. They bumped their way through the dark constricted space full of painfully angular furniture, and emerged into a tiny yard full of lumber at the back. The shopkeeper followed them out, showering them with imprecations. The wall at the back was of crumbling brick and tall enough that Taqla would never have dreamed of tackling it in her own shape. But Rafiq went straight over it with a leap and a scramble, and she had no choice but to follow. She was glad of the strength in her arms and shoulders, easily capable of hauling her own bodyweight. She couldn't help grinning even as they jumped down the rubble slope beyond. Her ear was burning as if it were on fire and her head was throbbing, but she was hardly conscious of the pain or the fear of the men behind her because she was exulting so much. She'd always tried to keep out of trouble and out of public notice, but she was coming to realize that Zahir's body liked a bit of a fight.

They'd come out into an open space hemmed in by buildings, and it was obvious from the stench that this was the area of the leather dyers. A honeycomb of limestone pits lay before them, each filled with a different colored slurry and each more caustic and stinking than the last, so Rafiq set off along the narrow stone kerbs between the pools, leaping the heaps of slimy hides, and she teetered in his wake. Her sense of balance was *worse* in a male body, she thought—or perhaps it was the blows to her head that were making her unsteady.

"You didn't have to join in the fight!" Rafiq called back. The dyers, nearly naked and painted to the thighs in the colors of their trade, had paused in their labors to stare.

"We hadn't finished our conversation."

"Ah—of course. Well, I am grateful. My business with those sons of donkeys might have distracted me permanently."

"Who were they?" she asked.

"Sons of the household of Hava." Rafiq skidded on a nameless lump of slime and wobbled dangerously over a vat of crimson. "They have a dispute of honor with me—I shouldn't have gone out into the city without guards."

"What did you do?" The Hava family was well known in the city.

"Nothing! Well, their mother—"

"Their *mother*? Sitt Khadiga? She's fifty if she's a day!"

"She's a handmaiden of Iblis!" Rafiq had clearly decided that there was no rescuing his good reputation as far as the household of Hava was concerned. "She came to my warehouse to buy silver plates and offered only the most ridiculous prices. When I wouldn't sell, she began to berate me, so I called a servant girl to usher her out, and the harridan tore off her own veil and swore that Bekla had done it."

"She didn't, then?"

"No—she did not! And no judge would have found in Khadiga's favor. It was only the word of her people against mine. But the damage was done because I was there. And because I can bear witness that she's uglier than the back end of a camel."

Taqla snorted. If Sitt Khadiga al-Hava had been unveiled in front of Rafiq, then regardless of whose fault it was, the insult to her honor would be avenged by the men of her family. "You could have given up the servant girl," she suggested.

Rafiq paused midstride to give her a hard look. "She was innocent." His glance drifted past her face. "And we're still being followed."

Three men were scrambling over the wall into the dyers' yard. Taqla, who was just beginning to think she might stop and catch her breath, hissed between her teeth. They hurried on, aiming for the buildings beyond the far wall. A mud-brick stair led up onto the roof of a house and they scrambled up, ducking beneath a palm-frond shade and running straight across the dyed hides that had been spread out to dry there. An old woman busy turning the skins shrieked abuse at them for that.

"We need to get down to the street," Taqla suggested, panting.

"Soon. First—jump!" Rafiq put on a burst of speed and launched himself off the edge of the roof, right over the narrow lane to the rooftop opposite. Taqla cursed him silently, hoped that this was a perfectly reasonable distance for a fit young man to cover, and threw herself after him. She hit the flat surface jarringly, stumbled but recovered, and vowed not to try that again—her toes had barely found the edge. She staggered clear of the two-storey drop.

"Where—where now?" A glance told her that this was a big building they were on, square in form but hollowed around a central courtyard. There was no obvious stair down. And their pursuers had not given up. The head of their leader bobbed into view over the first roof.

Rafiq didn't answer. He just went to the edge overlooking the central courtyard, squinted down, then turned and dropped to his belly and slid his legs over into the void. He hung there for a moment, lurched down until he was hanging by his hands then disappeared from sight.

What? Taqla mouthed, aghast. *Is this normal?* she wanted to demand—Did every Dimashqan man take to scrambling over the rooftops like an ape at the slightest provocation? Was she just supposed to follow him?

She didn't have much choice. Gritting her teeth, she did as Rafiq had done—and found, below the roofline, complex decorative piercework in wood, which allowed her to swing down onto the upper-storey balcony below. She nearly pulled her arms from their sockets doing it, and she cursed her sheltered upbringing.

"Quick." Rafiq signalled her into a doorway and they plunged into the building's interior. The shuttered rooms were in darkness and filled with sagging baskets and dusty bales, the finely tiled walls not making up for the reek of rat urine. Taqla knew what was going on—there were many grand old houses like this in the city nowadays. When the seat of the caliphate was moved from Dimashq to Baghdad, many of the wealthiest families had abandoned the city, locking up their houses and leaving them to decay under the care of a lone watchman. Squatters had moved into some buildings, others were used as storage spaces or stables. This one looked and smelled like it was full of sheep's fleeces all quietly rotting away in the gloom.

Voices and scuffling suggested their pursuers were not far behind. Rafiq drew his scimitar.

"No!" breathed Taqla warningly.

"No witnesses here," he whispered. But he relented with a shrug and pushed her into the angle behind a cupboard door in a dark corner, backing in after her as the voices grew louder. It was almost pitch-black, to Taqla's discomfort, and a shelf dug into her spine. Worse, it was an extremely confined space. As Rafiq squeezed in after her with his scimitar held at the ready, his back pressed up against her chest, radiating heat. She could smell his skin and his sweat over the general miasma of dry rot, and it smelled good in a way she was not ready for— hauntingly, disconcertingly good. She could feel the movement of his muscles through his clothes and it made her own muscles quiver and clench. She shrank away desperately, trying to minimise contact, but it was too late, her panicked mental efforts were not enough. Even as they both held their breath and as footfalls echoed in the chamber outside, the spell of shaping cracked into a thousand pieces and the form of Zahir abd-Umar dissolved into her own. The pain in her ear vanished. Bones shortened. Male muscle softened to feminine curves. Her bare nipples pressed against his shirt and she felt them pucker and harden at the contact.

Taqla prayed that Rafiq would not notice.

Feet passed up and down the hallways, in and out of rooms. Voices barked threats and complaints. Something clattered as it was thrown across a tiled floor. But the building was dark and big and the room layout complex. The noises passed back and forth, growing gradually fainter. Taqla tilted her head to heaven and bit her lip and tried to cross her arms in front of her breasts despite there being no space, hoping that her body scent, her stifled breathing, her reduced stature would not give her away.

"I think we're clear."

"Umm," she grunted, dropping her voice by an octave.

Rafiq slid cautiously out around the door. She gave it a moment then slipped out after him, leaving her too-large sandals behind and moving on silent feet. He was still looking intently up a corridor when she fled in the opposite direction.

She didn't go far. She had no idea where to go. She dived into a room and plunged toward the window in the wall opposite, throwing open the shutter with frantic hands. Daylight poured in, making her eyes water. Below her seethed a busy livestock market, the perfect place to get lost in. It was two storeys down but there was a shack of some sort built up against the wall and it would be simple enough to drop onto its roof and scramble down to the earth.

But she couldn't get out that way. An unveiled, bare-breasted woman running through the market would start a riot. She whirled, dizzy with fear. She needed time to recast the spell, she needed to get her mind under control and visualise Zahir once more—but it couldn't be done instantly. In the meantime, she could not be found in Zahir's clothes, she realized. If Rafiq walked in on her—and she had no doubt he would have glimpsed her retreat—then he would know. Her mask would be revealed for the fiction it was. And if Zahir became known as a sorceress in disguise, then Umar would be no safer. All her years of meticulously constructing his persona would be wasted in a day.

She didn't know what she'd have to do to silence Rafiq if he saw her like this.

She looked round the room, which was full of sacking and mounded fleeces, and made her decision. She flung off the rope coil and her clothes and stuffed them out of sight, then dived in the opposite direction onto a heap of wool, which sagged unpleasantly beneath her and released a waft of sheep's grease. Not a moment too soon, because Rafiq pushed open the door just then, sword in hand.

He saw the open window first and stepped toward it. Then he saw her and stopped dead, his eyes widening. Taqla clenched her forearm across her bare breasts and held the other hand over her lower face as a makeshift veil, scrunching up as much as possible. She knew he had an excellent view of her bare flanks and thighs, but that didn't matter. Or so she told herself—even as her skin heated with shame under his gaze.

"Ah." Rafiq's expression softened, a smile warming his eyes. "Forgive me."

She glared. Let him try anything and she would summon the snakes out of the walls, she promised herself, ignoring the treacherous gush of warmth to her sex.

"You are?"

"The watchman lets me sleep here," she whispered. "In exchange for..."

"Of course." He seemed to become aware that he was staring and made some effort to look away, laying his right hand on his breastbone in that Dimashqan gesture that had many subtle shades of meaning but in general expressed good intentions. "Have you...ah...did a youngish man come past here? Alone?"

She tilted her head, indicating the window. "Out that way."

"I see." He raised an eyebrow. "I thought he might wait for me. Never mind." He took a few steps toward the window, but then hesitated, his gaze caught once more upon her nakedness. "There are some men who've just broken into this house—I don't know where they've headed. You should get dressed and find the watchman."

She nodded warily.

"Good." With a last appreciative glance he climbed through the window frame, and she heard him drop to the roof below. Taqla let out a pent-up breath.

That had been far too close, she thought. And now she needed to get dressed and focus her will upon becoming Zahir once more. Strong, practical, invisible Zahir. But with Rafiq's smile burning in her mind's eye and the memory of his body imprinted on hers, it took her a surprisingly long time to make herself male again.

Chapter Three

*In which the most beautiful woman in the land
is rather taken by her portrait.*

"Fah! I hate poetry!" said Ahleme bint-Jamil, daughter of
the Amir of Dimashq, throwing her book down upon a cushion.
The white doves that had been pecking at the flagstones nearby
flew off in a panic.

Nura, who had been plucking the strings of an *oud* softly
while her mistress read, looked up, unimpressed by Ahleme's
vehemence. "Really, mistress?"

"They're liars! All of them. All this rubbish they write..."

Farida, another slave woman, yawned and stretched her
hand out to the tray of candied dates that sat between them.
Like Nura, she knew that Ahleme was too soft-hearted to beat
her slaves for minor impertinences, and they both tended to
take liberties. Farida liked her food. "You spend a great deal of
money, mistress, on that rubbish as you call it," she pointed
out.

Ahleme rolled her eyes. She knew that Farida was right,
but that didn't ease her frustration. If she really hated poetry,
she wouldn't send her slaves down to the Souk of Booksellers to
buy those precious little volumes, or spend so much time
reading their handwritten pages. Nor would she while away so
many hours composing her own verses, which she then hid in a
secret space beneath her window. "They only have three things
they want to write about," she complained. "They whinge about
how much they want to go back to the free desert life, they
whinge about the pain of love—and they bleat on like goats
about the consolations of wine when the whinging becomes too
much even for them."

Farida belched softly and smiled.

"That is poetry," Nura said. "You might as well protest that birds fly and fish swim."

"But I don't believe any of it! Do you think any of them have ever lived in the desert? Have you seen the desert tribesmen— do they look like *they* write poetry to you? All the poets are very comfortable here behind city walls, and if a jackal so much as howled nearby they would probably hide beneath their pillows. As for love—it's just stupid, what they say."

Farida glanced at Nura and lifted her eyebrows. "What would you know about that, mistress?"

Ahleme thrust her lower lip out. "What real man falls in love like the poets say, all sleepless nights and refusing food and tearing his robes? Can you imagine my father behaving like that? Do you imagine he wrote poetry to my mother and stood below her window weeping?"

Farida sniggered and Nura frowned.

"Well, your mother was nobly born, mistress, so of course no man wrote about her." The fact was that most love poems were paeans to slaves, since respectable women couldn't be the object of a stranger's desire without it leading to disaster and bloodshed.

Ahleme snorted. Her feelings on the subject were confused. "Maybe she wanted him to," she suggested, knowing she was being daring.

"Really!" Nura struck an angry chord, like a wasp's buzz. "Your father is a man of honor, mistress! He would never have disrespected one of his wives so."

"I meant after they married, of course," she amended.

"Well, what would be the point of that?" asked Nura. "Love is about the wanting, not the having. A man will do anything for you, but only if he cannot have you. That's why a maiden should never give a man what he is after."

"Hah," said Farida, smugly. "Some things are more rewarding than merely being wanted."

Nura wrinkled her nose. "And that is why no man has

asked permission to marry you, Farida. You are too accommodating."

"What do I need a husband for? My mistress provides for me."

"Your mistress does not provide you with sons!"

"Ah, if God willed me to have children, wouldn't I have seen it by now?"

It was an old argument and Ahleme wasn't interested. Shaking her head, she rose and walked a few paces over to the fig tree in the centre of the courtyard. She stared up into the branches, searching out the green fruit, looking for one ripe enough to pluck. The two slaves carried on their desultory bickering for a few moments before lapsing into a complacent truce.

Ahleme thought she understood the poets' nostalgia for open spaces. Though she'd never travelled into the desert, she knew exactly what it was to feel hemmed in by high walls and inactivity. Her own days blended into each other seamlessly without hurry or event or achievement. She would bathe, she would listen to music, she would pray and eat and listen to the gossip of her slaves and maidservants. She would spend hours in the carved *mashrabiya* balconies that jutted out from the outer walls of the Citadel and allowed the women of the amir's household to see the world outside without themselves being spied upon, where she would watch the light changing on the wooded slopes of the Jebel Qassioun outcrop to the north, or from another balcony gaze down upon the food market before the Citadel gates. She was fascinated by the smells that wafted up to her, so alien to the perfumed palace—smells of animal dung and rotting vegetables, bubbling oil and melted sugar and fresh bread. She loved the purple of the baskets of figs and mulberries, the pale green mounds of almonds still in their fuzzy shells, the sunset tint of persimmons and even the reds of the butchers' stalls. She knew by sight the guards and the hawkers and the porters who worked there, knew their routines and their quarrels, and sometimes found herself envying the market women all muffled in their headscarves who chopped cabbage and haggled and sang and conducted arguments at the tops of their voices. At least, she thought, they had a purpose in rising from bed each day.

And she understood too why the poets praised wine and the cool nights in which they drank it beneath the glittering stars. But she didn't understand why they talked of love— endlessly, its sorrow and its glory, the way it captured a heart and laid low the powerful, how the mightiest man might be rendered helpless by the flash of an eyelid or the arch of a delicate foot, or the flutter of blood in a slim neck. Ahleme did not believe this. She wanted to know where these men were, these deep souls with their raging emotions who loved like women did. From what she saw of men in her father's palace, women were either an afterthought or something to be consumed casually, like food. If you were poor and unmarried, she reasoned, like the young men who cooked in the kitchen or tended the formal gardens, you might dream of them, you might watch them with starving eyes, but you would no more feel enslaved to a pretty woman than enslaved to a tender joint of roast mutton. And if you were rich—well, her father had four wives still living and nearly forty concubines, and the thought that any one of those women could rule him through looks alone was laughable.

Of course if one of them had borne him a son...

Forty women—and yet no son and only one daughter grown to adulthood, they whispered in the palace corridors; *the Djinn must have put the Evil Eye upon him. Ah, but there is no Fate but the one given to us by God.*

So, Ahleme said to herself, admitting what she could never say even to her most trusted slaves, *I am a poetic fool. I read my poems of love here in the palace garden, sitting beneath the old tamarisk tree or by the edge of the fountain pool, weaving wreaths of jasmine in my fingers and wishing there could be a man who loves me with all his soul like the poets pretend is possible—and not because I'm the daughter of an amir but because the curve of my lips makes his heart leap and the flutter of my black lashes stops it dead. If I married such a man, I know that my passion would mirror his. If he were handsome and kind and loved me, then I would love him forever. It is what I dream of.*

Except that sometimes her dreams were stranger and more shameful, and she blamed the poets for that too. Even this last night she'd woken hot and agitated, flinging back her coverlet to let the air cool her wet skin, but unable to do anything about the melting sensation between her thighs. She'd dreamed she was lying in a room of gold—not gold leaf or plate but flowing, molten gold that ran down the walls and oozed from the ceiling. She'd opened her eyes in the dream but been dazzled by the glow and glint of the liquid metal, hardly able to see. There had been a man lying next to her, but he was so bright that she'd been unable to look at his face. He'd been covered in gold too, and so had she, every inch of their naked bodies slathered in the thick slippery melt. Not a strand of hair disrupted the slick smoothness of his body or head. He'd been touching her, running his hands over her firm breasts and across her slender waist and down between her thighs, his caresses heavy but almost frictionless, and he'd been kissing her throat and her breasts and pressing up against her. Ahleme quivered even now at the recollection. He'd been a big man, his hard muscles sharply defined even under the slippery gilding. He'd been very eager, and her response had been just as fierce. She could recall the thick bulk of his male member, like a gold bar under her hand. She could still remember the desire she'd felt for that hard shaft, and the searing pleasure as he'd parted her thighs and moved upon her, sliding that member deep into her needful body. Her spasm had shocked her awake, wet and trembling.

In the way of dreams, the whole scene—his hunger and hers—had possessed an intensity beyond anything she knew in waking life. It had made her moonlit room and the snoring slavegirls and the brush of her fingers across her own bare flesh seem faint and unreal. And all this day she'd clung to the memory of her dream, as if to the recollection of a momentous event.

This is all the fault of the poets, she told herself. They made her long for what was not hers—not yet at any rate, and perhaps never, unless her father chose for her someone as handsome and vital as the man of her dreams.

"I wish to go down and see the public audience," she announced, making Nura strike the wrong note, and stirring Farida out of her stupor.

It was boredom though, not hope, that drove her. This was the one day of the week when anybody could petition to be presented at the divan of the amir, though she knew there would be no handsome princes or their envoys seeking her hand, not today at least, because she would have heard of it in advance from the servants, gossip in the palace being as efficient as it was. The arrival of such an envoy was not an uncommon thing, but so far, despite the gifts and the flattery and the politicking, they had all been turned away disappointed. Ahleme sometimes wondered when her father would see fit to let her leave his house for another man's, or if he was holding out in hope of a marriage offer from the caliph himself.

Before descending to the audience chamber, she stole a look at the people waiting. There were interior balconies throughout the palace, of course, their gilded screens allowing a watch to be kept on almost every room, and the women of the amir's house made good use of them. A cluster of concubines and servants were spying and whispering, their giggles probably not entirely inaudible to those waiting below. They all made way for the amir's eldest and favourite daughter though, as she walked slowly around the upper floor, examining the faces below.

It was the usual collection of citizens, she thought. Those with enough money or influence to cut their way to the head of the queue, or enough persistence to take the long route. A trio of judges in close conference, their white beards nodding. A wealthy-looking widow, several merchants with gifts and taxes to present, a nervous-looking peasant chaperoning a slender girl with beautiful eyes who was probably hoping to be taken on as a concubine, a delegation of desert nomads with curved knives in their belts and arrogant, uncomfortable expressions. She scanned the faces, idly looking for the most handsome.

And there, *Oh yes.* Ahleme felt her interest quicken. He was standing against a marble pillar, dressed in the local style but very finely, his saffron-colored coat embroidered with gold thread. His hair hung low over his collar and his brows were knitted in what was a faint frown either of thoughtfulness or of impatience—both traits generally considered hazardous in the palace environs. *Very handsome*, she thought, feeling almost embarrassed at the warmth that bloomed inside her. Casually she signalled one of the household eunuchs to her side.

"Who is that man?" she asked, pointing at random at a haggard, bald fellow with an armful of scrolls.

"He's an artist I believe, my lady, hoping to receive commission from the amir."

"And that woman?"

"She's locked in a dispute with her neighbor over orchard land they both claim, and is asking the amir to adjudicate because the neighbor is a judge. He is the one at the end there, with the blue sash."

"And him? The one with the yellow coat?" She kept her voice bored.

"Rafiq ibn-Jurraia, called the Traveller. A merchant-master recently returned from Saba."

She yawned. She'd heard of Rafiq, whose journeys were always a source of interesting news and gossip, but never seen him before. She regretted that now. "I will be attending the audience at my father's side. Escort me there."

"As you wish, my lady."

So when Amir Jamil entered the audience chamber and all his subjects knelt and lowered their foreheads to the ground, Ahleme processed in with his entourage. She waited like all his councillors and judges and scribes to be told where to sit, and because Jamil was an indulgent father and proud of his eldest daughter, the ornament of the palace, he patted the divan at his left side and she sat next to him. They exchanged smiles and a few private words of greeting—Jamil liked to spend time with his children, and the affairs of the city left him little time to do it.

Ahleme in turn was pleased with her father's approval. She didn't remember her mother, who had died years ago, but the respect of this rather taciturn man, who let her have almost any luxury she wanted so long as those things were of no importance at all, meant more to her than all the jewels and pets and dresses he so often gave.

When the petitioners were allowed to lift their heads, there was the faintest ripple of appreciative surprise through the room. Ahleme was properly veiled of course, but because of her exceptional status, her veil was not the thick homespun cotton of the streets nor even the light silk affected by concubines, but a net of seed-pearls and silver beads that left her facial beauty undisguised while still adhering to the demands of propriety. Thus her fame had spread, and after today there would be more witnesses to pass on the word. Her rich, stiff dress was modelled on the colors of her family's emblem, in shimmering blue embroidered with peacock feather eyes, encrusted with emeralds. There were more gems in her long hair and gold bangles in rows about her forearms. Although she lowered her eyes modestly for the first few moments, she knew that her presence had brought pleasure to those who'd never seen her before. It made her want to laugh. What was the point of the whole world telling you were pretty when there wasn't one of them permitted to love you, or you him? She felt at times like these like an admired saluki bitch or a particularly well-formed mare.

So the audiences began. Much of the proceedings were repetitive and dull, with the petitioners tying themselves into verbal knots of extravagant politeness before their ruler. Only the play of her fingers on the fringe of her cushion betrayed Ahleme's impatience at these, because she was too well trained in the ways of the court. She did pay attention during the meat of the exchanges, because any novelty was of value to her, but she was pleased when it was the turn of Rafiq the Traveller to be called up from the mass of petitioners. Having returned from a trading journey with camel loads of frankincense and coffee beans, his caravan's goods value had been assessed by officials and he'd come to pay his tax. He also presented a gift to the amir, which was brought in by two court eunuchs—an ivory boat carved in wonderful detail, its hull filled with dull red crystals of dragons' blood. Her father leaned forward to inspect it and made appropriate noises of appreciation.

"You will have many interesting stories to tell us then, of the places you've been, Rafiq?"

The younger man looked up, meeting his gaze steadily. "Many, most wise of amirs."

He's a spy, thought Ahleme. *Of course he is.* It made sense that the amir gathered intelligence from travellers, and that he knew about events and plans in neighboring regions and their intentions toward Dimashq.

"Good. Perhaps you will wait behind after this audience, and entertain my vizier and myself with your tales."

"As you wish, father of the city."

"Very well." Jamil waved his hand graciously.

Is that all? Ahleme protested inwardly as Rafiq made to withdraw. She wanted to hear more from this man herself, and in particular she wanted him to look at her. "Traveller," she said with a bright guilelessness, "will you tell me something?"

His eyes flicked to hers. Whatever emotion he was feeling, it didn't show, but strictly speaking he shouldn't have held her gaze like that. Ahleme didn't care a bit. Her heart made a funny jump in her breast. She liked his warm eyes and the dark arches of his brows and the little line of enquiry between them. And the play of his lips as he answered, "Of course, my lady. What do you wish to know?"

She improvised with, "What sort of clothes do the women of Saba wear?" Then wished she hadn't picked a subject so vapid.

"Well, there are many tribes in Saba, my lady, and the women of each dress differently. Also there are traders from the Horn of Africa and from India, and they bring their families with them so there's a great mix of peoples on the coast. But very common is a fashion for wearing gold jewellery that is pierced through the side of the nose and hangs upon the cheek."

"You saw their faces?" She widened her eyes.

"Most of them go unveiled, though they cover their hair." The corner of his mouth twitched. "It's a terrible disappointment to learn that most women are no more great beauties than are most men."

Ahleme smiled. The amir lifted his hand gently.

"My daughter, you are keeping all these people waiting upon you. You must curb your curiosity for the moment."

Rafiq withdrew to the side then, and Ahleme had to hide her disappointment. The next petitioner brought forward was the artist, a tall, bony man who laid his scrolls upon a low table. He wished, he explained with slow, formal diction, to show the amir his work in the hope that he might find favour and perhaps future employment. In token of sincerity, he first wished to make a gift of a picture of great wonder and astronomical value, which had fallen into his hands during his sojourning in the East.

Ahleme, who had been sunk briefly in her own thoughts, started to listen at this point. There was something about that man with his long thin fingers and his deep-sunken eyes that she found oddly disconcerting. Something about him nagged at her instincts, as if reminding her of someone. Ahleme glanced at her father, but Jamil looked neither more nor less impressed than usual. The religious councillors were stirring—the argument about whether it was right to pictorially depict living beings or not was about to break out again, she suspected.

"What manner of painting?" the amir asked.

"Ah," said the artist, stooping to the biggest of the scrolls. "This comes from the land of China, most wise of amirs, where they paint upon silk. And the boast of this scroll is that upon it are depicted all the most beautiful things that exist in the world, without exception."

"Then it must include the Great Mosque here in Dimashq,"

said Jamil with a little smile, "and my own daughter."

"So it must." The artist lifted the scroll over his head and let it unfurl all the way to his feet. Everyone on and about the divan craned to get a look. Ahleme's view was better than most. She saw a landscape painting depicted in ink, all shades of grey and black. In the foreground at the bottom was a stand of reedlike plants and beyond that the land stretched away, full of tiny detail, to huge and impossibly steep mountains, their overhanging summits wreathed in cloud. The style was unlike anything she'd seen before, at once fantastic and beautiful and intensely melancholy.

"Vizier?" The amir was too dignified a person to get up and squint at a picture himself, so his highest official did the honors for him. He bent and peered at the middle ground, his brows furrowed.

"Where do you start? There is so much detail—cities, bridges, people. Oh—there! Yes, there it is!" He pointed at the scroll. "It's the Great Mosque of Al-Walid! I see the minarets and the shrine of the head of John the Baptist! Such detail! You can even see the mosaics on the inner walls!" His expression of pleasure warped. "That isn't possible. You could not paint such fine detail. And the trees there, the water—they're moving!"

"The picture is magical," said the artist, as if the vizier were a simpleton. There was a rumble of mistrust and excitement among everyone who heard those words. Magic was as always greeted with a confusion of fascination and great wariness. The vizier shrank back, looking conflicted.

"Is it safe?" Jamil asked, frowning.

"It is only a picture, oh father of wisdom. Do you not wish to see if your daughter is depicted among the most beautiful things in the world?"

Jamil's frown deepened.

"I will," Ahleme said quickly. She itched to see the marvellous painting, and that it might include her made it irresistible. When her father did not immediately say "No," she sprang to her feet and approached the tall man and the hanging scroll. For a moment she looked him in the face, and she felt a strange clench inside her, something half-fearful, that sense of recognition again. Then he bowed his head as if acknowledging her courage and that made her heart swell. She wondered if Rafiq was watching her but did not dare to look his way. Instead she focused on the scroll.

To her indescribable delight the vizier was right—the landscape was alive. Rivers flowed over waterfalls. Cranes skimmed over rippling lakes. Contorted pine trees shifted their needles in the breeze. Everywhere she looked new detail sprang out at her. Buildings that seemed tiny blocks at first glance became elegantly detailed when she peered closer, caves opened up to reveal their painted interiors. And from round a wind-carved rock on a narrow mountain road stepped a tiny figure in a robe of peacock feathers.

"That's me!" she cried joyfully, reaching with a finger to the ink-washed silk. "There I am!"

With those words she vanished from the room.

Rafiq, who had been watching the amir's daughter even though he could hear little of the conversation up there at the divan, knelt bolt upright, wondering what on earth had just happened. There was a horrible silence in the whole of the audience chamber. Even those who wanted to cry out in shock did not dare.

The amir lurched to his feet. "What have you done with my daughter?" he demanded, his voice barely raised but hoarse with rage.

The artist lifted ragged brows. "You mean, *my* wife," he corrected. The lower edge of the scroll burst into flames.

Jamil lifted a finger. "Seize him!" But as the guards ran forward from the edges of the room, the artist began to burn too, from his feet upward. Before the flames had reached his knees, his feet were ash and he was hanging in midair. Before the guards were within striking distance, there was nothing of him but head and shoulders and a sardonic grin, wreathed in pale flame. By the time the first blade cut downward there was nothing for it to cleave but a hanging cloud of blackened flakes, as if paper had been burned and the ashes crumpled and thrown about the room.

Chapter Four

In which two bargains are struck.

Taqla, wishing to make magic, had shut herself within an inner chamber whose carved shutters looked only into the courtyard of her house and not out into the street. Not that it was, as these things went, a particularly terrible magic. It was only a spell of illusion, an entertaining trifle. But Taqla felt horribly self-conscious on this occasion and she'd instructed her housekeeper Lelia that she wished to be left undisturbed.

Carefully she fanned the brazier of charcoal to hot white ash, then cast upon it frankincense and a bunch of green sage soaked in a rare perfume. She should not be doing this, she knew. Her own shame told her that. But stronger than the shame was the coiled sense of longing low in her belly, the ache that would not be appeased. She wanted to see him again, Rafiq the Traveller. The memory of him would not leave her alone and had kept her awake for half the night. Now her skin prickled with anticipation.

It's harmless, she told herself. She was not dishonoring herself, for no one would know. She just wanted to look.

As the smoke began to rise, she spoke the ancient words that compelled it, and instead of dispersing about the dim, blue-tiled room, the plume gathered and thickened, hanging in a compact cloud. The sage twigs shrivelled and the smoke became a milky knot, roiling in the air. Taqla emptied her lungs and then stepped forward to plunge her face into that cloud, drawing the smoke into her as she inhaled. As it burned her throat, sweet and acrid at the same time, she fixed her mind upon her recollections of Rafiq. The man running ahead of her over the rooftops. His body pressed to hers in the dark. The look in his eyes as he beheld her naked.

When her breast was nearly bursting, she exhaled again and the smoke flowed out from her lips, carrying her memories with it. This time the cloud took on human shape. Tinted with color as in life, it formed within moments into the image of Rafiq, standing upon the tiles before her and dressed as when she had seen him. He seemed quite solid, though Taqla knew the simulacrum was as intangible as smoke. He seemed to live—breath moved his chest and his eyes shone as he blinked, his gaze meeting hers. Taqla couldn't help the warmth that rose in her cheeks, or the little laugh that broke from her lips. The likeness was perfect, though what was discomforting was how hard his handsomeness smote her this time. She had to remind herself that this was nothing more than an illusion. There was no need for her to feel so shy.

When her father was alive, he would often, when relaxing, surround himself with dancing girls formed of smoke this same way.

"Rafiq," she whispered, enjoying the shape of his name on her tongue. He didn't answer—he couldn't speak, of course— but he smiled a little in response and she felt her heart bump. Taqla circled him slowly, taking the time to examine and appreciate him as she had not been able to do in the flesh, and though Rafiq simply stood there and let her, he turned his head to watch, his speculative expression as alert as her own.

Oh but he was handsome, she thought. Not bulky but strong. Sun-darkened skin framed by the neck of his shirt. Disordered hair flecked with dust from the abandoned house. Angled black brows. A mouth that hinted at humor and sensuality. Lean hands more callused than a merchant's should be. And a ready, confident tilt to his stance.

Coming full circle to face him again, she stepped backward to take in a full-length view. Rafiq instantly stepped forward, closing the space between them.

Despite herself, Taqla jumped a little. She laughed again, half nervous and half delighted. She knew that the simulacra had no real souls or wills, but they took their personas from those who created them and could appear autonomous. She couldn't help liking the way the quirk of his lips was darkened by the glint in his eye. It made her feel flustered and self-conscious and guiltily excited. As he eased forward, she moved back, retreating until her shoulders butted up against the chamber wall.

It's not real, she told herself, feeling her breath coming fast and shallow.

Soundlessly he placed his hands on the blue tiles to either side of her, not touching her but penning her in. His face inclined over hers. She could almost imagine she could feel his breath. She was deliciously aware of how much taller he was than her, how much broader his shoulders. She could feel the sudden hot trickle of her moisture, like a crack in the dam that held back her hunger.

Is this any way for a sorceress to be acting? complained the voice of pride inside her. *Is this how you squander your talents?* But it was a very small voice, and drowned by the roar of much fiercer and more primal needs. She was hooked like a fish on her own desire, ensnared by his eyes and by the way a tiny movement betrayed the biting of his inside lip.

For a moment Rafiq's gaze slid significantly down from her face to her breasts, and then he crooked an eyebrow as if pointedly posing a question.

"You want...?"she whispered.

He smiled—and that did incredible things to her insides. She wondered what it would feel like to kiss those lips, even as she knew she couldn't. But that unvoiced suggestion... Well. She'd bared herself to him once already. Was it so difficult to do so again?

"Well, if you really..." Her blouse crossed over at her breasts and tied with long tails about her waist. Blushing even more warmly, she pulled the knot open and loosened the cloth to expose the warm cleft between her breasts, the curving swells of soft, firm flesh. Her breasts felt heavy and her nipples tightened to hard points as they kissed the air. She looked up into his face nervously.

Rafiq's lips parted. She glimpsed the tip of his tongue playing across the edge of his teeth. Then, spreading his hands wider on the tiles, he stooped, making as if to kiss her bosom. Taqla gulped air, her breasts rising to meet his mouth. Of course she could feel nothing, but she could see the dark bulk of his head and the sweep of his lips, the individual hairs—soft or bristly—of his beard and brows and downcast lashes against her soft skin. She slid her hand across her belly, questing down between her thighs.

The door to her left shook under a fusillade of knocks.

Taqla jumped like a cat caught hooking goldfish from a courtyard pool. She flung her hands out, waving, and the false Rafiq broke up into wisps of aromatic smoke. "What?" she shouted, too loud but feeling rattled.

"Mistress?" The door quivered against its bolt again.

Hurriedly she knotted her disordered clothing about her. Her pulse was racing, and she was a little shocked to realize how deeply she had been immersed in her flirtation. The outside world had all but vanished. "What is it, Lelia?" she asked as she opened the door. "I said not to disturb me!"

The older woman on the other side frowned at her. "There's a man at the door wishing to speak to Umar the Scholar, mistress. His name is Rafiq and he sent this gift in token of his respect." She held out a small silver dish—in the centre was a pearl with a gray, lustrous surface.

Taqla tugged her clothes straight once again, her heart thumping hard. She bit her lip, picking up the pearl in order to put off speaking. It rolled around in her palm. It was a good size, she thought. It wasn't an ungenerous gift. "You'd better show him in to the *madafah*," she said. "And make him coffee. I'll meet him in a few minutes."

Lelia pulled a face. "Do you know him, mistress?"

"Zahir met him once."

"He looks like trouble to me."

Taqla wrinkled her nose. "He was."

She went into her own chamber in order to change into the guise of Umar the Scholar, laying the pearl in a small chest. She was embarrassed now by how foolishly she had behaved under her own enchantment, and it was a relief to take a moment to catch her breath and straighten her thoughts as she stripped off her rings into a brass tray. She wore many rings when she was in her own shape, each one significant to her calling—green jade from distant China, black lava from the island of Sicily, lapis from the Afghan mountains, smoky glass from Alexandria in Egypt, white gold from some barbarous infidel realm to the north, pink coral from the Gulf of Ayla. One was of very old green bronze and etched with Hebrew characters. As she laid them down, she glanced into her mirror, which was a fragile artifact of the old Roman Empire, a slice from a bubble blown in glass, with the interior coated in lead so that the glass reflected. It showed her her untidy hair and her strange green eyes. Her normally full lips were pursed to an anxious line. She breathed hard down her nose, annoyed with her uninspiring reflection and more annoyed with herself for being so flustered. So Rafiq had come to her house—what of it? He was not coming to see Taqla the Sorceress—Taqla the Whore as he would think of her, crouched among the moldering sheepskins—but Umar the Wise. He must have asked his way around the Souk of Glass to find the scholar's house.

She reprimanded herself once more for the way her disguise had been undone by the unthinking press of his body against hers.

Undressing, she laid her feminine clothes aside and shut her eyes, picturing the form of Umar she had perfected over the years, once even examining the corpse of an elderly man found drowned on the riverbank to get the flaccid musculature right. Passing her hand over her hair, she turned it from black and thick to gray and sparse with a few words. Umar had crooked legs, knobbly joints, prominent veins in his hands and calves, shrivelled genitalia, a sagging little belly and a white beard. Apart from his height, he did not resemble the real Taqla in any particular, but he was the very picture of a scholar. She donned a robe and, over it, a big white woollen cloak with a hood, and then wrapped a headcloth about her head and jowls in the fashion of a desert dweller. She'd learned from her last encounter with Rafiq. If her disguise was that fragile, then she wanted the maximum amount of cover from her clothing.

Leaning on a stick, she made her way downstairs to the *madafah*, the reception hall. This was roofless but shaded by high walls of white plaster, and a pool sprinkled with rose petals cooled the air still further. Rafiq, she saw at first glance, was sitting on the guests' cushions, quietly watching as Lelia heated water over a charcoal brazier and warmed the coffeepot. He was wearing much better clothes today; his jacket was of embroidered silk. Clothes to impress a stranger with whom one wished to negotiate, she surmised.

Her spell of shaping shivered but held firm and she smiled. Good. She was in better control of herself now. A handsome face—and oh, he was handsome, just as the smoke-Rafiq had been, but she couldn't let herself think of that—would not be enough to upset her purposes.

Rafiq rose as she stepped out from the shadow of the arch and they both bowed and made their greetings. Taqla told Lelia that she would take over coffee-making duties, which was a signal honor for the guest but caused the middle-aged woman to retreat with a pointed, openly warning glance entirely inappropriate for a housekeeper to cast upon her venerable master. Taqla clenched her teeth, thinking that she would have to have another forceful talk with Lelia when they were alone.

Host and visitor seated themselves comfortably on the cushions and made small talk while Taqla ground the pale green coffee beans with a brass pestle and mortar, roasted them in a flat pan over the coals and brought them to the boil three times, adding first cardamom then saffron, before transferring the liquid into a clean warmed pot for pouring. The whole process took some considerable time, during which they talked in a leisurely manner about Dimashq and the lands about, enquired after each other's health and families and shared a deal of gossip—all without once touching upon the news that burned upon the lips of everyone in the city, which made Taqla conclude that this was exactly what Rafiq had come to consult Umar about.

She drank the first half-cup herself, as was customary, to show that it was not harmful.

Finally, once he had sipped from the tiny cup of thick black coffee and made noises of appreciation at the flavor, Rafiq said casually, "Have you heard the news from the Citadel?"

"Nobody in Dimashq has not heard," Taqla answered, savouring her brew. "The beautiful Ahleme stolen away by magic in front of her father's very eyes. The amir's great rage and distress. His promise to any man who might return his daughter to him and restore his honor. I hear that half the young men in the city have bought the first camel they can lay their hands upon and ridden out to search for her. Dimashq echoes like an empty cistern."

"I was there when it happened."

"Really?" She glanced at him over the rim of her cup, her interest sharpened. "Is it true that she stepped into a painting that then burst into flames? As did the magician?"

Rafiq shook his head slightly. "She only touched the painting, and then vanished. I don't think she'd have been so foolish as to walk into it herself."

"Hm."

"Anyway, that's why I'm here to be honored with your hospitality today."

"Really?" Taqla's fist tightened under the sleeve of her robe. "Why is that, my friend?"

Rafiq laid his hand apologetically on his breast and the gesture made her heart thud, remembering his eyes upon her nakedness. "I mean no disrespect, believe me. But since the girl was stolen by magic it seemed to me that the best way to find her must be by magic also—and that all those men racing out into the desert and to the coast are wasting their time."

Taqla narrowed her eyes. "But I'm only a scholar, friend,

not a sorcerer. I study the action of glass lenses upon light and color, and I study the movement of the stars. True, I can cast a horoscope, but that is hardly magic."

He nodded. "Yet when I asked about the souks, you have a reputation as a scholar who knows where to find things that people have lost."

"A ring, a needle, a donkey...small things only. It's often a question of encouraging the owner to think clearly, that is all."

"And I met your slave Zahir in the streets yesterday, and something he said made me think that you might have some knowledge of the hidden arts."

"Zahir is a fool," Taqla growled.

"He's certainly rash. I might well owe him my life. I'm not suggesting you are a sorcerer, only that there are many strange objects of power in this world, and that you might in your wisdom know how to make use of them."

Taqla stared at him, trying to ignore the glow of pleasure at what he'd just said about her actions the previous day, wondering how much she could trust him. "I might advise you," she admitted grudgingly.

"I would be forever grateful."

"How grateful?" she wondered.

"Well." He wasn't perturbed. "I do have certain private resources at my disposal. But should I bring back Ahleme from her abductor I would have many more. Her father promises her hand in marriage, and that he will make the rescuer his grand vizier. And since he has no male heir..."

"That would put you in a very powerful and profitable position then."

"It would." He smiled a little, but his eyes stayed serious. "Of course you might harbour those ambitions yourself, my friend, in which case I am only using up your valuable time."

"Oh, I'm no adventurer—look at me." Taqla indicated her aged body with a sweep of her hand. "Nor fit to be the husband of a woman so young and lovely."

"Then are you willing to aid me? Name your price."

She tilted her head, putting aside the monetary question. "You're determined to find her?"

"It would be the greatest achievement any man of Dimashq could dream of."

"Ah." She chewed the inside of her lip. "Is the amir's daughter as beautiful as they say, then?"

Rafiq nodded. "She is..." he rolled his eyes skyward, "...quite extraordinary." A quick shake of his head conveyed awe. "Not much like her father to look upon, but her mother came from Aksum, they say."

"Ah," repeated Taqla, wishing that it didn't feel like glue were settling over her heart. *Stupid girl*, she reprimanded herself. *Who did you think he was after? Why are you upset that he should be thinking of another?* Still, she had to ask, "Doesn't it offend you that you won't be the first man to lie with her? Her abductor will most certainly have enjoyed his prize by now."

Rafiq frowned. "It's a pity, certainly, but her marriage to me will restore her honor." His mouth quirked. "Here I am mooning over the daughter of the amir as if she were some dancing girl— and as yet I've taken not one step toward finding her."

Taqla pushed away the sludge of disappointment that felt as if it were gumming up her insides. *Be sensible*, she told herself. *You've lost nothing; you never had it to start with. Think of the task at hand.* Brushing the tip of her nose with her index finger, she asked, "What color was the smoke?"

"Pardon?"

"When the magician burned and vanished—what color was the smoke? Yellow, like sulphur? Blue? It makes a difference."

"Oh." Rafiq shut his eyes to revisit his memories, and Taqla could only stare with painful fascination at the dark sweep of his lashes. "There was no smoke," he said decisively, looking up again. "None. Not even when the scroll burned. Flame but no smoke."

Taqla felt her spine crawl. "Oh," she said. "That's not good news. Are you sure?"

"What is it?"

"He wasn't a sorcerer. That was no earthly flame. He was a djinni."

"What?"

"As Mankind was made from the earth at our feet, so the Djinn were made of hidden flame. Fire without smoke. It means..." She blinked at the coffeepot. "It means she will be all but impossible to find. He could have taken her anywhere. Anywhere in all the world, you understand? Those men on their camels will be searching in vain. She hasn't just been smuggled out of the Citadel or the city. She's *gone*."

Rafiq's gaze was steady. "*All* but impossible, you say? There is some way of finding them, then?"

"Maybe."

"Tell me."

She knotted her fingers together, thinking hard. "None of the spells that I—that I have heard of are powerful enough to lead you to her. But there is a book. It's called the Scroll of Simon. It's said to contain a spell for finding anything you desire, anywhere under the sky or on the earth or in the sea."

"And will it tell me how to kill a djinni?"

"You can't kill a djinni," she snapped. "They are far too powerful. You can trick them and trap them and command them, but you can't fight them."

"Trapping and commanding will do. Will this book show me how to do that too?"

She ran her tongue across dry lips. "I can do that," she admitted cautiously, regretting every word. "I've never done it, but I know how you could do so. If you had to."

"Good! Then get this book and we will find the djinni and the girl."

"It's not that easy. I don't have the Scroll of Simon. So far as I know there is only one copy."

"Which is where?"

"Baghdad. In the House of Wisdom. All the ancient texts of the infidels are being gathered there by order of the caliph and translated into proper Arabic. There are books on medicine and science and geography—and magic."

"Well then." He calculated, talking almost to himself. "I have contacts in the City of Peace—friends who will help. I can pay for a look at this book. Baghdad is thirty days away by caravan, if you take the Palmyra route. A man riding alone might do it much faster, but it would be far more dangerous. So..."

"There's no hurry. All the amir's men on all his camels will not find a djinni before you do."

"Would you say *there's no hurry* if it were you, or your own daughter, in this creature's cruel hands?" asked Rafiq, and Taqla bit the inside of her mouth because the one thing she had not allowed herself to do was imagine what it must be like for the abducted Ahleme. In this disguise, she could not afford to. Annoyed, she swatted at a fly.

"The Djinn are not evil, you know. Not inherently. Like Mankind and unlike the Angels, they were created with free will."

"Truly? Well, I've seen fewer years than you and bow to your wisdom, but in my experience it's not much reassurance that they're no worse than us."

Taqla could not bring herself to argue over that one. "I can get you to Baghdad in two days, maybe less," she said in a low voice, "if that is what you choose to do. And I can help you trap the djinni, though you risk your life."

"Two days? You're sure?" His eyes lit up. "What would you ask from me in return?"

Oh yes. Of course she should demand a fee. Why else would Umar the Scholar offer his aid to a stranger? "In return I want..."

"Yes?"

"I want the captured djinni to be my own servant. And when you come into the highest office, if you do"—even here in private she was careful with her words—"then I want my choice of any magical device in the treasury of Dimashq."

Thoughtful, he nodded. "You have my word."

"Then you must prepare to leave for Baghdad."

"Tonight?"

"No. You'll be travelling by daylight. Tomorrow."

"But in the desert it's better to—"

"Are you telling me how best I should get you there? In *two days*?" she asked while privately agonising over the work she would need to do to prepare the device she had in mind.

Rafiq lifted his hands. "No. Of course not. Forgive me."

"Tomorrow is Friday. Come back here just before the afternoon call to prayer. You'll be leaving when the streets are at their emptiest." She scrambled to her feet, her mind already sunk in plans, and gasped when Umar's old bones refused to cooperate. Rafiq, rising, caught her arm to steady her and clasped his hand over hers. His grip was strong and confident, and she cringed as the spell of shaping bent.

"Thank you, wisest of scholars."

She turned away, hurriedly pulling the headscarf over her crumbling features. "And bring a saddle," she ordered gruffly.

Ahleme woke upon a bed spread with a fur coverlet and knew at once that it wasn't her own. She sat up, took a look at her surroundings, and as her eyes tried to make sense of what they saw and the memories filled her mind, she clapped both hands over her face.

She wasn't wearing a veil. A squeak of anxiety escaped her lips.

She wasn't wearing her own clothes either. The stiffly embroidered layers had been replaced with loose *shalwar* pantaloons and a tiny top of bronze-colored silk whose artfully slashed and filmy fabric made the minimum possible concession to her decency. Ahleme ran her hands over the silken scraps in amazement and horror. It was a costume even a dancing girl would have blushed at, but trimmed with fringes of gold coins in a manner similar to that she'd seen on the clothes of some desert women. Her hair was pulled back into a complex braid held with a golden filet and there were thick gold bangles coiled about her ankles and her wrists too. Strings of the coins hung across her bare midriff, and as she sprang out of bed, those coins made a tinkling noise. Her bare feet sank into mounded carpets and stumbled over cushions.

She couldn't make out the dimensions of the room. There were pillars certainly and arches too, and oil lamps hanging on chains from some of these, but the light was uncertain and shapes peculiar, and the shine and the shadow seemed to merge with each other in a manner that confounded the eye. Ahleme dug her nails into the palms of her hands and circled the big low bed, growing more frantic by the second. Under the rugs, the floor was level and did not creak. The pillars were translucent, bluish in color, reflecting glimmers of light at odd angles. Suddenly she glimpsed the moon overhead, but another step quenched its light, turning it to a distorted ghost. *Glass,* she thought, *the roof is glass. The pillars and arches are of glass. And the walls—*

The walls were not there.

She got to the edge of the rugs and there was a lip of thick blue glass and then nothing, a black void. The sound of rushing water rose up faintly as from a great depth. No walls, just faint rainbow arches of glass disappearing into the darkness beyond her and below her and above her. The room she was in, she realized as her stomach rose to meet her throat, was hanging in midair upon a web of glass strands like one of those brittle confections of spun sugar served at banquets. One false step and she would fall, and only God would know how far. Ahleme recoiled from the edge, retreating back upon the cushions, beginning to whimper.

"You will see better when dawn comes."

Ahleme whipped round and saw a woman standing between her and the bed, a young woman of great beauty, very tall and delicate and extraordinarily pale, with long, unbound hair the same white as the fur coverlet on the bed. Ahleme had never seen anyone like her and could not guess where she had appeared from. "Where have you brought me?" she cried.

"What's happening?"

"Hush. Be calm."

"The man with the scroll—is he here?" Ahleme gasped, moving toward her. "Did he bring me here?"

"Don't be afraid. I'm your friend," said the strange woman, and she caught Ahleme as she fell forward, seizing the stranger's skirts and bursting into tears. "Hush," the pale woman repeated, enfolding her in her arms and stroking her hair. "I feel your pain."

"Who are you?" Ahleme asked, sobbing, her voice muffled in the other's robe.

"I'm Zubaida, sister to the one who carried you here." At that, Ahleme lifted her head, shocked into silence. The woman added, "You're safe with me."

"What does he want?" She glanced around quickly. "Is he here?"

"Soon."

"What—?" Ahleme began to squeal but Zubaida laid a finger gently on her lips, trapping the words.

"Shh. Listen to me. Oh, you're younger than I thought. Listen and don't cry. My brother is great among the Djinn—" She broke off as Ahleme shrank from her embrace, realizing rather belatedly that this strange woman was not pinkly pale as certain of her father's concubines from beyond the Black Sea were, but the whitest shade of blue, and that her eyes were without color. Even her brows were like white gull feathers. Her long hair hung upon the air, undulating softly.

"A djinni!"

"He has seen your beauty and wants you for his wife."

"Me?" The news hit Ahleme like a blow. "He can't. I can't. My father won't allow it." She was aware she was babbling a little, but couldn't stop herself. "There was no contract, no judge to bear witness. I may not be married to him."

"Then you'll have to settle for being his concubine."

Ahleme mouthed *No!* but no sound came out. Her stomach felt as if it were full of lead.

"He desires you to be the mother of his children."

"No," she whispered. "You must let me go. Please!"

"The choice isn't mine. I'm as powerless in this as you are."

Ahleme was not used to feeling so helpless and she ground her knuckles against her lips. Zubaida stroked her cheek.

"Your pain is mine also, sister. This is a terrible thing he does."

"My father will not permit this. He will send soldiers. They will find me."

"Your father doesn't know where you are."

Ahleme bit her lip. She felt dizzy. "You're a djinniyah. Wish me away from here, safe back in my own room." She felt the other woman stiffen, but she was so distraught that she barely registered the flash of Zubaida's eyes.

"You think that will help you? You think I can go to war with my brother? Oh, you're quick to give orders, but you don't know what it is you're demanding."

"Then what am I to do?" she wailed.

"Are you asking my advice?"

"Please! Please help me, elder sister."

Zubaida sat back, eyes narrowing. "Well, I might be able to help you—but you must never let him know that I've done so."

"Of course not." Any hope was better than none, she thought, not caring what she had to promise.

"I can gift you with a magic. It must be subtly done, and work in line with your own will, or else Yazid will know that it's not your own doing."

"Yazid—that's his name? Is he very cruel?"

"He is...not one that someone so tender as yourself should be paired with."

"Oh." Ahleme shuddered. "What is this spell?"

"When he comes to lie with you, you must want to stop him, that's all. Can you do that? Can you want to drive him off?"

"I can want, but if he's stronger than me..."

"Don't worry about that. It's enough that with all your will you must reject him."

"Yes. Of course."

"Good. Open your mouth."

Ahleme hesitated.

"You don't have long, sister—he'll be here soon. You must trust me!"

With a droop of her eyelids she obeyed, parting her lips. Lightly Zubaida bent in and laid her own mouth open over hers and Ahleme quivered, feeling the soft heat of another woman's lips. Then Zubaida began to speak, lip to lip, passing the almost inaudible words direct from tongue to tongue. The syllables seemed to explode softly against Ahleme's palate, filling her head with steam, making her heart pound as the pale woman's tongue fluttered over hers. The chant went on for some moments, and then Zubaida pulled away, smiling.

"There."

Ahleme licked her lips cautiously, tasting rosewater. "Is that it?"

"It's good enough, child," said Zubaida, her eyes flashing somewhat, "so long as your will is strong."

"I'm...sorry." Her status as the daughter of a great amir was reasserting itself. She couldn't find her courage, but dignity and duty emerged through the fog of shock. "I thank you. May I send a message to my father? I can tell him where I am!"

Zubaida shook her head. "But I can let you see him, if that'll ease your heart."

She nodded.

"Come here then." Zubaida took her by the hand and led her to one of the glass pillars that rose from the floor into unseen spaces overhead. The glass was smooth but not regular. Zubaida stood behind her, directing her to look into the reflective surface, and Ahleme gawked. She had seen glass formed as beads and panes and pitchers before but never anything as big as this, which seemed like a waterfall turned to stone.

"What can you see?" Zubaida asked.

"Just myself." In that clouded mirror, her body didn't look like her own. She was shocked how alluring the concubine's clothing made her appear, from the barely restrained orbs of her breasts to the golden-brown sweep of her legs. Over her shoulder, Zubaida looked as pallid as something that had crawled out from under a stone.

"Look beyond yourself. See your father."

Carefully Ahleme focussed behind her own reflection and there, dimly at first, she saw another picture begin to form. Her father was standing over a map, a big one burned onto the spread-out hide of a white oryx. He was scowling and pointing at a symbol and then jabbing that finger at the men who waited upon him. Ahleme could hear no sound, but she recognized the captain of the palace guard and the vizier and the chief of spies. As she stared, the captain ordered soldiers out of the room, obviously barking at them.

"Father!"

"Quiet. He cannot hear you."

"They're searching for me," she said. "He's sending out his men to look for me." At those words the scene shifted and she saw the Citadel gate. A troop of soldiers was riding out on horseback, each man clad in black with the blue cloak of the Amir of Dimashq. In the centre of the market square, the troop split suddenly into nine smaller units and these rode off in different directions, heading, she realized, for each of the city's nine gates.

The scene shifted to the Bab Sharqi, the eastern gate of the city. She knew it because it was the oldest of them all and still stood as the Romans had built it, with three arches side by side. Troops were clattering out through the central aisle. But not just troops; there was a group of three men on camelback, whipping their beasts to a lumbering trot. And there were further knots of men visible on the pale road too, under a staring moon.

"Are they all looking for me?" The thought that the whole

city might be mobilised was like a rush of strength in her veins.

"My brother has kicked over the wasps' nest," said Zubaida. "It will be a while before it settles again."

The scene shifted to an interior, a large arched space with the characteristic striped brickwork walls and arches of one of Dimashq's caravanserais. In the foreground crouched Rafiq the Traveller; she recognized him at once. He was packing a set of saddlebags.

"This is someone you're looking for?" Zubaida asked, sounding almost amused.

"Me?" She couldn't disguise the unsteadiness of her voice. "No. I mean, that's not anyone I know."

Zubaida lifted a white eyebrow. And when Ahleme turned back to the glass the vision had melted away.

"Please, show me Dimashq again," she begged.

"Are you amusing my beloved in my absence, Zubaida?" said a deep voice behind them both. "That's most kind of you, Sister."

The djinni Yazid had arrived.

Chapter Five

In which a bad first impression is made, and two journeys begin.

"You can't go with this man!" Lelia protested as Taqla knotted a cloth bag of dried dates. "Days and nights out in the desert with him, alone!"

"I am not going anywhere. Zahir is going with him."

"Zahir?" Lelia planted her fists on her broad hips. "Oh—and that makes all the difference!"

"Of course it does. There can be nothing improper imputed to me."

"Because *Zahir* doesn't think that this Rafiq has a handsome face, does he?"

"Lelia!" Taqla went crimson. "Don't be ridiculous! Someone has to accompany Rafiq to make sure he brings back the Horse Most Swift."

"So you don't trust him?" she demanded with an air of impending triumph.

"Yes...I trust him." Taqla shook her head, flustered. "I'm sure he's an honorable man. But you have to be sensible about these things."

"Oh, that's what it's called now, is it? Being *sensible*?"

"Think about it. He's on a quest to rescue the daughter of the amir. If he succeeds, we will have a powerful ally in the Citadel."

"If he succeeds," the housekeeper countered, "there will be someone in the Citadel who knows exactly what you are. Never trust the man in power, girl. Don't you know anything? Don't you remember what that amir did to your great-grandfather?"

"Shut up." Taqla clenched her fists and bit her lip. "Of course I remember. But you have to trust someone sometime. I trust you, don't I?"

"You're not listening to me, I notice!"

"Because you're fussing over nothing. It's a journey of only a few days, that's all. Baghdad is safe and I will get to speak to the scholars in the House of Wisdom face-to-face instead of writing all those letters. That will be worth so much to my studies!"

"Well, I heard that this man tore the veil off Khadiga al-Hava and is not to be trusted."

"That's street gossip and belongs in the gutter with the dung. He told me the true story himself. Why would anyone want to see Khadiga's face?"

Lelia cooled her vehemence momentarily to consider this. "Well. I've seen her in the bathhouse and she's no beauty, that's for sure."

"See? And don't you think this is a good thing he's doing, rescuing this poor girl from the Djinn?"

The fire came back into Lelia's tone. "That's why you're risking your honor, is it? Out of the compassion of your heart?"

"I'm not risking my honor. I told you, Zahir will accompany Rafiq the Traveller. What possible law can be broken?"

"Oh, because Zahir doesn't think like Taqla, does he? Listen, girl, I'm not stupid. I've seen the look in your eyes when you say his name. Men may do their thinking with what hangs between their legs, but women are just as bad, believe me. Haven't I been married three times? I *know*. And that Rafiq with his fine face and his nice manners and his fancy stories is just the sort for a clever-clever girl like you to lose her head over."

Taqla drew herself up, feeling injured. "I have not lost my head!"

"You think you're any smarter than the rest of us when it comes to men? You're a little girl! You know nothing yet. You haven't even had your heart broken."

"Then maybe it's time I did," she snapped. "Since there's no chance of me marrying and I have no family name to uphold, what does it matter?"

Lelia seemed to shrivel. "Don't say that."

"Why not? It's true. You know it."

"You will marry. We will arrange it somehow, God willing."

"And leave this house to enter the harem of another family? No." She smiled savagely. "I would rather remain a sorceress and hidden from the world, forever."

"Don't say that!" Lelia made the sign to warn off the Evil Eye, then came forward and laid a hand on her arm. "I don't want him to hurt you," she said in a much more subdued voice, and Taqla relented slowly, stroking the older woman's calloused fingers.

"He won't hurt me. I know what it is he wants. He means to marry Ahleme, the Jewel of Dimashq. And so I'm going to help him do that. All of us will profit and he will never know who I really am, I promise."

Rafiq approached the house of Umar the Scholar on foot with the horse saddle and bags slung over his shoulders. He'd have preferred to have his servants do the carrying, but he understood Umar's need for discretion. For the same reason, despite his poor relations with the House al-Hava, he brought no guards, wearing instead his most nondescript travelling clothes and covering his face and head.

Having been let in by the housekeeper—and the woman honored him with the most disapproving mutters, which he failed to see he'd done anything to justify—he was shown into the courtyard where he found Zahir abd-Umar squatting on his haunches, picking his teeth indolently with a splinter.

"Zahir! Peace be upon you! God has preserved you, I see. You left me before I had a chance to thank you."

Zahir squinted up at him, half-grinning. "I thought you would follow through the window."

"I did, just not so quickly as you. Don't tell me you didn't see the girl in the room?"

"A girl?"

"With not a stitch of clothing on her."

Zahir shook his head. "Alas my blind eyes! Was she pretty?"

"Not bad at all." Rafiq smiled at the memory, though what he chiefly pictured in his mind was her furious glare, her eyes wilder than those of a hawk in a snare and, memorable in a predominantly dark-eyed city, green as pond water. He wouldn't forget eyes like that quickly.

"Ah." Zahir pulled an odd face. "Well, my luck was not in that day."

"I think mine was, meeting you. May you bite the noses off all my enemies!"

Zahir waved his hand vaguely then stood to his feet. "My master Umar regrets that he cannot be here to meet you, but has left you a message," he said, producing a piece of paper. "Would you like me to read it to you?"

"No, I can read." Rafiq took the note. The script was well-formed, he thought, in a scholarly hand. He read down past the formal salutations to the meat of the message.

I regret that I am unable to rise from my bed this day due to a complaint of the stomach from which I suffer, but I have instructed my slave Zahir that he is to accompany you to Baghdad and give you what assistance he may in your quest. He is most trustworthy and carries with him a letter of introduction to Hunayn ibn-Ishaq at the House of Wisdom. My good wishes and prayers go with you both. May God who sees all things and is most merciful preserve you.

"You know what it is I'm hoping to obtain in the City of Peace, Zahir?" he asked, folding the note away.

"My master told me what you are after."

"And what do you think of it?"

"Me?" Zahir looked surprised. "What should I think?" But he answered his own question quickly. "I hope you're as brave as you think you are, because it's a terrible thing to go up against a djinni. Even for the sake of the most beautiful woman in Dimashq."

"Ah—but you haven't seen her."

"No," agreed Zahir, and spat out his toothpick.

"Are we ready to go then?"

At that moment, the call of the *muezzin* echoed out across the rooftops of Dimashq, summoning the people to prayer. Zahir tilted his head. "We are now." From the folds of his clothes he brought out a tightly wound ball of silver wire of the kind often used to bind sword grips. "Horse Most Swift," he said, dropping the ball upon the floor before him.

The hair rose on Rafiq's neck as the ball shot into the air to the height of a horse's withers, trailing a silver wire behind it. Then it dropped a few feet, leaving a loop hanging in midair. Back and forth it shot, up and down, making overlaid circles great and small as if it were weaving on an invisible frame. There was far more wire in that little ball than Rafiq could have guessed, and as the ball rushed about, faster and faster, a form began to appear from the crisscrossing silver—a horse with a fine, arched neck.

Rafiq's fingers twitched as he stopped himself making the sign to avert the Evil Eye. It would not be polite in the circumstances, he thought, though this thing taking shape in front of him was deeply uncanny.

"This is the Horse Most Swift," said Zahir. "It will run faster than any beast alive, faster even than the caliph's hunting cheetahs. It can carry two men and not grow tired or need to eat. It can gallop across any surface however steep, and even across the surface of the sea, though at sunset it stands still and won't return to use before dawn. It will take us to Baghdad. You brought a saddle, I hope?"

"Yes. Of course."

"Good. It's murder on the rear end without one."

Rafiq blinked. "And where did your master come across such a thing—or did he make it himself?"

Zahir shook his head slightly. "It was made in ancient Persia. It's said to have belonged to the Emperor Darius the Great at one time, and he rode it into battle. Things like this are beyond the skill of any modern sorcerer, unless he's a djinni."

The ball slowed, unravelling down to the last few inches of wire, which carefully tucked themselves behind the Horse's ear. The two men were left staring at a beast of silver filigree, still obviously hollow but with the animal's features crafted in fine detail from its plaited tail to its flared nostrils. It was motionless.

"How does it work?" Rafiq came forward and laid a hand on its neck. The mesh was, to his surprise, inflexible. Crowning the Horse's withers were a pair of looped silver handles that looked like they were designed for holding on to, rather than, say, steering.

"Magic, of course."

"I mean, are there words you speak to animate it?"

"Yes, there are words. That's one of the reasons I am to go with you."

Rafiq took the rebuke with a nod. They saddled the horse between them and he lashed on his travelling bags.

"We should hurry. You mount up behind me, and hold my belt," Zahir instructed.

"Haven't you brought any baggage of your own?"

With a smile, Zahir indicated the empty pouch that hung from his belt. "Everything I need is in here." And Rafiq could only raise his eyebrows and accept this. The slave of the house of Umar mounted first then gave Rafiq a hand up behind him. The silver Horse stood like stone. Rafiq slipped a hand into the back of Zahir's belt and felt the man in front shift slightly, giving him more room on the saddle. Then, "Be ready," Zahir warned, and leaned forward to whisper in the Horse's silver ear.

The Horse Most Swift shuddered, stamped its feet on the flagstones and sidled nervously across the courtyard. Rafiq tried to pretend this was a perfectly ordinary steed he sat astride.

"Lelia—open the gate!" called Zahir. "Rafiq, my friend, duck your head!"

The courtyard door creaked open, the Horse sprang forward

and the two men crouched low as they surged under the lintel and out into the city beyond. The streets were all but deserted for Friday prayers, which was a good thing, because they tore down the narrow alleyways, twisting through corners and leaping goods laid out for sale. Rafiq forgot all pretensions to dignity and grabbed hold of Zahir, whose fingers were knotted white about the handles, both of them clinging on for dear life as they turned down Straight Street and headed for the city wall. The arches of the Bab Sharqi shot past in a blur and suddenly they were out on the open road and the Horse put on even more speed, its hooves thundering on the beaten rubble, tents and huts and trees flashing past as they headed, straight as an arrow, eastward—and Rafiq couldn't stop himself whooping with exhilaration.

The djinni Yazid was taller than his sister and not a delicate eggshell blue like her but white as marble, his skin shadowed with silver gray. The arms folded across his bare chest were ridged with muscle and hairless, yet the eyebrows angled across his bald forehead were black, like ink. His features were bluntly handsome, Ahleme supposed, but it was too harsh and proud a face to inspire anything but terror in a captive. She shrank back against Zubaida.

"Brother—are you trying to scare the girl out of her wits? Could you not have picked an appearance less imposing?"

"This?" He spread his arms and looked down at himself. His baggy *shalwar* were blue silk, his feet bare, his torso like his arms as hairless as a eunuch's but hard with muscle, narrowing from broad shoulders to a taut waist. "This is my most humble guise. I come to my bridal chamber girded for love, not war."

Ahleme whimpered under her breath and Zubaida shook her head. "Brother, this is wrong. You know it."

"Hush." He held up his hand. "I'll not hear more of this."

"You know that last time our kind bred with the Children of

Earth, a flood was sent to wipe out all trace of the offspring."

"I said hush." His eyes flashed. "If you have no sweet words for me, then it's time for you to leave."

"Please don't!" Ahleme begged, grabbing her arm.

"Yazid..."

"Go!"

Under Ahleme's hand, the other woman's flesh turned to nothing, and from where her solid form had stood an explosion of white moths rose up, fluttering and swooped around her, wings brushing her skin like kisses before the whole swarm flew apart and vanished among the glimmering planes of glass. Ahleme was left alone with her captor.

She put one hand over her mouth, the movement instinctive.

Yazid smiled. "Too late for that. I have admired your beauty for a long time, my beloved. You have nothing you need hide from me."

"I am not your beloved," Ahleme managed to get out, though all the power had gone momentarily from her voice and it was more like a whisper. "I am Ahleme bint-Jamil and you have no authority to take me from his house."

Yazid's heavy lids drooped in a cool blink. "Come here and sit with me, beloved. You must be hungry and thirsty by now. We'll eat together." A tilt of his hand revealed a low table laden with food that had not been there by the bed when she had risen from it. She could see plates of roast meats, fruit and flatbreads and quenching iced sherbets to drink. Ahleme was hungry—she guessed by the gnawing in her stomach that it was at least a day since she had last dined—but her hunger was not so strong as her wariness.

"No. You must let me go."

"Are you telling me what to do?"

She took a deep breath. "I remind you of your honor."

"Oh." He chuckled. Then to her confusion he answered, "If slaves had honor, then you might have that right."

"Are you a slave? Who is your master then?"

The humor died out of his eyes, leaving them cold. "Come here to me."

"No."

Without warning he vanished—only to appear instantaneously behind her and drop his hands on her bare shoulders. Ahleme squealed and tried to wriggle from his grasp. He caught her by the jaw and held her. His hands were warm and dry on her skin. Somehow she had expected someone that pallid to be clammy to the touch.

"You're very beautiful." He loomed over her, his face hovering over hers so close that she could feel his breath. He smelled of burning cedarwood. "There's no need to be afraid, I'm not going to harm you. You will bear me a son. A perfect Child of Earth and Fire, with his mother's blood, his father's power."

"No!" Ahleme twisted her face against the painful grip of his fingers.

"No?" Lifting her almost off her toes, he marched her backward, step by stumbling step, and pushed her onto the bed where she sprawled with mouth and eyes wide. He knelt over her, his eyes blazing. "Am I not good enough for you, Daughter of Earth? Is my line not noble enough?"

"You're not even human!" she gasped.

"How *dare* you!" He didn't raise his voice, but black lines of script began to form over his skin, even on his scalp. Those across his cheekbones looked like scars. "Your forebears were made of mud, little human, while mine blazed among the stars of heaven!"

"Then do not break the laws of God!" she cried, desperate. "Why can't you return me to my father and ask for my hand, with honor?"

"Ask? Ask his permission?" He bared teeth that were just a little bit too pointed to be human. "I do not need to stoop to *asking* any Child of Earth. Including you." With one hand on her breastbone, he shoved her flat on her back, pinning her. With the other he tore the flimsy silk of her top, baring her breasts.

For Ahleme there was no question of fighting him off. He was far too strong for that. There didn't even seem to be a question of screaming. She had hardly any air in her lungs with that heavy hand on her chest. She opened her mouth in a silent cry of protest as his expression filled with pleasure, his gaze feasting on her nakedness.

"Beautiful," he growled, almost in awe, his free hand moving to play across the swell of her breasts, hot on her tender skin, squeezing the softly firm flesh. For the first time in her life she felt a man's fingers close about her nipples, felt the pang as he tugged at her. "Perfect."

She shut her eyes, trying to gather her will. Zubaida had promised her aid. Zubaida had said...

Yazid's hand left her breast and slid down the length of her body, snapping the strings of coins, pressing hard on her stomach, groping under the low line of her *shalwar* trousers to cup the silky mound of her sex. He did it slowly, savouring her body. She squealed at the violation and tried to twist out of his reach, but he was kneeling astride her thighs by now and she couldn't escape.

"Stop that," he remonstrated.

She tried to clamp her legs together, but it was impossible to close them against the hand that was forcing its way into her tender folds. It hurt. Pain boiled up to join her terror and confusion. She sank her nails into his arms because she couldn't reach his face, and shrieked with panic as she tore at the hard muscle.

And she felt herself change. Her upper lip split to the nose, peeling back to reveal teeth and gums. Tusks thrust out of her lower jaw. Pustules bubbled up beneath her skin, bursting with a stink of pus. Her bones twisted out of symmetry and her left eye swelled up, going blind, bulging out of its socket. Her breasts withered to ragged flaps of skin and sprouted bristles while her stomach shrivelled clear down to her spine—and her virgin sex burst open like a gangrenous bladder, in a welter of rotted flesh.

"What!" Yazid roared, recoiling. "What's this?"

Ahleme couldn't answer, and could hardly think. Her blue, swollen tongue lolled out from between her jaws, drool slicking her crusted face. Her body felt like an alien thing, like a corpse in which she was trapped. She tried to pull herself up the bed, away from him, but though he wasn't holding her anymore, her sticklike limbs lacked the strength. She looked down at herself, but it was too much to bear. She vomited over her own chin.

"Daughter of a bitch! Stop this!"

"No," she spat. In the fevered depths of her mind she clung to one thought—*I revolt him.*

"Do you think I'm afraid of you?" he demanded. The script tattooed on his skin was nearly clear enough to read now, and there were long claws on his hands. "Do you think I cannot become just as monstrous?"

"Your son," she lisped thickly past her tusks and the clogging lumps of matter. "How will your perfect son turn out if I conceive him now?"

Yazid jumped to his feet, flushing a deep, dark blue from head to foot. He didn't say another word, but bellowing with fury, he smashed his foot down on the low table, turned into a column of blue flame and vanished upward, the glass palace glowing for a moment like a thousand streaks of lightning. Then it went silent and the only movement was the oil lamps rocking on their chains.

Ahleme laughed and laughed. Then she cried, and there was no distinguishing between the two noises. After that she lay back and shut her eyes and prayed to die.

When she opened them again, she thought that in her shock she must have dozed off momentarily. There was that same feeling of returning to the waking world. She lifted her hand to her face and stared for a long time at her narrow fingers, her flawless skin. She touched her face and felt the unbroken lips and narrow lines of teeth, and she licked the end of one finger with the delicate tip of her tongue. Only then did she dare to look down at herself. There was no sign of the foul transformation that had racked her body, and only her ripped clothing and the scattered coins showed what Yazid had attempted.

Rolling off the bed, she crawled wearily over to the table. The platters were scattered, the food strewn about on the rugs. She picked up a ewer that had held peach nectar. A small pool still remained in the hollow of its belly. Stifling a sob, she tilted the liquid to her dry lips.

Chapter Six

In which seekers come to the House of Wisdom,
and a noble maiden falls.

The Horse Most Swift didn't stop to eat or drink, but with its feet it consumed the miles. Out into the desert it galloped, over stony ridges and the sweeping plains of grit where its gait could grow smoother, and Taqla grew used to the sound of its hooves going *tarampara-rampara-ram* and the hot sun overhead and the endless shuddering surge of the silver beast beneath them. The flat desert became a flat, cultivated plain before they reached Baghdad, but it made no difference to the Horse Most Swift. Even the Euphrates River shot past beneath its silver hooves with the same hollow echoing beat.

The two riders didn't talk because the Horse Most Swift was steered by her will and she needed to concentrate on avoiding collisions. A rock or a tree could rear up from the landscape and they'd be on it in moments. And this was a good thing because it kept her mind off Rafiq. He sat right behind her and his thighs bumped against hers—not that she retained any foolish hopes in that direction, but was uncomfortable to be reminded.

At night, when the Horse Most Swift had drawn to a halt, she produced from the seemingly empty Bag That Holds the World, a goathair windbreak complete with struts, a bundle of kindling, a full set of pots for brewing coffee and enough food for both of them. Then there was time to talk, while the stars overhead wheeled around their axis and the moon rose over the empty land. Rafiq would draw from his clothing a wind-scoured slip of tree root or burnished bone that he had found while they were setting up camp, and carve away at it with a small knife while he spoke. The first night he whittled a fleeing hare and the tiny animal seemed to quiver with life in his palm.

And after dinner she bundled herself up in a hooded *aba* of thickest wool to sleep, aware that the shape of Zahir was not likely to last while she was unconscious, and watched the fire through a chink in the stifling folds of cloth. She had to be careful to wake early and renew her disguise under her bedclothes and a mantle of dew.

"So why aren't you married?" she asked on the first night. It was a legitimate question even for a casual acquaintance, since it was so unusual for a man of his age and status not to be.

Rafiq managed a shrug that involved both shoulders and facial expression. "I used to be, when I was much younger." He drew a paper-thin sliver of wood from the back of the animal he was carving, and then his hands fell still. "But while I was away on a trading journey to Medina she cut her hand on the hasp of a gate, and caught a fever from that wound. By the time I came home, thinking to find my wife about to bear my first child, all there was for me to see was her grave—hers and the unborn child with her."

She made a noise of sympathy in her throat, moved by his brooding eyes.

"I couldn't even see her off." His voice was soft. "That's how necessary I was."

Taqla stifled the desire to touch his arm. "Did you love her?"

He smiled, but sadly. "We used to fight all the time. I was very young, and very stupid. I thought that a wife was something like a bridle or a cart. Something that did its job well or badly. And I thought she was a bad wife because she nagged me." His mouth twisted. "But when she was gone I missed her. And it dawned on me that she'd had a life and a death that I was barely a part of. Like I was the one who wasn't real."

"There is no Fate but the one given to us by God," said Taqla, her lips shaping the familiar sympathetic words automatically.

"I haven't married again. I feel..." He sighed. "It's clear that the journeys I make are too dangerous to take a family with me. And I don't want to leave another wife behind like that. So..." He spread his hands in a resigned gesture.

"Or you could stop travelling."

"No." He lifted his gaze, his eyes glinting in the low firelight. "I could not. Not yet. I am only myself when I'm on the road. When I stay too long in Dimashq, I become someone I don't even recognize."

They entered the City of Peace on foot through the Bab al-Sham, the Horse Most Swift ravelled up into a ball of silver wire, and with its saddle concealed in Taqla's travelling pouch.

Baghdad was a terrible shock to her. She had rarely been outside the walls of Dimashq in her whole life, and never before this far. She tried to hide it, but she was occasionally aware that Zahir was gawping like a peasant. Dimashq was an ancient city built of brick and mud that had once been great, but was now as slumped and purposeless as an elderly widow, its buildings piled one on another as if they had crashed down from heaven, every road a twisted alley, its grand houses falling inexorably into decay. Baghdad in contrast was a new city less than seventy years from its foundation, a planned city with a massive circling wall that was as perfectly round as the sun and with straight broad streets that led from every point to the palace at the hub, a city of hewn marble that gleamed by moonlight and glared under the midday sun. It sat on the west bank of the Tigris where three great pontoon bridges spanned the river to the parks and palaces of the nobles on the other side. It was a place of aqueducts and fountains and the main streets were not of beaten earth and dung but, to Taqla's fascination, paved with bitumen and powdered limestone. She hadn't imagined any city could be so grand. In those streets the clothes and the language were predominantly Persian, but everywhere there was such a mix of tongues and peoples in every type of dress that she couldn't even guess where some of them had travelled from. She was secretly pleased that Rafiq had been before, that he could take rooms for them in a caravanserai he had a part ownership in, that he knew the geography and could lead them to the House of Wisdom. Not that it was difficult to find in the end, because it stood next to the palace, under the shadow of its green copper dome.

Hundreds of feet above the milling crowds, on the very top of that dome, was the statue of a mounted warrior. When Taqla gazed up, his lance was at rest, pointing at the ground. The people of the city boasted that he would point in the direction of any enemy approaching Baghdad.

The House of Wisdom itself was a square building with a tower for the observation of the stars and a grand courtyard, all surrounded by a garden full of flowering rosebushes. Small groups of people sat around in the garden playing chess and conversing. Above the main doorway was an inscription in gold lettering—

The world is supported by four things alone: the learning of the wise, the justice of the great, the prayers of the righteous and the valor of the brave.

Nevertheless Taqla was relieved to find that Rafiq, mindful of the fifth pillar of the world, had brought sufficient funds to pay various doorkeepers and functionaries, thus speeding the process of access to those of real importance. She was also impressed that he'd thought to bring a gift for the library—a bundle of the peerless paper of Samarqand.

Rafiq, she had to admit, did this sort of thing better than she did. He'd insisted that they change into their best clothes before applying for an interview, which of course made sense, but also that they visit one of the five thousand bathhouses that Baghdad was reputed to boast, in order to clean up beforehand. That had given Taqla occasion for enormous anxiety. The prospect of her magical disguise failing while Zahir wore only a twist of cloth about his hips was not pleasant, but as it turned out, the proximity of so many near-naked men—

paunchy and hairy, most of them—had only bolstered Zahir's sense of masculinity. The only bad moment had come when they were broiling in the steam room. She'd been lying facedown on the heated surface of the marble island when Rafiq had stretched out beside her, his skin sheened with sweat, his muscles as sculpted as sand dunes. She'd had to crawl toward the centre of the slab where the heat was actually painful in order to wrench her mind off the way the beads of perspiration stood upon his taut stomach, and had lain there with gritted teeth, pressing her forearms to the scorching marble. Luckily she'd been called away soon after by an attendant to submit to a soapy massage so ferocious that she'd thought her bones were being dislocated, followed by a deluge under a bucket of cold water that had truly put paid to any lingering lasciviousness.

She was still aching from that massage as the two of them were shown into the House of Wisdom, and she welcomed the pain. Pain anchored her to reality, she told herself, and shot down the twittering birds of foolish fancy.

The room they were ushered into and bade to sit down within was lined with niches, twelve rows of niches all the way to the ceiling, the higher ones only accessible by ladder. In every niche were piles of books and scrolls, each wrapped in a leather strap. Taqla's mouth watered. She longed to look through the volumes.

"Wait here," the servant of the House said, backing away as a slave entered with a single cup of thick black coffee for each of them. It was a polite but not effusive welcome and the slave stayed to keep an eye upon them. Taqla clenched her fists as she sat upon her cushion. There were more books in this one building than in any since the Library of Alexandria, she had heard, on every subject from alchemy through mathematics to ethics. More were being added every day, with the scribes of the House translating documents from every language in the world and the scholars of science and philosophy writing all they knew. This place held more precious treasure, as far as she was concerned, than the whole of the caliph's palace.

Rafiq, less awed, stood and ambled over to look at a niche.

"Don't touch!" snapped the slave as he laid his hand upon a scroll. "The books are in particular order and are not to be opened."

"Just looking," he rejoined mildly, turning his head to squint at the titles, which were tooled into the leather straps binding them shut. "*The Book of the King*—what's that about?"

"Medicine." Taqla seized the excuse to join him at the wall. "And there—*Ten Treatise on the Eye*."

Rafiq looked suitably impressed. "*The Spiritual Meadow of John Moschos*," he read out, switching to the niche above.

"Uh…it's a Nasrani text. A collection of their holy stories."

Rafiq dropped his voice. "And you say that this Ibn-Ishaq is a Nasrani too? How does the caliph trust him with the House of Wisdom?"

Taqla smiled. "He's beyond reproach. He once spent a year in prison for refusing to concoct a poison for the caliph's enemies, claiming that he had no right to bring harm to anyone."

Rafiq looked sceptical. "That makes him trustworthy?"

"The caliph has declared him a man of virtue." Taqla shifted to another shelf, her eyes devouring the titles—the *Physics* of Aristotle, the *Geography* of Ptolemy. She was only paying Rafiq partial attention, vaguely aware that he was drifting the other way down the shelves, until he spoke again, turning a scroll so he could read the title out.

"The *Book of Insects' Buzzing*? What does that mean?"

Then she was on top of him and knocking his hands away from the shelf before she even stopped to think. "No! Get off it!"

Rafiq stepped back and gave her a very hard look. "I wasn't doing anything!"

"Don't even touch it," she ordered, her stomach scrunched up tight against her heart. Then she grasped how strangely he was regarding her and tried to explain. "That one's a magical text."

"Are you this bossy with Umar?" he asked pointedly.

That hurt, to her surprise. "You are not my master," she

defended herself.

"Praise God, the Merciful and Compassionate!"

"Look, you don't understand—that book is dangerous."

"To *touch*?"

"Yes!" Then she took a deep breath. "Maybe. Just stay away from that sort of thing. It's something you shouldn't mess with. You have no idea what you're doing."

"But clearly you do, Zahir abd-Umar," said a voice behind them, and they both turned to see a middle-aged man with hair worn long in the Persian style and a gray beard, carrying their letter of introduction in one hand and a roll of papers in the other. Taqla bowed low, and in a moment Rafiq caught up and bowed too, though with greater reserve as befitted a free man.

"Please, sit with me," said Hunayn ibn-Ishaq after they had apologised for impinging upon his routine and he had waved away any suggestion that he might have better things to do than meet them, then enquired after their health and the health of Umar who had sent them. "Would you prefer that we converse in Syriac?"

"It's not necessary," Rafiq said, sounding a little cool. He'd taken Ibn-Ishaq to be suggesting that they were uneducated provincials, unable to cope with proper Arabic.

"A pity." The librarian smiled faintly. "It's my own first language and I miss the cadences." His eyes flicked slightly to indicate the slave waiting by the door. The slave looked like he was a Turk, as far Taqla could guess, and presumably did not speak the language of Al-Sham.

"If you so wish, Master of the House," she said smoothly in Syriac.

Ibn-Ishaq smiled. "You are kind." He put Umar's letter on the carpet between them. "Well, this is an unusual request. We get many people asking for copies of different books, or parts of books, and of course we do our best to honor such requests. But there are not many who would ask for an excerpt from this particular scroll."

"No?" asked Taqla blandly. She had corresponded with Ibn-

Ishaq in the name of Umar for a few years, but that didn't mean she knew the man. She was wary of condemning herself.

"There are not many who would know how to use the extract you request, either. Your master being an exception, I now assume. An incantation of finding." His eyes flicked to Rafiq. "Someone must have lost something very valuable."

They'd travelled so swiftly that the news from Dimashq hadn't yet reached Baghdad. Rafiq looked noncommittal. "What one man holds as precious is worthless to another."

"And yet the second may bargain to his advantage."

"We're willing to pay well for a true copy from the Scroll of Simon."

"In the original Greek," put in Taqla. "Exactly as written."

"I'm sure you are, having travelled so far for it." Ibn-Ishaq stroked his beard. "A true copy. That's what your master has told you he needs, is it? Why do you think that is?"

Taqla shrugged. "My master keeps his own council. Even I don't know his plans."

"Then it's a good thing that he has been so generous in the books he has loaned to us over the years for copying, and his name is favourably pronounced in the House of Wisdom. There are those—many of them, in high places—who would say that such a book as this scroll is dangerous and should be forbidden to the Faithful."

"Not nearly so dangerous as the one on your shelf there," Taqla pointed out.

"True. And if your master had asked for a copy from that I would have refused him. The Scroll of Simon...that is possible. In trustworthy hands it might do no harm." He cast Rafiq another long look, weighing him up. "You are Umar's agent in this, then? He describes you as a merchant-traveller."

"That's certainly accurate. I hold the purse for this transaction."

"And the nature of the text does not alarm you?"

Rafiq indicated Taqla with a tip of his chin. "Zahir has reassured me that the Art of Solomon is not just the provenance of the wicked."

Taqla bit the inside of her lip.

The librarian tapped his fingertips together. "For the friendship we owe Umar then, I will instruct my scribe to make one fair transcription of this passage you request."

Rafiq nodded. "We are grateful. Shall we agree upon a price?"

Ibn-Ishaq waved his hand languidly. "Very soon. Tell me, have you been to Saba?"

"Yes. This year." Rafiq looked quizzical, and Taqla wondered at the sudden change of subject.

"One of my scribes is working on a special project for a client. He's collating all the riddles that the Queen of Saba asked King Solomon the Wise, with their answers. Sadly the sources are fragmentary, and some of the answers are missing or clearly incorrect, so we've had to search them out. This one for example." He unrolled his papers and passed a slip across to Rafiq. "Have you heard it in your travels?"

Rafiq blinked, picked up the paper and read it out loud. *"Who is this man who weds two sisters, with no offense at his wedlock being taken by anyone? When waiting on one he waits exactly as well on the other too; husbands may be partial, but no bias is seen in him. His attentions increase as his beloveds grow old, and so does his generosity. How rare is that among married men!"*

Taqla frowned. She wanted—childishly, she knew—to answer the riddle before he did, and racked her brain. *A man at a well with two buckets?* she wondered. *A porter carrying a yoke with two baskets?* Neither answer fitted properly, and nor did any other she could think of straightaway. But when she looked up at her companion's face, his expression was as discontented as hers.

"No," he grunted. "I don't know the answer."

Taqla shook her head, irritated. Like all riddles, it left a feeling that the solution was imminent.

"That's a pity." Ibn-Ishaq stroked his beard again. "I'll tell you what. There is a man who'll know the answer. He lives only a day or so's travel south from here and is famous for his knowledge of such trifles. If you will go and get the answer from him, then by the time you return I will have a copy of the excerpt you requested awaiting you. There'll be no other charge."

"That's very generous. Why does it matter so much?" Rafiq asked.

He lifted an eyebrow. "It doesn't, in a sense. But we strive to complete our knowledge, and to have a book with all riddles but one answered..." He shook his head, pulling an expression of dismay.

"Why haven't you sent to this man before?" Taqla asked, more suspiciously.

"Ah. Well, he has a reputation. Not a good one, you see. He lives in the ruins of Taysafun and things are said of him that mean most of my messengers wouldn't care to find him. But you two...you are not frightened of such things, are you? You know how to protect yourselves."

"He's a sorcerer," concluded Rafiq grimly.

"He is usually titled a Seer, though perhaps it's the same thing in the end. It may all be nonsense of course. But it's better not to talk about these things too openly, as you know."

"And...Taysafun? What's that?" asked Taqla.

Rafiq could answer that one. "It's the old Persian capital. I've travelled past it on the road south—it was abandoned when Baghdad was built, wasn't it?"

Ibn-Ishaq inclined his head. "Much of the stonework used to build the City of Peace came from that place."

Rafiq looked at Taqla. "What do you think, Zahir—another few days? It won't make that much difference, will it?"

Taqla didn't answer for a moment. She didn't like the sound of this at all. Sorceress herself, she had never encountered another of her sort, other than her father, and had no great desire to cross swords with one. But, she reasoned, what would Rafiq do without her, if there was some magical danger? If she didn't aid him then he might have to give up his quest. She sighed. "What's this man's name?" she asked. "And what else can you tell us about him?"

Daylight showed Ahleme the glittering vertiginous extent of her prison, but brought no relief. No visitors either, and no fresh food or drink. She huddled in the centre of her bed where she felt least dizzy and wondered if she was being starved into submission or simply left to die. She hoped Zubaida might remember and have mercy, but those hopes bore no fruit. On the second day, after a night full of terrible dreams, she lost her temper and hurled a big silver ewer at a glass pillar, screaming her frustration and fear at the top of her lungs.

"What do you want?"

Ahleme turned swiftly. If her outburst had had any goal, it had certainly not been this—to summon Yazid. He stood with arms folded, his mouth a grim line. She drew herself up defiantly, licking her cracked lips. She'd knotted her torn clothing together into a semblance of propriety and she was determined he wouldn't have the joy of seeing her intimidated. But she couldn't bring any words to her lips.

"Well? Did you have something to say to me? What do you want?"

"Take me home," she said through gritted teeth.

He laughed without any pretense at humor. "Your conversation is repetitive, Flower of the Earth. You waste my time." He lifted his hand.

"Water," she said quickly, suddenly scared that he was about to leave.

"What?"

"I'm thirsty," she admitted.

Yazid's eyebrows lifted derisively, and in a flash of panic Ahleme's voice broke free.

"That's your plan, is it—starve me until I'm too weak to resist?" She would have spat if she'd had enough moisture in her parched mouth. "And to think we are told the Djinn are a proud race! You stoop lower than a dog."

"Starve you?" he growled.

She kicked an empty pitcher across the floor and said bitterly, "God curse you for your cruelty." She fully expected the djinni to fly into another rage, and in all honesty didn't care, but there was only silence in answer to her invective. Yazid's mouth opened but no sound came out, and at that moment Ahleme was smitten by a horrible suspicion.

"You do *know* that we die if we don't drink?" she asked.

Yazid's eyes flickered. "Of course I do." He made a hurried movement with his hand and a goblet carved of amber appeared at her feet, brimming with clear liquid. Ahleme couldn't help the little whimper that slipped from her lips. When she stooped to pick it up, she could smell the faint sweet odour of roses. She hesitated, a part of her convinced that this was a trick and that he would steal the drink away as quickly as he had offered it, but as the cup touched her lips, she felt cool, clean water flavored with petals wash over her tongue and down her throat like a blessing. She buried her face in the cup and slithered to her knees, and even after she had drained it it was a while before she lifted her head again.

"What's wrong with your eyes?" grumbled Yazid.

"They're trying to cry," she whispered, "but I've wept so much that I can't anymore."

He twitched his shoulders and turned to pace up and down the rug. "Why are you doing this to yourself?" he asked. "Are you so arrogant that this is worth it?"

"Arrogant?" She was confounded by the accusation.

"Do you really think you're too good for me?"

"Too good?" Ahleme blinked. She could not have felt less arrogant. She felt like a piece of soiled laundry that had been beaten to rags on a riverbank.

"Look at you—your red eyes, your grubby skin, your hair—" He grimaced. "What a mess you look! Is this the best Humankind has to offer?"

She nearly smiled. "You're not seeing me at my best." Then, as he took a few steps toward her, she added warningly, "or my worst." A seam appeared down the centre of her forehead, the skin drawing back to reveal the raw bone beneath. Yazid recoiled, and as he retreated to a safe distance, Ahleme relaxed, letting her skin repair itself. She tried to hide the trembling of her limbs.

"You think you can beat me," he growled.

I'm sure I can't, she thought bleakly, and shook her head. She'd had plenty of time to imagine how it was going to go. *I am just putting it off—until the moment you really lose your temper.*

"You want to humiliate me."

She winced. "No."

"You want a Son of Fire to bow his head to a Daughter of Earth so that all the world may mock us once more."

"No! I don't want to do anything to you. I just want to go home."

"Well, I will not let any mortal put their foot upon my neck!" He stooped to thrust his face closer to hers, his teeth bared.

"Just listen—"

He swept a hand toward her, and instantly they were both elsewhere. Outside. The sky yawed around her on all sides—above and below—and it was cold, so cold, colder than she had ever been in her whole life. Wind tore at her clothes. Her breath froze in her lungs as she drew it in, then fell in a glittering shower of ice as she exhaled. She looked down and saw a narrow curved bridge of pale blue glass beneath her feet, and below that, hundreds and hundreds of feet below, a savage mountain slope with reddish rock walls almost too steep for the snow that clung there. They were standing on the *outside* of the glass palace. Her bare feet skidded from beneath her and she fell flat with a shriek, spreading arms and legs, trying desperately to cling to the icy surface of the glass even though it was so frigid that it hurt to touch it. She screamed with terror.

"Not so arrogant now, Daughter of Earth?"

Twisting her head, Ahleme saw Yazid standing there as

calmly as if in a garden, his bare feet firm on the glass. She stretched out her hand and seized his ankle. It felt warm and solid and she grabbed the other one too, sobbing with fear. Hauling herself across the treacherous glass, she clung to his knees, her mouth open and her tears freezing upon her cheeks.

"That's right." He scooped her up beneath the arms to pull her upright against him, and she flung her arms around his waist. He didn't have to hold her, in fact he put his fists on his hips to make this quite clear. "I'm quite good enough for you now, aren't I? Suddenly you're more than happy to embrace me, I see."

Ahleme mashed her face to his bare chest and drew her first breath that wasn't a scream. He was solid and he was warm and that was all that mattered to her.

"You think you are so brave, so grand, defying me? Look at you! You are a slave of terror, a mewling wingless thing that cannot fly, only fall. Pathetic! You are nothing! Even to me you are nothing, you know. Your beauty—hah!—there are Djinn women who burn like the sun compared to you. Listen to me, Daughter of Earth, you are *nothing* to me. Only the son you will bear me matters."

Ahleme managed to raise her head. She looked into his angry, triumphant face and weighed his words against her fear. Then she pushed herself to arm's length, took two steps backward and, her eyes still locked on his, stepped off the edge of the glass and fell.

She didn't scream as she plunged through the thin mountain air. Not until Yazid, appearing out of nowhere, caught her in his arms hundreds of feet below, did she scream—and then she only let out one cry as all the breath left her lungs.

In an instant they were back in her room, standing on her rumpled bed.

"Why?" he shouted. "Why did you do that?"

Ahleme raised her stiff hands before her face, starting to gasp as she tasted the warm air, starting to shake as the terror flailed about within her. She lost all control of her limbs, trembling wildly and collapsing in his grasp. Yazid held her only briefly before shrinking away and laying her upon the coverlet where she curled up into a knot. His hand hovered over her hair but his face was a mask in which horror dominated. His rage collapsed in on itself.

"You must never do that," he whispered. "Never." Then he reached under the bed, pulling out a great length of golden chain, arm after arm of it. It had a thick coil of gold at one end, and he prised this open with his fingers and clasped it about her ankle, bending the metal to tighten it again. Ahleme was incapable even of protesting. "You must not fall," he told her.

She shut her eyes. If he had chosen to ravish her at that moment, she wouldn't have resisted because she was still looking her death in the face and the enormity of it made everything else unimportant. But he only sat and watched her, his mouth twisted and his eyes burning, until she finally stopped spasming with terror and merely shook with cold.

"You should bathe," he said then, standing to point out a sunken bath that had not previously been there. Its scented waters steamed. Beside it a low table was spread with a hot meal—cucumbers stuffed with lamb mince and rice, and a jug of heated wine.

In the moment it took for Ahleme to look that way, he vanished.

The chain was precisely judged, it turned out when she dragged herself to the waters. Long enough to let her bathe and move about the room, not long enough to let her approach the edges of her prison cell or throw herself off. Her one chance at escape, bleak as it was, had been lost.

Chapter Seven

*In which one woman sees her future
and another learns of the past.*

They had to leave Baghdad, through the Bab al-Basra and across the lower bridge, on foot so as not to excite comment, and for the same reason they spent most of the day walking southward along the road beside the eastern bank of the Tigris, through fields and over the bridges of irrigation canals, under the nodding heads of *shaduf* poles and the dusty fronds of date palms and the cloudless blue sky. A dry breeze blew steadily and made the heat bearable. There were many small villages visible on the flat plain, set among the green of the fields.

"Have you noticed that as we get farther away from the city, the villages have become walled?" Rafiq pointed out in the afternoon. "There must be something out here they fear." He was accustomed to walking alongside camel caravans and seemed tireless. Taqla, who was not used to marching far and whose feet were aching, merely grunted.

Soon after that they came to the edge of the fields. The road continued across the plain with the mounded bank of the Tigris visible to their right as usual, but the canals they crossed were no longer maintained and were full only of cracked mud, and the flat silt beneath their feet played host only to long weeds and thorny bushes. The change to the landscape was quite abrupt. Soon afterward the road swung away in a great curve in order to avoid running into an area of mounded banks and crumbled walls that sat hard by the river. This, they had been told, was the remains of the ruined city of Taysafun.

"Should we leave it till morning?" Taqla wondered as they gazed across at the blank-eyed windows and the broken domes visible even from here. It was late afternoon and the shadows were already lengthening.

"Another day? What are you worried about?"

"I don't know. Bandits maybe. Evil things are drawn to deserted houses and old ruins."

Rafiq pulled a face. "Well, if we camp here, we're very exposed. And bandits are likely to be keeping an eye on the road, if anything."

She worried that the normally fearless Zahir had lost face. They compromised by mounting the Horse Most Swift for the final approach to Taysafun's most obvious gate. It was only as they drew close that Taqla realized the scale on which these remnants were built. This city must have been in its time almost as imposing as Baghdad, and when the shattered façade of the palace came into view over the lesser rooflines, the gaping barrel vault of its central chamber, as empty as a throat, yawned wide as if it wanted to swallow the rest of the city whole.

Rafiq made an instinctive gesture to ward off evil and Taqla secretly reached into a pouch and slipped a couple of her rings onto her fingers, wedging them as far down as Zahir's thick masculine knuckles would allow.

"This isn't a pleasant place," said Rafiq in a low voice as they began their exploration on foot, passing the smoke-scorched doorway of a guardhouse. Under their feet, hardened silt from some past flood smothered the streets and thresholds, rendering most doorways so low they would have to stoop to enter. The scuffing of their sandals sounded hollow as it echoed from the silent walls. Although the sun hadn't yet set, darkness had already invaded the interiors of the buildings and lurked in the depths of alleyways. It wasn't hard to imagine that there were watchers hiding just out of sight in the shadows, and once imagined, the fancy was impossible to dismiss.

They'd been told that Safan the Seer made his dwelling in the ruin of the Fire Temple, and since such things were usually built on mounds, they made for the highest areas of ground

Heart of Flame

they could spot, as well as they could through the maze of unfamiliar streets. The ground plan of Taysafun was nearly as bad as that of Dimashq, so Taqla let her instincts lead her steps, trying to ignore the itch between her shoulder blades that insisted she turn around now and catch whoever—or whatever—it was spying upon them. It was a successful tactic, or at least when the sun finally dipped behind the western wall and the clamor of brass being struck over and over broke out from the top of an embankment, they found themselves quite close to the source of the noise.

It was a man, as they'd hoped. A skinny man clad in tattered rags standing upon a mound of rubble, arms swinging over his head, banging a ladle against a brass serving dish. He didn't seem to notice them as they toiled up the slope toward him, but he was making a great deal of noise, not just his percussion but his cries, "Come on! Come on, pets! Time to eat!" his face tilted to the sky all the time. Taqla squinted up, expecting to see pigeons, but the heavens were empty of all but the red-brown stain of dust hanging over the horizon. At last he fell silent, his arms dropping to his sides.

"Peace be upon you, Grandfather. Who are you calling to?"

Rafiq's calm question took the old man rather by surprise. Taqla's shock was a great deal worse however, when he dropped his face from the broad sky overhead and tilted it in their direction. "Who's asking?" he rasped. "Who's asking?"

He was blind, but not just blind. His eyelids had been sewn shut with sinew, the stitches angled like bird tracks across the withered leather of his face. Taqla tried not to cringe. Rafiq's expression merely stiffened. A travelled man, no doubt he was more used to life's variform cruelties.

"I apologise," he said. "We didn't mean to startle you. I'm—"

Taqla laid a hand on his arm and shook her head. He caught her meaning.

"—hoping that you're the famous seer Safan. We've come a long way to ask your advice."

"Famous, am I?" He scrambled down over the broken

stones, homing in on Rafiq's voice, feeling his way with cracked and yellowing feet that were missing several toes. Altogether he was the filthiest, boniest beggar Taqla had ever laid eyes on, almost an animate skeleton, but he moved quickly despite his blindness and the heavy pot in his off hand. He slithered up to Rafiq and lifted a hand to touch his chest and then his face. Taqla saw her companion steel himself not to recoil.

"Come miles to see me," Safan crooned, stroking his fingers across Rafiq's features. "A travelling man, companion of the road."

Taqla felt the hairs on her neck prickle. *Companion* was the literal meaning of Rafiq's name. He smiled uneasily.

"The road is good for you, isn't it?" Safan cackled. "Never the end, just the journey. You'd fuck without coming if you had the choice, wouldn't you?"

Taqla let out a hiss at the obscenity. Rafiq's lips tightened to a hard line.

"And who are you companion to?" Safan turned his attention to Taqla, groping toward her. She noticed the only point of color on his grimy form—a blue scarab beetle strung on a thong about his neck—before she shut her eyes as the filthy fingertips and the ragged nails swept her skin. The old man stank worse than a he-goat. "Oh no. *He's* definitely the handsome one," the seer announced, jerking his chin at Rafiq. "What a disappointment. Still, can't expect two of a kind, can I?" He grinned widely at Taqla, revealing brown teeth and black gums. "Pestle or mortar, my little chick," he mocked. "Have you made up your mind which you are yet?"

Taqla went cold. The world seemed to lurch. This old man was a sorcerer for certain, and with instincts sharper than anything she herself could aspire to. She suddenly knew she was in real danger here of being revealed and she had to fight to conceal her fear. "Who were you calling, Grandfather?" she said with silky politeness.

"The stars of heaven, of course. They need to come and eat."

"The stars?"

"Yes." He ran his fingers across the brass pot. "Every night I call them into the sky so they may graze. Every morning I shoo them out again."

"And what do they eat?"

"Our dreams, little chick, of course. Don't you know that? And a good thing they do, or else we'd all go mad."

Rafiq raised his eyebrows with pointed significance. "You're doing a fine job then," said Taqla weakly.

"Ah, but do I see any gratitude? Does the world beat a path to my door and strew it with rose petals? No. Only a few travellers with their questions. Questions, questions, always the same. *Will I seize the throne? Should I ally with the Romans or invade them? Shall I rule all the earth?* What about you two—do you want to rule all the earth?"

Taqla shook her head as if trying to dislodge his words from the interior of her skull. "No. Our interests are, uh, humbler than that."

"I doubt that. No one comes to Taysafun without very good reason anymore. It's accursed of God."

"We've come for the answer to a riddle."

"A riddle?" He smiled, wrinkling abominably. "I like a good game of riddles. It's been such a long time. Come and sit with me." Without waiting for an answer he scrabbled away over the boulders. Rafiq caught Taqla's eye and shrugged.

Safan led them to a ragged gap in the base of the pile of boulders, but thankfully he signed them to sit and wait before he disappeared into the darkness, sliding in with the practised facility of a scorpion under its rock. Taqla sat down, staring at the mound grimly. This was the first place in Taysafun she'd seen marble facing. Everywhere else all the marble, the ornate lintels and porticos, had been conspicuously stripped from the buildings that still stood. But this mound was made of great slabs of carved alabaster, cracked now and blackened by fire, crumbling to lime in some places. Just over the gap Safan had vanished into was a tilted and split stone bearing the winged disk sacred to the old Persian Empire.

"Is he a sorcerer?" asked Rafiq quietly.

Taqla nodded. "Be careful. Don't give him anything without my say-so." *Don't offend him,* she might have added, *don't promise him anything, don't believe what he tells you.*

Rafiq nodded and rested his hand on the hilt of his sword.

She twisted her rings, mentally preparing her defenses. No threat had yet been offered, but nothing about Safan inspired trust. What really worried her was that she couldn't help seeing something of herself in the mad old man. Was this a forewarning of what she was to become, she couldn't help wondering—deranged, repulsive, clinging to her life in a place where no normal human would live?

With a rattle of small stones Safan reappeared bearing a cloth bundle. Grunting, he settled himself in the dirt, picking at the knots. "There. Yes. I have my best cups for you. No coffee, not for years now, but there is wine. I found it in the royal tombs. No vultures for the great kings—no, that would be undignified—tombs of hewn stone and treasures for the afterlife. Luckily for us the Pale People can't stomach alcohol. They left that for me." He held up a metal cup, very dented but obviously gold from its undimmed gleam, and sniffed the interior. "Just a little dusty." Spitting into the cup, he wiped it vigorously round with the filthy rags about his waist. "There." Then he poured from a leather flask a wine so dull a red it looked brown and handed the cup to Rafiq. "For you, the chalice of a king."

Rafiq looked pained but took the cup and lifted it to his lips, miming a sip. *Good,* thought Taqla.

"And for you," Safan said to her with a leer, offering a cup set with turquoises, "the drinking vessel of an infidel queen."

"Thank you," said Taqla through gritted teeth. She had no intention of drinking, but it would have been grossly offensive to refuse outright. The cup was so heavy it was uncomfortable in the hand. She could quite believe it had been robbed from a royal tomb. The wine smelled like vinegar.

"Drink it all down," Safan cackled. "The best wine, this, fit for an emperor."

Rafiq gave a twisted smile. "Truly, a unique vintage. Incomparable."

"Oh then take it, take it. Save it for a wedding or something equally momentous. It'll come in useful I'm sure." He held the sloshing half-full flask out to Rafiq, and then added slyly, "For both of you."

Taqla gritted her teeth.

"You're the father of kindness." Rafiq stoppered the flask with a grimace and slipped it into an inner pocket.

"The guest is a king in my household. Have you any food on you, my royal visitors?"

"Um. A little." It was a relief to set the chalice aside and go looking in her bags. "Would you like some?"

"I haven't eaten in such a long time. The belly forgets, but the mouth remembers. I shall sew that up too, in time. Give me those dates. I smell their sweetness. Here," he added, stuffing his mouth with Taqla's food, "is a riddle for you. *I went hunting, and those I found I threw away, but those I could not find I kept.*"

"Lice," said Rafiq, not holding an entirely straight face.

"Very good!"

"Shall I ask you one?" With the utmost casualness he repeated the riddle of Hunayn ibn-Ishaq, which he'd memorised word for word as they walked. Taqla had to admire his cunning.

But Safan was quicker-witted yet. "Ah-ah-ah! It's against the rules to ask one that you don't know the answer to."

"What makes you think I don't?"

"You've a liar's tongue but not a liar's heart. That's the riddle you came to ask me about, isn't it?"

Rafiq admitted defeat with a smile and a dip of his head, though both were probably wasted on him. "As you say, old father. Your insight is what brought us here."

"I'd have thought your friend here would be able to solve it."

Taqla stiffened. Rafiq cast her a glance but answered

mildly, "He's a servant of wisdom, but he doesn't know the answer to that one."

"Doesn't he?" Safan sniggered and picked at the stitches of his eyelids. "Well, what will you give me for answering this riddle for you?"

"I wouldn't have thought you have much use for money out here, Father, but we will pay you." He caught Taqla's alarmed look and added, "once we have agreed upon a price."

"So much choice then! He wrapped his sticklike arms around himself and rocked back and forth in delight. "A year of your life? Your nextborn child? Your innermost heart?"

Rafiq started to look alarmed.

"Heh-heh-heh. It's been years since I had anyone's arms around me. Perhaps I should ask a kiss from your boy."

"No," said Taqla coldly before Rafiq could react.

"You shy, ugly boy?"

"I know what else can be stolen with a kiss," she answered. "No, no tricks of that sort. We leave here intact. And no promises. No debts."

Safan hunched his shoulders, his dead-man's mouth spreading in a lipless grin. "I see. It's like that, is it? Well, I will tell you what I'll accept as payment for the answer to your riddle. South of here, but before you reach Basra, there lies a great swamp that's fed by the Euphrates and the Tigris. In the middle of the swamp is an island, and on the island grows a tree. If you want your riddle answered that badly, then you'll bring me a fruit from that tree."

The prospect of being sent off on another errand knocked all the sense out of Taqla's mouth. "That's ridiculous."

"Is it? I'm not negotiating. That's my price for your answer."

"I know the swamp," said Rafiq, frowning. "How will we know which tree?"

"Oh, you'll know it. It grew from an apple core that was thrown into the Tigris a very long time ago, in a garden at the river's headwaters. A very *old* garden, do you understand? It'll be unmistakable."

Taqla clenched her fists until her nails bit the skin.

"It's also forbidden, isn't it?" said Rafiq, his voice grim.

Safan laughed at that. "See these eyes of mine? I sewed them shut when I chose to no longer believe the illusions of the world. Bring me the fruit so that I might see with new eyes— that I might see all things as they truly are."

"That's a lot to ask," said Taqla faintly, "for a riddle."

"Then leave it unanswered. Go home. Give it up, whatever it is you are trying to achieve. It can't be very important, can it?" Scuttling backward like an insect, he retreated legs first into his hole and disappeared from view.

Rafiq then shook himself as if waking from a dream and when Taqla, blinking, looked around, she saw that somehow the night had crept up around them and the stars were all out overhead.

"You might know something about magic," said Rafiq, weariness and irritation fighting for the upper hand in his voice, "but, Zahir, you're really no good at negotiation."

Ahleme had washed her hair and was braiding it up again. She'd discovered that the sunken bath in her prison would fill with fresh water, hot or cool as she preferred, at a word of command, that the bottles of perfumes and soaps and unguents at its rim never ran out no matter how much she used, and that there was always a set of clean though perilously scanty clothing laid out for her upon the bed when she had bathed. She'd also discovered that without the assistance of her slaves she was hopelessly maladroit at her toilette, and that it took hours to groom herself. So between eating and sleeping and trying to recreate the dancesteps she had once watched her slaves perform—it was shameful, but it was the only amusement she could think of on her own and she itched for exercise to relieve her frustration—she bathed a lot. She was aware that it might be cleverer in this place to let her beauty decay, but she couldn't bring herself to do it. And there was absolutely nothing else to do in her airy cell. She'd spent all her life surrounded by the women and eunuchs of the *haremlek,* and now she didn't know how to deal with solitude.

When she looked up, Zubaida was sitting on the bed, watching her with an oddly intense expression. Ahleme jumped.

"Oh!"

"I came to see how you were." A smile crept up Zubaida's face, reaching her mouth disconcertingly in advance of her eyes. "Well, by the looks of things."

"Yes." Ahleme felt strangely embarrassed, as if it would have been more proper to be discovered broken and starving. "I mean..."

"You have enough to eat and drink?" She swept a sideways look at the table, laden as always with tempting dishes.

"Yes. Now."

"Good. Keep your strength up. But don't let it soften your resolve, Ahleme."

"Of course not." The suggestion that she might be bribed into concupiscence by a few goods meals was hurtful when what she needed was comfort and reassurance.

"Your own beauty is your enemy now. So why do I see you working at maintaining it?"

She stuck her bottom lip out and let her gaze fall to the carpet. "If I looked at myself and hated what I saw, do you think I would have the will to resist him?"

Zubaida snorted. "You're a strange people, you Children of Earth. Full of contradictions. Your strength becomes your weakness and your weakness becomes your strength, always."

Ahleme didn't answer that.

"Anyway, I came to tell you that I've been to Dimashq."

"Oh—is my father...?" Ahleme couldn't finish the question. She couldn't imagine what she should hope her father was doing.

"The whole city is in uproar. Every man able to bear arms and ride is searching for you. The land is being turned upside down. Only hold out, Ahleme. Rescue is on its way."

She bowed her head, swallowing down the hope that filled her throat and made it hard to breathe. "Will they...will they be long?"

"It's up to you to refuse Yazid, however long it takes. Use the magic I've given you. Whatever happens, you must not yield to him."

She looked up from under her long lashes. "It's not going to work. If I make him too angry, in the end he will force me from spite, or just kill me."

Zubaida's mouth twisted at that. "No he won't."

"He has a terrible temper!"

"He won't kill you." There was such emphasis in her light voice that the glass bottles by the bath tinkled together. "He can't. Haven't you heard of Solomon the Wise?"

"Of course."

"Hundreds of years ago he and the sorceress Bilqis made a great magic together to bind every djinni that lived, and they put upon my people great strictures in order to protect Mankind. One of his bonds was that whatever hurt a djinni does to one of your sort, he must suffer in himself." She smiled, but oddly it did nothing good to her beautiful face. "If Yazid were to kill you, he would slay himself. If he wounds you, he feels the hurt in his own flesh."

Ahleme shrank into herself.

"I said he *can't*. You have nothing to fear, so steel yourself."

"That's what the writing on his skin is, then?" she whispered.

Zubaida nodded, and though Ahleme's impulse was then to question her about her own glacial complexion, she thought better of it before the words left her lips.

"That explains it then," she said almost to herself.

"Explains what?"

"Why you leave us alone. Mostly."

"You flatter your race," she said silkily, but Ahleme hardly heard.

"And why you haven't taken the whole world as your

domain. I mean, with the power you have, you Djinn could enslave Mankind and rule the earth. Easily. But Solomon has stopped you."

Zubaida's lips pursed. She lifted her eyebrows politely but couldn't quite hide her derision. "Enslave Mankind?" she asked. "Why?"

"Well, you could make us do anything you wanted."

"For us?"

"Yes."

"Why would that be of any value?" She lifted her hand and a flame danced in her palm. It turned into an enormous ruby, then a rose with ruby petals, then a persimmon pearled with dew, then a golden mouse that leapt off her hand and ran away across the rugs. "I can do everything I want without the need for slaves weaker than myself."

"But—"

"This house was molded by my brother out of his imaginings, because he desires to live here. It isn't mine. I come and I go as I please. It's his, and if he wants to unmake it and build another tomorrow at the bottom of the ocean, then he'll do it in a moment. What does he need anyone else for? We Djinn don't have servants or subjects. We rarely even live together, but you humans swarm in packs and fight for your place in that pack, as dogs do."

Ahleme bridled at the monstrous insult. "My father is not a *dog*, he's a great—"

"It's hard for you to understand, isn't it? We're not like you. For us it's enough to have power, but you want *power over*—you measure yourselves by how many others you can thwart. There are so many things we do have in common—love and anger and pride and joy and the law of God. But we don't have the sickness that lurks in the heart of all men. We don't have your terrible need for dominion."

Ahleme stuck out her bottom lip. "Then what is Yazid doing to me then? What does he need?"

"Freedom. We need *freedom*." She stood and walked away

toward the edge.

"Don't go!" Ahleme gasped. "Stay and talk to me. I'm so—"

But a cloud of white petals rose on the updraft and blew away over the chasm below.

Chapter Eight

In which many disguises are revealed.

"Basra really isn't that far," Rafiq said. He was still sore with disappointment and his voice betrayed his mood. "I've done the Basra to Baghdad run. It's a good-sized port, bigger than Ayla."

"You've been through the swamp?"

"Well, the road skirts the edge, on an embankment. Yes, it's a big swamp. But we've got the Horse Most Swift. We could be there in a day."

"It's not the getting there that worries me." Taqla shouldered her bag and looked around uneasily. The ruins of Taysafun had looked eerie enough by day. Under the glow of the rising moon every shadow and every broken doorway seemed cut from primordial darkness.

"What does then? The Tree? Why?"

"If such a sapling of the Tree of Knowledge does exist—and I've never heard of it, I mean my master Umar has never once breathed a word about it—then I think we're getting in way over our heads."

"You're afraid of the wrath of God?"

"Look, a thing like that won't just be sitting there waiting for every urchin boy to steal a handful of apples. It's been kept secret. And what I'm scared of is that it'll be guarded too."

"By something more dangerous than a djinni? That is what I'm looking to take on, remember. Umar promised to help me that much."

Taqla opened her mouth to argue and then shut it again, like a fish. "Can we have this discussion somewhere safer than the middle of a cursed ruin, in the dark?" she wondered.

"Fine. If we cut south through the city, we can pick up the Basra road."

So they went that way, though Taqla was far from having made up her mind that she would be heading to Basra. What she wanted most at the moment was to get out of the ruins. Her mood didn't improve as they walked either, though they stuck to the broadest roads where the shadows loomed less closely. Strange sounds accompanied their progress, the clatter of a falling rock to one side or another, a creak as if of a door—though all doors had long fallen from their hinges here—and once, from a wellhead, a hollow whispering. High in a tower whose crumbling state made it unlikely that anything human could have climbed up there, a pale light like marsh gas shone in a single window. Taqla warned Rafiq not to look at it and they pressed on.

The palace of the emperors was the worst. Heading south took them directly in front of that monstrous façade and the black sweep of the central archway, so high that it seemed to be a second, and starless, night sky. She was grateful for the uncertain moonlight after that.

But they escaped Taysafun without harm in the end, scrambling through a breach in the southern curve of the wall. And they had the road in sight and were just hurrying past what might have been an orchard once, for the branchless stumps of dead trees stood in a cluster, when three fluttering white figures stepped out from behind a ruined outhouse straight in front of them. Taqla yelled a warning, Rafiq whipped his sword out and lunged forward to push the foremost of the three back on his heels. More cries went up, among which the words "We are under your protection!" were audible.

It was the traditional formula for surrender. Rafiq stopped making cuts in the air, and moved to a guarded stance, blade raised. "Who's there?" he demanded.

"Pilgrims!" quavered the tallest, cowering but also trying to draw the smallest back behind him. "Mercy, prince of kindness!"

As Taqla moved closer, she could confirm that their ghostly pallor was due to the seamless white pilgrim cloths wrapped about them. Three men—no, two and a boy. The one who had spoken had a gray beard and a shaven head.

"Pilgrims?" Rafiq's voice was harsh. "What are you doing out here, in the name of God?"

"Our party has camped a little way from the road, kind master—but there are women in the group so we came away in order to make water in private."

They looked terrified, the whites of their eyes catching the moonlight. They repeated their assurances over again in the next few minutes, that they were only pilgrims, they carried no wealth and were not worth robbing, that God would bless those who treated them with mercy. Eventually Rafiq persuaded them that he had no murderous intentions and sheathed his sword. Then they asked, "Will you come and share our camp tonight, kind friends?"

Rafiq turned to Taqla and she shrugged. Out on the road, safety was always sought in numbers, and protection was offered to pilgrims as an act of piety. It was certain that these two elderly men and the nervous adolescent were unarmed and offered no threat in themselves.

So they all went back to the pilgrims' camp together in the end, finding a group more than two-dozen strong squatting in the shelter of the orchard wall. Their arrival was greeted with some excitement, everyone clustering around to meet them.

"Peace be upon you," said Taqla for the twentieth time, trying to make sense of the indistinct moonlit faces and the murmuring voices. There were women here, and a few youths too. There was no sign of any mules or baggage camels. This was a gathering of humble people.

"Have you not lit a fire?" Rafiq asked. "Is there danger of some sort?"

"We didn't want to be seen from the road," someone answered.

"Here, I'll light one in the angle of the wall. If we keep it low and smokeless, it won't be seen. And there's plenty of dead wood." He wandered off on his mission and Taqla was left with the half of the group who did not follow him. They stood around her in a semicircle as if she were absolutely entrancing.

"Where did you set off from?" she asked.

"Baghdad," one of the women answered, after a strange hesitation.

"You're heading to Mecca?"

They looked at each other, shuffling a little. "Yes," said the woman. Then they all went back to staring at her. Taqla felt a little uneasy. She longed to sit down and rest, but there didn't seem to be anywhere but the dust to do it. She was getting the strange impression that no one in her audience had blinked yet, but that was undoubtedly a trick of the moonlight.

"Hey," she said, smiling. The smallest pilgrim, a boy, had shifted right up to her side and was gazing at her intently, his mouth a little open. He didn't answer but a soft distinct noise came to her ears—he was sniffing at her. Her skin crept. Reaching under her outer coat, she delved in her travelling bag for the last few dates Safan had left them, and held out the sticky morsel to the lad. "Want something to eat?"

His gaze dropped to the dark lump in her open palm and he wrinkled his nose with a snort. Very slightly he shook his head.

Taqla felt a worm of misgiving slide up her spine, clammy enough to make her shiver.

"He's taken a vow of fasting," the woman explained.

Taqla had never heard of a child so young being made to fast. She shoved her hand back into her bag, casting a quick surreptitious glance to try to locate Rafiq. "What about a piece of this?" she said casually, producing a bundle of dried salted meat and tearing off a flat strip. She held it out to the boy and he nearly took the ends of her fingers off as he snatched it, cramming it into his mouth. Taqla took a step back. Everyone else took a step forward. She looked up to see a dozen faces fixed on her, devoid of any readable expression but so intent that it made her heart clench. "Why don't you share it out?" she whispered, passing the whole package of dried camel meat to the nearest adult. Then she retreated smartly as the pilgrims crowded in without a word on that man, reaching for the meat eagerly, pulling it from hand to hand as they passed it round.

She walked quickly to the wall, finding Rafiq there on his knees coaxing a fire into existence, surrounded by a loose ring of watching pilgrims. A big tangle of dead branches had been swept into the corner of the wall by some flood, promising a proper blaze in time. She squatted down over him. The first flames were licking up the curls of resinous tinder he had kindled the fire upon.

"Rafiq." She kept her voice low. "We're in trouble. You're going to have to fight."

He looked up at her and then round at the circle. The elderly man they'd met first smiled and nodded at him. "Zahir," he muttered, "they're pilgrims."

"They aren't. Get up."

He looked up at her with his jaw set. "*Pilgrims*," he repeated, and she recognized the exaggerated reverence of a not particularly pious man for those prepared to put in more effort than he. Not to mention a man still in an irritated mood over the setback with the seer. She took another despairing look at their audience and was sure they were closer than before, blank eyed and poised. She wished the moonlight were brighter and she could see them more clearly. There were dark stains on some of those white robes that she would really like to identify. Maybe—*maybe*—they didn't have weapons, but the two of them were hopelessly outnumbered and would be dragged down before she had the chance to cast a spell to help them. She clenched her fist. "Rafiq—look at them."

He sat up. "Zahir!"

The pilgrims shifted forward.

She didn't have time to cast a spell, so the single word she spoke was not a spell. It was a word that undid magic, a word that restored all things to their true seeming. She said it loudly, and as it fell on the assembled company they warped, casting off the appearance of pilgrims, growing bulkier and more hunched as massive doglike jaws thrust forward from their faces. They tore off their white robes with hooked claws, revealing hairless, corpse-gray and entirely inhuman bodies beneath, and they kicked the rags away with hoofed feet. The stench of an open grave rolled over the two travellers.

Rafiq's exclamation was blasphemous, but he had the sense to draw his sword as he jumped up.

"The bond of salt!" Taqla screamed, her voice suddenly high. "You took the meat I offered you! Three days safe conduct! You ate my salt!" And the monsters farther toward the back hesitated, snarling.

"Maybe some did," said a voice behind them, almost human but distorted by teeth and jaws like a hyena's. "But I didn't." As they turned, a pallid form launched itself from the closest mob. There was only a split second to react to the blur of its movement, and in that moment Rafiq whipped up his steel blade to intercept its rush with the full strength of his torso. The monster's head hit the dirt well beyond arm's reach of its body. Its claws spasmed in death.

The mob howled, but they shrank back. Taqla reached down with her ring of black lava and seized the nascent flame from the hearth at her feet, lifting the ball of fire in her open hand over her head. Two more of the beasts who had been gathering themselves for a rush visibly changed their minds. Back to back, she and Rafiq faced the encircling monsters, she with flame and he with a naked blade stained black with blood. As the noise settled to a poisonous hiss, she tried to draw breath. Two dozen pairs of eyes glowed green in the firelight.

"Just how hungry do you think you are?" Rafiq warned.

"Magic!" hissed a beast. "Isn't one sorcerer in Taysafun enough?"

"Safan's bones are too old and dry for you, are they?" Rafiq's grin, though not nearly so impressive as the fangs bared on all sides around them, still carried a threatening edge. "Don't think ours will be any easier for you to taste!"

Taqla was too busy trying to hold the fire's shape and heat in her mind to speak, but she lifted her hand a little higher and the flames turned white, roaring softly. Snarling, the beasts averted their eyes from the light.

"The bond of salt will be honored," said a different monster, slouching to the front. This one had an eye missing and a face marked, though hardly made fouler, by old scars. Its long white tongue licked drool from its chin. "We'll give you three days of safe passage from this hour. After that...if you're on the road or in the desert, we will hunt you down. How far can you run in three days, meat?"

"We'll see," answered Rafiq.

"And now you will give us back our comrade. The fallen belong to us."

"You're welcome to him."

The circle bent out of shape as he and Taqla retreated warily from the corpse, and then three or four of the monsters snagged both body and severed head with their claws, dragging the parts away into the darkness. The little crowd followed, growling and reluctant at first, then increasingly focused on their fallen friend, leaving the two humans alone. Rafiq straightened slowly, relaxing his sword arm.

"They're ghouls, aren't they?"

"Yes." Taqla lowered her shaking hand. She felt dizzy. "They can take on the form of...someone they've previously eaten." She pressed her other hand to her lips as muffled but unmistakable noises became audible from the night, not nearly far enough away for comfort. "The Pale People," she whispered. That was what Safan had called them.

"I've heard stories, but I've never seen one." Rafiq was keeping his eyes on the scrum of ghouls just visible beyond their circle of light.

"Nor me." She could hardly grasp that they'd come so close to being torn apart and devoured. She was a scholar and a quiet citizen of Dimashq—what on earth was she doing out here?

"But you saw the danger." There was a stiffness in his voice that did not suggest any form of apology.

"Uh-huh."

"I'm guessing there's no point in us moving out until daylight?"

"They'll keep up with us easily."

"That's what I thought. But not with the Horse, I'm hoping."

"No. I'm going...I'm going to have to put the fire back on the wood now." She moved over to the makeshift hearth, piled up a few more sticks then let the flame flow from her hand back to where it belonged. It turned yellow and homely at once. She stared out into the dark but the ghouls were busy at their horrible repast, paying the two humans no attention at all. Then she looked up at Rafiq. He was watching her, his jaw clenched. Belatedly she plucked the *jabbayah* headscarf she wore around her shoulders and pulled it over her head, wrapping it to veil her lower face. Because, of course, the word that had revealed the true form of the ghouls had torn her disguise to shreds too.

Rafiq uttered a harsh laugh. "Why bother with that?"

"Don't look at me." She averted her face.

"Sorry." He didn't sound it. "Let me not offend your sensibilities." He rubbed his hand over his forehead. "So. Not a slave at all then. A witch like Safan, all the time."

Taqla clenched her teeth. "Not like him."

He laughed. Then he walked around a few paces before speaking up again. "I knew, you realize. I've known—I've guessed—for a couple of days."

"What?"

"You talk in your sleep, you know. With a woman's voice."

Taqla's jaw dropped. How was she supposed to have guessed she did that? "What did I say?" she stammered.

He gave her a guarded look. "Nothing clear enough to make out. But your voice is female. And once I noticed that...well, there were other things that catch the attention. You don't make eye contact when you talk, you don't like to stand too close—and no offense, but you fight very dirty, like a woman does." He tightened his lips, his eyes as hard as the edge of a sword. "I took you to the bathhouse to make sure, but after that I thought that if it's a disguise, it's a very good one. *Magic.*" He said the word like it stained his mouth.

Taqla bit her lip.

"You're the girl from the empty house, aren't you? The watchman's trull." He smiled humorlessly. "I recognize that glare."

"The spell finished early," she said, feeling like she were talking through a mouthful of ashes. "I was stuck for an explanation."

"Ah. And does your master Umar know about your real identity?" He paused. "Or, seeing as how I've not seen Zahir and Umar together, can I assume that you're Umar too?"

Taqla said nothing, feeling sick. She just wished he wasn't so sharp. *I'll have to leave Dimashq,* she thought. *All my household—we will have to leave forever.*

"Wonderful. So now I've been lured into the wasteland where I'm surrounded by ghouls with a witch to keep me company. This isn't one of my good days, I'd say."

Taqla's anger flared. It was probably a good thing that he couldn't see her mouth because she was baring her teeth at him now. "Lured? You're the one who came looking for sorcerous help! This quest was your plan!"

"So what's yours then? What were you meaning to do to me?"

"Do to you? We had an agreement, I thought."

"I had an agreement with Umar the Scholar as I recall—not with a witch." His voice had risen to match hers. A couple of the ghouls looked up briefly, curious.

"And I'm so much less to be trusted than the nice old man!" she hissed.

"Oh, should I be taking the deceit as a sign of your good faith? Or is there some justification for your duplicity?"

"Don't be a fool," she snapped. "Would you have made the

same bargain with a sorceress?"

"If I thought she was being honest with me!"

"Could I have come out alone with you into the desert if you'd known I was a woman?"

"All right, you tell me. Why the hell would you want to?"

For a horrible moment the words choked in her throat. "You already know that. You get the amir's daughter. I get the djinni and payment later. That was the deal. We both agreed to it and that's what I wanted." She swallowed. "Anyway, it's all over now." He'd moved disconcertingly close while they shouted at each other, she realized. "You should be keeping an eye on the ghouls right now," she pointed out, gritting her teeth. "Not on me. I'm not the one who wants to kill you."

He snorted but turned away. For a moment there was silence except for the distant crunching of bones. "Why is it all over?" he asked at last, in a much quieter voice.

Taqla bent to throw some wood on the fire. "I'd have thought that was obvious. You can't trust me and I can't trust you. Our pact is finished."

"You can't trust me?" He actually sounded hurt. "I'd like to point out I'm not the one who's been doing all the lying."

"I didn't lie!"

"No?"

"If I did," she amended, "it was in self-defense, not treachery."

"I gathered that." He seemed much less argumentative with his back turned, she was relieved to find. "What do you plan to do tomorrow?" he asked.

"Go home."

"You're leaving me here? With the ghouls on my trail?"

She hadn't thought of that. "You should make it to the Baghdad walls by nightfall."

"Probably. And there is always a chance, God willing, that on my own and on foot and without bodyguards I still won't be robbed and left for dead, or for the ghouls to find. But I'm not overly optimistic."

She bit her lip. "I'll let you ride with me to Baghdad then."

"Take me south."

"What?"

"You said it yourself. You want the djinni, I want Ahleme. We had an agreement. Let's see it through."

She smiled but it was not really a smile. "No. That's impossible now. You know that."

"I don't see why not. It's not as if there's anyone around to pass judgment on you. And hard though it may be for you to believe, I am capable of resisting your allure." He might as well have spat on her as spoken those words, but though Taqla froze, Rafiq, facing away from the fire, didn't notice. "I want to rescue Ahleme. That's all I want from you, I promise."

Taqla felt her stomach turn to stone.

"We've come this far already. To give up when we know the route..." He looked back over his shoulder. "I'm sorry I got angry with you. I don't like being lied to. But if we can trust each other, then we can work together to win our great prize."

Taqla felt the air go out of her lungs. It was like he were using the same hand to beat and caress her alternately, and she didn't know which hurt more. But she was honest enough with herself not to pretend that she wanted to leave him, even now. However unpleasant his words, she was too proud to abandon him. And of course, without her, he had no chance of continuing his search. She could picture too well his failure and his disappointment if he was forced to give up, and though she had no place in his imagined future, she wanted to see him triumphant. She lifted a hand, making a gesture that was intended only to ask for a moment's delay while she collected herself.

"Besides," he added, "I'd have thought a sorceress like you would want to see the Tree of Knowledge for herself."

"Don't do that," she said softly. "Don't try to manipulate me. If you want honesty, then it must go both ways."

His eyebrows rose but then he smiled, and it was a different kind of smile to any that she'd seen in his face before, warmer and more relaxed. "Fair enough." Then he came over and knelt near the fire so as to be face–to–face with her. "You don't have anything to fear from me, I promise. I give you my word, you will be as a sister-in-law to me."

She wondered at the slightly odd choice of words. "The usual form of words is 'as a sister'," she said stiffly.

"My sisters bossed me about cruelly when I was a little boy." His mouth twitched. "I'm hoping for a little peace this time round. Though from what I've known of Zahir..."

"Ha. Funny man."

The relationship between a brother- and sister-in-law was not so bad, she decided after consideration—an alliance that was mutually respectful but not intimate. It was in its own way like a veil, allowing her to move in his world without exposing herself to criticism or unwanted attentions. *As if I wouldn't welcome his attentions*, she mocked herself. Then, more soberly, she refuted her own accusation. *His desire is all for Ahleme. He'd only be making a whore of me if he did turn my way.*

"So...? Do we have an agreement?"

"I don't know. I'll think about it."

"Well. Good." He sat back. "In the meantime I'm going to sit over here on this pile of bricks. I don't know what the word of a ghoul is worth but I doubt sleeping is the best idea tonight. You might sit at the other end if you like."

"All right."

They both sat within reach of the fire's warmth, but not within reach of each other. Taqla wondered if she should set about making coffee but it felt awkward performing that courtesy for him, as if it would be letting down a defense. She put her chin in her hand.

"So what's your name, you-who-are-not-Zahir?"

She couldn't think of a good reason not to tell him. "Taqla."

"That's Greek, isn't it?"

"My father's mother was a Greek from Constantinople, I believe."

"Well, it's a pretty name."

She shook her head. "You've got to stop doing that too."

"What?"

"Being nice with me. Flirting."

"Was I flirting?" There was a hint of humor in his tone, and she suspected there was no right answer to that question.

"You should treat me just like you would Zahir."

Rafiq sighed. "I didn't see him as sister-in-law material." She gave him a sharp look and he spread his hands. "But if that's what you want..."

"Yes."

"I'll try."

There was silence for a while.

"Taqla?"

"Yes?"

"I'm planning to stay awake all night. I'm happy to prepare coffee for us, but could you get the pots out of your magic bag there? And some food?"

It was almost a relief when Yazid made a reappearance. Not, Ahleme hastened to tell herself, because she wanted to see him, but because she was so lonely and bored that anything that broke her solitude was welcome, even if it was followed at once by fear. She laid her hand over the barely clothed slopes of her breasts, feeling the painful lurch of her heart. He was so *big*—somehow it took her by surprise every time—and taller and broader than any of her father's guards. The mere physical fact of his presence was terrifying. It made her aware of her own fragility.

"Ahleme." He dipped his head in a minimally polite greeting. Despite the dense line of his brows, he didn't look particularly angry today, and his skin was the luminous gray of a clouded sky. But still his eyes burned, like pale embers.

Hesitantly, she bowed in return. She'd had a lot of time to consider what Zubaida had told her and it had left her very confused. From the very start she'd taken it for granted that

Yazid's fury was due to her refusal to submit to him. Was it really more complex than that? Had she provoked him in some way, without realizing it?

"Are you comfortable now?" he enquired. "You've food and drink. Is there anything else I might bring to you?"

Every time previously she'd demanded that he release her. This time she tried another tack. "If you would be so kind," she said softly, "I'm alone for so many hours. Please—" She didn't miss the spark that lit his eyes when she said the word. "Please would you bring me some books? And paper and pen? Or a lute perhaps, so that I can practice my music?"

He spread his arms, his broad chest expanding with the gesture. Suddenly the floor of her cell was covered with books, one stacked on another, and a chess set there too with familiar gilded and ebony pieces, and a five-stringed *oud* lute, and a frame on which a piece of silk was stretched, half embroidered with a peacock design.

"Here—everything from your room. Every book on your shelves. Your embroidery. So that you may amuse yourself when you're not in my arms."

Ahleme was so pleased she didn't object to the implication of his words. With a squeak of excitement and a rattle of her chain, she jumped off the bed and ran over to a pile of books, seizing the one from the top. Yes, there it was, her favourite book of poems just as she remembered it. There was even a red stain on the third page where she'd once allowed a drop of wine to spill upon the paper. She flicked through, her eyes devouring the lines and making themselves familiar once more with the tiny jewel-bright illustrations of flowers and birds.

"You seem pleased."

She glanced up. "Yes. Thank you."

Yazid picked up a book at random and flicked through. The volume looked tiny in his big hands. "Can you play the lute?" he wondered.

"Yes."

"Play something for me."

Ahleme nodded. This was better than anything he had required of her so far. She took up the instrument, tested the strings then began to pluck out a tune she knew well. The notes fell like ice water.

Yazid dropped his book and picked up another, frowning. Then another.

After a few bars she began to sing the words of a simple *ghazal*, keeping her voice low and, she hoped, pleasing.

"You hypocrite!" His cry of disgust shattered the song.

"What?"

"Hypocrite! All these books are full of love poetry! Every one!" He hurled a volume down with some force. "Such passion, such frustrated desire, such heartfelt yearning! Is this what you read about all day? Your books are full of love but you won't take the love I offer you!"

Ahleme started to tremble, and she thrust her lip out to keep her voice steady as she replied, "What you offer isn't love!"

"No?"

"No! Would your heart fill with joy at my smallest smile? Would you pour out your passion for me in poetry?"

"That's love, is it?"

"Yes!"

"It's the posturing of failures and eunuchs!"

She set the lute aside because she didn't want to drop it. "It's love, though you've never felt it. A man who writes one of those poems bares his soul. He bleeds with love. He gifts his beloved his pain and his hope because he wants her to know how much he'd do for her, how much she has cost him. Because he wants her to share that emotion."

"Hah! The emotions of a wine-addled poet! What do they matter?"

"The emotions of the *woman* matter. That's why poetry moves the beloved—because what she feels matters to him." She gathered up handfuls of the chain from around her feet and brandished it at him. "Is this love, according to you? This is captivity."

Yazid drew himself up. "The chain is there to keep you safe."

"And the way you treated me on this bed?"

He took a step forward. "My desire for you is like a raging fire. Do you doubt my love? I'll prove it willingly." He gestured at his crotch.

She started to retreat. "That's not what you said outside," she reminded him. "You said I was nothing."

"I..." His jaw worked. "I spoke in anger."

"Why do I make you angry? If you love me, then why this rage?"

"Because you are full of lies like a dead horse is full of maggots!" He snatched at the air in frustration. "Because of your arrogance and hypocrisy! One day you won't love me because I haven't your father's permission, but today you will not love me because I don't express myself in tender poetry. Which is it, Daughter of Earth? If a poor man wrote you poems, would you love him? If the day comes when your father chooses you a husband, will you refuse him for being too old and dry and not being sick with longing for you?"

Ahleme's mouth fell open.

"Well, which is it—duty or passion? I see no connection between the flames that burn in those books of yours and the rich powerful man your father will undoubtedly pick. Do you?"

"It's an ideal," she whispered. She gestured toward the books. "That's what I want from my husband."

"But he won't be like that, will he?"

"I...I'm not..." He was pushing her back step-by-step and it was impossible for her to think. His eyes wouldn't leave her alone. They ate her.

"Which matters most to you?" Yazid had the look of an eagle about to fall upon its prey. "If you loved with all your heart a man who wasn't suited to your father's purposes, what would you do? Which would you chose—happiness or duty?"

"I would choose honor," she said in a ghost of a voice.

For a moment he faltered, obviously taken aback. "Why?"

"Because...because..." She felt dizzy. She laid a hand upon a glass pillar and began to retreat around it. Everything that Zubaida had said about Mankind whirled around in her head. "Because we do," she admitted. "Honor is status. Status is power. We're human. We would rather have power than anything."

"Even love?"

"Yes."

Yazid put his shoulder to the pillar and stared at her, uncomprehending. "Why?" he pleaded.

Her voice was shaking. "Because we're afraid."

"Afraid?"

"Yes. We're not like you. We can't change the world with a snap of our fingers. We can't live alone; we're too weak. We live...in packs." She took one more step around the pillar and the chain at her ankle locked, nearly tripping her. When she spoke next, it was almost breathlessly. "So we cannot really bear the freedom that poets write about. We live by laws and honor and obedience instead."

He circled the pillar until he was almost on top of her. "You must be miserable all your short lives," he growled.

She averted her face, pivoting on her trapped ankle to turn her back on him. "I suppose we are. It isn't important." She rested one flank against the pillar, feeling the cool glass against her thigh and left breast.

"How can you say that?" He was standing right over her now. She could feel his breath on her hair when he spoke. "I would make you happy, Ahleme, if you'd let me."

"You'd make me your slave," she whispered.

"I would set you free." His hand descended on her thick braid at the nape of her neck and she jerked.

"No!" she warned as spines broke through the skin of her shoulders. Yazid hissed and withdrew his hand.

"Don't—I'm not going to hurt you. Not even touch you. Just your hair, Ahleme. Let me stroke your hair."

She pressed her face to the pillar, gathering her will to repel him. Then he laid his hand on her head gently and ran it down her braided hair, and she nearly whimpered.

"There. There. It's not hurting you, is it?"

He wasn't hurting her. Her resistance wavered. The spines shrank into their cusps of flesh.

"You've beautiful hair, like darkest honey." His voice was a low murmur, and Ahleme felt her bones turn to water at its purr. She was tired and scared and she dreaded the thought of mutilating herself once more—every part of her recoiled from that thought—but she would do it to stop his assault, she was ready for that if she must. If he did. If he didn't just stand there stroking her hair, twining the long tail of her braid with his fingertip, dipping his face to the top of her head to breathe the scent of the rosewater she'd washed her hair with. She shut her eyes. He wasn't hurting her. It didn't feel bad. It even felt good, this slow caress, because it had been so long since she'd been touched or embraced or comforted by anyone she knew. She was accustomed to physical contact every day with her women, and she'd missed those soothing fingers massaging or anointing or combing out her hair. It was good now just to feel the contact, the rhythm of his stroking hand, the warmth radiating from his skin, the brush of his fingers on her spine...

She shivered.

"Oh... Your skin is so soft." Yazid traced the line of her backbone from the cloth stretched across her shoulder blades all the way down to the hem of her *shalwar* just above the cleft of her bottom, exploring each dimple of her spine. He was very gentle and she couldn't feel even the tip of his claw. She wanted to feel angry but she couldn't. It would have been so much easier if he'd made her angry. She could have turned into a monster in a moment. She couldn't even feel scared now, not really, although in one way she was as dizzy with terror as if she were back outside standing on that high arch. Yet it wasn't a fear that made her recoil or fight. It made her press herself to the glass, aware of every inch of her skin as he repeated the motion. Her scalp pricked and shivers chased the length of her back, raising gooseflesh, which he soothed away with the warm sweep of his palm. "Don't be frightened," he whispered.

She was frightened. And yet she wasn't, not at all. She didn't understand how she was feeling, only that that there wasn't room to step back and analyse it, only to react to that gentle, searing touch. One way or the other.

"Let me just stroke you." Yazid's spread hand nearly encompassed the whole width of her waist. "You're so beautiful. I just want to..." His hand slid over the firm orb of her bottom cheek.

"No!" she groaned, stiffening instantly. No—that was too far, she knew that. That crossed the line. Yazid removed his hand.

"All right. It's all right. Just your back. You don't mind me touching your back, do you?"

How could she say no, when she'd let him already? When he returned to stroking her back it was such a relief, and such pleasure. Even when he hooked a finger under the stretched cloth of her top and the fabric turned to dust that fell shimmering down her smooth skin like sprinkles of gold. Ahleme gasped and pressed her bare breasts to the glass, her breath fogging the blue surface. Yazid laid his hand flat between her shoulder blades, on the bit that always itched, rubbing in slow circles.

"Don't be afraid. You're beautiful, my Jewel of the Earth." His voice was the growl of a lion, but so quiet, so very quiet that he had to lower his mouth to her temple and utter the words with his lips brushing her ear, something that sent shivers prickling all over her skin. He sensed the movement and scratched her gently between the shoulder blades, which made her gasp with gratitude. Then he ran his claws down her back, tenderly, all the way to the rising sweep of her bottom, and that made her groan out loud. "Oh yes," he breathed.

Dimly she realized she wasn't thinking straight anymore, that somewhere along the line sensation had become too important, that her body was overriding her better judgment. Somewhere in her head she was still scared and outraged by the djinni, but not enough to drive him off. Not even when he buried his face in her hair and breathed deeply the scent there, not even when his bare chest brushed against her bare back, his heat making up for the cold of the glass he was pushing her up against, the cold that was pinching her nipples to stiff points. Not even when he stopped talking and just breathed hard and quick. She couldn't see any part of him and didn't have the experience to realize what he might be doing with his other hand, the one that wasn't stroking the lower half of her back over and over, firmer and firmer, kneading her firm smooth flesh and pressing her harder against the glass. She only felt the flush of heat to his chest and the change of his stance and the hitch in his throat, and while she was still confused, he uttered a groan that sounded like despair and lurched up against her, the whole length of his body pressed hard against hers, his thighs rigid and his silk *shalwar* clammy on his perspiring legs.

Ahleme was too stunned to react. She just held on to the pillar as Yazid held her, the tension easing from his big frame. Even when he finally stepped away she couldn't turn and face him—she was topless and he would see her breasts. She wouldn't have turned to face him though, not even if she had been wearing the thickest of winter *abas*. Her cheeks were burning, her heart pounding. Her whole body roiled with confusion and shame and unfulfilled arousal. She pressed her forehead to the glass and gnawed her lip to stop herself losing control.

Without a word Yazid lifted her hair aside and stooped to press his lips to her neck. She could feel the heat of his mouth and the indent of her skin under his teeth. His thumb traced one last path down her backbone. Then he was gone.

Chapter Nine
In which a poem is read.

As the sun rose, the ghouls withdrew, creeping into the ruined outhouses and into holes beneath the rubble.

Taqla had managed to doze for a few hours with her head cradled on her knees. As soon as it was safe, she rose and stumbled away to find some privacy, and while she was hidden behind a wall she took the opportunity to cast her spell and revert to Zahir's shape once more. Then she strode back, taking the ball of silver wire out of her bag.

Rafiq looked at her once-more masculine face and his brow puckered faintly but he said nothing. He rubbed at his neck with the slow movements of one who ached in a number of places. In the light of dawn, he looked tired out, all narrowed eyes and stubble. He hadn't slept at all through the night and, looking at him, Taqla felt a pang of guilt. She'd simply assumed that he would be the one to sit watch, and he hadn't asked her to take a turn. She gave him the last piece of meat to make up for it, breakfasting herself on dry bread, and then she prepared the Horse Most Swift for their departure. They would need to get as far away as possible, she told herself, to escape the ghouls. They had to make it pointless for the Pale People to pursue them.

But once she was sitting up on the Horse and Rafiq swung into place behind her, it all went wrong. The moment he settled against her, even though he clung no closer than he'd done before and was in fact assiduously careful, she became overwhelmingly aware of his thighs enfolding hers, his groin against her backside, the bulk of his chest at her back. She was sitting within the compass of his arms and that was too much to ignore. The spell of shaping shivered into a thousand little shards. Taqla swore, threw her leg over the Horse's neck and jumped to the ground.

"What's wrong?" Rafiq asked. Then he recognized how her clothes hung on her suddenly smaller frame. "Oh. I see." With a sigh he dismounted too, leaning back against the Horse's flank and folding his arms. He watched as she adjusted her headscarf. "What happened to the spell?"

"The spell..." Taqla stomped up and down. "The spell is fragile." She swore in a manner that would have sounded coarse coming from Zahir, clenching her fists. "I can't keep it up if you get close. You're—" She swallowed. "You know now that it's an illusion. That weakens it. Your disbelief." *And I am lying to him again,* she told herself in disgust.

"Right." Rafiq rubbed the heel of his hand across his forehead. "Well then, I suppose you'll have to stay as Taqla. It'll look odd you wearing men's clothes, but it can't be helped. It won't matter."

"No." Her lip was stuck out. "You can't sit behind me."

"Ah." He looked away, but he didn't argue with that one. "Then...maybe I should go in front and you sit behind me. That would be less...improper."

"No. No chance."

"Why not?" He wasn't impatient this time. Exhaustion seemed to have humbled him.

"Because then you will have to have to command and steer the Horse," she admitted.

"Is there any reason I can't?"

She didn't answer. She just glowered.

"Ah." His eyebrows flashed as understanding sank in. "Look, I'm not going to steal your Horse, Taqla."

"That's easy to say." She was horribly aware that she was being pushed back into a choice between abandoning him or taking steps she never wanted to take.

"I swear it on my life. And I've not lied to you yet."

She turned away and looked at the tumbled walls and the

dead trees, knotting her fingers and twisting her rings.

"We do have to get a move on," Rafiq reminded her in a low voice.

"Shush. Let me think."

He was quiet after that, though he watched her thoughtfully as she squatted and covered her head with her hands and wrestled with her insecurity and her mistrust. She couldn't let him sit at her back. That was simply impossible. So she must let him sit before her. Or she could take the Horse and leave—and then he was on his own. What if he didn't make it safely back to Baghdad? What if the Pale People were prepared to follow him into the city? Could she live with that dread, that not knowing?"

"The command words are in Persian," she said in a voice ragged with dismay, standing again.

"That's all right."

She looked him in the eye, unblinking. "There's a command to bring the Horse to life and start it running. There's another to stop it. In between, you just have to steer it by concentration of your mind. The Horse wants to run at full speed in a straight line. The really hard bit is getting it to slow when you need to. You'll fight to keep it to a trot."

He nodded slowly.

"The command to start it is," she said, taking a deep breath, "in Persian, 'In the name of Ahura Mazda the Most High God, run for me.' To stop it you say, 'In the name of Ahura Mazda the Most High God, stand still.'"

Rafiq's mouth opened as if he was about to say something, but no words came out. Only his eyes spoke his wariness. Taqla braced herself, marshalling her arguments. *It's only a form of words, nothing more, and doesn't mean I'm invoking the infidel gods. It's the form required by the Horse's makers, and not my choice.*

But in the end he just lifted one shoulder in a shrug and nodded. *A pragmatist,* she thought. *As all sorcerers must be. Which is why we don't trust even each other.*

"Let's get going then." He turned to the saddle. "Do you want to get up first, Taqla?"

"No." It was a nice gesture, she recognized, but no more. If he did intend to dump her and ride off at any point, a good hard jab in her ribs would be enough now that he knew how to control the Horse.

So Rafiq mounted and offered her his hand to help her up behind him. It stung, to have to sit at his back on the broadest part of the saddle and slip her hand into his belt, to see him survey the land then lean forward to speak in the Horse's ear. For a moment black despair rose up in Taqla's heart. She was once more female, and known as female in the eyes of the world, and thus inevitably had lost some of her power. Because of the shape of her body, the Horse Most Swift was no longer hers to control. Because of the slot between her legs she must put herself at this man's mercy. She must fear him. She must placate him. She must never trust him. For a moment she was so angry that the world seemed to turn dark about her.

Then he spoke the words and the Horse leapt forward with such a spring that they both nearly slipped from the saddle, and she threw her arms around him and held on with all her might, her cheek pressed to his back, his hair whipping in her eyes.

Yazid didn't reappear for nearly two days. When he did, he was a smoldering dark blue, and Ahleme, who had learned to take that color as a sign of his wrath, scrambled hastily to her feet and backed off.

"That looks well on you," he growled. Ahleme flushed from head to toe at the words. The clothes she'd found that morning had been no more than two narrow strips of white silk, one to wind about her hips and groin, the other to tie over her breasts—but both so transparent that her darkly golden skin glowed through.

"Keep away," she whispered. Her shame was beyond words,

but the blood raced through her veins without the heavy nausea of true dread.

He glowered at her. Then he lifted a piece of paper in his hand and began to read from it.

Where have you gone—you who lit love's flame?
Across the sands I seek the light of your camp flame.

When I approach, the ashes of your hearth are cold.
You hurry ahead, and dawn turns the world to flame.

The infidels worshipped fire upon the hills
And tended day and night their sacred flame.

So I offer all that my eyes see, all my thoughts;
The furnishings of my life to feed my heart's flame.

You have made of me an idolater, lost to God.
You have cast me still living into hell's flame.

Desire will burn me to ashes while you laugh
And warm your hands over the dying flame.

"There," he said when he'd finished. "Did that please you?"

"You wrote that?" she asked. Her eyes were wide with shock.

"You think it's rubbish, don't you?" he snapped.

"No..." So it wasn't a good poem, not by a long way—the internal metre was all over the place—but that he'd written one at all astonished her. He'd written it for *her*. He'd listened to her. She couldn't think of the last time a man had really listened to her.

"I knew you'd laugh at me!" Yazid crumpled the paper and flung it down at his feet.

"I'm not laughing." She took a step toward him, almost

inadvertently. He crossed his arms, blue and black flushes rippling across his skin. "Please. Can I hear it again?"

He bared his teeth in contempt. They looked very long and white in his midnight-blue face.

"Then I'll read it," she whispered. Step-by-step she made herself approach, and then knelt to pick the paper from the floor. She looked up at him when she was down there. His face was the color of a thunderhead, but all the anger had drained out of it. She knew she must appear absolutely vulnerable, kneeling there at his feet, but she could only guess at how tempted he found himself. Slowly and as gracefully as possible she stood again, smoothed out the crumpled paper, and then let her gaze fall to the inked lines.

He wrote it for me. The thought sent her mind into chaos, making reading difficult. She took a long time.

"Yazid..." She looked up. But he was gone.

Chapter Ten

*In which both fish and fowl are encountered
and a game of chess commences.*

Tarampara-rampara-ram.

The swamps just north of Basra, where the Euphrates and
Tigris met, were a new world so far as Taqla was concerned, a
world of lush, green *qasib* reeds three times as tall as a man
and as thick as his thumb, through which a maze of watery
paths wound their way. It was a world of ducks and waterfowl,
of the constant whispering susurration of leaves, of close
horizons and sudden open stretches of silvery water that turned
out to be bottomless black mud if you accidentally set foot in it.
On the drier islands were tall groves of trees and, Rafiq warned,
both lions and fierce wild boar. Though none of those beasts
were encountered, there was no shortage of mosquitoes aiming
to eat the travellers alive in their stead, at least until Taqla wove
a charm about them both. The place made her nervous.

There were people out here too, by all accounts. Rafiq
called them the Madan, and said they lived on islands of heaped
rushes and fished from narrow *mashoof* boats for a living.

"Are they friendly?" Taqla asked.

"Well, if you're on the road, they're happy enough to trade.
They get very jumpy if anyone enters their territory though."

So they avoided the floating villages and their little herds of
wading water buffalo, and since they were both city dwellers
and had no skill at hunting or fishing, spent a hungry night
huddled on an island. Rafiq, exhausted, managed the king's
share of sleep that time while Taqla sat watch and listened to
the eerie calls of the night birds, her nerves prickling. She
watched Rafiq too, finding a strange sort of satisfaction in the

droop of his relaxed hand and the slow rise and fall of his chest. The vulnerability of the sleeping man spoke to something deep inside her.

As soon as daylight permitted, they were in the saddle again, spiralling through the marsh at a steady canter. Light danced off the spray in their wake.

"How will we find the Tree?" Rafiq asked once.

"We'll know it when we see it," she reminded him, less sure than she sounded of seeing anything in the dense reed beds.

"Whether we see it or not, we need to be at Basra before sunset if we want to eat today."

They spent hours riding through a labyrinth that seemed devoid of landmarks, before Taqla said abruptly, "There, turn down that channel."

The Horse swung down the narrow tunnel she had indicated, the reeds almost brushing their knees.

"Why this way?" Rafiq's tone was just the safe side of doubtful.

"Why not?"

"That's not the answer I was hoping for."

"Then just trust me." An empty stomach made her sharp. "There's more to being a sorceress than an expensive collection of toys, you know."

"I'd noticed that a tongue like a whip came into it somewhere," he said, and though his back was to her, she could hear the rueful twist of his lips. Her impulse was to apologise, but that made her angry. Why should she apologise to him when he was the one being rude? Yet she could think of no riposte, so in the end, she said nothing.

Then the reeds opened out to either side so that they emerged onto a stretch of open water, and Rafiq slowed the Horse to a prancing trot as they stared around them. There was a low mist here, rising about their knees like a faint steam but rendered more opaque by distance, and the sun had turned it to the palest gold color. Over the veil of mist, the darker bulk of what looked like treetops loomed ahead where there seemed to be higher ground, and circling over the upraised branches were a great number of birds.

"Vultures?" said Taqla uncertainly.

"I can't tell. If this were the desert, then yes, there would be death up ahead there."

But this isn't the desert, she said to herself, the skin on her neck turning to gooseflesh for no reason she could express. "We should head that way."

The Horse Most Swift picked up speed, its hooves thrumming on the surface of the water. Then, without warning, the surface of the swamp heaved up before them and something long and sleek broke the surface. By sheer instinct Rafiq managed to get the Horse to shy sideways and they just evaded the lunge, the flick of a finned tail, the gurgling splash. They wheeled to the left, kicking water into spray. The foul smell of disturbed mud rolled into their nostrils.

"There's something in the water!" Taqla shouted.

"And it's quick," replied Rafiq through gritted teeth as the silver surface broke into a V-shaped cut and that something angled back toward them. It was impossible to tell what color it was because it had the same slick shine as the swamp itself, but it was possible to tell that it was big. Three or four times the length of the Horse at least, Taqla guessed.

With a superfluous kick of his heels, Rafiq unleashed the Horse Most Swift's pent-up speed, and they bolted away across the marsh. The lake fled beneath them. Taqla even risked a glance behind and saw only the ripples of their wake still spreading across the silvered mirror of the mere. In moments they were approaching the island ahead, and then Rafiq had to slow the Horse abruptly to stop them running up the shallow bank and colliding violently with the tree that grew there. In fact, he spoke the words to bring it to a halt just in time to stop the Horse on the foreshore, in a narrow margin between the arboreal giant and the swamp behind them—but at least, Taqla thought with relief, safely on dry land. They sat on the silver statue for a while and just stared.

Birds shrieked and scolded and mewed overhead.

There was only one tree on this island, that much was obvious from even a cursory glance. And it looked nothing like an apple tree. It was a great sprawling evergreen with thick handlike leaves and low-drooping branches that swept down to rest on the earth before rising to their tips. In the centre of this great green hillock was a trunk presumably, supporting the hulking mound of the central mass, but that center could only be guessed at from where they stood, so low were the branches and so dense the leaves. Taqla thought that maybe it was a fig tree of some sort, except that it bore in places clusters of white starlike flowers unlike anything else she'd seen before, and yellow fruit drooped high up among the farthest branches.

"What on earth is that?" said Rafiq to himself in an undertone. Taqla followed the line of his gaze to a high limb.

"A peacock?" she suggested, seizing on the outline of its long tail.

"No, it's not. The little thing sitting by its leg is a peacock."

It took a moment for Taqla to readjust her sense of scale. The whole tree was a perch for countless birds, and more circled constantly overhead, their calls making a chaotic din. But she hadn't realized until now what sort of birds they were. Not vultures, or at least no more than one or two were vultures. There were swans and geese and gulls and herons and delicate snow-white egrets, hoopoes and peacocks as well as countless smaller fowl that she couldn't name. There were eagles. And they were all smaller than the one big coppery bird Rafiq had pointed out. As she compared that to its smaller entourage, Taqla finally admitted to herself that it had to be bigger in the body than a camel—and that the Tree it was sitting upon was *vast*, by far and away the broadest she had ever seen.

With a fluid movement Rafiq dismounted. "Do you think he's the Bird King?"

Taqla didn't reply at once. She missed her books desperately, those volumes of lore that provided all the answers to such esoteric questions.

"He's not big enough to be a roc, is he? I mean, they're the size of elephants." Rafiq kept his voice low but sounded worried. He laid his hand on the grip of his sword. As if to mock him, a goose waddled past his feet, plucking busily at the short grass. It didn't even spare him a glance. Taqla swung down from the saddle. Now that they were still, she could smell a sweet floral scent, presumably from those starry flowers. It reminded her of night jasmine.

"I've never heard of rocs holding court like this," she said.

"Think he'll let me climb up and get one of those fruit?" He shook his head suddenly, and blinked. Then he looked back at her properly for the first time since their arrival. "The Tree of All Knowledge, both Good and Evil," he said, his eyes a-glitter. "You've got to be tempted, Taqla."

She was so tempted she felt dizzy. "That was its parent," she temporised. "I doubt this one is as significant."

"Maybe not. We can—"

Taqla saw his expression change abruptly but didn't have time to work out in what way. There was a noise, a huge noise, and she didn't have time to recognize that either, other than that it came from behind her. There was just an enormous blow that struck her whole body, and then it went dark and she wasn't on her feet anymore, and her last thought was *What spell do I need?* before it went so dark that even her thoughts winked out.

Yazid had taken to the concept of wooing, Ahleme thought. His gift this day was an egg of polished crystal that felt warm as it nestled in the palm of her hand and trembled slightly. Then it split open and out came a sparrow of gold, every feather a work of art, with tiny sapphires for eyes. It flew around her head and perched on her finger and twittered as it preened its metal plumage.

"Do you like it?"

Ahleme did actually. It was a relief to see anything here

that had a semblance of independent life, even if it were only a magic clockwork sparrow. But she didn't answer at once. In Dimashq, or any human city, this little toy would be a priceless wonder. But she doubted that it had cost the djinni anything at all, neither money nor effort. It was only an amusing toy to him, a trifle for a woman-child. "Yes, but I prefer the poem," she said, allowing him a tentative smile.

Yazid tightened his lips, but she could see the satisfaction in his eyes. "Now I will sit with you on the bed," he announced. His refusal even to pretend to ask her permission didn't escape Ahleme's notice.

"Sit where you wish," she said softly, rising to her feet. "And I will stand at the end of my chain."

Yazid paced past her to the bed and mounted it as if it were a throne, sitting cross-legged. Ahleme tried to walk away but nearly fell over. Her ankle chain had shortened to a single link, pinning her to the bed frame. For a second she nearly panicked. "Is this the next stage of my bondage?" she snapped over her shoulder.

"It is a joke," he replied silkily. "You said the end of your chain. You didn't say how long that would be."

She pulled a face. Then it occurred to her that she had better sit down because, as she stood there, his face would be on a level with the twin cheeks of her silk-swathed bottom and there was nothing she could do to stop him looking. So she sat on the edge of the bed, thinking that at least he was only facing the back of her head now.

"Shall we play chess?" A small table appeared by her knee with a chess set upon it. Ahleme jumped slightly. She found things blinking into existence profoundly unsettling. But Yazid just reclined on his elbow so that he could stretch out a hand to the board and set the pieces back to their starting positions. Of course, in doing so he had to reach past her hip and his forearm strayed dangerously near to her bare skin.

"You are so powerful," she said to distract him. "Is there anything you cannot do?"

"Of course. There are limits." He sounded unusually somber. His fingers set the ebony Shah upright. "No one is omnipotent but God. But by your standards the limits are few."

"Then why don't you make yourself a golden Ahleme?" she asked, her voice wobbling a little. "She would do anything you wanted her to."

"And could she bear me a child?"

"You could always marry a djinniya."

"Anyway," he went on as if she hadn't answered. "I don't want your obedience."

"No?" She didn't hide her disbelief.

"No. You start."

Ahleme shifted a pawn into a standard opening move without thinking about it. "Yes, master," she said sarcastically.

Yazid was certainly in an unusual mood. He didn't seem to notice her snippiness and he kept his voice low and even. "I want you to love me. Passionately. As your body was shaped to do."

Ahleme closed her eyes for a moment. "I can't do that. I've told you."

He jumped a knight over the forward rank of pawns. "Would it help if I looked different?" he asked, his gaze drifting up from the chessboard, over the indent of her waist and the swell of her breast and the delicate angle of her cheek. "I can, you know. I can look like anyone you want."

"No," said Ahleme quickly before she could dwell on this thought, "it wouldn't make any difference."

"Not if I looked like the caliph?" His smile was a little wicked. "Would you not find it easy to love me then?" In a twinkling his body warped and shrank. Suddenly there lay on the bed next to her, not a brawny semi-naked djinni, but a middle-aged man in cloth-of-gold clothes, with a narrow foxy face and clever eyes, his long beard speckled with gray hairs.

"No!" she squeaked, shocked. Then, unable to help herself, "Is that what he looks like?"

"Caliph Al-Ma'mun, Commander of all the Faithful." His

voice was unchanged, and it sounded even deeper coming from that incongruous frame. "Doesn't he inspire you with flames of passion?"

"Stop it," she said, twisting her hands together, before remembering to add, "please."

"What about this?" His next transformation was even more disconcerting. He became an amber-skinned youth, younger than she was, with black ringlets and full lips and poetic, indolent eyes. "Am I not beautiful?"

"Please!" she gasped. "Go back to your own shape!"

"You'd prefer that?"

"Yes!"

He switched back at once, his irises bleaching from black to white in a single heartbeat. His lips moved to a smirk, but those eyes were almost anxious. "I'm not so unpleasing to your eyes then?"

"No," she admitted, biting her full lower lip. Of course he wasn't displeasing. He was handsome enough, in a brutish, overwhelming way. It just took some getting used to, that was all. And he wasn't what she'd dreamed of in a man, all her fervent virginal years. Her shadowy ideal had always had fine features and a certain athletic suppleness—like that man Rafiq the Traveller, she thought distractedly, only younger. Closer to her own age. "Is it your real shape?" she asked, suddenly suspicious.

"It's my own shape when I'm here," he said. "In other places I take forms appropriate."

"Other places?"

"We're not confined to the surface of the Earth as you are. I could take you to so many..." His voice sank. "I could show you sights you've never seen, lands you've never dreamed of treading." He sounded almost wistful.

"That wouldn't require much," she sighed.

"Then let me." He sat up sharply, looming in over her shoulder to put out his hand for hers. So close to begging permission of her, his discomfort revealed itself in the drawing back of his lips, a flash of fire in his eyes. The sharp points of his incisors served Ahleme as a belated reminder of the horror of her situation. She looked down at his open palm over her smooth thigh and noted the curved claws that tipped his fingers. If he gripped her hard, he could rip her open, she thought, her mouth drying. She shrank away minutely.

"No. Please don't. No more."

For a moment shadows chased across his skin and she thought he was going to explode, but he swallowed hard and held his temper. "Then let me touch you," he said, drawing one finger across the small of her back.

"No, not again—" she whispered.

"Your beauty drives me mad with love." His breath was hot on her bare shoulder. "I've watched you and watched you, and wanted so much to—" He sensed her flinching. "Are you still frightened? Don't you want to be loved like this?"

"Don't," she whimpered. It couldn't be mistaken for a command. His lips brushed her shoulder, silk on silk.

"Then play chess with me," he whispered, the purr of his voice igniting little flashes of sensation across her skin, "and the moment you win, then I will leave you in peace. Hm?" When she made no answer, he reclined on his elbow again, so close to her that she could feel the radiant warmth of his body. "Your move."

It was a slim chance of a dignified way out of her situation, but it had to be seized. Ahleme knew she wasn't bad at chess— often it was the only way to pass the long hours in the palace, even if she had no outstanding talent. She narrowed her eyes and considered the pieces, finally making a move.

Unhurriedly, Yazid reached past her for his rook. But when he withdrew his hand, he placed it on the small of her back. Ahleme jumped a little.

"Please don't touch me," she said in a small voice. "It's distracting."

He chuckled, and his teasing fingertips withdrew. There was the faintest hiss of skin on silk, and a long exhalation of breath from behind her. Ahleme's eyes widened. Recent experience was branded on her mind. "Please don't do that either," she whispered.

"You said not to touch you. It's hardly fair to stipulate what else I might touch. Your move."

They played in silence for a few moves—or near silence, anyway. Ahleme was torn between wanting to win and wanting to get her moves done quickly. *The quicker the better*, she told herself. Yazid was more leisurely. Of course, in every way it was in his interests to play for as long as possible. Her one advantage was that his chess moves were unfocused and grew more so as his breathing became irregular. She heard the click of his tongue as he moistened his dry lips.

"Check," she whispered. Without a word he rose to press his face to her back, his lips to her skin. Ahleme stiffened, pulled away and half-turned to snap a warning, frightened glare at him, and at once Yazid fell back on the bed, his eyes fixed on her and aglow with need.

She looked. She shouldn't have done, but she did, the merest glance down to his groin. He was still clothed, for which she was profoundly grateful. His fingers rested over his lower belly, frozen in mid-caress. Quite visible under the silk was the bulk of his arousal, outlined by the sheen of the silk, flat against his belly, straight as a beam, and to Ahleme's inexperienced eyes, improbably large. She clenched her jaw and tried to turn away, but somehow couldn't stop looking.

Yazid's fingers strayed to the drawstring of his *shalwar*. He cleared his throat. "Take this," he said huskily.

She shook her head, pressing her lips together.

"Oh, come on, my virgin princess. Aren't you curious? Don't you want to know what you do to me?" He traced his length reverently with his fingers, and it twitched beneath the silk, making the breath catch in Ahleme's throat.

He was right of course. She was horribly, shamefully curious. Like every other young woman of rank, she'd seen pictures in instructional books intended to prepare girls for their marriage duties, but those tiny painted miniatures with their garden settings and their sharp outlines and their convolutions of limbs seemed to bear no relation to this, here now, so simple and huge and solid. The suggestion that this was her doing, that this was some sort of power she had over him, squirmed deep in her belly. She felt too hot all of a sudden, despite her scanty clothes.

"Have you seen this before?" His voice was husky.

Her chin jerked to signify no.

"You're cruel, my princess. You torment me like this, then you do nothing to comfort me." Despite his mass and his muscle, he seemed oddly vulnerable and exposed, lying down while she sat at his side, hip to hip. He was laid out for her scrutiny. She couldn't help wondering what he would feel like under her hands if she ran them over that smooth torso. Were his muscles as hard as they looked? Would that rippled stomach resist the pressure of her fingers? Would his—?

She caught the illegitimate thought and in a panic squashed it, flushing. But she didn't look away.

Slowly, watching her face for reaction, Yazid wrapped the end of the drawstring tie around two of his fingers, turn after turn. Then he began to pull. The silk string went taut then lengthened. Knots popped. Suddenly the generous gathered material about his waist was free, and loose enough for him to draw the cloth down, revealing himself.

"There. That's what you do to me, Flower of the Earth."

His fingers looked pale against the iron-gray flush of his flesh. Ahleme's mouth had gone dry. He looked... *Muscular* was the only way she could put it. Like the neck of a proud stallion, it invited her touch. She curled her fingers into a fist. It fascinated her. She could feel somewhere deep in her mind things shifting about, pieces sliding into place, doors opening— a mystery had been revealed at last. She needed time to take this new knowledge into her soul.

"Want to touch it?" Yazid's hand moved as if he were caressing a small but strong animal. He shifted his shoulders and gray shadows flickered up his torso from his crotch to his ribs. "Do you want to find out how hard it is? How much it wants to be inside you?"

The manifest impossibility of something that size fitting into any woman almost made her laugh—it seemed like another limb. She bit her lip. He reached out his left hand and trailed the back of his knuckles over her thigh. His right hand moved upon himself, up and down, up and down.

"Then just let me look at you," he rasped. She licked her lips. For some reason this made him groan. "Let me...let me..." His eyes looked dark and his throat was marbled with blue. "Oh God—touch me..." And that couldn't be taken for anything other than a plea. Ahleme was moved almost to pity.

Her hand was moved by something else though, a curiosity all of its own. Bewildered, she saw it steal out. She hadn't meant to do it, she hadn't consciously intended to lay her fingers on that hot, charged length. She hadn't allowed herself to really think about what it would be like. And yet, there she was doing it. Her fingers must have felt icy cold to him because he was like burning silk under her touch, silk that moved over a mahogany hardness. She coiled her hand around its girth and squeezed, testing the obdurate mass. Squeezed again.

With a cry, he erupted. *Like quicksilver*, she thought with the part of her mind that was watching in surprise everything that had happened, everything she was doing. *Just exactly like alchemists' quicksilver.* It splashed on his belly and puddled in his navel and tricked down his sides to the bed as he heaved and arched. And then in moments it sublimed, vanishing from his skin into the air. Leaving him trembling and hot with fresh sweat and staring.

And a voice inside her that she hardly recognized cried out in awe and triumph, *I did that! I did that to him!*

Chapter Eleven
In which keeping warm is what matters.

Rafiq saw the water surge at Taqla's back and the creature launch itself from the waters, but the attack was so quick that he didn't manage to cry a warning. The monster—glistening gray with the mud of the swamp's depths, its broad, piscine head all mouth and grasping barbels—flung its front half onto the shore of the island, struck Taqla hard from behind and, as she fell, engulfed her from the waist up in its maw. The Horse Most Swift was knocked aside and fell with legs sticking stiffly out. Then the fish twisted about, thrashing the water to spume with its tail as it tried to return to the marsh. Its tiny eyes, dark and soulless, were set wide at the sides of its head and the interior of its gills gaped as white as the briefly glimpsed inside of its mouth. The stiff feelers projecting from its jaw waved like the legs of an overturned crab.

Rafiq threw himself forward. He didn't try to draw his sword. This was not the right situation for a scimitar. He just threw himself onto the creature and rammed his arm up to the shoulder in its gill slit, grabbing on to the interior ridges as it surged forward and yanked him off his feet. The water struck him hard in the face and he closed his eyes, holding his breath as they crashed beneath the surface. It was rare for any man of Dimashq to be able to swim—as boys they had no more than the shallow and less-than-fragrant Barada river to splash about in—but Rafiq had sailed from Basra and Ayla and Tyre, and he'd learned to be competent in water. He even opened his eyes as his free hand found, at his belt, the straight knife he'd carried since the day he was attacked by the Al-Hava family.

From beneath, the water was yellow and clouded with silt, and he could see little but the gray flank of the monstrous fish he clung to and a churning of silvery bubbles. His knife hand looked as pallid as a corpse's. Clenching his teeth, Rafiq reached forward to stab the blade into what he hoped was the beast's right eye. A small, dark cloud stained the water as he twisted the blade, yanked it out, and then plunged it in again. The monster twitched from head to tail, clamping its gill shut bruisingly tight on Rafiq's left arm. A great, dark plume of murk billowed over them both as it plunged toward the bottom of the swamp. But it couldn't go deep; there wasn't enough water for that. After plowing the thick mud of the bottom, it burst upward again as Rafiq gouged at its slimy skin for the third and fourth time. He had every intention of cutting the creature until he passed out from lack of breath, but there was a muscular thrashing, and suddenly through the piss-colored water, Taqla's limp form swirled into view, her clothes billowing about her. Rafiq let go of the gill and kicked away from the fish, reaching out to catch her as she sank past him. His lungs were desperate now. He pulled her to his side and cast one last look around for the fish. Seeing nothing through the hailstorm of swirling dirt, he kicked for the surface.

The air he gasped undoubtedly stank of rotted pondweed, but to him it was sweet and pure. He cupped Taqla's chin in one hand, keeping her face above water as he sculled back toward the island of the Tree. He didn't dare resheath his knife, so progress was even slower, but eventually he approached the slope of the foreshore and found enough resistance beneath his feet to try to stand. Thick goo squidged up between his toes, and when he tried to walk it sucked at his legs. He staggered painfully slowly through the shallows, Taqla's body cradled in his arms, and even when there was grass beneath his filthy feet, he kept walking away from the water. Only when he was under the shelter of the outermost branches did he drop the knife and sink to his knees, laboring for breath. Gently he laid her on the ground.

She didn't move, though there was no sign of any wound on her body. The clothes plastered to her form and the wet headcloth draped over her face were horribly reminiscent of the tight winding-sheet of a corpse. With clumsy fingers he pulled the veil unceremoniously from about her head. Her face looked gray, and the whites of her eyes showed under half-closed lids.

Rafiq swore. Then he called her name, shaking her face. When she didn't react, he picked her up and rolled her over so she was sagging from his arms. Balling his fist under her ribs, he tipped her forward and squeezed her torso hard. Water vomited from her mouth as her stomach emptied, but it wasn't accompanied by coughing. He tried again, deliberately squashing her chest cavity. More water, and this time blood too. He felt like he'd been kicked when he saw that. "No," he said over and over again as he laid her down. He tried to find a pulse at her throat but his hands were numb with cold and he could feel nothing. He even opened her mouth and blew his own breath in, as shepherds did with stillborn lambs. Her chest moved but deflated as he released her and didn't rise again. When he lifted his head, there was blood on his lips.

"Taqla," he groaned. "Oh God. Oh God." Sitting down hard, he covered his face with his hands. Given the choice, he would have fled even further from reality.

There was a thump nearby and a low haunting whistle, as if from a flute. Rafiq raised his head, too numb with shock to be scared.

Sitting a few feet away was the huge copper-colored bird they'd seen in the treetop. The peacock-like tail lay behind it like the train of a king's cloak. Its eyes were as golden orange as an owl's. Only it was not a bird, because it had pricked ears like a massive dog—a dog's head with a curved bird's beak, a beak with teeth in it.

Rafiq stared. The thing was bigger than he was by some way, but he felt no particular inclination to draw his sword and defend himself from this hybrid, only a sense of bewilderment. Taqla's fate seemed at least as much an offense against nature.

The creature trilled, a sweet, low note.

"Step back." The words arrived in Rafiq's head without passing through his ears. It didn't even sound like someone

else's voice, he simply knew that the words had been spoken. He rose to his knees, eyes locked on the creature, mind in a spin. The thought of what it might intend made his stomach clench. Among the Faithful, dogs had a bad reputation. They were scavengers and grave robbers and as unclean as an animal could be. But he was vaguely aware that this had not always been the case here in Persia, that they'd once had a higher status.

He withdrew slightly, with reluctance.

The bird hopped forward and stooped over Taqla's body. Its inhuman eyes flickered. Then it lifted its long tail from the earth, and with a series of shakes spread the feathers into a fan. Rafiq's jaw sagged. An ordinary peacock tail was magnificent enough in its blues and greens. This bird was adorned in golds and reds and purples, though dozens of colors scintillated there. Royal colors, he thought, dazzled. And as it shivered those feathers, the bird stooped and brushed its spread wings over Taqla's motionless breast and her colorless lips, and made a noise like the lowest note of a Sufi flute.

"Wake up, daughter." The words, unspoken, were perfectly clear.

A flush of blood rose to her cheeks. She took a deep breath.

Taqla tried to stay burrowed away from the cold for as long as she could, but in the end it woke her. She had never in her whole life been so cold. Every bit of her was stiff and protesting, except for her back—that was warm. And her left hand. Someone had taken that hand and was rubbing it between their own warm ones, from fingertips to forearm. She cracked open her eyes and mistily recognized her bent knees, and beyond them a fire burning. Almost everything else was in darkness. The fire had been laid on a raised bed of baked mud and there were earthenware pots on trivets in the hot embers. Her clothes, she realized with distaste, were soaked through and clammy. She shut her eyes again, tired by the effort of waking.

Her back was warm. She was sitting in front of a fire, propped up by someone else. As the realization sank in, Taqla's eyes shot open again. Her legs were framed by another pair. She was sitting between someone's knees and she didn't recognize the dark shirtsleeve she could see on the hand chafing her wrist. Weakly, she tried to sit up. Pain twinged in every joint and a forearm went round her, pinning her in place.

"It's all right, it's me," said Rafiq's voice right in her ear. "You're safe."

She twisted in his embrace so that she could see his face at least partly, and managed to groan, "What's happening?"

"We're in a village of the Madan. In their guesthouse. It's all right."

Her head was bare. Her head was bare and she was sitting in Rafiq's embrace and she could hear a murmur of nearby voices in the gloom. Her limbs convulsed in a panicked attempt to roll away from him. At once his arm clamped tighter.

"Don't worry, it's just the women in here."

"Let go!" she gasped.

"Don't." He'd dropped abruptly into Syriac. "I told them you were my wife."

"What?"

"What else was I supposed to say?" he hissed through gritted teeth. "Lie still."

She went limp, largely because she had no strength to fight him, and stared round. She could see shadowy forms beyond the fire's light, and hear muffled giggles and whispers. His arm was warm. She couldn't think of anything to do but go along with his plan.

"There," he murmured. "You know, I think they're pleased to have a chance to come into the guesthouse. It's usually men only."

"What happened?" she asked, licking her lips. "Why am I wet?"

"You don't remember?"

"I remember..." She searched the muddled pictures in her

head. "The Tree."

"And the Anfish?"

"What?"

"That's what the people here call it. It came out of the swamp and swallowed you up like a piece of bread."

Another memory surfaced. "Something hit me—so hard that I couldn't breathe."

"Yes. It pulled you down into the water. So I jumped in after you and stabbed it in the eye and it spat you right out again." His tone was light. "Do you remember the great bird?"

"Uh... Yes. I think so."

"It healed you." There was momentarily an odd unsteadiness to his voice. "Then it led me here to this village. The people took us in because of the bird. They call it the Simurgh and believe it's holy."

"The Senmurw," she said faintly. "The Bird of Compassion. The one who nursed Prince Zal in the old Persian story."

"Ah. Well, it saved you."

She decided she would think about that when she was feeling better. "And the Horse Most Swift?" she asked, suddenly fearful.

"Don't worry—it's in the hut here. I couldn't work out how to ravel it up though."

She nodded. "I'm cold," she whispered. "I can hardly feel the fire." She could hardly feel her hands either. She had to lift them up to count the rings on her fingers and check they were all still there. Misunderstanding the gesture, Rafiq folded his hands around hers. She was grateful for the warmth, however self-conscious it made her feel. Shutting her eyes, she felt herself begin to slide back into sleep.

"Taqla?"

Muzzily she lifted her head from where it had fallen back against his shoulder, to see a woman bending before them holding out a steaming bowl.

"Here. Soup," said she, passing it to Rafiq's hand. Then she laid a folded wad of cloth at Taqla's feet. "And dry clothes for you."

"Thank you," she whispered.

Rafiq cupped the bowl before her chest. "Can you hold this?" But when she tried to take it from him, her fingers were too stiff and clumsy. "It's all right," he repeated, "just drink." Then he held the bowl to her lips for her to sip the broth. It was a fish stew, it turned out, bulked out with rice. Taqla's stomach seemed to unfurl from its tight knot as its heat and richness seeped into her. She wanted to cry with gratitude, so good was the taste. Nevertheless it took her a long time to empty the bowl.

"Do you want some?" she remembered to ask Rafiq after the first mouthfuls of fish-meat.

"I ate while you were asleep."

It was funny how his holding her bowl for her took her back to being a child again. When she'd been ill as a little girl, Lelia had fed her and stroked her hair. Taqla wondered wistfully if Rafiq would stroke her hair, and then caught herself in a moment of lucidity and thrust the idea away.

But when she'd eaten, he wouldn't let her doze off again. "You need to get changed now," he told her. "Those wet clothes can't stay on."

"Then you need to leave the hut," she said in Syriac, feeling more resolved now there was some heat in her belly.

"That would look very strange," he replied in kind, "if I really were your husband. Come on, on your feet." He half lifted, half pushed her to her feet and she staggered, shocked at how weak her legs were.

"You can't look," she said through gritted teeth, pulling out of his arms. She nearly fell then, but one of the women came forward and caught her.

"Do you need help?" She spoke accented Arabic.

"Yes. Please."

Rafiq took the opportunity to squat down near the fire, toasting his hands and the front of his shirt and trousers, which were damp from her touch. Casually he turned his face away. Taqla found herself in the charge of three women. "Get out!" she hissed to him in Syriac, but he ignored her.

"What's wrong?" one of the villagers asked her.

"Nothing." She fought a wave of dizziness and they had to support her as she swayed. Luckily that seemed to take their minds off the agitation she'd been displaying toward her husband. They worked her out of Zahir's revoltingly clingy shirt and baggy trousers, clucking and commenting on how foreign women seemed to dress just like their men. Taqla just concentrated on staying on her feet and simply hoped that Rafiq wasn't watching. Her skin was so cold the slightest movement of air felt like it were cutting her, and she was shocked to find tears brimming in her eyes, tears that felt hot enough to scald her cheeks.

The women bundled her into a long cotton robe that smelled strongly of smoke. "Get into bed," they ordered her. One went and spread her wet clothes out over a framework of dried cane next to the fire. Rafiq's own clothes were already toasting there, she saw, and steaming. So was her headscarf.

"Bed?" Taqla wrapped her arms around herself. The eldest of the women pointed at the heap of woven rush mats Rafiq had been sitting on as he held her, with a blanket carefully folded at one end.

"We'll leave you two to warm each other up."

Then the whole group of them filed out, leaving only their blessings for a safe night. Taqla stood speechless with discomfort, then stumbled to the fire and hunched over it. Rafiq had hardly moved, it seemed. He knelt there with his chin in his hand, looking drawn and thoughtful.

"No way are we sleeping in the same bed," she whispered.

His gaze flicked toward her. "You see more than one bed? More than one blanket?" He eased himself to his feet, moving with effort.

"Then you'll have to—"

"Taqla, I'm cold and I'm tired—and you're even worse. I'm going to lie down and turn my back, and you can lie down and turn your back, and we can share the blanket and it'll be fine."

"No. Never."

"What," he asked wearily, "have I ever done that you should distrust me?"

"Apart from having being born a man, you mean?"

"Well, you can't blame me for that. It's hardly something I could help."

"Yes. And it's all the other things that men 'can't help' that have got me worried."

She regretted the words the moment they were out of her mouth, but his response was to break into a crooked chuckle. "You're feeling better then, I see."

Taqla crossed her hands over her breast, trying to stop the shivering that was taking possession of her body. "I wish I was."

"Believe me," he said, going over to the blanket and unfurling it decisively, "I'm so tired, Taqla, that all the houris of Paradise couldn't get anything out of me tonight. I'm going to lie down now and you...you do what you want. I'll see you in the morning." He stretched out full length, turned his back to the fire and covered himself with the thick woollen blanket. Taqla opened her mouth to protest, but got no further. She stayed huddled over the glowing embers for a few minutes as if she'd like to press herself to their warmth, feeling the exhaustion wash through her in waves.

He'd left her with the fire side of the mattress, she noted blearily. That was kind of him.

Very soon his breathing became slow and regular, and almost inaudible over the chattering of her teeth. Giving up in despair, she forced her aching limbs from the fire's glow and slipped in under the blanket, her back to his, her jaw clenched. She settled with her shoulder blades nearly touching his, her legs curled up, her fists crushed into the pit of her stomach. The blanket was heavy and promised warmth in time, but the rush matting beneath her was chilly. She thought it would be a long time before she slept—if she ever dared.

It was moments.

Taqla woke gradually, slipping in and out of awareness. So gradually that there was no feeling of shock as she came fully awake, just a sense of calm and ease and comfort. And warmth. She was warm again, even down to her toes.

There was, she realized, good reason for that. She lay partly on her side, leaning back against Rafiq, her head cradled on his arm. His other arm was draped around her, heavy and comforting, and his face was buried in her hair. She could feel the slow tide of his breath as his chest rose and fell. She could feel the curl of his fingers against her ribs. The warmth and the peace of him had soaked into her bones, and for a while she did nothing but blink her eyes slowly into focus, and breathe and listen to him breathing, as if those things made up the whole world.

A pale light illuminated the interior of the hut, the great hooped pillars and barrel vault of the roof they supported—all made out of rushes. She could faintly hear voices and the lowing of cattle outside. It must be morning. It must be time to get up. This quiet moment was something she'd somehow stolen from the harsh reality of the day.

She could just lie there, she told herself. She could just lie in his arms until he woke too and then he would kiss the back of her neck and pull up the robe that had already ridden up to her thighs and then... Her imagination failed her at that point. Heat stirred deep down in her, a hungry ache, and she pressed her lips together to stop an animal noise of need escaping them. She wondered how her body could be so stupid as to persist in hoping. This self-indulgence was insane. And dangerous.

As softly as she could, she tried to slide out from under his arm and the blanket. She almost made it, but Rafiq stirred as the first cold draft thrust into their warm nest, made a grumbling noise and pulled her firmly back against him, working her backside into his crotch. His hand slipped up to cup a breast and her nipple tightened deliciously in response.

Worse than that—Taqla suddenly had hard evidence that a physical quirk she'd noticed on the few occasions she'd both fallen asleep and woken up in male shape was not unique to Zahir. Her eyes flew wide open.

"Rafiq—get off!" she said in a strangled voice. He jumped.

"What?" His arm recoiled. As he released her, she rolled out from under the blanket and ended up hunched on the floor, hugging her knees to her chest with one arm, the other crooked over her mouth. "What?" he repeated, looking around and blinking as he struggled to sit up. "I was asleep." He focused on her and ran his fingers over his face and through his tousled hair. "Oh..."

"Get up and out," she ordered him. "I need to get dressed."

"Taqla, I'm sorry—"

"Go!"

"Right." He half rose then a look of consternation flitted across his face. "You won't mind me taking the blanket," he muttered, furling it about him before heading for the doorway.

She got dressed as quick as she could, changing the borrowed robe for Zahir's spare clothes from the Bag That Holds the World—which were as dry as if the little sack had never been dunked in the swamp. She tried not to think about Rafiq's embrace and tried not to miss its lost warmth. She failed on both counts.

When she was ready to face him, she drew back the roll of matting that served as a door and stepped outside. The air was damp. She saw that they were right on the edge of the water, and under her feet the leafy ground was eerily soft and springy. To her right, a small group of men sat on their haunches, Rafiq among them. They seemed to be talking and eating. There were no women in sight. Of course, she thought, the women would be working.

It would have been unthinkably brazen to approach the group of men without being called over, so she turned the other way and went to sit by the edge of the water. In among the shoots of growing rushes, a couple of black oxen stood chest deep in the swamp and munched at leaves with the dreamy look of cows everywhere.

This was an upside-down world, she thought to herself, staring out at the little islands that dotted the marsh nearby, each a precarious-looking foundation for a hut or two. It was as different as imaginable from her homeland. Here water was common and dry land precious. Here the colors were green and silver, not brown. Here the sky was enclosed by tall walls of reed and cows swam and fish—

Memory surfaced from a haze as thick as swamp mud. She'd been standing on the island. That was the last thing she remembered.

Here fish attack on dry land. She shuddered. It must have knocked her clean out when it hit, to leave everything since such a blank.

Rafiq broke her reverie by squatting down beside her, and put a flatbread into her hand. Surprised, she thanked him and slipped the bread under her veil.

"Feeling a bit steadier?"

She nodded, her mouth already full of dough. The bread was stuffed with salted curd cheese, making it sticky. "Are we going back today?" she mumbled, swallowing. "To the Tree, I mean. I have an idea how I can hold off the Anfish, you see, and—"

"We're not going back. We can go forward."

She looked at him questioningly, still chewing hard. Rafiq scratched his stubbled chin and stared out across the water. "The Senmurw spoke to me," he said, sounding self-conscious. "Not like a man speaks...but when it sang, the words were there in my head. It asked me why we'd come to the Tree, and I said it was for one of the fruit, and it said it would give us one if...if we brought its egg back to it. It laid its only egg years ago, you see, and it was stolen and taken away to the Temple of Yaghuth. It wants it back."

Taqla ran her tongue over her teeth, unable to speak for a moment. The word *Yaghuth* sounded naggingly familiar but she couldn't place the name. "You said yes?" she asked at last.

"Uh-huh."

"You're not upset?"

"I wasn't in a position to be ungrateful. The bird saved your life."

That was an unsettling thought. She tore her piece of bread into smaller pieces. "Do you know where this temple is then?"

"It's in the Abu Bahr, it said. Which happens to be an area in the Empty Quarter."

"What? That's *hundreds* of miles south."

"And deep desert. Yes, I know." He looked at his hands. "No water, no shelter, no people. We don't have to go. We can give up now."

She frowned. "You've changed."

"Taqla, we both nearly drowned yesterday." His voice was suddenly hoarse. "I thought for a while that you had. It scared me half to death. I mean...I need you to say alive for this." He gave a twisted grin. "I need me to stay alive too, of course. Having you alive will definitely help on that front."

"But you still want to keep going?"

"Yes." He didn't hesitate over that one.

Taqla felt a prickle of—what? Disappointment? Fear? Relief? "Then we go forward," she said firmly. Then added, slightly shamefaced, "And can we go via Basra? I really need a hot bath."

Chapter Twelve
In which a storm rises.

Tarampara-rampara-ram.

The sand was green. It wasn't obvious if she picked up a handful, so pale was the color, but when it lay in a sweep at her feet, the delicate shade couldn't be mistaken. The jade-hued crests of the dunes rose and fell in unending succession on every side, right to the horizon, like fossilised waves. That was presumably, Taqla thought, how the Abu Bahr—which meant *Father of the Sea*—had received its name, and how this area of dunes came to be remembered distinctly when so few people ever ventured even into the margins of the Empty Quarter. This was nothing like the familiar flat desert of home that was stippled with low thorny tussocks that provided sparse browsing for goats and camels. There were no pilgrim trails here, no caravan routes, no wells or villages, not the smallest tree or patch of thorns to break the monotony of a landscape wholly dead. Only the crippling heat of the sun during the day and the old stories of cities like Ad and Irem of the Golden Pillars, long since swallowed by the sands—places cursed by God for their wickedness.

Green sand and ancient evil. The Temple of Yaghuth was not, they gathered, going to be an exception. The odd familiarity of that strange name had been solved by one of the old men back in the swamp village. It was written of in the holy Qur'an, he told them, as the name of an idol worshipped in the time of Noah.

They travelled only in the mornings and the evenings. During the worst heat of the day, if no rock outcrop could be found, then they erected the windbreak and sat in its meagre shade. Taqla walked as much as she could because she felt better able to read the subtle strands of Fate when she was in contact with the earth and moving slowly. It was hard work striding over the soft sand. As she headed off in whatever direction took her fancy best, mesmerised by the puffs of grit thrown out before her sandals with each step, Rafiq would ride spiral sweeps centered around her plodding figure, urging the Horse to the top of dunes to get a look down the hidden slopes and investigating the crags of greenish bedrock that emerged through the skin of the sand like jagged bones. But none turned out to be the ruins of an ancient temple.

At night the desert changed. They noticed it when first the moon rose. Rafiq stirred, staring out around them. "What on earth—?"

Taqla, using the corners of her vision in the dim light, swung in a circle. The hair stood up on the nape of her neck as she saw that the landscape around them had altered, that the barren skyline of rolling dunes was now broken by strange shapes. Most were featureless mounds or clustered tiers of angles but one nearby had the branched silhouette of a lumpy tree. And among its branches something moved, shimmering. "Over there," she whispered, pointing. "What's that?"

With a flick, the dim light shot behind a dark mass and vanished. Taqla was left staring at her own hand. As she'd pointed, her hand had left a greenish phosphorescent trail hanging in the air. She waved her fingers experimentally, and the glow outlined her rings.

"I'm alight."

"So are they," said Rafiq and she turned to look behind her. Globular, almost feathery glows of light hung above them, motionless except for the faintest pulsing. And a whole swarm of smaller glows was headed in their direction, flitting over the new contours of the ground. The swarm hovered over a mound momentarily, and Taqla glimpsed the pink blush of a domed surface as convoluted as an exposed brain.

"Coral?" said Rafiq disbelievingly. Then the swarm was

upon them and Taqla saw that it was about a dozen cuttlefish each as long as her hand, moving through the air as if it were water. They clustered about the two travellers, colors chasing across their transparent skins. Apart from the blushes of color, she realized, the animals were see-through, beings made of dim light. One jetted close to her face and she put up a hand to intercept it, causing the cephalopod to flit away and swim in a circle before returning. It swam straight through her hand then, and though she felt nothing, she jumped.

"Ghosts," she whispered, anxiety giving way to wonder. The whole swarm of cuttlefish was gathering about her now, entranced by the phosphorescent swirls she left in water only they could feel. They followed each move of her arm and she found she could conduct them in a strange dance. "They're like ghosts."

"The ghost of a whole sea," Rafiq said, stepping to the leafless tree of coral and scything his arm through the branches without meeting any resistance. "All around us."

Taqla had never seen the sea. She laughed, turning on her toes as the cuttlefish danced around and through her. The sand she stirred puffed up and hung in the moonlit air before falling slowly back. The undersea color show was muted but lovely, an unearthly glimmering that barely illuminated more than a fleeting glimpse of feathery or rugose corals. "It's beautiful."

The moonlight picked out Rafiq's grin.

"What are they, do you think?" she asked, pointing at the eerie blobs of light.

"Well, those look like jellyfish."

"And those?" She waved at a cluster of three round spiralform objects, as big as millstones, that defied gravity just like the jellyfish. Each seemed to sport a cluster of tentacles.

"No idea. I've never seen anything like them."

They stood and goggled at the lantern-festival display, which strengthened as the moon rose. Everything was sketched in delicate glimmers, everything as insubstantial as mist. But when a beast bigger than all the others came soaring over a crest and angled in their direction, Taqla couldn't help her heart jumping into her mouth.

"Whoa! Don't move!" Rafiq snapped, but neither of them took his advice when it became clear how big the thing was—as long as an ocean-going dhow, with a heavy neck and a mouth longer than a grown man, filled with jutting, snaggled teeth. Four huge paddle limbs propelled the monster. Taqla and Rafiq both took an involuntary step back and together, leaving a green glow to outline their retreat. The creature twitched its head and bore down in their direction, its crocodilian maw easing open. "Oh no," Rafiq groaned, reaching for his sword.

Taqla grabbed her fear in both hands, lifted it high over her head and spoke the words that would ignite it. White light, painfully bright, shot from between her fingers, illuminating for a long moment the sands around them—empty, barren and leached of color, their own shadows thrown down like ink upon the pallor.

When the light went out, they were both blind. It took a long time for their eyes to readjust to the moonlight.

"You didn't have to do that," said Rafiq a little unsteadily. "It couldn't actually eat us."

"It couldn't eat our *bodies*," she replied dubiously. The Ghost Sea had gone, even when she was able to make out the outlines of the dunes once more. "You know what that was?" she said, flushing with relief and pride. "That was the Behemoth. We saw the ghost of the Behemoth!"

After that they slept. In the morning when Taqla awoke, she found a fragment of coral in a fold of her clothes, like a tiny flower of stone.

"Be patient," Taqla said as they waited out another afternoon's scorching sun. "Did you think God was going to hand you a map?"

"Do you really believe we will find it?" Rafiq was carving a piece of sun-bleached goat bone with his knife. It was a round knob broken from a femur and this time he was picking out the shape of a human head from it.

"Yes." She shut her eyes. "I feel...something. It's near. It tastes bad."

"This is sorcery, is it?"

"Part of it."

"Hm."

From under her lashes, she watched the tiny face taking form beneath his clever hands. It was a woman's face. *Ahleme, the Flower of Dimashq*, she thought. He had seen the girl once and been engulfed in the flames of love. Now every moment apart from her was a burning torment. Taqla wasn't unsympathetic. She understood how love was. The pain, and the need to quench that fire, took over the lover's life. She'd heard it said and sung a thousand times, and now knew for herself how it felt because she too burned.

No, she corrected herself. If she had been foolish enough to give way to her feelings, then she'd have been love's victim too, but she'd been smart enough to recognize the trap and strong enough to resist it. She wasn't helpless. She did not love.

Rafiq suddenly seemed to become aware of what it was he was carving, and covered the little face in his hand. "How did you become a sorceress then?" he asked, snagging the waterskin from between them and lifting it to his lips. "Did you...make a pact?"

"With Iblis himself, you mean?" she said, smiling. "No. You have to be born to it. I was seven years old when it first became clear I had the Art. And it runs in my family. My father and my grandfather and *his* father were sorcerers."

"Your mother too?"

She stopped smiling and brushed some sand carefully off her knee. "No. In our family it wasn't considered wise to make marriage-links with outsiders. Too many questions might have been asked by strangers, you see. So the mothers of my line were all slaves bought at the market, not free women. But they had to be maidens—it's almost always the firstborn child that has the Art."

"Why's that?"

"No one knows. Magic seems to root better in a virgin womb." She ran her tongue across her lips, but they stayed dry, and out of somewhere very deep inside her, words came and pressed up against them, struggling out into the air like wasps crawling from their hidden nest. "That was how they found out I was my father's heir. When I was seven, I told my father that the baby my mother was carrying in her belly wasn't his. I thought it was obvious. I thought he knew." She blinked. "I was just a little girl. I didn't know what it meant."

Rafiq frowned. "What happened?"

"He sold her. I don't know who to."

"Oh."

Taqla shrugged. "It's the lot of slaves and wives to be disposable."

Rafiq looked pained. "Not all of them."

She didn't reply, only ran her fingers through the sand between her feet, wondering why she had told him her story. She hadn't spoken a word about it to anyone, even Lelia, since leaving childhood behind.

"He broke the law, you know," said Rafiq cautiously. "She'd already borne his child, so she should have been safe from being sold on."

"Yes, well." Her throat felt like it were coated in ash. "*Legally* he could have had her executed. I suppose he might have been being merciful, just selling her." She remembered her father's stern face. "I doubt it though. He was always very...proper. Very disciplined."

Rafiq rubbed at his jaw. "Is your father still alive?"

"No." Perhaps once this point had been raw, but by now it was covered by layers of scar tissue. "He went out into the desert one day with a mule load of aloes and sandalwood. He meant, I assume, to lure and trap a djinni. His servants found him with his skull and his belly burst and every bone in his body broken, as if he'd been dropped from a great height."

"My condolences." Rafiq's tone was completely flat.

Needled, Taqla drew herself up a little straighter and thrust out her lip. "He was always good to me." She recalled long hours of study, his dedication to her excellence in the Art, and her fierce determination to win his approval. He could have disowned her or ignored her, but he'd chosen to school his daughter in his own path. She did not underestimate the value of that care. "He made me his heir and he taught me...so much."

"I can see that," Rafiq answered a little grimly.

She shot him a hard glance and then wished she hadn't. His eyes seemed to look right inside her. "We can move on," she muttered, looking around for her belongings. "It's not so hot now."

"What went wrong?"

"Pardon?"

"What went wrong when he tried to capture the djinni?"

"Oh. I don't know." Without thinking, she began to rotate the little bronze ring about her finger. "Maybe he took too long getting the words of binding out. Maybe he encountered one who couldn't hear him. They have to hear to obey, you know. Some of them, the Ifrit especially, took awls to their ears and made themselves deaf so that they couldn't ever be enslaved. They'd rather spend their lives in silence than submit to us." Rafiq looked shocked, so she went on. "They fear and resent us, you know. We are inferior to them in almost every way, and yet God has favoured Mankind and made us their masters."

"That's...good to know," he said. "Let's hope the one we're chasing isn't deaf. Or fast. Or, God willing, awake."

She found a stone. At first it simply caught her eye as she walked up, a shiny piece of flint in the coarse sand and pebbles at her feet. She took one pace past, stopped and turned. It lay there, gray and sharp-edged against the green blur of the sand. It nagged at her mind's eye. Stopping, she examined the flake, turning it over in her palm. It was an arrowhead, she decided after a moment, though the tip had been broken off. It felt warm and smooth—and somehow a little unclean. She had an unaccountable urge to wipe her hands on her clothes.

Instead she looked around, but only the featureless dunes rolled about her, wave after wave, and even Rafiq wasn't in sight. There were no similar shards in view—this was a desert of sand, not flint. So she sat down, and with the arrowhead resting before her, loosened her headscarf to bare the nape of her neck so that she could unbind her hair from the clumsy braid there. Once loose, it felt uncomfortably warm on her skin. She plucked nine long individual hairs, then braided them together to make a short string that she looped about the stone arrowhead. The small weight hung from its tether, swaying back and forth. She stood carefully and watched to see which way it would twist, pivoting on the balls of her feet and humming a particular little tune under her breath. Only then did she notice that Rafiq had reappeared, and was sitting on the motionless Horse under a nearby dune crest, watching her.

Rather clumsily she looped her *jabbayah* one-handed over her head once more, loose strands of hair blowing in her eyes and sticking unpleasantly to her throat, but she didn't stop humming. The arrowhead swung and she concentrated on which direction the tug felt the strongest. When she was sure, she indicated to him with her hand in which direction they were to go, and set off again.

Two hours later, Rafiq rode up and told her she was going in circles.

"What?"

"We're circling back on our own footprints."

She looked around her, blinking. The light reflecting off the sand was so hard she could hardly focus. "Then it's here somewhere," she said, peering in vain across the sand for some sign of an ancient temple.

"Are you sure?"

She was too hot to give him more than an exasperated look.

"That's a pity—because we're going to have to leave."

"What for?"

He nodded to the horizon over her shoulder. "See that? I don't like the look of it at all."

She stared. A greenish haze like the oldest of bruises was building low in the sky.

"Sandstorm," said Rafiq, leaning forward in the saddle and looking grim. "We can almost certainly outrun it on the Horse, but we need to get going."

She shook her head. "No."

"Why not?"

"We found this place. We're meant to be here."

"We've found nothing much," he answered dubiously. "And I'd rather not be caught in a sandstorm."

"We're here." She set her jaw. "At the right time. Storm or not."

"I've seen men killed by these storms," he said quietly. "Are you sure?"

She nodded, wishing she felt more confident. Sorcery was such a tenuous, fragile link to the world. She trusted her instinct, but had never put it to such a test before.

"All right then."

They prepared a camp and what little shelter they could. Rafiq was anxious, far more so than he would ever have admitted to Taqla or to anyone. He'd survived a two-day sandstorm some years back and had seen flesh stripped down to bone and eye sockets scoured blind. He'd seen men who'd been buried by sand, only their hands or feet protruding from its waves. The worst threat though, he knew, was from suffocation. Fine dust could work its way everywhere, including down throats and into lungs. Not normally preoccupied with his own mortality, the one death Rafiq did recoil from was suffocation. He wanted an enemy he could react to, and though he'd learned like every traveller that there were some things—

heat, thirst, pain—that could only be endured, it was a terribly hard thing for him to prepare to lie passively before the assault of the storm when it would have been so easy for them to flee.

Trust her, he told himself, *she knows what she's doing.* The thought made him smile to himself because he'd spent most of his adult life refusing to respect any judgment but his own, and here he was entrusting his life to a sorceress. Choosing a spot near the top of a slope—he thought it too easy for the dune to march over their heads if they sheltered at its base—he pushed the Horse Most Swift over on its side and they set up their goathair shelter against its metal belly.

As the air began to taste sour and grow heavy, djinn could be seen stalking the dunes—or at any rate the whirls of dust that betrayed their invisible presence. The light grew greenish yellow as the shadow of the storm blocked out the sun.

"Stay sat upright, if you can," he told Taqla, as they drew the thick, rank-smelling cloth over their heads. "Create an air pocket for yourself—but keep your eyes shut."

Then the storm was upon them, at first with angry gusts and a rattle of sand, and then with a continuous pressure. Rafiq hunched his shoulders and cradled his head in his hands as the light under the cloth dimmed. He'd wrapped his headscarf tightly about his mouth and nose but couldn't bring himself to swathe his eyes, so he just screwed them shut. He could feel the wind pounding against his shoulders and taste dust on his tongue. Sliding lower into the shelter offered by the Horse's body, he clenched his teeth against the waves of inner rebellion as their tent collapsed slowly over their heads, cocooning them in darkness, leaving them no choice but to endure the hours of misery.

He could hear Taqla, he realized. Even over the continuous roar of the wind her voice was audible. At first he thought—rather surprised—that she was praying, but listening more closely, he worked out that she was muttering in a language he'd never heard, repeating the same three nonsense phrases over and over again. It was a spell, he supposed. A spell for their safety or to calm the winds or something. The repetitions were hypnotic. Only occasionally would she pause to huff out sand or clear her throat.

The thought of her being smothered inexorably an arm's length from his own corpse burned in his mind. In the darkness he groped toward her, finding her shoulder first. She was lying on her side with her arms over her head, the tent pressed against her neck by the weight of drifted sand behind it. Rafiq pulled her into the downwind lee of his own body and she didn't protest, hardly even skipping a beat of her chant as he settled her against the bulk of his torso, her head nested against his chest. It was probably illusory, the notion that he could shelter her, but it gave him some comfort.

After that, listening to her murmuring voice, his cheek pressed to the crown of her head, he fell into a kind of stupor while over their heads the sandstorm raced on. When, late into the night, the wind slackened at last and Taqla's tired murmur dwindled to nothing, he even dozed off.

But when dawn came he was first on his feet, throwing back the goathair flap and its burden of sand to crawl out into the open. Blinking, he took one stupefied look at the landscape before him then called, "Taqla! Come and see this!"

Because there, unmistakably, was the Temple of Yaghuth.

Standing before the glass surface of a pillar, Ahleme stared at the reflection of herself in its blue-green depths.

When she'd woken that morning, she'd found no clothing awaiting her but these—a skirt made up of strings of pearls, and a top barely long enough to cover her breasts, made of strung pearls too, worked in an open mesh. She'd put them on because she'd had no choice—unless it was to drape herself in the furs of the bed. She'd put them on because nothing had happened for hours and she was curious to see what she looked like. Now she stared. The white beads showed up well in the mirror, shining against her warm flesh, and against her skin they felt cool and heavy. From a distance, the ensemble might even appear decent. Only when one looked closely was it clear that there was nothing between these jewels of the sea to protect her modesty, that her nipples peeked out like two dark pearls among the pale ones, that the secret split of her velvety sex could be glimpsed whenever the strings shifted.

Ahleme swung a little on her toes, watching the way the heavy beads swung and then fell back against her legs. She couldn't help feeling shocked by how tempting she looked in this costume, and guiltily pleased. Of course she knew she shouldn't be vain, but...

But she looked beautiful. There was no denying the pleasure she felt at that. A woman ought to dress modestly and this was anything but, yet oh how it suited her. Every time she turned away from the mirror, she turned back, fascinated. She ran her hand over the bare span of her narrow waist then stroked the pearls over her breasts, whose own points stood up nearly as hard.

Her eyes in the reflection were troubled, fearful, and bright with a potential that might be terror, or just as easily might be anticipation.

He has not sullied me, she told her reflection. *I am still a virgin.*

The trouble was that she didn't look like one.

Chapter Thirteen
In which a very old voice is heard.

Taqla, crawling out from beneath their collapsed shelter, noticed first that the green sand had got everywhere during the storm, into every layer of clothing and every fold of skin. *Everywhere.* She shook it out of her hair and beat weakly at her clothes as she stood, blinking in the new sunlight. Around her the landscape had been resculpted, dunes replaced by valleys and low places turned to hills. The dune she remembered to their left had been partially swept away, and revealed in its place was the great pale dome of a building.

Rafiq turned to her with a huge grin as he shook out his headscarf and it fluttered like a flag from his hand. "That's it! You were right!"

Taqla grinned too, behind the safety of her veil. "Yes. By the will of God."

"Come on."

"Just a moment." She turned back to the Horse Most Swift, which lay almost buried. Its hollow body had filled with sand and would have been impossible to lift upright, so Taqla ravelled it up into its ball of silver wire. Then she followed Rafiq toward the temple.

The closer she got, the uneasier she felt. Whatever pale stone the building had been hewn from—and there were no joint lines visible in the dome, nor had it been split by the weight of sand—it had the color and texture of worn bone, and even in a place as strange as the Abu Bahr it struck the eye uncomfortably. Sand was still heaped about the walls, but at one point it ebbed low enough to show a porchlike structure jutting from the circular main building, and in that the lintel of a doorway, level with their feet. Most of the building must still be buried.

"We're going to have to dig," Rafiq said, kneeling to scoop sand away with his hands from that straight edge of stone.

"Wait." Taqla dropped the silver wire at her feet. "Lion Most Strong," she commanded.

The wire rose as it usually did, flying back and forth to create a mesh of strands, but this time it wove the form of a maned Lion, not the Horse. It was lower built than the steed but broader. Rafiq said nothing but his eyebrows went up and his eyes spoke volumes.

Why should I tell you everything? Taqla wanted to ask, nettled, but she said only, "It'll do the digging for us."

"Feel free."

They stood aside while the silver beast dug, front paws scooping the sand untiringly and much faster than any human being could. By the time Taqla let it fall still a large double door had been revealed—two leaves of corroded bronze. They looked like they opened inward, and stood slightly ajar, a handswidth of complete darkness gaping between them. Rafiq slid down the slope and took a grip on one of the doors.

"Wait," said Taqla. "I should go first."

He cast her a hard look. "Why?"

"It might be dangerous."

Heat shimmered in his gaze but he kept his voice calm. "What on earth do you think might still able to threaten us, after all these centuries? Do you imagine the priests are still alive?"

"No. But there's the god."

He blinked. "There is no god but God," he reminded her.

"Mm. That's... You might find that's more a doctrinal statement than a factual one," she said uncomfortably.

He gave her a long, thoughtful stare. "Then I had definitely better go in first," he concluded. "And if I get into trouble it'll be easier for you to rescue me than the other way round."

She didn't argue. In all honesty she felt a little bit relieved to let him take the lead into that uncanny black space. He put his shoulder to it and eased the door open, the hinges protesting and showering dust. Then he slipped inside and she, clenching her jaw, followed.

There were no windows inside, of course. If there had been then the interior would have filled with sand long ago, she supposed, so they had to wait just within the threshold for their eyes to adjust to the gloom. There was no sand beyond the small antechamber; a lightly dusted flight of steps led down into the great circular space within.

She felt an almost overpowering desire to rush out and wash herself—or scratch off her skin—anything to escape the feeling of uncleanliness that crept over her skin in cold waves. It wasn't a sensation she normally associated with sorcery, in fact she'd never felt anything like it before. Putting her palms together, she made a tiny light between them, a cool blue glow, and then looked questioningly at Rafiq. He nodded, so she let the light drift away from her cupped hands, a wisp like a night insect that floated down the steps and illuminated their way.

One tread at a time, Rafiq descended into that space, looking about him carefully. He waited once he reached the last step, and Taqla, her senses straining, crept down to join him. Her little sorcerous glow hung in midair, casting the faintest of lights, the faintest of shadows. There was no scent but slightly dusty air, no sound but the small ones they were making themselves, yet every fibre of her body was taut with the conviction that they were not alone. Across the domed chamber, the pale bulk of an enormous statue loomed and she stared toward it.

Without a word, Rafiq touched her lightly on the arm and pointed up. Taqla switched her gaze to the dome overhead and shivered. The roof was unsupported by any pillars. Equally unsupported, in fact more so because they did not seem to be strung from any wires or rafters but just hung like needles from a lodestone, were the blades clustered all over the interior of the dome. They looked like spears of dark metal and they hung point down, their tips swaying ever so gently.

Rafiq touched his index finger to her lips through the veil, an action that rattled Taqla at least as much as the implicit threat overhead, then stepped carefully across the bare rock floor. She forced herself to look up, keeping a watch on the lances, but they didn't stir. When Rafiq had made it all the way across the chamber toward the idol, she gritted her teeth and followed.

Any last hope she'd entertained that Yaghuth had been a beneficent heathen deity of healing died then. There was an altar stone, which had a groove for fluids about the rim and a channel for drawing them off. It stood within a great stone basin just before the idol, and that basin was full of crumbled human skulls. The statue itself was, she guessed, crafted of jade, a single unimaginably large block of the stone crudely but effectively carved. Yaghuth had a human torso with two vulture heads sprouting from the neck. These stared at each other beak to beak, giving him the strangest bifurcated countenance, and he had no legs but four snake tails upon which he stood upright. He had four arms too—one hand raised as a fist in threat, one stretching out as if to seize something, and two turned over holding objects in their cupped palms. It looked like one of those objects was another human skull—it was difficult to see clearly from below, so tall was the idol and so dim the light—but the other was a copper-colored egg as big as a watermelon.

Rafiq indicated this last discovery with a flick of his eyes, pulled a rueful "wish me luck" face, and then stepped up onto the edge of the basin.

Then the idol spoke.

"Give to Yaghuth the red offering."

The voice was ancient, weary and distant, but it whispered across the chamber, stirring the dust on the skulls and making the blades overhead sway. Taqla had to clench her teeth against a wave of nausea. Rafiq dropped back from the basin lip to the floor, looking swiftly around.

"Give to Yaghuth the bending of the knee. Give to Yaghuth

the smiting of the breast. Give to Yaghuth the red offering."

"Go back to sleep, old one," said Rafiq to the empty air.

Taqla was shocked by his audacity. Possibly the god was too, because there was a marked pause before that poisonous whisper spoke again. *"Give to Yaghuth—"*

"No," said Rafiq. "Your time has long gone. Go back to sleep."

"Yaghuth gives victory. Yaghuth gives power."

"Not for thousands of years, old one. The world has changed."

"Yaghuth sleeps."

"That's right."

It wasn't overly bright, this god, she decided.

"Yaghuth wakes. Yaghuth hears the steps of the little man. The little man wakes Yaghuth."

"Not intentionally," said Rafiq with a wry flash of his teeth. *He's enjoying this*, thought Taqla through her nausea. *It's like the chase across the rooftops. He likes to test his Fate.* She shook her head.

"The little man comes to the fane of Yaghuth. Tell Yaghuth why."

It was Rafiq's turn to hesitate. "You have the Egg of the Senmurw," he said at last. "You've hoarded it long enough."

"The little man wants the Egg."

Rafiq tilted his chin.

"Yaghuth breaks the Egg."

To Taqla's horror the statue moved, the great open hand beginning to curl into a fist around the Egg. Dust showered from the shifting stone. They both cried out in a single voice.

The idol went still, blunt claws curved about the Senmurw's Egg.

"Give to Yaghuth the bending of the knee."

"Never," he answered, eyes wide and teeth set.

"Give to Yaghuth... Give to Yaghuth the feet and the words."

"What?"

"The little man wants the Egg. The little man goes. Give to Yaghuth the going. Go to Banebshenan Banebshenan Adhur-Anahid for Yaghuth."

"Uh," said Rafiq with an expression of dawning alarm.

"Say to Adhur-Anahid to give the bending of the knee to Yaghuth. Say to Adhur-Anahid to surrender that which she promised to Yaghuth. Say to Adhur-Anahid the time has come."

"All right. I understand." He cast Taqla a worried look. "I think I do, anyway."

"Give to Yaghuth the going, and Yaghuth will give the little man the Egg."

"Yes," he said. "I see. Why not."

Taqla shook her head, but Rafiq wasn't paying her attention any more. He started to back away from the idol, motioning her to move too, and that at least was a plan she wasn't arguing with. They stumbled from the temple and scrambled on hands and knees up the slope of sand, not stopping until they were several hundred paces away from the building. There Taqla pitched onto her knees, pulled down her veil and dry-retched.

"Are you all right?" she heard him demand.

"Yes." She wiped her hair from her lips. "I think. Oh...I don't think you should have agreed to that."

"I'd have agreed to nearly anything to get us out of there." He shuddered. "It moved, Taqla. The idol moved! I'd no idea it could do that!"

"Nor me." Taqla rammed her knuckles under her breastbone, swallowing her revulsion, and groaned.

"What's wrong?"

"Couldn't you feel it in there? It was like breathing sewage."

He shook his head. "I didn't smell anything."

Taqla didn't bother to correct him. She covered her face again and sank her head in her hands. She'd be better in a few moments, she told herself.

"You ever heard of this Adhur-Anahid woman?"

She shook her head.

"It sounds like a Persian name," mused Rafiq.

"It is. Banebshenan Banebshenan means 'Queen of Queens'. She must have been the wife of one of their emperors, I imagine."

"Well that does it, doesn't it? That thing in there has no idea how long it's been buried under the sand—there's no Persian Empire left."

"No."

"So we're finished."

"Perhaps."

"Where would we be finding a Persian queen these days?"

"Oh, there's one obvious place," she said quietly.

"Where?" Rafiq stepped round to stare her in the face.

"Well, there must be imperial tombs somewhere, mustn't there?"

He laughed, bitterly. "Ah. There's the problem. You did notice that word 'tomb', Taqla? We've hit the cliff-face."

"I can talk to the dead." She said it softly, unhappily.

"What?"

"I've never done it before," she amended hastily. "But I know how."

"Oh no." He turned and walked away, back and forth, shaking his head. "No, no, no."

Taqla watched him stomp up and down, and then turn back in her direction. His face was set in lines of consternation, his eyes full of dark eagerness. She thought that she would do anything for that face, that look.

"Could you?" he asked.

In a room without walls, Ahleme basked under the glimmering light of a hundred lamps, in a sea of furs, by the side of the djinni. A thousand flames were hazily reflected by the net of pearls across her breasts and in the ropes of pearls that lay across her thighs. Between the pearls her skin gleamed no less enticingly.

It was not only her attire that had changed since first she came to this place, and not only the fact that she no longer recoiled from his presence. Her expression this night was one of fascinated concentration. She was reclining on her side. Yazid lay on his back, hands knotted safely out of the way behind his neck, his broad chest like a sea rock upon which she had been cast up. His breastbone rose and fell accompanied by the sigh of waves. Her cheek was propped in the palm of her hand. She had wondered about laying her head upon his chest, but thought not—that was too intimate an embrace. It might give him ideas he should not be having.

She still guarded her family's honor, whatever this scene might look like to anyone else. Whatever the mocking little voice inside her said. There were, she insisted, still boundaries of propriety.

It was just...the boundaries had moved, as the desert's edge moves, driven by the wind.

Ahleme's free hand was in motion, as unhurried as the wash of Yazid's breath, as the caress of the waves on a beach. Back and forth, up the marble-smooth, marble-hard length of his virility. Every exploratory squeeze, every turn of her wrist, every rub of her thumb brought forth its response. His eyelids quivered to the rhythm of her touch, his breath gathered and released to the stroke of her hand.

She had never imagined that there was such power in giving. A pulse throbbed in the crease of her thigh.

"Harder," he whispered, "please."

She tightened her grip until the muscles in her forearm protested and he gasped. Then she let go altogether. His eyes flew open, torment in his pale gaze. With a faint smile, she reached down to cup him, finding his purse of stones clenched. She trailed fingertips over the creases and slid her hot fingers back up his length, delighted at its response, its eager jerks and nudges.

"Ahleme," he groaned, as if in terror.

Pushing herself up on her elbow, she watched the work of

her hand, her dark fingers and her gilded nails. The contrast with what they held was shocking. His helpless need for release mocked his power and his strength. The djinni's flesh wept a milky tear in shame.

Without a word—she had yet to learn the words for this—and without thinking—her reactions were instinctive—Ahleme stooped upon him, moist lips parting, to offer the comfort of her kiss.

Chapter Fourteen
In which a king makes confession and an angel sings.

Tarampara-rampara-ram.

Within a circle described by a silk rope and inscribed with Greek letters, Taqla stood in the sand before the Tower of Silence on the hill above the ruined palace of Firuzabad. If she chose to look down that way, she could see that building huddled on the bank of a green pool, and a little farther off, more ruins surrounded by a round ditch, and the clustered buildings of an inhabited village among the fields of the plain. A bowl of myrrh burned at her feet. The sun was dipping toward the horizon. Rafiq sat cross-legged, his bare sword lying across his knees, flipping a pebble from one hand to the other and back again. His mouth was set in a thin line.

They were both anxious, not just because they were there to commit necromancy, though that was reason enough, but because they were almost certainly visible from the village to any sharp pair of eyes. Taqla didn't know if the local people were still fire-worshippers—there were still enclaves of them in the caliphate because their religion was tolerated to a degree. That would mean that she and Rafiq were trespassing upon their sacred funerary site. But equally, if these villagers were of the Faithful they were unlikely to approve of strangers messing about in the half-crumbled tower of the infidel dead.

Necromancy was on no one's list of approved activities.

The arched gateway to the Tower of Silence gaped. Inside could be glimpsed brick stairs ascending. Taqla had a theoretical knowledge of what they ascended to—an open platform on which were laid the bodies of the dead for the birds to pick clean and the sun to desiccate, a pit of jumbled bones in the centre. If the old ways had died out when the palace and city were sacked, then those bones would be splinters and dust. If the locals were still infidels then... Then she did not want to picture the contents of the platform. Fire-worshippers did not bury or burn their dead for fear of polluting the elements. They marked no graves with inscriptions, kept no individual space in death. It made it that much more difficult to locate a body to talk to.

Theoretically, her chances of success would have been improved with the blood of a black ram, but she hadn't even bothered suggesting that to Rafiq.

The skin on the back of her neck creeping, Taqla chanted, "I call forth Banebshenan Banebshenan Adhur-Anahid to speak with me," for the seventy-fifth time. If this didn't work, then they would have to return to Taysafun and try there but, regardless, she wanted to be out of here before dark. Necromancy after nightfall was far more dangerous. It had a tendency to attract the attention of entities neither desired nor amiably inclined.

Maybe, she thought, her lips and hands still moving in the prescribed patterns, this Adhur-Anahid was older than the empire of the fire-worshippers. Maybe they would have to search back farther into Persia's past, to the empires of Cyrus or Xerxes.

"I call forth Banebshenan Banebshenan Adhur-Anahid to speak with me." The seventy-seventh repetition. Taqla fell silent, holding her breath. The afternoon sun was turning the hills orange. For a moment there was only the sound of insects faintly droning. Then a breeze blew up. It stirred the grass and it blew through the stones of the Tower of Silence and it brought to Taqla's nostrils the rank smell of death even through the incense smoke. Then even the breeze was gone.

From the gate of the tower came flies, a swarm of them. They swept out in a cloud, motes of darkness gathering into a spiral, a cluster, a cloud so dense it almost had solid form. She watched it glide across from the door toward her, swirling and shifting shape, and then gather itself into a pillar that stood between her and the sun. Her eyes watered as she tried to look at it without staring into the light. It seemed to coalesce into the form of a man.

"She is not here." It spoke with the tormented buzz of countless carrion flies. "She never was."

Taqla was half aware of Rafiq rising to his feet, sword readied, but she was trying to concentrate on the thing that hovered before her.

"I see. Then...who are you?" She'd never heard that the dead were eager to rise to a summons. They didn't consort with necromancers out of choice.

"I am Ardashir. I was Shahanshah of all this realm." It might have been an auditory trick that loaned the buzz a bitter tone. "I built the palace you see below, and the city and the fire-temple. I raised up my people against our Parthian overlords and gave them freedom. I conquered an empire. I sired sons. I am Ardashir, the first in centuries to wear the crown of King of Kings."

"I'm sorry to have disturbed you," she whispered.

"And Adhur-Anahid was my Queen of Queens. But she is not here. You seek in vain."

"My apologies, father of the Persians." Taqla pressed her hand to her breast.

"She is not dead."

"What?" Surprise robbed her of courtesy.

"She did not die. I died, after the fullness of years. But I cannot rest. And that is because of Adhur-Anahid."

"Please...I don't understand."

"Centuries before your people conquered mine, I laid upon my people the laws of the Prophet of Ahura Mazda. Great was the empire, and in all its lands I did righteously oppress the unbelievers, the Christians and the Jews and the worshippers of the old gods. But there was a hole in my mantle of righteousness. I left a place for the followers of one of the gods of stone. I let the cult of the *daeva* Yaghuth go free and unharmed because I had made a bargain with him. I had made it before I took the throne, and the bargain was instigated by Adhur-Anahid, may her bones be consumed, may Ahura Mazda turn his face from her on the Day of Judgment, may the earth refuse to bear her up."

Taqla's heart was clattering like the hooves of a spooked horse. "You bargained with him in exchange for...for an empire, did you?"

"I was the younger son. My brother Shipur was our father's heir." The buzzing tone was emotionless except for that bitter edge. "I listened to Adhur-Anahid, and she gave to me a stone to eat and words to say, and then the roof fell upon Shipur. How could a falling roof be the fault of a man? I took a vassal kingdom and made it an empire. I bathed in piety and cloaked myself in righteousness all my days. But now I cannot rest, I cannot leave these bones."

Taqla couldn't quite bring herself to feel any sympathy for Ardashir—or for any emperor, come to that. "Then you made a poor bargain," she said.

"I will make another."

"Oh?"

"With you."

"Oh no..."

"I will tell you where to find my Queen of Queens, if you will help me rest."

Taqla bent forward as if bowing, braced her hands upon her knees and shut her eyes. It must have looked strange to Rafiq, but it was all she could do not to slop to the floor in exhaustion, wrenching at her hair. She straightened with painful effort. "And how would I do that?"

The cloud of flies belled out, whirling, then recoalesced to a form man-shaped and man-sized, but made up of points of living jet. "The bitter stone stayed in my belly until the day of my death. It was laid down with my bones. Take the stone to the sea—the *daeva* Yaghuth has no power over the sea. Cast the stone into the waves. The sea will wash his taint from my bones and free me for Judgment."

"And where is this stone?" she whispered.

"Within the Tower of Silence."

She winced, but even as she did so knew that it could have been much worse. "Give me your word that you will do neither me nor my companion harm."

"I pledge by the Almighty, by Ahura Mazda."

The oath wasn't really necessary, she thought. The dead didn't lie. It was one of their better points. Grimly, she nodded. Then she turned from Ardashir to meet Rafiq's gaze. "All right. I have to go..." She pointed at the tower gateway. "In there."

He looked pale, and he pulled a face, but he nodded and took a step that way.

"No." She flinched. "Rafiq, can you wait out here?" She didn't want him to be part of whatever filthy grubbing about she would have to do in there. Certain aspects of sorcery were distasteful, even barbaric. She didn't want him to see her like that.

"And leave you on your own with...that?" His glance lanced the dead Emperor.

"Please...you know I'm good at finding things."

He frowned, his eyes pools of doubt. "Then call me if you need me. And listen for my voice too. I think I saw movement at the bottom of the hill. Be quick."

She nodded. Then, taking a deep breath, she stepped from the circle and followed the dead man into the charnel house.

By the time she emerged, Rafiq had called her three or four times, his voice winding faintly through the thick stone walls of the Tower of Silence. She ran down the last few crumbled steps, her right fist clenched tight about her prize, and out into golden sunset light. One glance across the hilltop revealed their predicament. Rafiq stood defensively between her gateway and the men who had emerged upon the hilltop, a group about a dozen strong. They were dressed like farmers and carried spears, the sort used for driving off leopards and jackals. Not sophisticated weapons by any means, but it gave them the reach over Rafiq's curved sword. They looked angry, and when she emerged, they were shouting in Persian at Rafiq—"What are you doing here? What are you doing?" As soon as Taqla emerged into view, the cry went up—"Look—there's the other one!"

"Get on the Horse," Rafiq ordered, not daring to look round at her. It was doubtful if the farmers understood him, but as Taqla scurried to the side where the Horse Most Swift waited, a couple of them broke from the group and ran to intercept her. Rafiq however, moved quicker, running in on the first spearman, grabbing the shaft just behind the crude point and thrusting it aside as he smacked the wielder hard in the face with the pommel of his sword. Taqla was half aware of the first farmer falling to the ground as Rafiq wrested the spear from his fingers and whipped the butt end round into the side of the next man's head, felling him too. But she was too busy to see anything else as she scrambled into the saddle, leaned into the Horse's neck and gasped the words that animated it.

The Horse Most Swift leaped forward from a standing start and Taqla wrestled it in a circle, groping desperately for the stirrups with her feet, stuffing a fold of her veil between her teeth. The farmers cried out at the sorcery, scattering as she bore down on them, their faces sallow circles framing their open mouths. Taqla skidded the Horse into a turn then sent it ramping toward Rafiq, who stood fending off an opponent with his sword and the stolen spear.

"Go! Go!" he shouted as she drew level with him, nearly knocking his opponent aside bodily. The silver Horse shied beneath her as she tried to hold it steady for one more moment. Flinging aside the spear, Rafiq jumped, grabbed her round the waist hard enough to nearly unseat her, and clung on like the Old Man of the Sea as they surged into a gallop. He only just had time to get his legs astride the saddle before they were right on the cliff edge.

It hadn't looked like a cliff on the way up; it had looked like a steep, barren hillside. From this angle, teetering on the edge, it looked sheer. Taqla held the Horse on the crumbling edge for one desperate moment, then as it jerked forward and began to drop, she pitched facedown with it, hanging on to the handgrips for her life as she stared into the throat of the drop. Rafiq threw himself backward instead. He was practically sitting on her as the Horse began to slide stiff-legged down the hillside in a plume of dust. There was one horrible moment when Taqla thought that Rafiq's weight was going to force her off over the Horse's head. She saw his legs kicking wildly for purchase against its shoulders, but he must have grabbed the back of the saddle or the Horse's tail because he just—*just*—managed to hold his weight and keep his balance. Taqla clung on, her thumbs nearly dislocated by the pressure, until the gradient suddenly levelled out once more, and with a thump the Horse was back on all fours. Taqla barely avoided getting her nose broken on its metal neck as it righted itself and bolted off like a startled hare into the plain, hooves beating a triumphant tattoo—*tarampara-rampara-ram*. She sat back hard, nearly smacking Rafiq in the face in turn, and he grabbed her roughly in his efforts to keep from being unhorsed.

"In the name of God!" he shouted, and she couldn't tell whether it was elation or horror or both. "You rode off the edge of the cliff!"

She had a fold of cloth clenched between her teeth so she didn't shout back. But she heard him break into laughter.

"Taqla the crazy!" he shouted. "The witch with no fear! See her ride upside down! See her ride on the dust!"

Eyes blurring, she pointed the Horse at the open land and gave it its head. They raced onward.

She should have stopped, really. She should have given them a chance to swap places in the saddle, because Rafiq was sitting tight up against her, holding her waist, his thighs embracing hers. But the sun was setting over the green plain and she didn't know how much longer they had left. Already the golden orb was slipping behind the line of the hills and the shadows were long. So they rode and rode, until their panting had calmed, until their hearts had stopped pounding, until the light turned to faintest blue and suddenly the Horse slowed to an amble, set its feet and stood motionless.

They were stranded in a wide valley of sparse grasses.

Taqla waited for Rafiq to dismount. His hand was resting right over the delta beneath her ribs, above her navel. When he didn't move, she twitched her shoulders uncomfortably, and only then did her release her. She ignored the unexpected sensation of loss, threw her leg over the Horse's neck and jumped to earth, irritated and anxious. Rafiq sat still for a moment more then slid down on the other side. They stared at each other over the saddle. Rafiq's wild mood had vanished. He looked troubled, a thoughtful line between his black brows, unspoken words in his eyes.

"Taqla," he said, then bit the inside of his cheek.

Why? she thought, suddenly wretched and hurt. *Every time I use sorcery he goes like this on me. Haven't I done it for his sake too? If I'm so offensive then why does he accept my help?* Avoiding his eyes, she bowed her head over her open palm and blew out the fold of her veil from between her lips. The little pebble landed in her hand.

"I've got it," she muttered.

"What?"

"The token Ardashir wants rid of."

Rafiq blinked, for all the world as if he had forgotten. "Right. Let's see."

She held it out, a slip of jade, about the size of a thumbnail, perfectly polished. It would be easy enough to swallow, if one had to. That was one reason Taqla hadn't put it in her unshielded mouth when she'd needed both hands to ride. "Have you got a pouch?" she asked. "I don't want to hold it."

"Uh? Oh, yes, of course." He began to unknot the flap of the saddle bag. "Is it...?"

"It's horrible." Just holding it made her skin creep. "Tomorrow we'll throw it into the sea." From the corner of her eye she could see a couple of flies circling the Horse's ears, just as if it were a real animal.

Between them they deposited the little pebble into an empty cloth bag that had once held milled grain. Taqla then tucked it into Zahir's magical travelling purse.

"Taqla..." That dark look was back in Rafiq's eyes. She knew what he was about to say and she cringed. He wanted to ask her about finding it, about what had happened in the Tower of Silence.

"I don't feel like talking," she growled.

He dropped his gaze. "Fair enough, then."

"We should walk on until we can get out of sight. Those farmers..."

"I doubt they'll try and follow us on foot."

"They might raise the local amir and his men."

"They might."

In near silence they repacked and shouldered their bags, and Taqla ravelled up the Horse Most Swift. Then they walked on toward the far range of hills. But every time she paused to look back behind them at the valley under the rising moon, she caught Rafiq watching her, his expression somber and charged with unease.

Yazid appeared out of the air, clearly flustered, blue shadows chasing across his skin. "Get up," he ordered.

"What? What's happening?" Ahleme dropped the book she'd been reading but didn't rise from her cushion.

"I have to take you away from here." He scooped her up under the arms and pulled her to her feet. "We have to go."

"Go?" She was so surprised she just hung limply in his grip. "Where?"

Yazid clenched his teeth. "Away. You have to consent."

Ahleme stared. "I don't—"

"Just consent!" His eyes flashed.

"No! Not unless you tell me what I am consenting to!"

The djinni's hands tightened. She had a nasty feeling he was barely holding back from shaking her, but that only made her more scared and more determined. "It's...one of the laws of Solomon," he rasped. "I can't remove you without your consent. And I need to take you away now."

Ahleme stuck out her bottom lip. "Why?"

"You're in danger here. Please listen to me. I have to hide you elsewhere."

"Hide me?" That really did make her suspicious. "From whom? Or what?"

Yazid rolled his eyes then swung her bodily around to face across her chamber. There was a flash of light and the pillars of glass—all of them, those close around her bed and those in the receding distance, every reflective surface her eye could encompass, lit with an inner illumination. She saw sunlight and clouds and hillsides and trees, and she gasped. Like the visions of Dimashq that Zubaida had shown her before, this false yet living landscape seemed close enough to step into, though trapped behind walls of glass.

"There," he grunted. "See it?"

Ahleme tried to focus. She was looking down from a high place, she thought, at the head of a valley. Straight before her she could see the blue line of what she guessed was the sea. To either side craggy rocks rose to high cliffs. On the slope of the dry river bed below her something was moving.

"What is it?" It was almost impossible to make out—a shimmer of light, a flicker of movement without shadow or solidity.

"It's an angel. I heard it singing. It's crossed the sea and is heading this way."

"An angel?" The hairs stood up on the back of her neck. "Is it looking for us?"

"I don't know. But you don't want it to find you."

"Don't I?" She wrenched out of his grip to look him in the face. "Will it be angry at you for what you've done to me?"

His face twisted. "Angry? It will kill us both."

She gaped. "Why?"

"Because God decreed in the days of Noah that Fire and

Earth must not mix. That the Sons of Flame shall not lie with the Daughters of Dust. We have broken the law, you and I."

"No we haven't!" she shouted. "Not yet!"

"No?"

"And anyway, it wasn't my fault! You stole me away!"

"You think the angel will listen to your excuses?"

"God is merciful!"

"God may be, if He chooses. Angels are not."

"But they're good!"

He shook his head. "No. They aren't. They're only obedient." He lifted his hands and gestured as if shaping his thoughts between them, clearly trying to explain something that he had never needed to teach another. "They are without free will, Ahleme. Their consciences are clear. Don't you understand how terrible a thing that is? They obey the laws of God, and that's all. They don't struggle. They don't know temptation, or confusion, or doubt. They have...no imagination. They can't understand that someone else might feel differently. They can't make allowances. They have no compassion, and no pity."

Ahleme bit her lip, turning back to the vision in the glass. The angelic form was larger now, as if level with the nonexistent watcher in the valley. Its shine flickered steadily, like the beat of many invisible wings, she thought. Or the flash of scything blades. She could see that its progress whipped up dust in a thin plume. And now a flock of birds flew out of the grass and the bushes, circling it. She could see them with throats wide, heads back, fluttering frantic wings to keep up.

"Are they singing?" she whispered, mesmerised.

"Yes. The Angels sing the praises of God, always. It's the most beautiful sound in the universe."

The birds, fat little quail, flew one by one into the blurred boundary of the shimmering angelic body and disappeared in a spray of red mist, even their feathers reduced to shreds. They seemed insensible of the danger, vanishing one after the other. The angel did not slow or alter its course. Ahleme cringed.

"Is this true?" she asked. She put her hand on Yazid's bare

arm. He felt cold to the touch and was clammy with sweat. "You're not lying to me?"

He shook his head, eyes fixing on hers. "Please," he breathed. "I have to hide you."

"Where?"

"Another...place. You won't be found. Just let me take you."

She nodded.

Gathering her in his arms, he put his hand over her eyes. She felt the floor drop from beneath her feet and for a moment her weight was all on him, and then just as suddenly there was a solid surface beneath her again and a thrumming noise in her ears. Her bare feet felt no cold though, nor any sensation of heat. They were curiously numb. She couldn't feel the chill of Yazid's flesh either, she realized, not even where his fingers rested over her eyelids. Nor did he remove that hand.

"I've made you safe here," he murmured low in her ear, audible over the background roar. "No harm will come to you while I'm away."

"You're not leaving me!"

"I have to go back to turn the angel away. I won't be long. Listen to me, Ahleme—you mustn't move. You mustn't make any noise. It would be better not to open your eyes. Just wait for me."

"Where are we?"

He growled with exasperation. "We are in the Realm of Hidden Fire, the birthplace and home of my people. Do you understand? There are djinn here who have never walked the surface of the Earth, and who have never been enslaved by Solomon. If you draw their attention, you will not be safe from them."

"Oh!"

"Can you do this? Can you wait?"

She nodded against his chest and dug her fingers into his skin, wondering why she could barely feel him.

"Good. Remember, make no noise."

He was gone. She swayed a little then clasped her arms

around herself. The roar seemed louder without his sheltering mass. She could feel her hair blowing a little in a breeze. She sniffed but could smell nothing, not even her own perfume. She rolled the pearls of her scanty top between her fingers nervously.

It would be better not to open your eyes, he'd said.

She screwed them tighter shut, but after a few moments her brow began to ache. She let her face relax. A red glow crept under her lashes.

All around her, the roar of flames.

Cautiously she opened one eye, then both—wide with horror. She was standing in the middle of a lake of fire.

Chapter Fifteen

*In which the sea shows its reluctance
and the fire too much enthusiasm.*

Tarampara-rampara-ram.

They couldn't lose the flies, no matter how far or fast they travelled. Whenever they stopped the Horse, there were always a few buzzing about their heads, but Taqla gritted her teeth and didn't attempt a spell to drive them off. And when they reached the coast, the fat insistent flies of the interior were replaced by smaller ones that were less loud but more prone to biting, and a constant irritation.

The coast was a narrow strip of white surf between low, yellow cliffs and the dark blue sea. It stretched to left and right as far as the eye could discern, without a sign of so much as a fishing village.

Rafiq slowed the Horse Most Swift to a dancing trot along the sand. "Are you ready with the stone?" he asked.

"Ready." Taqla clenched the slip of jade in her palm.

"Let's get it right out beyond the breakers," he said, turning toward the ocean and giving the Horse its head. They surged forward. They'd done this before. When riding from the Empty Quarter to the tower at Firuzabad, they'd charged straight out to sea, the Horse's hooves drumming upon the waves' surface. Taqla—to her shame—had been as nervous as a cat over the watery depths, but the Horse had coped as well with salt water as with marsh or dry land, and only the uneven pitch and drop of their progress had made it any different to any other terrain.

This time it was different. As they rode forward, the sea retreated. With a great sucking sound it sank away before them and mounded up to either side, exposing the sandy bed of the beach and islands of coral. They were heading between two arms of the sea, just as Moses must have done when pursued by the soldiers of Pharaoh. As they cantered forward, the slope dropped beneath their feet and the walls of water towered up overhead. Rafiq made a noise of disbelief and slowed the Horse.

"What's going on?"

"I don't know!"

Taqla could smell the brine and the mud underfoot. She could see stranded fish flopping in exposed basins of sodden coral, and then, suddenly, a shivery glimpse of a great pale-bellied shark swimming in the blue wall above their heads. Its bevelled nose poked out through that plane into the air and then it twitched its tail and fled.

"Is it the stone?" Rafiq wheeled the Horse in a wide circle, but the water withdrew just as swiftly as they moved forward. The way back to the beach had closed behind them and they were now pacing the sea floor at the bottom of a wide hole, a cone of air. Flatfish struggled in the muddy sand underfoot, panicked by their inexplicable loss.

"Maybe." Taqla brushed the sweat from her eyes, feeling nearly as frantic as the suffocating fish. She'd not anticipated— never imagined—such an unnatural reaction to the stone's proximity.

"What do we do?"

"I don't know!" she gasped. Then, "Take us back to the beach!" Inwardly she cried *I'm not keeping it!*

Rafiq turned the Horse uphill and they mounted back up from the muddy depths through the zone of coral, jumping the craggy blocks. Behind them the sea roared in again, with a noise like satisfaction. In a few moments they were up above the surface again, in the clean air, and then they were on the beach, and when they looked behind them, the sea lay as calm and innocent as ever, blue waves sparkling as they caught the light.

"Jump down," said Rafiq. "I want to be sure." He swung her down from the saddle then thudded away in a spray of sand, out to sea again. Taqla watched as he galloped a wide circle across the tops of the waves, exactly as they'd both expected to do only a short time ago—a miracle rendered normal.

With a tattoo of hoofbeats, Rafiq rode in again, stopped the Horse a few yards from her and leaned forward in the saddle. "It's the stone, isn't it?"

"The sea's refusing it," she said, her mouth dry.

"So what do we do?"

Taqla shrugged helplessly. Rafiq jumped down from the saddle, waved away a fly and reached for the waterskin.

"Come on," he said, uncorking the skin. "We've got to be able to think of an answer."

They sat in the sand, trying to conjure a solution for some time, and then Rafiq excused himself and went off up the beach to answer the call of nature. Taqla, left alone, rolled the innocuous-looking jade pebble between her fingers and chewed the tip of her finger through her veil. If they couldn't sink the stone, they wouldn't learn the whereabouts of Adhur-Anahid. If they couldn't deliver their message to her then the demon-god Yaghuth wouldn't give them the Egg. If they couldn't return the Egg to the Senmurw then it wouldn't grant them one of the fruits from its Tree. If they hadn't a fruit with which to pay the sorcerer Safan then he wouldn't answer the riddle for the House of Wisdom. Which meant they would not obtain the spell from the Scroll of Simon, and Rafiq wouldn't be able to pursue the prize he sought.

Her head ached. The flies around her ears were an incessant irritation. She groped her way to the answer at last, though. It wasn't the answer she wanted, but it made sense. With a feeling almost of physical pain she took the Bag That Holds the World from her belt. The little travelling pouch had the lustre of silk and a pattern, barely visible even by bright sunlight, worked into its cloth, a pattern that reminded her of clouds. Trapping her lower lip between her teeth, she set to emptying the Bag of all its contents, one piece at a time—the goathair shelter, the coffee and cooking pots, two sheepskins for sleeping upon, a bundle of kindling, her change of clothes and personal effects, rope and spare straps, three waterskins, parcels of dried food, her thick *aba* overmantle for cold nights, a purse of coins that Rafiq had given into her safekeeping. It made quite a sizable heap by the time she'd finished.

Into the empty bag she dropped the tiny piece of jade, wiping her hand upon the sand the moment it was free. She knotted the mouth of the bag and then, because she was afraid that it wouldn't sink, that it might be washed ashore elsewhere, she dropped the Bag That Holds the World back into the empty grain bag and she scooped sand in on top. When she tied off the second sack the little bundle was satisfyingly heavy.

Her heart was slamming in her chest as she mounted the Horse Most Swift and spoke the words to wake it. Turning it toward the waterline, she let the mount fly, and they galloped down the beach and across the sea—hooves rattling on the wave tops, rainbows shining in the clouds of spray that hung at the Horse's heels.

Taqla should have been pleased to find her surmise vindicated, but she felt no better. She took the Horse right out over the deeps of the sea until the pastel corals were left far behind and even the cliff over the shore was a narrow stripe. Then she circled, and lifted the bag of sand out at arm's length, and let it slip from her fingers. The little sack hit the water with a plop and sank instantly, only a glimpse of pallor burned in her mind before it vanished forever. Taqla knuckled her queasy stomach with her fist then turned back to the beach, the salt wind burning her eyes.

Back on dry land, Rafiq was standing over the heap of belongings, his brow knotted.

"It's all done," she said when she'd brought the Horse to a halt.

"I trust you'll be able to replace the bag easily?"

Taqla slid from the saddle, planting her feet in the sand. She felt like some indefinable part of her ached. "I doubt it," she muttered. "It came from China." It had been woven by one of the Eight Immortals, she understood—though she had no idea who those personages might be.

"Then why did you throw it away like that?"

She turned to glare at him. "It was the only way."

"Was it? You didn't even ask me—you just took off!"

She felt her hackles rise. "Should I have asked your permission?" she demanded.

"I thought we were in this together!"

"So now you tell me what I may do with my own property?"

He threw up his hands. "I just meant, we might have come up with another way if we'd both had time to think about it. It's stupid to waste something so precious if there's an alternative!"

Taqla started to shake. Her voice came out in a rasp. "I did it for you and your quest, in case you've forgotten. Like all the magic I do. And don't you *dare* call me stupid."

"I didn't—"

"Do you think this is easy? You think I *like* raising the dead and grubbing round among corpses and carrying you halfway across the world and putting up with that—that thing I was carrying?" Her voice was starting to break apart. "I had to get rid of the stone," she managed to croak before she had to cover her face with her hand because she was starting to leak tears and she couldn't bear the thought of him seeing her cry—and she didn't even know why she was weeping except that the jade had filled her with such loathing, and she was feeling physically sick at the thought of having thrown away her precious Bag That Holds the World. She was so busy fighting her swollen throat and stinging tears that she was only half-aware of his hands suddenly on her shoulders, one of them moving to her face—

A hail of flies swept between them. Both Taqla and Rafiq recoiled, finding themselves yards apart. Between them formed a black cloud, a shape of swarming sandflies and waterfleas and black wasps, roiling into the outline of a human being.

"It's gone," the shape buzzed. "I am free."

Taqla choked back her unborn sobs.

"Keep your promise," Rafiq whispered.

"I will. Adhur-Anahid lives and rules in the city of Bokhara," said the dead King of Kings. "And now I go."

His voice disintegrated into the buzz of a hundred thousand desert insects as the swarm broke up into a formless cloud that spun away into its individual parts. For a moment Taqla was blinded by the rush of insect wings in her face and she staggered a little, swatting at those that bit her exposed skin. When she'd recovered her composure, she turned wide eyes and wet cheeks—the latter mercifully veiled—to Rafiq again, her jaw clenched to offset the lingering tremble of her lips.

He bit his own lip, his gaze intense. "Taqla..."

I've made him doubt my strength, she thought, despising herself. She drew herself up straight. "So where on earth is Bokhara?" she asked.

Ahleme remembered Yazid's injunction to make no noise, and she managed not to scream. She put her hands over her face instead and stared out through the cage of her fingers, her gasping breath loud in her own ears.

She should be dead. That much was clear. She should not be able to stand here and still breathe, or bear the terrible heat. Yet it was a heat that she couldn't even feel. Under her feet was a pillar of black obsidian no wider across than her own shoulders, and it jutted from a heaving sea of molten metal that stretched to the horizon on every side. She could see by its glow, red hot in most places, white where bubbles of flaming liquid pushed to the surface and burst. Everything was in constant roiling motion, like in a pan of simmering sugar syrup. The air shimmered with heat. Ahleme lifted her eyes to heaven, but overhead it was pitch-black, without stars. She couldn't even tell if she was outdoors or in some immense underground space because there was only the sea of fire and the rock at her feet and her, quaking and shrunken, a pale dot in an incandescent world.

No wonder the angel couldn't follow her here, she thought. This must surely be Hell.

When she held out her hand, she could see the red glow upon the undersurface, but she felt nothing. That had to be Yazid's doing. He had put some sort of protection upon her. Despite her surroundings, she shivered. How long would it last, this immunity? Would it last even if the angel killed him? Not that she could imagine that happening. He was too strong and too protean, surely?

But what if the angel somehow—*somehow*—she had no comprehension of what the rules were of this political game— what if the angel stopped him coming back for her? How long could she last here? What would happen when she got too tired to stay awake? What if she fainted? Her island wasn't big enough to lie flat upon. If she fell into the boiling flames would she burn or drown or simply sink forever?

Imagining herself feeling faint, Ahleme sank to her haunches and clasped her arms around her knees. The pearls of her skirt looked orange in this light. She licked her lips then realized how dry her mouth was and how she was longing for a drink of sherbet, and wished the realization had never come into her mind.

"Yazid," she whispered miserably.

Was he fighting the angel at this moment? She could imagine him fighting. With his great frame, he looked like he was born for battle. She was less able to imagine him tricking or talking his way out of the situation. *Could* you lie to an angel? Could you fight one? Angels had laid waste to whole cities in the past, she remembered. But then hadn't the Patriarch Jacob wrestled with one once?

Ahleme shook her head a little. She knew nothing of theology. The pearls strung from her hair brushed her forehead. She didn't want Yazid to be punished. Yes, he'd stolen her from her father's house and put her family honor to shame but... She struggled with the thought for a moment—he hadn't hurt her.

Was that what mattered to her above everything else? she asked herself, slightly shocked. Whether he hurt her? Not her honor or her family but only her flesh, her feelings? And her feelings were so muddled. He'd done less to her than many a mortal man might in the same situation. With all his power and pride and temper he had been restrained, somehow. Sometimes he was almost tender. And she had...

Ahleme blushed to herself. He deserved divine retribution no more than she did, surely? It wasn't true that he'd forced her to all the things she'd done. She'd made certain choices, even though they hadn't felt like choices at the time. They had just felt instinctive. She didn't feel guilty even now. She didn't feel deserving of punishment. She felt almost angry.

"Leave us alone," she shaped with her lips.

Far out upon the fiery ocean, something moved. Ahleme sat up with a jerk, frightened her defiance had been noted by angelic powers. But it was simply a spout of flame, rising from the seethe and arcing over to splash back down again. Molten splashes blazed against the dark sky like flowers of fire. As soon as the spout had fallen another rose a little way off. The rumble of the molten spume reached Ahleme's ears some time after.

Arc after arc of flame lit the darkness. It took Ahleme awhile to realize that there were two distinct spouts and never more at any time, though they moved around on the face of the deep, jumping over each other. *They're dancing*, she realized with a start. *They're dancing together.*

Perhaps it wasn't dancing, perhaps it was some strange form of battle or even conversation, but she grew more and more convinced that she was watching two beings, two giants of formless flame. She even thought she could hear in their rumble a kind of vocalisation, more like thunder than words. The sight was both beautiful and terrifying. She hunched down smaller, hoping that she couldn't be noticed by such colossal entities, and she watched them with a mute awe as they moved across the sea of flame. She watched for a long time, too anxious to look away, too scared to think concretely of anything but how she wanted Yazid to come back for her.

Be safe. Be on your way back to me, she begged over and over in her head.

So mesmerised was she that she almost missed the sound behind her when it first came. It was a hiss, an exhalation so huge that it might have been the breath of a god. It made her loose hair dance about her face. Ahleme looked over her shoulder.

Behind her the fiery lake was mounded up, white hot where it bulged. As she stared, from the liquid rock rose a column of yellow flame, many many times taller than a human, billowing and dancing. Strange shadows flitted in the pillar of light, lending it almost the semblance of a form, though it was a form that never stayed constant. Ahleme caught glimpses of a vast head on vast shoulders, incandescent hair, features molded from nothing but burning gas, a mouth like a furnace, eyes that were blank suns. And suddenly she thought she recognized that face.

"Zubaida?" she squeaked.

The huge lips curved in a smile. At that scale, there was something horrible about the expression, a lack of any kindliness. Then the face turned away.

"Zu—!" she opened her lips to shriek, almost forgetting every warning. She clapped her hands over her mouth, stifling the sound.

The smile broadened. Then the titanic figure slid back beneath the surface of the lake, leaving a seethe that spread out, becoming smooth and slick like oil on water. All around the molten surface continued to heave and bubble, but this great round patch grew mirrorlike in its gloss. What was the djinniyah doing, Ahleme wondered?—and startled as she saw the first picture form within its reflective pool.

There, that was the Palace of Glass, clinging to a sheer wall of red rock like a wasps' nest of spun blue sugar, its multiple spiralling petals looking as delicate as threads from this distance. She'd only ever seen it from within or close to, and its scale was daunting. Ahleme bit her lip, searching for any sign of movement in the vision, any sign of conflict. She braced her hands on her thighs, leaning forward—so that when the whole Palace shattered, noiselessly and in an instant, into fragments, she almost lost her balance in shock.

"Yazid?" she gasped, gulping the word into her breast.

The dust fell, glittering, into the valley below, where it rose for a moment in a billowing cloud. When that settled she saw a tiny, dark figure kneeling in the drift, head bowed. For a moment Ahleme thought that she was falling into the vision, as the figure grew and became recognizable as Yazid, then she thought that the djinni was enlarging himself, and only finally did she realize that the vision was moving closer to the naked figure. He was dark blue all over, as murky as the ocean under a gray sky, and she could not guess whether this was due to effort or to anger.

Ahleme glanced anxiously about her, wondering if Zubaida was still there, longing for an explanation and for reassurance. But further movement in the mirror of fire drew back her attention as the angel slid into the scene, shimmering with light and surrounded by a rainbow halo of glass dust, its grace almost serpentine. It halted before Yazid, who lifted his head. A look of stoic resolve was stamped across the djinni's face. For a moment the divine messenger grew still and a little more visible. It had several pairs of arms, Ahleme thought, perhaps feathered or spiked somehow. They were arms that were closer to fanned blades than to anything else. Its head was plumed too, or perhaps crowned, it was still too hard to tell. Light shifted within its complex, transparent form, a constant confusing shimmer like the glitter of sunlight on wavelets or the flicker of desert lightning.

Yazid's mouth moved. He was saying something. A pause and then he spoke again, shaking his head. Accusation and denial, thought Ahleme, her throat tightening. She clenched her hands against her thighs. Little blue flames licked about Yazid's head and ran down his skin, dancing in the crystal powder about his knees. For some time the conversation went on, Yazid adamantly denying his interrogator. But it reached an abrupt conclusion when the angel reached out to pluck the djinni up and hold him by the throat, his bare feet kicking in the air.

Somewhere deep inside Ahleme there built a squeal of outrage. *Fight back!* she wanted to urge him. *Fight him, Yazid! You're an amir of the Djinn! You can't let him do this to you!* His forbearance appalled her. He lifted curled hands but made no attempt to attack the limb pinning him. She struggled to understand. Where was his temper and his pride now? Where was her roaring, blustering abductor?

It was with a sensation of sickening vertigo that she realized that his forbearance and endurance were for her sake. He was protecting her.

That was almost too much to bear.

There was no release from the fear. He refrained from defending himself at all, just hung there in the angel's grip as its free hands passed back and forth over his body. Ahleme couldn't make out what it was doing, the flame and the dust and the glitter too confusing. She could only see the fluid sweeps of its arms as the locked pair began to rotate in circles like a spinning dervish, and then for a moment the flame and the dust rose about them in a curtain. When that fell, so did Yazid. The angel flung him down on the rocks of the valley floor.

Terror kicked in Ahleme's belly. The djinni's chest was split wide open, and within she could see a roaring furnace of golden fire. His heart was a burning flame. Yazid's hands clawed at the rocks beneath him, his face locked in a rictus of pain, his eyes bulging. The sacrifice was complete—and she felt his wounds as if they were her own. In the merest sliver of a moment she knew all the horror of a woman seeing her lover torn and broken before her.

"Yazid!" she screamed, for that instant losing all sense of her own peril, as the anguish within her burst out in a shriek.

And like a monstrous echo of her own cry, Ahleme heard behind her a thunderous yell. She jerked back round, nearly losing her footing on the plinth of rock. The two arches of flame had turned to towers of fire. For a moment they simply hovered.

Then they both dove below the surface, headed straight for her.

Half of her didn't believe anything could be worse than witnessing Yazid being broken as she had just done. The other half recognized the threat with a surge of terror.

"Have mercy! Please! Zubaida!" she screamed, calling her only ally left as the twin titans surged toward her, surfacing like dolphins in arcing leaps from the sea of fire. But Zubaida, if it was her she'd seen in the magma and she hadn't just imagined it, was gone.

In moments the giants were upon her, rising up about her tiny island like walls of flame. She half-glimpsed faces on them too, and arms and hands and rippling muscles, but they were too large and too brightly shining for her to focus upon. They laughed to see her, not a malicious sound but joyous and careless and terrible. Then one snatched her up. A hand bigger than she was curled around her, though she felt nothing solid, only an immense force that plucked her from her tiny sanctuary without effort. She screamed once, "Yazid!" It was a cry wrought of despair.

That was her only opportunity for words. With her next breath she screamed again in simple terror, but after that she had no chance. It was all she could do to keep air in her lungs as they tossed her aloft and threw her between them like cats playing with a ball made of rags, or a captured mouse. That was all she was, she realized dimly, as she was buffeted back and forth—a novel plaything, a toy. She clenched her arms over her head to stop it being torn off, but she had no other control, no protection. She was hurled hundreds of feet into the air, heels over head, sent tumbling and spinning, legs flailing. She could see nothing but boiling clouds of flame. Their voices booming in her ears drowned all other sounds. *I'm going to die*, she thought.

Her bodice of pearls was wrenched apart. They fell like hail, some striking her in the face. The first inkling of heat flared along the skin of her thighs and belly and pushed up between her legs.

Oh merciful God, if they break the spell of protection I will burn like straw.

They were laughing, laughing, laughing. Then there was a roar, a different note. Furious anger. A tone she recognized, dimly, through her terror and shock.

A titan hand seized her with a wrench that nearly cracked her back, and suddenly she was rushing upward so fast she felt her cheeks pressing against her teeth. Seamlessly the hand became a great arm, and then that arm became two of normal size holding her to a broad chest. Then the fire went out and everything went black, nothing but blackness and a sensation of terrible speed, and then, although they didn't change direction, they were no longer climbing, they were plunging headlong, through cloud.

They flipped. Ahleme caught enough breath to let out a gasp. She was held in Yazid's arms, naked against his bare torso, and he was standing in midair, thunderheads arrayed behind him like wings.

"Ahleme!" he cried.

She flung her arms around his neck and pressed her lips to his, wild with relief and delight.

"You're alive!" she shouted, but her voice was whipped away on the roaring air.

Then the wind caught them and they were flung sideways and up, the purple clouds boiling below. Then they dropped, and the wind turned them end over end over end. It was like being played with by the fiery titans all over again—except that this time Yazid was holding her tight in his embrace, and he was keeping her safe from the elemental forces. This time there was no pain and no fear, just elation. Every buffeting blow of the winds struck through their tight-pressed forms with a thrilling shock. Any words would have been inaudible, but Ahleme shrieked with excitement and opened her thighs to wrap them about his hips. The ride was a glorious assault on all her senses and every inch of her body. She didn't really register that she was pressing against Yazid with every lurch and swoop. She only knew that the winds had taken possession of her, that she felt as if she had wings. That she was flying, and that it was most wonderful thing that had ever happened to her, and she was on fire with joy. She threw wide her arms and let her head fall back in his hand and surrendered every particle of her body to the wind, to his strength, to the sensations thrilling through her.

When the buffeting finally ceased, she was laughing and weeping and breathless. She opened her eyes and realized they were hovering far above the storm, the clouds billowing beneath them like gray waves. Up here the air was thin and the light blinding. Yazid turned them both so that the sun wasn't shining in her eyes.

"Ahleme." That soft-spoken word was a prayer, and it gentled her in an instant. She looked up with new wonder into his face. Somewhere between the fire and the wind she had been shorn, at last, of her fears and her defenses and her past. Up here above the clouds there was nothing and no one else but the two of them, together. His pale eyes were burning with an emotion that was both joy and pain, and she remembered her glimpse of his blazing heart.

He'd defied an angel for her.

With her thighs wrapped about his naked body, she was in no doubt as to his state of arousal. It didn't frighten her. It hadn't frightened her in many, many days. But now, for the first time, she fully acknowledged her own desire, and she knew that that no longer frightened her either.

Wordlessly she nodded, and lifted her lips to his.

Chapter Sixteen
In which a message is delivered to a heartless tyrant.

Tarampara-rampara-ram.

The city of Bokhara lay in the land of the Turks, on the Silk Road west of Samarqand, in the lush Zerafshan valley that was counted one of the four famous Earthly Paradises. Rafiq had, in fact, been there once, years back. It was ruled, they ascertained at the caravanserai within an hour of arrival, by the Amir Mutamin al-Fayiz, who was a member of the Samanid royal family and thus a Persian—an elderly man of corpulent frame, impeccable religious orthodoxy and accredited ancestry.

"Well," said Rafiq, "he might rule in name. But perhaps he has a wife or a mother or a concubine who is the real power behind the throne."

So when Taqla went to the women's bathhouse, she made enquiries too. But she learned nothing to their advantage. No one had heard of an Adhur-Anahid in Bokhara.

"We need to get a look inside the palace," said Rafiq. "The amir holds a public audience every week. We should attend tomorrow."

"It would be a start," Taqla agreed.

So they dressed in their best clothes and went to the palace gate, a domed and tiled building very much in the Persian style, the next morning. A queue was already forming, watched over by guards. Rafiq slipped coins to a succession of officials with the result that the two of them were moved up the line ahead of the local petitioners, through a number of rooms and into a chamber where everyone was well dressed. More guards stood at the double doors beyond, checking everyone who passed through for weapons. Although they, like most of the local people, were Turks, the language of the court was Persian and that was what they were barking their orders in.

"Do you carry a sword?" they demanded of Rafiq as he reached the head of the line.

"Not today." He'd left his weapon along with most of their belongings in the caravanserai. Their saddle and the desert shelter they'd had to stash behind a rock when they walked to the city gate, since the stuff was too bulky for the two of them to carry by hand. Taqla had the ball of silver wire in the deepest pocket of her outer robe. She refused to let that out of her possession.

"What about you?" said a second guard, gesturing to Taqla. "Hey, what's a woman doing in men's clothes?"

She opened her mouth, ready with an excuse—they'd travelled far and thought it safer that way. But she didn't get the chance. He hooked his fingers over the fold of her headcloth and yanked it down to bare her face.

Rafiq reacted with a speed that took everyone by surprise. Launching himself at the guard, he grabbed the man by the front of his jacket and slammed him against a wall so hard that his head bounced off the tiles. If he hadn't been wearing a helmet, his skull would have been cracked. The guard went limp. Rafiq took a step back and dropped him, and then found himself surrounded by soldiers, four sword-points aimed at his throat.

"She's my *wife*," he snarled.

"Then maybe you should dress her like one," said the guard captain with cold anger.

Taqla, staring and holding her veil up in her hand, scrabbled wildly for a spell that would get them out of this. A deep darkness perhaps...or a stormwind...or a—

"What is going on here?" A new voice had entered the fray. A tall man stood at the entrance to the inner courtyard of the amir. He was clearly not a soldier, being dressed in sumptuous silk robes of many colors, but he carried himself with immense authority. He had a neat beard striped in gray and black, and eyes like jet.

"Vizier Najib," said the guard captain, with a little bow. "This man attacked one of my guards. He will be punished."

"He unveiled my wife, *sayyid*," said Rafiq through gritted teeth. His chin was being forced back on the point of a blade.

"Is that true, Captain?" The vizier looked from face to face, his gaze resting momentarily on Taqla. "Did he lay hands on this woman?"

"He did." The captain sounded grudging.

"That's against the laws of Bokhara and of God. He knows that."

Taqla, wondering what on earth Rafiq had been thinking of to play the injured husband and let fly like that, allowed her gaze to slip to his face. She was shocked to realize he hadn't been thinking at all. She could see the rage in his eyes and there was nothing feigned about it. He was shaking with fury. *What?* she thought. *What's brought this on?*

"On the other hand," said the vizier grimly, "no one lifts his hand to the amir's guards with impunity."

Taqla focused sharply. She took hold of the ring of smoky glass on her little finger and shaped the first words of the spell of darkness—and instantly the vizier lashed out, striking her hard enough across the face to knock her off her feet. Taqla was so shocked that it took a moment for her to even register the pain, or the blood running into her mouth where she'd cut the inside of her cheek on her own teeth.

"Gag her," said the vizier, as the room spun around her. He bent briefly to her ear. "We wouldn't want you pulling that sort of trick in the palace, would we?" he murmured, so low that no one else in the room could have heard. Then he straightened again. "Bind them both and take them to the chamber of questioning."

A twist of cloth was forced between Taqla's teeth and knotted at the back of her head, and then she was dragged to her feet. The overriding physical need in those first moments was to keep swallowing the blood seeping into her mouth so that she could breathe. She threw a desperate glance at Rafiq, but his arms were being tied behind his back. They weren't particularly gentle with him either, and he took several cuffs to the face. Together they were marched through the halls of the palace of Bokhara, down dim, tiled corridors and across courtyards where fountains played, until finally they were prodded and hauled up a spiral staircase to an upper floor and into a room.

It wasn't an unpleasant chamber, except that it was oddly bare. Carved *mashrabiya* screens covered the windows from outside eyes and kept the interior dim. A single divan couch and a low table faced three columns, and Rafiq and Taqla were quickly bound with their backs to two of those pillars. There were no carpets on the floor, just a layering of dark splatters upon the boards. Taqla took that particular feature in and her eyes opened wide. She tried to catch Rafiq's glance but he had problems of his own. As soon as the guards had secured his wrists around the pillar and bound them with cord, the captain stepped round in front of him and clenched his fist.

"This is for my soldier," he said, and punched Rafiq hard in the stomach. Taqla squealed with protest through her gag as Rafiq folded, stopped from collapsing only by his bonds. He didn't cry out but he did groan, and the guards laughed at that. Then the captain crossed over to the column where she was pinned. He pulled down her headcloth, which was half secured by the gag, and looked her deliberately and lingeringly in the face. Taqla's eyes would have spat fire if they'd been able, but he didn't seem to notice, being too busy making his point. He pinched her cheek disparagingly and cast a derisive and challenging glance back over at Rafiq. Then he signalled his men and they marched out of the room, all except one who stood with scimitar drawn by the door.

Her face burning, Taqla risked a glance in Rafiq's direction. He was slumped against his bonds as if his head was too heavy to lift, still gasping, his expression filled with pain. Taqla's stomach roiled with conflicting emotions. She was both frightened and angry, and that anger was directed partly at

Rafiq who had ditched them in this situation. But at the same time she ached to go over and stroke back the hair fallen across his face and comfort him and assure herself that he was all right.

Rafiq lifted his head and looked at her, stricken, his eyes burning. "Taqla—"

"Shut up!" The guard by the door hefted his sword. Rafiq fell silent and straightened up gingerly. Taqla thought how much she wanted to take his face in her hands and touch her lips to his, and knowing this, and that she was unveiled, she turned her face away self-consciously. Her mind was fooling with her, she reprimanded herself with some disgust. It was trying to avoid the terror of the situation by throwing up these distracting phantoms. She should be trying to think of a way out, not wasting her time.

But what could she could do without speech?

She didn't have long to think about it, to her surprise. Within a few minutes the door opened again and in walked Vizier Najib. He was a big, handsome man, some part of her recognized grudgingly. The gray in his beard did not hide the breadth of his shoulders or the fact that he stalked like a leopard. Around his lean waist was a thickly embroidered sash into which was thrust a curved Turk-style dagger and a scabbarded scimitar. He placed a goblet of wine down on the table and looked at them both thoughtfully.

"Leave us," he told the guard. Then when the three of them were alone, he folded his arms over his chest. "I have at least an hour before the amir is due to admit the throng into his august presence and will require my advice. The notion occurred to me—why should I not spend it with two disturbers of the peace? So, who will talk to me?" He glanced at Taqla and smiled. "Not you, I think." His gaze flitted back to Rafiq. "You then."

"Right Hand of the amir," Rafiq said, guardedly. His face was bruised and his lip cut and swollen.

"So who are you?"

"My name is Rafiq ibn-Jurraia al-Dimashq, *sayyid*, and I'm a merchant. Ask at the caravanserai for those who will vouch for me."

"I will. A merchant selling what?"

"Nothing at the moment. Our caravan was washed away by a flash flood in a wadi, our camels drowned, our companions scattered. We came to Bokhara seeking shelter."

"Really? A fine story. Now tell me why you tried to bring a sorceress into the amir's presence."

"A sorceress? Her? As I told you, she's my wife."

Najib waved a hand negligently and walked over to Taqla, looking her in the face with some interest. She lowered her eyes, not out of shyness but out of desire that he see her as nothing but a respectable and wronged woman. It didn't work for a moment. "She's a witch." He ran his hands over the pouches hanging at her belt, taking the time to measure the shape of her waist and hips and slide a hand between her legs. She jerked in shock.

"*Sayyid*, you are mistaken," said Rafiq very coldly.

The vizier found the hard bulge that betrayed the ball of silver wire and extracted it from its pocket. "Interesting. What's this?" He cocked an eyebrow. Taqla couldn't stop her eyes flashing in protest as she fought a wave of panic.

"Just silver," said Rafiq. "Easier to exchange than coin in some places."

"Hmm." The vizier put the ball down on the table and approached Taqla again, walking around her with a knowing smile. "A fine collection of rings you have there," he remarked, taking her bound hands in his.

Taqla clenched her fists, feeling the cord bite into her wrists.

Najib sighed. "I can always cut them off," he murmured into her ear and she shivered, knowing she had little choice. When she opened her hands again, he stripped the rings from her fingers, examined them one by one and laid them out in a line upon the table. It was painful to be parted from the tools she relied upon. She could feel sweat gathering at her temples.

"We came only to ask the favour of the amir," said Rafiq through gritted teeth. "We mean no trouble in Bokhara."

The vizier ignored that. He returned to Taqla yet again. "Any more?" he asked her, reaching for her throat. Under Zahir's stout outer jacket, which he tugged open, she was wearing a high-necked shirt of fine cotton. He took that between his hands and ripped it, baring her breastbone. Taqla tried to swivel away, but he grabbed her shoulder with a heavy hand, pinning her in place so he could grope under the torn fabric.

"Get your hands off her!" Rafiq roared.

"You have a hasty temper, friend," said Najib, squeezing Taqla's breast. "Very nice," he added, eyes glittering, as she protested through the sodden gag. He pinched her nipple, twisting it painfully, and then, just as abruptly, he let go and walked away, confronting Rafiq eye to eye. "She's most appealing, isn't she? Have you had her in the form of a boy yet? She can do that, you know. She can take any form that pleases you."

Taqla, her right nipple stinging and swollen, nearly choked as she tried to draw gasping breaths through her gag. She felt her eyes fill with welling tears and she swallowed wildly, her jaw aching. Meanwhile Rafiq opened his mouth, very obviously to utter an imprecation as offensive as humanly possible, but then bit down on the words, his breath hissing through his bared teeth.

"Talk to me, my friend," said Najib lazily. "Do you understand your situation? I am the vizier here and it's my position to protect the amir. He's an old, frail man who just wishes to be left alone to enjoy his hashish and his women. Tell me what you two were planning here...or believe me I will do things to the girl that you will not enjoy watching."

Rafiq snapped his head back in frustration, banging it against the pillar. "I'm a merchant—a trader!"

"And the witch?"

"My bodyguard," he said, his grin belying the cold hate in

his eyes.

The vizier laughed appreciatively. "Better. What were you planning to do?"

"I carry a message, that's all, for the ruler of Bokhara."

"Is that so?"

"It's something I'm often paid to do when I travel—take messages."

"Show me."

"It's not written down."

"Then what have you been paid to say?"

"I can't tell you that. It's for the recipient alone."

"From whom?"

"Again, I cannot say."

Dazed and frantic, Taqla was aware that Rafiq had remembered her warnings that the instructions of the god should be carried out very literally—if the message were to reach Adhur-Anahid through gossip or a third party the compact would certainly be void.

"That's...very interesting." The vizier leaned in closer, and from the expression on his face he seemed to be enjoying himself immensely. "Now, you see, you have piqued my curiosity. What do I have to do to get you to talk, my friend?"

He sank his hand into Rafiq's crotch. Taqla stopped breathing. Rafiq seemed to gain several inches of height as his spine straightened and all expression left his face. The two men stared into each other's eyes, faces almost touching.

"Ah now, no protests this time?" The vizier chuckled lightly. "In all honesty you're as much to my taste as the little sorceress, friend. Why don't I cut out the bit where she gets hurt and just move straight on to hurting you? Or do you like it rough?" His hand, buried in the loose cloth of Rafiq's trousers, moved with lavish purpose.

"Adhur-Anahid," said Rafiq in a clear voice. "You must give to Yaghuth the bending of the knee. You are to surrender to Yaghuth that which you promised him. He says to tell you that the time has come."

Vizier Najib froze. Taqla saw the color drain out of his face until he was quite gray, like a dyed rag that had been left to weather outdoors for too long. "What did you call me?" he said, taking a step back.

"Banebshenan Banebshenan Adhur-Anahid is what I named you. Why—had you forgotten the name?" There was a grim triumph burning in Rafiq's eyes. He was surer of himself by the heartbeat. "How many years since you last heard it?"

The vizier ran his tongue across his dry lips. "That name turned to dust long ago."

"But you didn't. And now the time of payment has come."

Najib backed away and sat down on the divan. "Already?"

"Already," said Rafiq remorselessly.

"But I had such plans..."

"Nevertheless."

Swallowing, the vizier nodded. "How did he find me? I thought I was well hidden."

"Ardashir betrayed you."

"Ah. That's cruel." He turned briefly toward Taqla. "I should have guessed that Yaghuth had sent you."

"Then perhaps you wouldn't have treated her so shoddily. Do you think he's a forgiving god? Or a patient one?"

Najib's mouth pulled into an ugly shape. "No. You'll return to him?"

Taqla saw Rafiq hesitate before he said, "God willing."

"Then you must take what I owe him." The vizier stood abruptly and dropped his multi-colored robe from his shoulders, letting it hang from his belt. The silk shirt beneath was swept off over his head revealing a hard torso flecked with tight gray curls of hair, and then he unsheathed his knife from its steel scabbard. Taqla felt a bolt of panic strike her in the entrails as it occurred to her that what was owed to Yaghuth was a blood-sacrifice, and she saw the same realization hit Rafiq too as Najib stood and approached him, stepping round to his rear. Her companion was completely vulnerable from that position, his throat unshielded. Rafiq turned his head and looked her in the face, his expression full of such intense purpose that her heart nearly stopped in her chest. She lurched in her bonds, struggling despite the futility to get her hands free, until the cord cut into the raw flesh of her wrists. All the while searching desperately for the solution his eyes begged for.

"Taqla—" he said roughly.

The knife swept out and down, through the cord at his wrists, seeming to part the rope at a touch. Rafiq nearly fell forward off the pillar.

"May you have as much joy of his service as I," said the vizier bitterly—then turned the knife to his own belly, just below the ribs on his left side, and plunged the blade in to the hilt. By the time Rafiq had turned and realized what was happening, Najib had opened a gash a span wide in the skin.

Taqla couldn't scream, but she made a groan in her throat of utter revulsion. There was no blood. She'd been expecting a great deal of blood. Instead there was only a black trickle like hot lacquer seeping from the edges of the wound—even when the vizier dropped the knife and thrust his right hand deep into the cut and right up to the wrist and beyond in his own chest cavity. His face twisted. The muscles of his chest and arm clenched and worked. Sweat sprang up on every inch of his skin. Then with obviously immense effort, he wrenched his hand free again—and in it was clutched a lump of green stone the size of two joined fists, webbed with black slime.

"Here," he said, holding it out to Rafiq, who stood aghast. "Take it."

He had the presence of mind not to touch the thing, which, Taqla could just about make out, was carved in the shape of a heart with protruding veins and arteries—but picked up the broad end of his cloth belt and reluctantly accepted the jade in that.

Najib sighed. "Never enough time," he said under his breath, and then his eyes rolled up and his knees folded and he collapsed slowly to the bare floor.

For a long time both of them just stared. Then Rafiq set his jaw and wordlessly knotted the stone up in the trailing end of his belt, to make a little bundle that sat over his hip. Stooping, he picked up the knife and wiped it clean on the fallen man's robe. Taqla shut her eyes and tried to pull enough air through her nose to stop herself passing out.

She opened them again when she heard his footfalls approach, and the heart she was sure had stopped in her chest began to thump painfully. Once more she was horribly aware of her torn clothing, her exposure. "Don't look at me," she tried to say, but through the gag it came out only as a kind of whimper. Nevertheless Rafiq understood. She saw in his face that he was trying not to look at the raw edges of the shirt and the inner curves of her breasts that the rent revealed. He tried, but he failed, and as his gaze fell on her he slowed, as if his veins were filling with lead. She in turn tried to hold herself motionless, but she couldn't stop the heave of her chest.

His gaze lifted to her face again. He looked, she thought, tired and needful and dangerous. He stepped to her side, laid one hand on her shoulder and, with the other, hooked the curved knife blade under the cords that bound her wrists and sliced through them. She felt every strand as they gave way. But as she shifted her aching arms back in front of her and flexed her bloodless fingers, he didn't remove his hand. It stayed on her shoulder, heavy, not uncomfortable, almost a caress—but not quite. The treacherous part of her wanted nothing more than to turn and burrow into that embrace, to grab him and crush her body against his in relief and reassurance that he was alive and unharmed and he was freeing her. More, her right nipple was still burning and she couldn't help but imagine how his fingers would soothe and comfort that.

Why does he wait? asked that secret, shameless, voice inside her. Just as so often before he had stepped over the line of propriety, but no further. Was he waiting for her to respond? If she said the right words, made the right gesture, would he touch her breast and not just her shoulder?

It felt as if something inside her were twisted to the point of tearing. She was barely aware that she was reaching up with one hand to fumble for the knot at the back of her head.

"Hold still," said Rafiq softly. He insinuated the point of the knife between the gag and the bare flesh of her cheek, and the cloth gave way with a tiny purr only audible to her. She shivered as the touch of the metal raised an instinctive alarm. The treacherous voice inside her fell silent.

"There's an enchantment," she said, pulling the gag from her mouth. Her voice was hoarse and her jaw ached.

"What?"

"On that blade. I'm guessing Najib would have been immune to normal weapons. Keep it carefully." She folded one hand over her bare breastbone and stepped away from him, not daring to look back. Fumbling a little because her fingers were still numb, she tugged her outer layer back over her torn shirt and secured them as best she could. At the same time she crammed every one of her turbulent emotions back into the confines of her heart. Only when she'd pulled her headscarf back into place did she dare turn again. Rafiq hadn't moved, except to lay one hand on the pillar and brace upon the arm as if weary to exhaustion. "How did you know?" she asked. "That he was Adhur-Anahid, I mean?"

"Mm?" He shrugged slightly. "I didn't. It was a guess. But he was so sure you were a sorceress that I thought *it takes one to know one.*" He managed to crack a wry little smile at that point. "Besides, after Zahir, I have my suspicions about every man we meet."

Behind her veil, Taqla smiled in answer, though no doubt it was a wasted gesture. Then her smile died. "I thought he was going to cut your throat," she admitted.

"So did I for a moment. Luckily—" He stopped, swallowed and shook his head. "Oh God, how do you live with a stone heart?"

She shivered. "Any way you like, I imagine."

Rafiq's battered mouth curved into a smile. There was a moment of quiet before he spoke. "So. We have what was owed to Yaghuth."

"Then we've done it, haven't we? We've got what we need?"

He nodded. "Looks like it. Time to pull the chain all the way back in, link by link."

"We need to get out of here first." She bent to the table and started jamming the rings back on her fingers one by one. Rafiq crossed to the window and peered out through the fretwork.

"Get the Horse set up."

"We can ride from here?"

"Across the rooftops."

She threw down the silver ball and watched it start to weave the shape of the Horse Most Swift. In the meantime, Rafiq returned to the vizier's body and stripped from it his sword and scabbard. The new knife was already sheathed at his belt.

"We've no saddle," Taqla reminded him.

"Then you'll have to hang on tight to me." Returning to the window, he chopped at the wood brutally, weakening the screen until he was able to kick a chunk out and look down. "Good. First step is a drop down to the outside of that dome. After that it's nearly a flat run to the city walls. God willing."

"What about our stuff? At the caravanserai?"

"Ah, now you're trying to make things difficult. All right, but that's going to need us to be quick...and lucky."

As the Horse completed its formation, he vaulted up onto the metal back and held out his arm to help Taqla up. She dropped into her familiar position behind him and thrust her hands into his belt as usual, troubled by how slippery the steed felt beneath her. Without a word, Rafiq grabbed both her hands in his and pulled them forward, crossing them over his navel so that she could grip her own wrists. Taqla found herself squashed up against his back, her breasts pressed to the vertical wall of his muscle. She made a nervous gasp.

"Hold *tight*," said Rafiq firmly. "Don't let go, whatever. Keep your head down." Then he spoke the words triggering the Horse into life.

Taqla shut her eyes just before they hit the broken window screen and crashed through into the drop beyond. Her stomach seemed to squash up into her throat for a moment. Then she felt the jar as the Horse's hooves connected with something solid, but she had little idea of what the footing was or what angle they rode at. She just clung to Rafiq as tightly as she could and hoped.

Chapter Seventeen
In which footsteps are retraced and several decisions taken.

Tarampara-rampara-ram.

The temple in the Empty Quarter stood much as they had left it, except that sand had poured down the slope they'd dug and in through the open door. The pale dome looked more like bone than ever, Taqla thought. Like the skull of some unimaginable monster. The wind had swept their footprints away.

Jumping down from the Horse, it took her awhile to realize that Rafiq wasn't following her toward the door. She swung around to see him standing in her trail, head cocked, looking grim.

"Don't you want to get this over with?" she asked.

"I don't know."

She walked back. "What's wrong?"

"Taqla...I'm wondering if it's right for us to do this. Give something up to an evil infidel god, I mean. Something that he wants."

"You mean you think its idolatry?"

"No, I mean I think it might have consequences. For the world."

The same thought had occurred to her. "He's barely a god," she said, keeping her voice low nonetheless. "Just the stump of one—a shadow. He has no worshippers left, no power..."

"Maybe. But we don't know what he wants this stone heart for. We don't know what he can do."

She looked down. "I think the time of the idols is over, whatever we do."

"And I think we still need to take responsibility for our

actions."

She bit her lip, trying to hide her surprise, and nodded reluctantly. "Listen," she began, searching for the right words. "I think that this journey you're on is one meant for you. I think there is purpose in it. At every stage it would have been easy for us to run up against a cliff, for there to be no way forward. Yet every time there's been a path." She made herself meet his gaze confidently, though it was hard for her to speak of the secret thoughts on her mind. "I think it's your Fate to fulfil this task, to rescue the daughter of the amir—and there is no Fate but that given to us by God. Take heart. I believe you will do as you're meant to."

"You believe in me?" A smile crept into his dark eyes.

"I believe in Fate," she answered, turning away hastily. "So are we going in there?"

"All right then. But bring the Lion Most Strong, would you? It would make me feel better."

So down they crept into the temple, as before, with the great silver Lion shadowing their heels. Under the windowless dome all was in darkness, and Taqla once more released a little spark of light to hang there, revealing the pale green bulk of the idol, the blades hanging overhead and—the only thing that had apparently changed—a scattering of dead birds strewn over the floor. She turned the nearest corpse over with the toe of her sandal and recognized a swallow, its pale breast unmarked but its claws clenched like tiny fists. Taqla was perturbed. Every spring the swallows visited her house in Dimashq, rummaging noisily among the vines that grew up the courtyard wall. Most flew on, but a few always stayed to build their mud nests under the arch of her outer door. She always looked forward to seeing the swallows, and though she didn't know what had lured these birds to their deaths, she now swore to herself that she would shut the door to the temple when they left. She glared up at the statue. It stood exactly as they had left it... No, not as they had left it, as they had found it the first time. The stone fist that had clenched around the Senmurw's Egg was open once more, displaying its trophy. Had it ever really been different, she wondered? Had they been fooled by illusion into seeing the idol move?

"Yaghuth," said Rafiq. There was no answer, though they both held their breath in anticipation of that corrosive whisper. With a certain amount of hesitation he unknotted his belt end, revealing the jade heart. "We return with that which Adhur-Anahid owed you. We've fulfilled our side of the bargain. Uphold your own."

Here in the gloom of the fane, Taqla could see a green glow deep in the translucent stone. The sickly light beat slowly, like a pulse, throwing into relief the carved contours of the heart, its chambers and blood vessels. Taqla felt her skin creep.

"The little man." Yaghuth's voice was faint, but the blades overhead shivered. *"He returns. Give to Yaghuth that which was promised."*

"Give to us that which you promised," he insisted.

"Give to the hand of Yaghuth the heart of Yaghuth. Take from the hand of Yaghuth the Egg of the Senmurw bird."

Rafiq looked for Taqla's nod, which she gave reluctantly, and then sized up the statue with its four arms. It was, Taqla thought, probable that someone standing atop the altar in the basin would be able to reach, at a stretch, both of the hands held out to receive offerings. To reach the altar would mean wading through the sea of skulls and putting oneself within the grasp of those arms.

Setting his jaw, Rafiq jumped up onto the lip of the basin and then stepped down upon the ancient bones, which crunched and crumbled beneath his feet with no more resistance than dead leaves. He sent up little clouds of dust as he trudged to the altar stone and Taqla tried not to imagine what that short journey would have looked like in the heyday of the temple, when the heads were newer hewn. *Be careful!* she wanted to tell him, but how he could be careful she couldn't say. With a grimace, he vaulted up onto the broad altar, still holding the end of his belt out in one hand and the green stone within, and stood upright. He looked small and far too vulnerable against the monstrous green bulk of the god. Carefully he checked from side to side, examining the two spread palms, one of which held a skull, the other the Egg they needed. Then, abruptly decisive, he flicked the skull off into the mass below and nearly threw the jade heart into the vacated palm, his bare fingers grasping the stone for only the briefest of moments. Turning to the other claw he grabbed the Egg in both hands and hugged it to his chest before jumping down.

Yaghuth sighed. The green glow in his hand grew stronger, casting strange shadows up on his carved double face. Taqla saw the whole surface of the idol suddenly begin to craze, as if something were bulging beneath the cracking stone. She didn't think that Rafiq saw it.

"Give to Yaghuth the bending of the knee."

Rafiq gritted his teeth and began the crunching path back through the bones.

"Give to Yaghuth the red offering. Give to Yaghuth the woman in offering, and Yaghuth will raise the little man over all men."

Unwisely perhaps, Rafiq responded—with an instruction that even a god might find difficult to follow.

There was a sudden splintering sound, and from the hairline cracks all over the idol a liquid squirted—green liquid like the algae slurry of corpse-fouled wells, that became solid as it met the air, a web of slender filaments that reached out and joined and became ropes of iridescent slime. The thickest of these whipped about and wrapped around Rafiq's waist and chest, hauling him into the air as lightly as a man lifts a baby—and squeezed. Rafiq groaned and let drop the Egg, which struck the flagstones with a horrible crack.

Taqla opened her mouth but had no time to spare for any utterance. She plunged for the Egg, her fingers snagging on the rough copper surface, and snatched it from the floor. It was warm and heavy, a part of her mind noted, though not as heavy as an egg of solid metal. She crushed it to her heart. When she lifted her eyes, Rafiq was being shaken about like a leveret by a

Saluki dog. His eyes were wide, his mouth open, but no sound came from his throat.

"GIVE TO YAGHUTH!"

"No!" she screamed, throwing into that word and the one that came after it—a word in a language known only to Djinn and Angels and those with the hubris to deal with such beings—all her terror and anger and need. All her desire to save went into those syllables, and from the Egg burst out a wave of red-gold light that struck the green strings of slime and fried them instantly to stinking smoke. Rafiq was flung out and crashed to the temple floor. For a moment there was a sickening silence.

"A sorceress." Yaghuth's voice was less loud, but no less malicious. The god who, until this moment, had taken not the slightest notice of Taqla, turned his focus upon her, and she felt her legs buckle.

"Give to Yaghuth the bending of the knee, sorceress."

She couldn't answer. She couldn't even breathe. She was distantly aware that Rafiq was heaving himself to his feet, clutching his ribs, but almost all her consciousness was the prisoner of the deity whose terrible attention was finally upon her. And in that moment, she realized that all her nausea and fear was not the reaction of someone confronted with the repulsive, but in actuality that of someone staggering at the edge of an unimaginable abyss. It was vertigo. She looked with her jade-green eyes into his own, and saw a great void filled with innumerable years and unbearable understanding and the shadows of things not human either in form or mind.

"Give to Yaghuth the bending of the knee." The god sounded almost wheedling. *"Give to Yaghuth the red heart, and take from Yaghuth the green—and Yaghuth will give to you words of power, sorceress. Yaghuth will give to you the forgotten names. Yaghuth will give to you the secrets of the ages. Yaghuth will give to you freedom and power and all the world to take in his name."*

Her tongue felt like leather, her throat as dry as sand. She wanted to scorn him as easily as Rafiq had done, but she was far too aware of the consequences—what the punishment would be, and what she would be giving up. From the corner of her eye she saw Rafiq limping toward her. She thought of what it would be like to have a god on her side and to fear nothing ever again.

"Yaghuth will give to you life everlasting. Just give to Yaghuth the bending of the knee."

If she refused him, then she would die, because the Egg of the Bird of Compassion, no matter what strength it might lend to help rescue another, had no power to help her defend herself. And if she died, then how would she get Rafiq out of there? Was she really ready to condemn them both?

Would he forgive her if she did anything else?

"No," she whispered, because that was all the volume she could muster. "Never."

There was a moment's pause. Then Yaghuth started to howl with rage and a black rain began to fall. Rafiq lurched forward and slammed into her, bowling her over bodily, his own form hunched over hers. She had no time to work out what was happening before he threw her underneath the belly of the Lion Most Strong. Something clanged off the silver overhead, and all around them the stone floor spoke in tones like the striking of small gongs. Rafiq hooked his fingers into the silver filigree of the Lion's belly and tried to crawl in on top of her—and then he gave a cry and rolled on his side, his face twisted. Taqla glimpsed a slender black tail stuck up behind him—and then one of the iron rods plunging from the roof and breaking into rusty fragments on the floor, and she had just time to realize that he was carrying one of the spears stuck through the small of his back before another, with an audible thunk, pinned him brutally through the flesh of the thigh.

Taqla didn't stop to think. She hooked her leg around his and hauled his trailing limbs under the sheltering Lion, dropping the Egg for a moment as she rolled him nearly on top of her. He made a horrible noise of pain as the rod through his back struck against the beast's silver belly, but then the rusted metal snapped. For a moment they just lay there while the voice of the thwarted god roared around them and the spears from the roof clanged off the Lion and splintered around them. They'd ended up face-to-face, on their sides, Rafiq's eyes blank with pain and his teeth clenched, and between them his breath coming in gasps on which flew flecks of blood.

"GIVE TO YAGHUTH THE BENDING OF THE KNEE!" chanted the god, over and over again.

Taqla took a deep breath. Rafiq had one hand on her shoulder and his fingers were biting in so hard she thought he would break the skin. There was no help coming from him just now. She wrenched his hand off and then reached to his waist, unknotting his sash belt and pulling out the knife thrust through the folds. Since the cloth went three times around his middle there was a fair length of it, and she shoved one end through a gap in the silver wire over her face, threading it through the Lion's chest. Then she knotted it in a loop under his arms and behind his back. She worked as quickly as she could, but it took some time, and by the time she had done, he was wringing with sweat and his pupils had contracted to tiny points as if he were gazing into a furnace.

"Yes," he managed to grunt, despite it all, taking hold of the belt. Taqla, wondering how much weight that cloth could hold, shoved the knife inside her own shirt and then took the Egg in the crook of her arm. She hooked the fingers of one hand in the filigree before she found the Lion Most Strong with her mind.

"Step," she ordered.

The Lion Most Strong, unlike the Horse Most Swift, did not follow its own nose. Its default attitude was to stand motionless unless ordered otherwise. So it took a single pace forward, dragging Rafiq beneath it in his sling, and Taqla scrambled with them, gritting her teeth against the pain of the wire biting into her fingers and using her legs to push.

Step. Step. Step. Slowly they shuffled across the floor of the temple toward the door, and every step was accompanied by a rain of deadly spikes, some of which even pierced the Lion's back and rattled around inside its belly. Taqla was thankful that Rafiq was still conscious, though she knew this mostly from his intermittent swearing.

"Hold on," she urged him. "We're nearly there." The daylight grew around them as they neared the outside world.

Then the doors swung shut and they were in darkness.

"*Give to Yaghuth! Give to Yaghuth!*" the vile voice burbled with malicious pleasure.

Taqla bit her lip, trying to remember whether there were any of the hanging spears here in the temple porch and what the double doors were made of. Bronze leaf, she thought, over old wood. She let go of the silver wire and grabbed on to the sling holding Rafiq. "Lion—break them down!" she ordered.

The Lion reared up on its hind legs and for a moment they were pulled upright, before it lurched forward and smashed at the doors with its forepaws. Chest to chest, the two humans dangling beneath it were flung about. Wood and bronze alike were rent asunder. Yaghuth's voice rose in a wordless scream.

Then they were outside and climbing the slope of sand, step, step, step, sand washing into their clothes and pouring over their faces, and it was all Taqla could to keep her eyes and mouth clenched shut and keep the Lion moving until they were no longer going up but only away. The moment she let her will slacken, the Lion stood foursquare. Taqla let go, dropped to the sand and rolled away from beneath its belly.

Behind them the temple of Yaghuth gaped, its smashed doorway like a mouth from which the teeth had been beaten, and from which faint howls could still be heard.

From then on things got worse.

Taqla managed to slip Rafiq from his sling and lay him down in the sand, sending the Lion away a few paces. She could see that there were two spikes through his body. The lower pierced the outside of his right thigh and thankfully not the inside where the big blood vessels were. The higher went straight through his torso between his pelvis and his ribs, on the left side, just above the drawstring of his trousers. About a handspan of metal stuck out at his back, and half that much at the front. Blood was welling up and staining his clothes. She touched him fearfully, not knowing what on earth to do. He rolled onto his injured leg; the belly wound seemed to be giving him the more trouble. Rafiq's eyes were narrowed to slits now, his neck corded with pain. He slid his hand down and touched the spearpoint jutting out from his belly, and hissed through clenched teeth.

"Heal me," he groaned.

She wanted to scream.

"Rafiq...I don't know any healing!" she had to confess. Why, after all, should she? Healing was something you learned if you lived among others. Safe behind the walls of her home, keeping herself to herself, she had never needed to worry about injury. "I'm sorry—I'm so sorry!"

"Ah. Pity." His understatement was bitter.

"Just hold on." She struggled to come up with a plan. It was impossible to imagine bundling him onto the Horse Most Swift. She doubted he would be able to cling on even at a walking pace, never mind when it was at full pelt. "I'll ride to the coast, find a city, a doctor—I'll bring him back before nightfall," she gabbled.

"No use." His bloody fingers groped for her and found her wrist. His grip was clammy, his breath coming in tight twists. "It's a gut wound. I'm dead." He tried to crack a grin, and it was horrible because there was blood all over his teeth—either Yaghuth's grip or the fall to the temple floor had broken his ribs, she guessed, and he was bleeding into his lungs. "Looks like you misread my Fate after all." His attempt at levity was followed by a spasm of pain and his eyes rolled back in his head. "Don't leave," he whispered, slumping back onto the sand, his fingers locked in hers.

Taqla ran her free hand over her face and slammed her fist against her breastbone, fighting down panic and despair. She made no cry, but inside she could feel a scream building. "Rafiq," she moaned, her mouth twisted all out of shape, hating herself for being a sorceress who could do nothing. She needed help. She needed a miracle. Only then did she remember the Egg.

It was the first time she'd looked at it since she'd used it to ward off the god, and one glance told her that something was wrong. In the temple of Yaghuth, the Egg had remained undimmed, its surface a mottled copper that gleamed like real metal freshly polished. But now it was patchy and dull, as gray as lead in parts, only a web of sunken coppery veins showing the original color. She had drawn too much power from it already, she realized queasily, and had come close to killing the nascent virtue it held.

And now, sitting there with the Egg in one hand clasped to her breasts, the other hand clinging to Rafiq's slackening grasp, she understood she had one more chance and another choice. But this time she must do it knowingly, and it was all but unbearable. This was the Egg of the Senmurw, the unique offspring of the Bird of Compassion, the holy creature's chance to continue its line and its presence on the Earth. How could she possibly burn up that last vessel of grace? What right had she to deprive the world of its healing and its hope? Yet...how could she let Rafiq die?

It was her choice. No one else was there to make it for her, or to bear the consequences.

Biting the inside of her lip, she extracted her fingers from his and shifted the Egg to that arm, drawing it tight to her stomach. Rafiq didn't resist her going, in fact he seemed barely conscious, his breathing shallow and immensely strained. As gently as she could, she wrapped her free hand around the spike that pierced his entrails. The slippery metal grated beneath the pressure of her fingers, not because it was loose in its sheath of flesh but because it was corroded to the point of collapse. She had no doubt that any attempt to pull it out would only leave shards of rusted iron embedded deep in him. "Help me," she whispered to the Egg. "Help him."

Then she began her spell. She knew nothing of healing, but in Dimashq, under Umar's name, she did have a reputation for being able to find things that were lost. She could call to small objects—a mislaid key, a ring that had slipped from a finger, a coin that had fallen down a crack in a flagstone—and draw them to her. Focusing her mind, she began to coax the metal in her hand with words only it understood. Gently she called to the iron spike, and it loosened in its socket. Blood began to well up from the wound and that nearly broke her concentration— she had never anticipated that it would be so *hot*—but she set her jaw and kept the spell going, the words spilling from her lips in a liquid babble. And as she spoke, she listened, and other words that she did not know formed themselves in her innermost ear, words whispered by the unborn creature cradled against her, words that knitted together torn tissue and repaired what was broken. She wove those words into her familiar sorcery. She wove too Rafiq's name and her need for him to live. It took a long time. First the main stem of the spike came loose in her hand so that she could cast it aside, and then one by one the smaller flecks of metal followed, burrowing to the surface through the torn tissue, snuggling between her fingers like tiny animals begging for a caress. Every single piece had to be extracted, all the way from his back to his belly, and as they moved, the vessels had to be staunched about them. It was obvious that she was causing him further pain, but she had to ignore his reactions. She had to ignore the blood and the stink. She had to ignore the ache in her head and the guilt in her gut and everything but the task, until it was done.

Then she did it all again, pulling his cracked and splintered ribs back into place before he drowned in the seep of his own blood into his lungs. Then she extracted the spearpoint through his thigh.

She passed out at last without even knowing it, slumping forward over Rafiq's chest as he lay there, the Egg of the Senmurw tucked against her belly like an unborn child—and now silent.

Taqla woke when something touched the back of her neck.

She opened bleary eyes on a shoal of moving lights, and as they focused, she recognized the glimmering outlines of ghostly squid drifting past her. Night had fallen and the moon was up over the Abu Bahr, recalling the dead ocean to life.

The thought made her spasm and she shot to a sitting position, twitching off the cold thing that lay against her neck. Then she stared down at Rafiq, whose hand flopped limply to the sand. Moonlight didn't make it easy to read his expression. She had to put a hand back on his chest to be sure he was breathing.

"How are you feeling?" she rasped, her throat parched.

"Thirsty," he whispered. "Cold."

"Does it hurt anywhere?"

He shook his head very slightly. Taqla wanted to fling herself on him and embrace him, but instead she contented herself with feeling for the pulse at his throat. It was thready but regular. She groped down his body, finding his shirt and trousers a sheet of black, stiffened blood. It would stink by tomorrow, she thought, running her fingertips over his stomach but finding no rent in the skin. "I'll get you some water."

The Egg of the Senmurw fell from her lap as she stood, and for a moment she swayed, feeling dizzy. Under the moonlight it had no sheen, its metallic surface lead-dull. She said nothing but she had to wipe at her face, with the back of her sleeve because her hands were too filthy, before setting the Egg by Rafiq's head.

Their little heap of baggage was half-hidden in a grove of ghostly seaweed. Taqla sorted through as quickly as she could, finding a blanket and a waterskin and some dates. Every so often she glanced over to where the pale bulge of the temple dome bulked above the dunes. She couldn't quite see the doorway from here but she knew that it gaped wide and the thought made her itch with unease. She felt nervous being separated from Rafiq too, as if his recovery might turn out to be an illusion after all, but when she turned back, he wasn't lying still but, on the contrary, struggling to sit up. For a moment he almost succeeded too, before his arms gave way and he sagged back into the sand. Carefully she lifted his head and helped him sip from the waterskin.

"I'm so weak," he gasped when he'd had enough.

"You lost a lot of blood."

"But you did mend me, after all." He started to shiver, as if he hadn't had the strength to before drinking. She ran her tongue over her dry lips, though he couldn't see the gesture. When he found out what she'd done, he would start shouting at her, she thought, but he wasn't strong enough to cope with that yet.

"Are you hungry?"

"No. Oh...but I'd kill a thousand armed men for a coffee. If I could sit up, you understand."

"I would join you. Well, we'll go find a town as soon as you're fit to ride, God willing. But now you need to get some rest. Maybe you'll be ready to move out, come the morning."

She spread the blanket over him and he curled up on his side like a child while she tried to scrub her hands.

"I'm freezing," he mumbled, shuddering.

Without a word she went round behind him, slipped under the blanket and wrapped her warm body to his chilled one. She draped one arm over him, still cautious, making sure that her hand rested only on his arm, thinking how much broader his shoulders were than hers and how solid he was. Rafiq gave a little sigh and fell asleep immediately. She felt his spine relax.

She stayed awake somewhat longer, watching the glimmer of the undersea denizens and feeling the blind gaze of the temple of Yaghuth between her shoulder blades.

Tarampara-rampara-ram.

Sunlight barely filtered through the thick canopy of the Tree, and they stood in a green-tinted gloom under the branches as if in a room roofed with leaves. Overhead birds of every species fluttered and hopped, most of them unseen among the foliage, but all their attention was on the great Senmurw bird before them, decked in glorious plumage, as regal as an emperor. It looked at them from wild orange eyes and uttered a fluting note with a questioning lilt.

Taqla stepped forward. This was the first time she'd seen the Senmurw close up and its sheer size would have made her tremble even if guilt and awe hadn't. It was beautiful. It made her feel like a small child. "I'm sorry, holy one," she said miserably, unwrapping the Egg she carried in her arms and bowing to set it on the ground. The shell was now pitted and crazed with hairline cracks, all hint of color gone. That which had been warm and alive with power was now as cold as an egg of plaster.

She stepped back next to Rafiq then, not because she thought him capable of defending her physically—he'd been tired and dizzy since the desert, though he was getting better—but simply to give the Senmurw space.

Rafiq hadn't shouted when she'd told him what she'd done. He hadn't said a word in reproach or even looked angry, just thoughtful, his eyes shadowed with pain. But he had insisted that they return the dead Egg to the swamp near Basra. "She has a right to know," he'd said.

"She?"

"The Senmurw. Of course it's a she. How many cock-birds do you know of that lay eggs? She's lost her only child."

If anything could have made Taqla feel worse, it was that. She'd been sick with self-reproach on the journey there, unable even to talk.

Now the Bird of Compassion hopped forward across the leathery dead leaves underfoot, cocking its head from side to side to stare at the Egg.

"What happened?" Its voice was a soundless echo in Taqla's head.

"It's my fault, holy one," she said. "My companion was injured, on the brink of death, and I made use of the Egg to heal him." She swallowed. "I understand what a terrible thing

I've done. I accept the punishment you choose to mete out."

Rafiq stirred uneasily and his fingers brushed the back of her sleeve, but she ignored him.

The Senmurw arched its head and half-unfurled its great tail, sending reflected light dancing across the underside of the canopy. *"Punishment, daughter? You mistake who I am. Do not ask me for punishment."*

Taqla's heart clenched. The prospect of being forgiven for a transgression so terrible was unbearable. How would she be able to live with herself? "I ask you to be just, holy one."

The Senmurw fluttered its wings. *"Just? I know nothing of justice. What is just in this case?"*

She shook her head slowly. "I killed your offspring. I robbed the world. Please...don't pretend it doesn't matter."

From the Senmurw's throat a strange warbling note issued. *"Daughter! Do you imagine that love perishes by being exercised?"* Standing on one leg, it reached out with the other claw and scooped up the Egg, turning it over to display it to the two humans. *"It's just the opposite! For three thousand years my egg lay untouched. Only because you used it to save is it now ready to hatch."*

The great bronze talons clenched around the shell, which shattered like dry bread and turned to dust, leaving within the cage of the Senmurw's talons a coiled bird of burning gold. It lifted its head and stretched out feathered wings, and as the Bird of Compassion opened its claw, the fledgling took flight, a miniature of its parent, and rose in a frantically beating spiral into the air. Its voice trilled like the highest of reed flutes.

Every bird on the island fell silent to hear it.

"Oh," said Taqla as tears of relief began to spill from her eyes. She slipped to her knees, blotting hastily at her face with her veil. The fledgling rose higher and higher through the canopy, turning the green leaves gold as it passed until it slipped out of sight, though its song remained audible long after it had vanished from view, like that of a steppe lark.

As lightly as a bird a hundredth its size, the Senmurw

sprang to an overhead bough, plucked among the leaves with its beak, then dropped back to earth before them. It bent its neck and dropped an object into Taqla's lap, something itself the size of an ostrich egg, oval and golden and fuzzy to the touch—the fruit of the Tree of Knowledge of Good and Evil.

"*There,*" said the Senmurw. "*This is yours, daughter. And earned well.*"

Tarampara-rampara-ram.

The fruit was warm in her hands and stayed that way even after the sun set. Taqla sat with it after they made camp among the hissing reeds, watching the play of firelight on its velvet skin. It smelled sweet too, as perfumed as a quince, and she couldn't resist brushing it against her cheek.

"There's something I need to tell you," said Rafiq, dropping another stick on the fire. With his face underlit, his eyes were oddly shadowed.

"Yes?"

"The fruit is yours, Taqla. Not mine, not ours. It's up to you to decide what you're doing with it."

"Why's that?"

He sighed. "The first time I met the Senmurw—and mind, I may not have been all that coherent, given the circumstances— she asked me what I had come there for and I told her that it was for a fruit for the Seer. I think she thought I meant you. I'm sure she did, in fact."

Taqla felt the strange urge to giggle. "You lied to the Bird of Compassion?" she asked.

"No, I didn't lie, not intentionally. It was just a mistake. Which is why the fruit is yours. I won't betray the Senmurw's trust. She thought from the start that it was for you to eat, not some madman in Taysafun. So you can keep it if you want...and I'm sure you do. It must mean a lot to you. I won't try to take it."

She groped for words. "You mean that?"

"Would I have said anything about it if I didn't?"

"And what will you do, if I keep it for myself?"

"Me? I'll go back to being a trader in frankincense and coffee. There will be no harm done—except to the girl, which is not our fault. And I'll have lost nothing but a dream." He smiled wryly, because *dream* was the literal meaning of the name Ahleme.

Taqla stared at the fruit, hefting its weight in her hand, trying to imagine what it would taste like, what it would be to bite into that firm flesh, what it would be like to know all things.

"Of course," added Rafiq softly, sitting down opposite her across the fire, "if you do eat the fruit, we won't need Safan. You'd know the answer to the riddle yourself. You'd even know where Ahleme is being held—we wouldn't need the spell from the Scroll of Simon at all, would we?"

She shook her head. "I don't know if that's the way it works. I mean, the last people to eat of the Tree of Knowledge..." She shivered. "Do you think they were thrown from the Garden for anything as trivial as being able to answer riddles?"

"They were thrown out for disobedience, as I understand it—but you have permission."

"Then why was the Tree forbidden in the first place?"

He shrugged. "I'm not a theologian, Taqla."

"I think it must be more a kind of spiritual knowledge conferred. A knowledge of mysteries." What had Safan said—something about being able to see things as they truly were? She didn't think that sounded entirely comfortable. It required hubris that even as a sorceress she did not possess. It was hard to speak, but she confessed at last, "I'm not certain I'm ready for that."

"Does it frighten you?"

She nodded.

"Well, the choice is yours." He sounded quite patient. "Only you can know if you want to take it on."

Quietly she covered the fruit with her right hand, as if

comforting a small animal. The fruit did feel oddly alive, she thought, being so warm and fuzzy, and she could even feel the presence of a single pip like a heart centred in the fruit's flesh. Tempting as such ultimate wisdom was, she was too nervous to really want it—or at least not tonight. Not now, while she was young and still had so much to learn by more mundane methods.

That was the notion that brought with it inspiration.

Without saying anything else to Rafiq, she began to chant. She used the same spell she'd used to draw out the flakes of iron from his entrails, and she used too the words of healing the Egg had taught her that day. Gently, gently, she drew the stone out from the fruit, healing the flesh in its wake. It split the velvet skin and dropped into her palm in an ooze of juice, and then she repaired the wound, leaving the fruit as unblemished as it had ever been, if a little softer. The seed was dark brown and shaped like a kidney.

"I'll take the seed," she said, meeting Rafiq's questioning gaze. "Give the fruit to Safan, because that's what he bargained for. I'll plant the seed in my garden in Dimashq and *if* it grows, and *if* I live long enough to see that tree bear fruit in years to come... Well, then I will know that I'm ready to eat."

Tarampara-rampara-ram.

"What took you so long?" complained Safan.

"There were complications," Rafiq said. "We're here now. And we have the fruit you asked for."

"I can smell it," the blind man agreed, flaring his nostrils as he took a sniff, and then groping crabwise toward Taqla. She stood her ground as he sidled up to her and pawed at her sleeve. "Sweet and juicy," he leered.

Taqla hadn't bothered to put on the guise of Zahir since the seer knew all about it. But she colored slightly despite herself. "Hands off," she growled, and was ignored.

"You gave up on the Ugly Boy, did you?"

The question was directed at her. "He left," Rafiq answered nonetheless, and she could see by the shift of his shoulders that he was readying himself to intervene physically. She shook her head at him.

"And this one pleases you better, I imagine?" That question was lobbed at Rafiq.

"I consider it an improvement."

"Remember your manners, Grandfather," she said, extracting her forearm from his grip with some determination. "We're here to trade, not to waste time." They had in fact made very sure to arrive in Taysafun in bright daylight so as to avoid the Pale People, but that didn't mean she had any desire to linger.

"Oh, time spent with you couldn't be wasted, little chick." He wiped his clawlike hands up and down his rags, clutching himself between the legs. "Now, what have you got for me?"

Taqla unwrapped the fruit from its protective cloth, but she kept a firm grip as his fingertips brushed its peachy skin.

"Oh!" he moaned, wetting his lips in a manner that made her flesh creep.

"First the riddle."

"The riddle? What riddle is that? I don't even remember your trivial question."

Rafiq recited it once again. *"Who is this man who weds two sisters, with no offense at his wedlock being taken by anyone? When waiting on one he waits exactly as well on the other too; husbands may be partial, but no bias is seen in him. His attentions increase as his beloveds grow old, and so does his generosity: how rare is that among married men!"*

"Such a woefully little thing to ask of me. Still, fools must be beggars, eh?"

"Give us the answer," Taqla said. "Only then is the fruit yours."

"One of the riddles of the Queen of Saba? Didn't you work it out, little chick? You should have, you know."

Taqla felt a sudden pang of anxiety. Had it been something

only a sorcerer should have been able to work out, then? Some aspect of a magical process perhaps, or some detail from mystic legend? The Queen of Saba had been both wise and powerful. Her riddles had been meant for the ears of the greatest magician ever born. Couldn't the answer have had something to do with their shared thaumaturgy? Could she, Taqla, have kept claim to the fruit of the Tree of Knowledge after all? But no last-moment inspiration came to mind no matter how she racked her brains.

"Tell me," she said through gritted teeth.

"It's kohl, little chick. A stick of kohl applied to the eyes."

"What?" she said idiotically, and Rafiq groaned.

"Now give me the fruit as promised."

Still shocked by how obvious the answer was if only she'd seen it, she dropped the fruit into his outstretched hand with hardly a thought. For a moment Safan just cradled it in his palms, head weaving back and forth as he savoured its aroma. "Yes," he whispered.

Taqla began to back away, though she couldn't have said why. She felt obscurely as if it were about to burst into flames in his grasp.

"Now go. Both of you. Leave me."

"We've no argument with that," said Rafiq, catching Taqla's sleeve and steering her toward the rubble path, and following on behind with his face still turned to the seer and his hand on his sword hilt. When there was enough distance between them and the old man, he stopped retreating and turned to hurry. Taqla looked back once as they rounded a broken wall. She saw Safan squatting on his haunches, the golden fruit pressed to his lips, his shoulders hunched and quivering. The fruit was the only thing in that picture that had any color to it, and she suppressed a twinge of guilt almost as sharp as if it were a child that she were leaving in that desolate place to be devoured.

"We've done it!" said Rafiq as they walked away, lengthening their strides. It would have been fatal to try to ride the Horse Most Swift in that labyrinth of ruins, so they both had to head to the city boundary on foot. "We've got the answer! You can cast the spell now!" He sounded almost giddy with triumph.

"Yes." She smiled behind her veil. She was relieved too, though she couldn't forget the dangers and difficulties that lay ahead of them still.

"Back to Baghdad now, and once we get the scroll, we'll be ready to take on the djinni."

"I don't think it'll be quite as easy as—" Taqla stopped talking and drew to a halt as a horrible sound pierced her ears. "What's that?" she asked, twisting about.

Rafiq cocked his head. "Safan's laughing."

It was laughter, a wild, unpleasant, hysterical laughter. Taqla shuddered and pressed on. They'd only taken a few more paces when the noise changed its note, though it grew no quieter.

"He's not laughing now," said Rafiq grimly.

"Oh God," said Taqla faintly, wanting to stop her ears.

"Come on." Rafiq urged her over the next set of crumbled walls. "Looks like you made the right decision."

So Taqla put her head down and they walked without speaking until they were beyond earshot, and all the time she wondered what Safan had seen.

But Rafiq's serious mood didn't last. Before they reached the walls of Taysafun he was smiling to himself. "The old man was right though," he said. "You should have guessed that one."

"*I* should have?" She was goaded.

"Yes. You'd have saved us a lot of travelling—not to mention all that coming eye to eye with death and a *whole* lot of money—if you'd just thought of eyeliner."

"Why should I have?" she demanded. "I don't wear kohl!"

He smiled sideways at her. "Well, true enough. I suppose you don't need it."

"What does that mean?"

"It means you have beautiful eyes anyway. Particularly when you're glaring at me. Yes—like that. Wow."

"Stop that!" she complained, but there was no bite in her voice.

"What? Your eyes are wonderful. I'm sorry—but if the face is covered then of course a man notices the eyes more. What about you, when you go about in Zahir's shape? Do you notice? I mean—do you feel things differently when you're male?" He spun on one foot to walk backward, grinning. "Do you find yourself longing after women...?"

"Shut up!" she cried. "I'm *not* talking about it."

He laughed for a long time at that one.

Chapter Eighteen
In which a magical scroll is read and a djinni moves home.

Tarampara-rampara-ram.

Taqla sat on a rug overlooking the roofs of Baghdad with a narghile at her side, and tried not to betray any unseemly impatience as she drew upon the ivory mouthpiece and watched the sun sink in a dusty haze toward the western horizon. The stones of the marble city turned from white to gold as she watched, and the bubbles gurgled through the water in the pipe with a soothing sigh, and every time she caught the anxiety knotting up her stomach, she would force herself to relax, to savour the mild mint-scented smoke and the sensation of being well-fed, clean and dressed in fresh clothes, and to enjoy the view.

Baghdad, she thought, her eyes sweeping the stepped roofscape, was undoubtedly the greatest city on Earth, casting even ancient Dimashq into its shade. And up here she had one of the best possible views. The caravanserai had been full when they had arrived, but the steward had offered to set up rugs and an awning on the flat roof, and in all honesty, Taqla was very pleased with the arrangement because they had more space and light and were farther away from the smells and noises of the animals penned in the ground floor.

With each inhalation, the charcoal at the top of the stem glowed red, the pipe bubbled, the taste of mint and tobacco filled her throat. With each exhalation, fragrant smoke drifted from her lips to join the scents of evening cooking fires.

Below her in the hidden cleft of the streets, goats bleated and children running home from the schools called to each other. A woman sang. And somewhere, she allowed herself to hope, Rafiq was hurrying back from the House of Wisdom with a scroll in his hand. She hadn't accompanied him because she didn't trust her spell of disguise to last in such an emotionally charged moment—and she didn't dare associate her real face with the name of Umar the Scholar. Rafiq couldn't depart the House of Wisdom with Zahir and return with a woman, she'd decided. So she'd stayed to sit watch over their baggage and drink sherbet, and to smoke, and to wait.

She was good at waiting, she told herself acidly. Sometimes it felt like she had spent her whole life waiting.

The wooden ladder from the floor below creaked and, as Taqla watched, a servant scrambled up, somehow managing to balance a brass tray on one hand. He was followed by Rafiq, who flashed a grin of triumph. Quietly Taqla averted her face so as not to catch the servant's eye as he bowed and set out a long-spouted jug of coffee and two goblets and a bowl of salted pistachios. She set the narghile stem down and waved him away with what she hoped was proper nonchalance as Rafiq seated himself cross-legged on the rug facing her.

"I have it," he said in a low voice, reaching into his shirt. There was no one else up on the roof at the moment, but it wasn't the sort of thing they wanted overheard.

"Are you sure?" The small scroll was slightly warm in her hand as she took it from him, his body heat clinging to the parchment. It was fastened with the unbroken seal of the House of Wisdom, she was careful to note.

"A fair copy in the original Greek. I talked to Hunayn ibn-Ishaq himself. He was most pleased to know we'd been successful. And he kicked himself when he heard the answer to the riddle."

"Feh."

"He also asked me what a man of Dimashq might be looking for in such troubled times. He's sharp, that one."

"She hasn't been found yet?" No such word had come to the caravanserai or the bathhouses they had already culled the gossip from, but Taqla knew that official channels would be swifter.

"No sign of her."

Taqla cracked the seal with her thumbnail but then hesitated.

"Go on. Aren't you going to read it? This is it, you know."

"I know." She spread the scroll between her hands and let her gaze rest on the inked letters within while her mind shifted into the right patterns for the foreign script. *"An invocation for the finding of that which is most desired, wheresoever it may be, on earth or at sea or in far lands,"* she read out.

Rafiq nodded, biting his lip, then, too restless to sit still, busied his hands pouring coffee for them both while Taqla scanned down the page. Aware that he was waiting, she managed to mutter as she read, "Yes, I understand...quite straightforward...there's an incantation to be said...and a potion to be brewed and drunk...of 'ingredients most rare in all the world'."

The jug nearly slipped from his fingers. "You're telling me we have to go looking for those now? More travelling?"

"Hold on..." She held up her hand. "I haven't got that far yet."

"God have mercy! Hasn't it been hard enough already?" He sounded, oddly enough, amused rather than angry, but Taqla wasn't paying attention to him, too fixated on the words she was translating.

"If you'll just—" She stopped then, frowning.

"What's wrong?"

"The ingredients... I'm so sorry, Rafiq." Her voice wobbled as doubt crept over her. "I think I might have led you on a wild-goose chase. I'm not sure this is a spell at all."

"What do you mean?"

"It looks like a joke...or a parable. The ingredients it demands for the potion are...impossible. Wilfully impossible. It might just be a way of saying that the thing you desire most will be forever out of reach." She lifted her eyes to his and found them intent and interrogative. "I'm sorry."

"What are they?"

She glanced back at the scroll. "Five ingredients, to be mixed and burned and consumed by the seeker. Firstly, the heart's blood of an immortal. Second, the wine of Hades. Third, the—"

"Hades? Who's that?"

"Uh...it's an old Greek word for the place the infidel dead go—the Grave. We can hardly be expected to travel to the underworld, can we?" She licked her lips. "Third, the seed of understanding. Fourth, sand from the depths of a sail-less ocean... No," she corrected herself, "it's not just no sail...an ocean that has *never* been sailed upon. What ocean has never been sailed?" Taqla shook her head, even as somewhere at the back of her mind something stirred.

"Well, hold on," Rafiq interrupted. "I have one of those. The heart-blood of an immortal, you say? How much?"

"It doesn't say. Just blood."

Turning to their piles of baggage, he opened a saddle bag and pulled out his travelling clothes. He'd thrown out his bloodied shirt and trousers when they'd bought new ones, but his old belt was still there. Sorting through to the end of the sash, he showed Taqla the cloth—which was smeared with black stains from the jade heart of Vizier Najib.

"Well?" Pulling out his knife, he sliced off the end of the belt and dropped the dirtied piece in front of her. "She was immortal, until she cut the stone out."

"You're the seeker." Taqla's mouth had gone dry. "You do know you'll have to consume it if you choose to go ahead?"

"You think it's dangerous?"

"I just meant that it's *haraam* to eat blood."

He pulled a face. "Of course. But you know what you said about my Fate? I'm beginning to believe you."

"All right then." She was wearing Zahir's travelling robe, as usual, over new clothes. She shrugged it off, then took her eating knife and cut the stitches of its heavy hem. The robe had been washed and patched, but was much the worse for wear following their travels. From the inside of the hem she poured out a stream of green sand onto the body of the cloth, the last detritus of the storm in the Abu Bahr. She remembered with a shiver that ghostly undersea realm with its monsters and its strange beauty. "Sand from an ocean that's never been sailed," she admitted, starting to feel lightheaded.

Rafiq nodded. Then he reached into his pack for the leather flask of wine that Safan had gifted him with. "The wine of the dead," he murmured, laying it upon the small heap of sand.

"You still have that?" she said disbelievingly.

"I forgot it, to be honest. But he did say it would come in useful."

After that they just looked at each other in silence, both knowing what had to happen next. It took effort for Taqla to move her fingers to the pouch she had strung around her neck, to the seed that nestled warm and precious between her breasts. She laid it on the cloth between them. Rafiq lifted an eyebrow questioningly, but she nodded.

"Thank you." His hand strayed out as if it would clasp hers, and she withdrew her fingers hurriedly. Rafiq's gaze fell. "What's the fifth ingredient?" he asked. "You said there were five."

Taqla looked at the last on the list and felt her stomach fill with cold as she worked it out and knew it was up to her. "Don't worry. I can get that," she said in a gray, even voice.

"What is it?"

"You'd be happier not knowing." She had no intention of telling him, not if the Archangel Jibreel himself dropped from the sky and ordered her to.

Rafiq wrinkled his nose. "Something to do with graveyards again?"

Let him think that, she told herself, feeling relieved. She shrugged her eyebrows in a noncommittal way that confirmed his worst fears, and he shook his head.

"I'm eating this lot? Ack."

"It'll be burned to ash, most of it." She stood. "Well, I'll go do my bit. In the meantime we need a brazier, and a coffeepot that's never been used, and cinnamon sticks and frankincense. Charcoal, wine, a flask with a stopper. Oh—and a pestle and mortar—again, never used. Can you get that stuff?"

"No problem. I can find them all without leaving this building." He tucked the seed, the scroll and the scarf scrap back into an inner robe pocket for safe-keeping, leaving the innocuous little heap of sand on her *aba*. He folded the garment over that to stop it blowing away on any breeze.

"Good. Meet you back here. She walked away without hesitation or glancing back, not allowing herself to look anywhere but forward at the task awaiting her. Heading down the ladder and out into the twilit city—not toward any graveyard but to the women's bathhouse, which was the only place she could purchase the solitude she needed.

Rafiq finished his tasks and was back on the rooftop well before Taqla, despite having to share a cup of wine and a sticky pastry with every one of the merchants he'd called on for his purchases. He was a bit surprised to find himself on his own up there, and he sent a servant off for lamps. Then he sat down to wait. The moon was rising in a perfect indigo sky and he sat for a while and watched the stars come out. Dogs barked in the alleys below. On a lower roof nearby a lame old man was crawling on all fours, and he watched the movement idly. But that distraction didn't work for long. Eventually he took the Scroll of Simon out from his shirt and unrolled it.

He could, in fact, read Greek, having spent a year as a very young man in Antioch, up on the border where the Caliphate of the Faithful met the Byzantine Empire. The two were deeply hostile to each other but that didn't stop trade of various kinds taking place over the borders, and there being many Greek speakers living in caliphate territories. Certainly his reading was rusty, but that didn't stop him wanting a look at the scroll he'd put so much effort into finding.

He scanned the text, finding the first part densely written and near gibberish. The list of ingredients for the potion was easy to spot though, being set in its own paragraph. *Firstly, the heart's blood of an immortal. Second, the wine of Hades. Third, the seed of understanding. Fourth, sand from the depths of an unsailed sea.*

Then he found the fifth ingredient—and as he read the line his jaw clenched.

Fifth, the maidenhead of your mother.

His first response was to be both offended and revolted, and the two together were so strong that he nearly flung the scroll away. What stopped him, and what proved stronger still, was puzzlement. How in the name of munificent God did Taqla think that she could get hold of such a thing? If his mother were still alive—which she was not—and still in possession of her maidenhead—which was patently impossible—then she would be in Dimashq where she'd lived her whole life. What was Taqla up to?

He stared blindly out across the city. Below him, the crippled man took a leap from one rooftop to another and scrambled like a spider up a buttress, but Rafiq was so distracted in his bewildered anger that he didn't even consciously register the motion until some seconds later.

With a lurch of his stomach, he realized he'd misread the scroll. The text did not literally say *mother*. It said *she who loves you most*, but the phrase was so common that he had automatically glossed it.

She who loves you most.

Understanding pierced Rafiq like a knife blade, cold and keen, at a point located between his heart and his stomach. He lifted his head and took a deep breath, and when he swallowed, the taste in his mouth was as metallic and bitter as blood. He read and reread the words.

From the alleys all around, dogs were howling.

Something crawled up over the edge of the caravanserai wall, and at last Rafiq managed to turn his vision outward. The object was a hand. An old man's hand, the skin wrinkled and blotched with age spots. It was joined on the sill by its twin, and then a head rose into view between them and grinned, revealing a mouthful of blackened stumps.

What? thought Rafiq, suddenly cold with alarm, kicking to his feet and snatching up his sword from the rug. This decrepit ancient had just—impossibly—climbed the wall of the caravanserai.

"Peace be upon you," the stranger said, boosting himself effortlessly up onto the top of the wall. His pupils reflected the lamplight with a green fire, like the eyes of a desert fox.

"And upon you also." Rafiq's throat felt like it was full of glue. "And upon all the Pale People."

"Heh." The old man laid his right hand upon his bony breast in acknowledgement and let his illusory appearance slip for the briefest moment, revealing the pallid dog jaws beneath the human disguise. Drool gleamed in the lamp's glow. "You travel quickly, and by daylight, we note. But we heard the sound of your horse's hooves. Not like any other steed in this land, that. Where's the sorceress?"

"Nowhere you will find her, friend." Rafiq threw aside the rope belt from his scimitar.

"Heh—Don't worry yourself. We know the Law of God better than you. We don't hunt within city walls. Only the meat of the desert is given to us for our sustenance."

"God is merciful."

"And you have found mercy, my friend."

"Yet you pursue us still."

"On an errand of honor. A debt must be repaid." Reaching a hand inside his stolen, blood-smirched clothes, the ghoul drew out a small object and let it dangle from its fingers—a thong on which was strung a small blue beetle in the style of old Egypt. Rafiq had often seen such jewels and understood that they were looted from tombs. Some were of turquoise and others only faience. He couldn't tell from a distance which sort this was, but he remembered seeing one just like it recently.

"That belongs to Safan the Seer."

"Safan is gone."

"Dead?" He tried to keep the creep of horror out of his voice.

"Gone." The ghoul smirked, showing teeth too large and savage for the mouth of any human. "We're grateful. Tell the sorceress that. Taysafun is ours."

"I'll make sure I do."

With another twitch, the ghoul dropped the necklace at Rafiq's feet. "She can have it."

"Her gratitude will be beyond measure."

"You never know, meat." With a twitch the ghoul swung itself partially over the wall edge and hung there for a moment on its arms, eyeing Rafiq up. "Peace be upon you and all your descendants," it cackled. Then it dropped and was gone.

They plunged earthward, the two of them together, Ahleme wrapped in Yazid's embrace, and as they fell the clouds rolled back as if the fire in her veins was boiling them away. She couldn't be afraid, not now, not any longer. Glory danced in her very fingertips, and she felt as though should he let her go, she too would fly. She didn't resist when he flipped her in his arms, her back suddenly to his chest, though she did cry out when she saw the landscape twinkling below her, but it was in shock and delight, not terror. A lake—no, a string of lakes—reflected the blue sky like a necklace of sapphires, set in lush shores greener than any she had ever seen and cupped by towering snow-clad mountains.

They fell until they were only moments above the surface of the largest lake and then Yazid scooped her slight weight in his arms and they flew, faster than a falcon, above the water. Ahleme glimpsed waterlilies and flocks of ducks and low boats before they were just as suddenly scudding over dry land— meadows full of blazing wild flowers, rising to foothills, and then there was snow beneath them again and rising walls of rock and they were ascending the bright mountain air like it were a palace stair. Then there was a shoulder of the mountain below her and Yazid brought them to a halt, hovering in midair, while the ice on the flattest point of the ridge cracked and rose and twisted, forming shapes like filigree, like poetry frozen in midair, to make an elaborate bower no bigger than two people might occupy.

With a wave of his hand, the djinni snatched a shred of mountain mist and turned it to a pelt of thick gray fur, which he flung down to line the nest. Then they sank gently together between the intricate ice walls and Ahleme's feet at last touched ground again, sinking into the pelt to her ankles.

They stood together in silence while she got her breath back, Yazid's arms furled about her nakedness. Without warning the invisible skin that had protected her from both heat and cold dissolved, and she shivered as the keen air struck those parts not embraced by his warmth. Her nipples puckered in protest and he cupped one breast tenderly.

"Where are we?" she whispered. The elaborately sculpted ice walls did nothing to hide the view of the lake below and the mountains about. This was not the same view as she had seen from the Palace of Glass, nor anything like the barren mountain slopes she'd glimpsed there.

"This is the land of Kashmir," Yazid said, his voice the rumble of a purring lion, "the most beautiful of all places in the world. Do you like it?"

"Very much."

"I had to destroy my house. I shall build a new one here and you will be the jewel in its heart."

For a fleeting moment Ahleme thought of her books and her lute and all her possessions, destroyed with the Palace of Glass. Then she brushed them from her mind and turned to face him, looking his body up and down and searching it with her fingertips. She found long pale scars, as thin as thread and straight as the edge of a sword, and almost invisible on his ash-white skin. A starburst of scar-tissue was centred on his chest.

"The angel hurt you," she exclaimed, starting to shake. "He cut you open."

"He wished to examine my heart. He found no guilt."

"I thought he'd killed you!"

"Oh, Daughter of Earth," he murmured, gathering her in his arms and laying her down among the furs, drawing the pelts over them both to shield her. "I would suffer it a hundred times over for this." His own body made the roof of her tent and she was filled with warmth. Then he kissed her mouth, and she felt the embers lit within her fan to a new glow. "Were you afraid?" he asked, as he drew back to let her catch her breath.

She nodded once, unable to speak.

"There's no need to fear anymore." His smile was fragile, his pale eyes intense. His body warmth surrounded her with the scent of cedarwood. Face-to-face, each drank in the sight of each other, strangely uncertain at this moment, holding it at the cusp as if it might shatter. Ahleme knew the touch and the taste of him intimately, yet at this moment she was pinned by the weight of awe, as if a mystery were being revealed. She touched his face and trembled.

"Cold?"

"No."

Very gently he stooped to kiss the rise of her breastbone, his mouth moving with exquisite delicacy on her skin. Ahleme made a little moan. She didn't resist when he moved to one breast and then the other and kissed each soft mound in turn, his lips closing over the buds of her nipples, his tongue swirling in circles and plucking them against his teeth. She only squirmed her thighs a little against his. She didn't protest as he worked his way down her body a kiss at a time. She didn't even think to use the defense Zubaida had gifted her with.

Yazid had learned patience. He was unhurried in his banquet, tasting each inch of her skin, drawing the furs over to keep her warm where he had left his trail. When he reached the meeting of her thighs he sat back a little and lifted her right leg, wrapping it over his shoulder before he stooped again. His hot breath and exquisite kisses caressed her inner thigh, working their way up to the mound that she'd kept plucked and velvety, and the sweet little pout of her cleft. It was warm and moist and yielding, just as her mouth had been.

He'd never tried this before. Until this day, Ahleme would have refused him outright. Even now, as she looked down the length of her body and saw his bowed shoulders and his head working between her legs, she could hardly believe it was happening. She flushed as he slid a finger deep inside her, and would have denied that she could be so wet if the evidence had not been overwhelming. But hardest of all was believing that anything could feel so good as did the lap and swirl and tease of his tongue. Even the nip of his teeth was a revelation. She arched her back and wriggled her thighs and clutched at his head, her cries growing more and more unguarded as the vestiges of her honor were overrun by the armies of pleasure. And when they stormed the citadel and threw down her sovereign dignity, she squealed and begged and flung the furs open to bare her quivering breasts to the chill, her skin flushed and glazed with sudden damp.

He lifted his head after a final kiss, delight balanced across a knife-edge with trepidation. Then he slid from under her thigh and rose over her while she was still lost for words, and guided the blunt-prowed tip of his member to the harbour it had sought so long. "Flower of the Earth," he groaned under his breath. "Ahleme."

Ahleme bit her lip. She knew only too well from hand and mouth how thick the girth of that member was. "Will it hurt?" she gasped, sliding her hands over his torso.

"Both of us, as one," he groaned, exploring her for entry, slippery with her wetness.

"Don't stop," she gasped, daring to command him one more time.

He didn't. And it did hurt, despite all his attempts to be gentle—but only briefly, and then the sensation was beyond all imagining as he filled her and pressed her down and spread her wide, so wide that she couldn't close herself off from the pleasure with which he filled her, so much pleasure that she was brought to bursting. Then he held her tight in his arms and cried her name as he moved upon her, and all around them the snow burned with a pale flame.

Chapter Nineteen

In which many betrayals take place.

When Taqla returned from the bathhouse, Rafiq was sitting, waiting for her by the light of a single lamp. She'd expected him to be excited but he was somber, almost motionless, his eyes fixing upon her with a look that she'd learned to associate with bottled ire.

"Is everything well?" he asked. His voice was low, on the other hand, not harsh at all.

"Yes." She sat herself down, slightly gingerly.

"Did you get it?"

She showed him the scrap of silk between her fingers, folded tight in such a way that the blood didn't show. He didn't need to see that, she thought. "All done."

Rafiq caught his upper lip in his teeth, eyes narrowing. She wished he wouldn't look at her like that, as if he were stripping her of her veil and her defenses and staring into the depths of her soul. But he only nodded, and said nothing.

"I'll brew it now," she said, turning to the little brazier he had ready.

So for the next watch that was what she did, working in near silence under his gaze. She put the sand into the bottom of the pot and heated it. She put the two pieces of cloth in to char with the sand, and she crushed the seed from the Tree of Knowledge in the mortar. She'd obtained the fifth ingredient with her teeth set and her eyes dry, but she wept silently when she broke open the seed and pounded it to flour. Yet she was careful to wipe the tears away with her sleeve and not to let them fall into the mix. Tears were too magically potent and she didn't want them to interfere with the spell.

Once every dry ingredient was in the pot, she set it to heat until the combustible ingredients were reduced to soot and ash, and then she mixed in the wine from Safan's flask and let the mixture reduce to a gritty black paste. There were no grand invocations to make at this stage, no dramatic gestures, only a few lines to be sung repeatedly under her breath. Anyone observing her at work would only have seen a couple sitting together, she preparing food over the fire and humming while her husband watched. A harmless and domestic scene.

"That's it," she said when the mixture had cooled somewhat. She poured in new wine and stirred the lot together as it hissed and spat. "It will be efficacious, I imagine, for as long as it remains in your body—a few days at least. You need to drink it at dawn so that we have the maximum time to ride. We'll have to leave the city and find somewhere to set the Horse up before the sun rises."

"You're coming with me, then?" It was the first time he'd spoken in an hour.

"Of course," she answered. "We're in this together." She opened the new flask, ready to decant the philtre.

"Yes." Rafiq looked thoughtful. "But I do think I should ask you now—you said you had a means by which I could capture the djinni. I think you should teach me. Once we're on the road, things might come to a head quickly and there not be time for a tutorial."

Taqla was relieved that whatever it was he'd had on his mind, it wasn't an argument—unless he expected her to argue over this point. It was undoubtedly true that if it came to leaping about and seizing things, Rafiq was better at it than she. She remembered how quick he'd been to get her into shelter in the temple of Yaghuth. "It's a ring," she said, drawing off the thin bronze one with the incised Hebrew characters. "You must touch the djinni—that's the hard bit—and command him, 'In the name of Solomon the Wise, I bind you as my slave.' It's very simple."

Rafiq repeated the line then took the ring from her. It had

fitted on her third finger, but he had to slide it over his smallest. Taqla set her jaw against her inner pang of loss.

"Well, I suppose we should get a few hours' rest," he suggested. "We'll need to be up soon enough. Not that I think I'm going to be able to sleep."

She clenched her damp palms. "It's your last night in the city." *Maybe forever*, she could have added, but there was no need. "Go find a coffeehouse if you prefer. I'm sure there are...diversions to be found in Baghdad."

He looked at her with a little frown and then almost visibly shook himself. "No. I don't think so," he said in a gentle voice. "I'll ask the servants to bring up two fresh narghiles and something to eat. Have I told you the story of my journey to the Isle of Madagascar? You will be amazed at the things I saw there. I have to tell you about the trees..."

"The trees?" she said with a faint smile.

"Oh yes!"

So they spent the rest of the evening relaxed together, he reclining, she sat up against their saddle, talking through old adventures while the stars turned overhead and Fate hurried to meet them.

It was a basic call of nature that woke Ahleme. She lifted her head from the furs, took a breath of the mountain air, and then rolled to look at Yazid. The djinni lay asleep. She'd never seen him sleep before, had not even been sure that he did, and the sight fascinated her. He had no need of the furs and lay on top of them, naked in the rosy evening light, his beautiful muscular body in prefect repose, his chest rising and falling. Unconscious, he looked a little less human than he normally did before her, she noticed with some amusement—his ears were definitely pointed. She grinned to herself. She wanted to slide her fingers down his ribs and his ridged stomach and to provoke the thing that lay curved and smooth between his thighs. She wanted to lick his dark blue nipples and see if they would respond to her teasing as they were so clearly refusing to respond to the cold.

But first, she needed to make water. She glanced beyond the filigree walls of their bower at the mountain towering overhead, wondering if it would be possible for her to get out and do it quickly or whether she needed to wake him and ask him for some protective warmth. There didn't seem to be a breath of wind and she was quite cozy here in the furs, but she doubted somehow that that would last when she cast the pelts off.

Carefully she rolled onto her other side to face the nearest wall of their nest—and she nearly emptied her bladder right there and then because Zubaida was there on hands and knees in the snow, her face a finger's breadth beyond the ice screen, her pointed teeth bared in a snarl. Ahleme sat up with a convulsive movement, face-to-face with the djinniyah, whose weight did not even dimple the snow she knelt upon.

"So you didn't resist him after all," Zubaida hissed. "I gave you a weapon and you didn't even raise it to defend yourself. Coward."

Ahleme tried to stop gasping. "It's not like that!" she whispered. "I mean...we're... Elder sister, it's all right now."

"All right? Because you want to play the whore with him? Because you're happy to shame your people and his? It that all right, then?"

Ahleme's mouth fell open as color flooded to her cheeks. "I..."

"Is it going to be all right when you conceive a monster by him?"

"What?" She was stunned.

"Whore," breathed Zubaida. "You will destroy us all."

Ahleme drew a breath to call Yazid awake, but before any sound could escape her throat Zubaida dissolved into a flurry of stinging ice particles that blew away over the snow and the rocks and over the lip of the ridge, down among the long shadows that stretched like fingers toward the valley below.

Rafiq paid the guards handsomely to open the gate and allow them out in the middle of the night. He and Taqla set up their equipment in the shelter of an orange tree grove, and there she performed the final stage of the rite and he choked down the flask of bitter liquid, struggling to swallow the sand but determined to drink it all.

"Think of Ahleme," she told him. "Keep saying her name."

So he said it, and the philtre lay like lead in his stomach, and then he felt the tug, a drawing on his body as strong and sure as the pull of the North upon a lodestone. "That way," he said, pointing. Then, with a look at the rising sun and the city walls behind them, "East. Dead-on due east."

They mounted the Horse and rode without stopping all day long, up into the Zagros Mountains and down into the lands beyond, which turned rapidly to desert beneath their flying hooves. When the sun set they ravelled up the silver ball and walked until midnight, falling asleep under a sheltering rockface.

Exhausted, Taqla slept more heavily than she ought. She woke some time after dawn and looked blearily around her. Into the fold of her *aba* was tucked a blue bead on a thong. It fell to the stones as she sat and she picked it up, confused. A scarab beetle, her eyes told her. The prickle in her skin told her rather more. She frowned, recognizing what it was from descriptions in several of her books. Where in all the world had he got this from?

But when she looked around she saw no glimpse of Rafiq— and equally, she realized with a lurch of her stomach, no sign of the saddle. Checking frantically in her robe pockets, she found the fabric slit—and the Horse Most Swift gone.

Once she understood Rafiq's betrayal, Taqla felt as if she'd been hamstrung. Her legs wouldn't hold her up and she had to sit down hard. She sat for a long time, just staring, her hands clenched under her breasts. A breeze lifted the ashes of their little campfire, but though her eyes followed the movement of the ash, she didn't see, and nor did she blink.

She didn't believe it at first. She couldn't believe that he would have treated her the way he did—like a sister-in-law, he had promised—only to rob and desert her, that he could have risked his life repeatedly for her sake only to abandon her in the middle of the wilderness like this.

Crawling to their baggage, she checked through it. He had taken very little—some food, a single waterskin. He'd left everything else including his bags of money, departing with only the clothes he stood up in, his weapons, the saddle, the Ring of the Djinn—and the Horse Most Swift.

Then she found she did believe it, and she blamed herself. What real reason had she had to believe he wouldn't betray her? They weren't related. He was a merchant out to maximise his profits, and she was a woman of no family who happened to possess some very valuable goods. He must be used to women falling for his generous smile and his wry charm—it was part of his repertoire as a vendor. The Horse must have been a source of temptation beyond all endurance. He'd only waited for the optimum moment. He had the Horse and a way to find Ahleme and the means by which to defeat the djinni all at his command. The Ring of the Djinn was all he had been waiting for. She'd been a fool to imagine that by following him round like a lost puppy she would ever gain any hold on his loyalty, his affection or his respect, and now the thought of how she'd debased herself by trusting the man made her feel nauseous.

After that she got angry, so angry that a smoke seemed to rise in her head and blind her. She got to her feet and clenched her trembling fists. Shame on her for being such a gullible fool, but that gave him no right to steal from her. She focused on that, on the theft of the Horse. It was hers. She had never offered it to him. She would take it back. And she had prepared for this eventuality.

Lifting her fist to her mouth, she kissed a ring on her right hand, the simple twist of silver wire identical to the strands that made up the Horse Most Swift. "In the name of Ahura Mazda the Most High God, stand still," she whispered. Then, "Lion Most Strong." Then, after a calculated number of exhalations, "Pin him. Hold him. Do not let him escape."

She wasn't helpless and she wasn't stranded there. She had ways of travelling other than her own feet and the Horse Most Swift. They had a cost, but in this instance she was willing to bear it. After making a survey of what she needed to take, Taqla began a spell of shape-changing. It wasn't anything so simple as the transformation into Zahir or Umar because they at least had been human and around her own size, and she had made the shift naked. This time she intended to take her clothes and her rings with her. It took longer to cast, and it hurt in every fibre of her body, every pinion breaking through her skin like a needle, but she did it in the end, folding herself down into the shape of a desert falcon. She wanted something fast, and she wanted it to have good eyesight. She knew exactly which direction they had been heading, but if he'd been lying about that too she intended to be able to spot the Horse's trail in the sandy places. With a bitter screech she leapt from a rock and flew eastward.

It took several hours pursuing the tracks of the magical mount, but she caught up with him eventually. She saw the Lion Most Strong from a good way off, standing motionless in the middle of the broken landscape with its silver body catching the sunlight, and as she neared, she saw that it stood with one heavy paw on the chest of a supine Rafiq, pinning him to the ground. His waterskin lay to hand. He had crooked an elbow over his face to shield it from the afternoon sun, and she was perversely annoyed that he wasn't struggling, even though he'd been held captive for hours and must have given up long ago. She would have liked to have seen him struggle and rage. Taqla slipped back into her own form a little way off, and sat for some time while she got her breath back and the ache faded from her shoulders. Though she watched him, she didn't see Rafiq stir any more than to shift a leg or lift a hand.

When she was ready, she approached on foot and ordered the Lion Most Strong to stand back, and it released Rafiq who let out a grunt of surprise. He struggled up onto his knees, blinking at her, his face crusted with sand. "Taqla," he groaned.

She stepped in as he lurched to his feet and punched him as hard as she could in the face. At the last moment he saw her fist and flinched away so her knuckles stuck him only a glancing blow, which was perhaps a good thing because she managed to skin her knuckles on his teeth and split his lip even so. He staggered a little. She clenched her stinging fist, shocked how much it had hurt her and blaming him for that too.

"Bastard! Thief!"

"Taqla—" He lifted a hand in dismay to his bleeding lip.

"You stole my Horse! You dumped me in the desert! You son of a whore!" She was burning too hotly with fury to judge her attacks. When she struck again at his face, he grabbed her wrist and pulled her hard against him, seizing the other hand as it flailed, and wrestling both wrists behind her to pin them at the small of her back. She was still too angry to be afraid. "How could you?" she spat. "After everything we've been through! Everything you promised!"

"Taqla!" he shouted as she twisted furiously in his arms. "Shut up! Stop it! Listen to me!"

"I hope street dogs eat your corpse!"

"Stop!"

She stopped struggling to draw breath, snarling. He was very strong and held her easily, his face over hers.

"Taqla, I'm sorry." His eyes burned. "Listen. Listen. I haven't betrayed you. Believe me."

"You left me!"

"I had to take the Horse. I am sorry, but I need it to find the house of the djinni. I had no choice. I would have returned it when I could."

"Tell me your ass is made of solid gold and you shit diamonds! Shall I believe that too?"

He shook his head, teeth bared. "Taqla—I left because I

couldn't bring you with me and see you hurt."

"Me—hurt? Haven't I saved your life before now? Haven't you needed me every step of this journey?"

"Yes!" He turned his face aside so he could spit blood into the sand, then caught her gaze again, his eyes hot with anguish. "Yes. I've needed you. But this is different. There's so much chance of you getting killed—"

"You think I'm afraid?"

"No. Never. Taqla, listen to me. I couldn't see you hurt for my sake. I couldn't bear it."

"We had a bargain," she snapped. "We were in it together. You get what you want and I get what I want."

He shook his head as if in pain, and when he spoke again it was under his breath. "I read the scroll."

"What?"

"The spell in the Scroll of Simon."

She felt as if she'd been kicked in the stomach. "Oh," she said while the import of his words sank in and the desert seemed to reel about her. It had never occurred to her that he would be able to read Greek. She was suddenly horribly conscious of the way he was holding her up tight against his hard body. "No," she whispered, trying to shrink away from him. She couldn't move an inch.

"How could I let myself hurt she who loves me the most?"

"I..."

"Look, Taqla, I saw you drown in the swamps of Basra. I couldn't do that to you again—not now. I couldn't let you risk your life out of love for me." His voice was soft, all shouting done.

"No, you've misunderstood..."

"Taqla, why are you scared of admitting it?"

"I... It isn't like that..."

"Isn't it? What is it like then? Tell me."

She groaned. His lips curved, self-deprecating, as if knowing he was inviting another blow.

"I think I know exactly how it feels. Taqla, is it not obvious that I've been falling in love with you this whole time?"

She went still, her eyes widening.

He smiled lopsidedly because of his split lip. "I've been like a man sliding down a sand dune, trying to keep on my feet and all the time falling. Can't you see that?"

She tried to speak but for once had no words. Not even when he bent his head and kissed her through her veil. She felt the warm softness of his lips on hers and the ghost of his breath through the silk. Her heart slammed painfully in her chest, sending the blood roaring through her head.

Quietly, while his lips still held hers, he let go of her wrists. One hand stayed to hold her close to him, but the other rose to touch her face through the folds of her headscarf. Then he drew back a little so he could look into her eyes. She could read his intent. She knew what he was going to do and the voices of warning were roaring in the back of her mind, but still she didn't resist when he gently drew down the fold of her veil and bared her face, though she shivered at the touch of his fingertips. A warm pleasure danced in his eyes. He brushed his thumb across her lips and whispered her name.

"As honey on my lips, I love you. As breath in my lungs, as water in the desert, I love you." Then he stooped again to kiss her for the second time, his mouth bruised and sweet and— under the gentleness—hungry. He tasted of blood.

Taqla's inner voices of reason and propriety were shrieking with dismay now. Rafiq had crossed a line that should never be crossed. She was in terrible danger, they told her. She was a fool, and he was an opportunistic dog, and this was the worst move she'd ever made.

She heard them all, and she let them go. She gave up thinking. She let the future fly from her grasp so that she could feel what was happening to her now, in this wonderful, terrifying moment when the whole world turned inside out and his hands were on her and her body was melting against his in a way that she could never even have imagined. When they broke for breath, she reached up and touched his jaw, tracing her fingers over the hard bone and the inflorescence of dark stubble as if to convince herself he was real. A new world of textures and sensations was opening to her. She brushed the outline of his lips and he bit softly at her fingertips.

"I was right," he murmured. "You do have a beautiful smile."

She hadn't even been aware she was smiling. It wasn't a wide one, just a tentative curve of her lips.

"I've never seen it till now, you know."

"I'm sorry," she whispered.

"What for?"

Sorry for hiding her smile from him? Sorry for being afraid? She hardly knew. She touched the bloody contusion on his lip. "For hurting you."

"Oh, I can take worse."

She flashed him a startled look.

"Better that you hurt me than I hurt you," said he.

"I've been hurting day and night," she said simply, no longer caring how dangerous it was to confess. His eyes darkened and his hands tightened on her.

"Truly?"

"Yes."

"Taqla...I want..." Rafiq shook his head, ashamed of his sudden incoherence. "You've enslaved me, my sorceress. That's the truth. I've never met anyone like you. You cut me open with a glance. I've never..."

She gazed up at him, wide-eyed, and he swallowed hard.

"Never before needed a woman to look at me the way you do." He stooped for another kiss, the third, and this time she slid her arms around his neck. She had to, for support, because this kiss was longer and deeper and he was bearing into her, arching her back. Something was changing between them, something happening in both their bodies, a wordless contract of intention being drawn up without any reference to her will.

This is alchemy, she thought, *the mystery of changing matter.* What was soft became hard, what was firm became liquid, what was cool began to fill with urgent heat—a heat fuelled by the meeting of lips and tongues, by the mingled scents of skin on skin, by the pressing of thighs and the slide of hands. And when his hands came round until he was holding her only by the hips and his thumbs slipped down the twin creases of her thighs toward her delta, that insistent touch was enough to make Taqla feel she would crumple in his grasp. Without meaning to, she moaned into his mouth, and then pulled away in shock and embarrassment. But not far. His hands held her there. His gaze pinned her even as she blushed and squirmed.

"Taqla..." It wasn't a question—and yet somehow it was. Rafiq's voice had changed subtly. It was deeper, and held an undercurrent of wildness. His eyes simultaneously promised and pleaded, and where their two bodies met, the extent of his arousal was indisputably apparent. As for her own sex, she wasn't sure whether she was going to melt or burst into flames. She lifted her lips to his mouth but didn't kiss him, instead she brushed her cheek to his, her nose to his, tasting his skin scent and sharing his breath. The aching tension between the two of them was painfully taut.

She left it to him to break it.

Quietly he moved his hand to the knot of her belt, and as she looked up at him through her lashes, he pulled the sash free from about her waist, letting her robe fall open. He dropped the belt and then treated her headscarf the same, so that her black hair hung about her throat. He ran his fingers through her hair then lifted a lock to his lips, kissing it. And all the time he gazed into her eyes, as if there was a magical bond between them that couldn't be broken. Even when he shrugged off his own outer robe, he kept focused upon her. Only when he laid it in the patch of shade cast by the Lion Most Strong did he glance briefly away. Then he offered her his hand.

Taqla felt her heart in her throat. There was no resistance left in her, not to him and not to the tide of her desire, as strong as an ocean. She set her fingers in his and let him lead her to stand upon his robe. His deft hands opened the man's jacket she wore beneath her outer *aba*. Beneath that she wore a woman's blouse, which wrapped over at the front and knotted about her waist. When he loosed that knot and drew the cotton aside, her breasts were bared for the first time—to the daylight, to the surrounding wilderness, to his hands and his glance. She read the delight in the gleam of his eyes and the quirk of his mouth, and she lowered her gaze, shy. But his touch was gentle—gentle and tender—and he cupped her and stroked her with caresses that offered such exquisite pleasure that she sagged against him, her legs weakening. He pulled her tighter to him and claimed the stiffened buds of her nipples again.

"Oh!" she said. It was all she could think of to say. She said it several times and then bit her lip, frightened she was babbling.

Then Rafiq went down on his knees before her. He did it so that he could kiss her breasts and take their sweet points in his mouth and breathe the scent of her skin as she quivered against him. He did it so he could bury his face in the cleft of her breasts and groan with desire even as he licked the salt off her skin. He did it so that he could unfasten her sandals and draw out the drawstring knot that held up her *shalwar* trousers and let them fall to her feet, and so that he could mouth the warm, taut skin of her stomach and slip his hand up between her thighs and cup the hot softness of her sex—and feel her as slippery between his fingers as a ripe peach whose juice escapes at the first squeeze.

Taqla nearly fell over. She locked her fingers in his hair as he kissed her, his tongue tracing paths below the declivity of her navel, and his hands doing things to her that no man had ever done. For a while she forgot to breathe, aware only of the pleasure of his touch and the burgeoning demand in her body and the hunger of his mouth.

Then, still kneeling, he sat back and took both her hands, drawing her down slowly on top of him to straddle his thighs. He revisited her breasts again with his kisses as she settled, and then, once she was held in his embrace, kissed her mouth once more. It was strange to be sitting eye to eye with him, even a little taller. His thighs were slab hard under hers. She was still wearing her long travelling robe that draped over them both but it was open all the way down the front so that he could slip his hands under and hold her bare bottom, taking her weight to keep her balanced.

"All right?" he whispered.

She nodded. "Will you take your shirt off?" she asked tentatively, and he grinned.

"You do it."

A certain amount of wriggling by both of them was needed to get his shirt off over his head, but Taqla thought it well worth the effort. She wanted to be able to see him. She wanted the brush of her bare breasts against his chest. She wanted the hard slats of muscle under her fingers, the dark flare of chest hair and the thump of his heart. Rafiq had muscled shoulders and lean hips and everything between was a delight. She was torn between feeling wanton and feeling self-conscious, and she blushed and squirmed on his lap as he laughed softly under his breath.

"You're wonderful," he told her.

"Am I?" His words didn't make any sense to her, but at this moment nothing made sense. All her emotions seemed to have exploded out of her body and to be whirling around like pigeons. She felt wonderful certainly, but she also felt frightened and ravenous and foolish. She wanted both to run away and to throw him down, to slam his fingers inside her and to faint. She needed him to catch all these desires and pin their thrashing wings and put them back inside her. She needed him to make sense of the chaos.

"Do you want me, Taqla?" he asked, the laughter fading from his expression, the darkness welling in his eyes.

"Yes."

He nodded. Then he reached to his waistband and released his own clothes with a tug. The loose cloth fell away and he freed himself from the folds. Taqla couldn't help but look and blush, as she saw for the first time the full proud length standing between his thighs. He was hot and velvety, as hard as marble and aching with eagerness, and when she dared to slip her fingers around his girth, he had to bite his lip. "This is the first time," he promised, the edge of a growl in his throat. "But not the last."

He lifted her bodily to nuzzle her breasts once more and then let her slide down his torso, impaling her wetness. He was too much for her inexperienced body. She made a noise of protest and tried to slow it down, clinging to his shoulders. Sweat sprang out on her skin. Rafiq slipped one hand under her rear to hold her up then the other hand between them, his thumb easing her with caresses as he opened her and entered her. She thought she would never be able to do it, never take that merciless thickness, never take that whole unyielding length. But she did. He moved his hips beneath her and a finger's width at a time she surrendered to him. Sometimes he lifted her and slid out, only to conquer more ground on his return. She started to make noises, plaintive at first and then hungry, she hauled down on his shoulders and he braced himself, his muscles standing out. She began to pant as the fear gave way to pleasure and the pleasure gave way to need. She closed her eyes and rubbed herself against him, and he licked her straining throat as the ecstasy burst open within her like a long-stoppered flask shattering at last, flooding her with a joy so keen that it made her cry out. Then she collapsed.

"Rafiq," she whimpered, shocked at herself.

"Shush. It's good. Oh, it's good."

He held her for a while, both arms wrapped around her shaking body. Then he gently tipped her over to lay her upon her back on his robe, and his own bulk pressed her into the desert earth. Taqla laced her legs about his hips as he began to move upon her. She'd been wet before; she was wetter now. She was made for him, a perfect fit, and every motion he made molded her to his increasingly urgent desire. His eyes grew shadowed, his breath shallower, his thrusts sharper, but still she beat him to his crisis, unfurling inside and entering into her own Paradise quite suddenly, straining beneath him as she felt each thrust all the way to her core. His teeth flashed and in the end he took her hard—harder perhaps than he'd intended—but Taqla, despite her cries, had no complaints at all.

Groaning her name as he filled her, he shuddered to his climax.

It did not stop there.

It was late in the day by the time they finished. Rafiq rose first, left Taqla wrapped in his robe and wandered about for a while gathering dry thorns for a fire. He cooked the food he'd brought over the flames and they shared a frugal meal as the sun set. After that he undressed completely, and in the flickering light of the fire, using hands and mouth and body, he laid bare her many secret treasures like a man unlocking drawer after drawer of a box of precious jewels. He kissed her in places she'd never imagined being kissed, and wrung from her noises she had not realized herself capable of making. She surprised him too, with the depth and endurance of her need for him. And after they were both sated, he rolled on his back and pulled her on top of him, full length, so that he could run his fingertips through her hair and stroke them down her back.

"Aren't I heavy?" she whispered, her cheek upon his breastbone.

Rafiq only chuckled.

Taqla woke in the warm compass of Rafiq's arms, her head against his chest and his heartbeat slow in her ear. For a long time she lay there, basking in a happiness as rare and fragile as body heat under the desert sky at night. *This is it*, she told herself. *I will never be happier than this moment.* Then she wriggled from his embrace and he half-woke.

"You all right?" he mumbled, reaching for her. His body was warm and firm and every inch of her skin wanted to press itself to him.

"Yes. Go back to sleep."

He turned his face to the cloak upon which they lay and his

breathing deepened. As she slid out from under the saddle blanket they'd been using for cover, she glimpsed the smooth muscle of his upper arm and the bare skin of his back, and her insides clenched with desire.

She took up her discarded clothing and dressed quickly, and though she draped the headscarf about her shoulders she didn't bother to veil her face. Then she climbed to the top of a dirt rise and found a slope facing east to watch the dawn, seated in the cold sand. Slowly the gold light washed across the desert before her, turning the shadows blue and highlighting her dark hair in a fugitive halo of chestnut brown. The landscape was beautiful, but so empty and lonely. She sat on her own for a long time.

Her headscarf sported a little brown spot where Rafiq had blotted his bloody lip. *Funny*, she thought, not smiling. It wasn't a Dimashq custom, but she knew that among some of the desert tribes a maiden's last-worn veil was used to soak and preserve the evidence of her torn virginity, and then as a married woman she would wear a new veil of different design. Well, she'd had no maidenhead to wipe up last night. Rafiq's blood was only a substitute.

The trouble with a new dawn is that you can see everything clearly, she realized.

Shortly after the sun's disk cleared the horizon, Rafiq made his appearance, toiling over the crest of the rise. He walked up wordlessly behind her and sat at her back, embracing her thighs with his, wrapping his arms about her body. He pressed his face to her hair to breathe its scent then kissed her temple and her ear and her cheek lingeringly. She shivered as his cool fingers caressed her. Her nipples thrilled to the brush of his hand and she lifted her chin, letting his mouth nuzzle her throat. The wave of arousal that washed over her left her dizzy. Just his touch, the scent of his skin, the whisper of his smile— these were enough to overwhelm her. It was terrifying that anyone should have such power.

Rafiq took her face in his hand to turn it to him, but when his thumb found the wet tracks on her cheek, he grew still.

"What's wrong?" he murmured. "Did you think that my love would've grown old with the night?"

She shook her head slightly, but it was more a shiver than an answer.

"Is it that I've dishonored you?"

She was on surer ground here, and found her voice. "I have no family to dishonor—do with me as you like."

"Well." He tightened his arms around her. "When this is all over, we will find the first judge we can and have marriage papers drawn up, I promise. I love you, Taqla."

She couldn't stop the warm, painful blossom in her breast, or keep the tremble from her voice as she admonished him, "No one marries for love."

"I will," he whispered, his lips warm on the whorls of her ear. "Or if you think that belittling, I will marry you for your wisdom and your courage—and your habit of saving my skin. There's no woman on earth who would make me a better wife, Taqla."

Marriage for a man was easy, easy, easy, she thought bitterly. They walked in and out of it as if it were a bathhouse. As for her, it was as if she were standing on the lip of a precipice. She took a deep breath and stepped off with the words, "Don't you think that that's going to cause trouble with Ahleme?"

The tiniest quiver went through Rafiq's frame. He didn't resist as she slid out of his arms and stood to face him. One look at his face told her what she'd guessed—that it hadn't previously even crossed his mind what a proposal to her would mean. It was almost funny in a horrible way, a part of her thought.

"Her father is the Amir of Dimashq, after all," Taqla continued, her voice coming out cold and hard even though inside she felt a burning heat. "I don't think he'll take it too well to have his daughter as your *second* wife."

"You have a point." Rafiq's eyes betrayed the furious working of his mind as he tried to unscramble the ramifications.

"So perhaps it would be better to marry her first and me second?" She hated the cold voice, but she didn't seem able to stop it.

Rafiq had gone pale. He knew he was somehow in the middle of a fight, and he had no idea which way he was facing or where to find solid ground to stand on. "That would be sensible," he said, his lips barely moving, his eyes fixed on hers.

"So I must bear living in the shadow of the most beautiful woman in Al-Sham?"

"Oh," he said, and then to himself, "Oh no."

"And look at it from Ahleme's point of view. Here she is, the loveliest woman in the land, and straight after taking her to bed you contract with a woman older and plainer. Won't she take that as an insult?"

"She'll have to put up with it," he snapped, "if that's what I want." The moment the words were out of his mouth he knew he'd made a mistake. That was quite visible, but she had no mercy on him. Her eyes flashed.

"Oh? That's how it's going to be with your wives, is it?" Taqla could feel her limbs trembling. "We put up with your every whim? However many of us there are you decide to marry?"

"Oh *shit.*" Rafiq scrambled to his feet too, his brows knotted. "Look, it's obvious—if I'm to be grand vizier or amir someday, then of course I will have more than one wife! What else do you expect? It doesn't make any difference to how I feel about *you.*"

"So generous," she said through bared teeth.

"What have I done wrong? Taqla, I swear to God that if I become amir, you will be my vizier, and to hell with tradition."

"I see. And what if I don't want to be what you tell me to be? What if I don't want to be wife number two, or even number one?"

"Then what is it that you want?" he cried. "Do you want me to leave this girl to the djinni—is that it?"

Yes! her most selfish inner voice cried, but "No," she snapped. "Don't be a fool."

His temper was rising to match hers. "Do you want me to give up on the hope of ruling Dimashq? Do you? Tell me! Because right now I have no idea what it is you do want from me, you crazy witch."

"That's what you think of me, is it?"

He shut his eyes, grinding his teeth. "Taqla—"

"The crazy witch you tumbled in the sand?"

"Shit—"

"What I want," she said from the depths of her bitterness, her voice ragged, "is for all this to be over and done with. I want to be home. I want you to rescue your beautiful girl and get the hell out of my life. I want you to be *gone*." She pulled the silver ring off her finger and flung it to the ground at his feet. "Go on—take the Horse. I don't need it, and you don't need me anymore. Take it," she snarled, "and get out!"

Rafiq stood, his mouth set in a grim line and his chin high. His eyes burned with fury. For a moment she thought he was going to say something more, but he shook his head once, bent to snatch up the ring and stalked off without a word.

Taqla slithered to her knees. She stared at the barren hillside until she heard the drumming of the Horse's hooves, and as that sound faded away, she crumpled slowly and the first gasp of pain squeezed from her throat.

Chapter Twenty

In which djinn go to war.

It was fortunate that riding the Horse Most Swift demanded the utmost concentration because it left no room in Rafiq's head for other thoughts. He took all his anger and shoved it down into his belly where it burned like hot coals, and he left it to smolder there as he rode east, the sun first rising in his eyes and then moving over his shoulder as the day wore on. He stopped only a few times, mostly to drink, once in a tiny village where the inhabitants shut themselves in their stone huts and he left a silver dirham for the loaves of bread he stole from a windowsill. The miles turned to hundreds beneath the Horse's silver hooves. He kept as much speed up as possible even when the land rose to barren hills and then rugged mountains where he had to pick his route more carefully. Always the tug in his gut drew him eastward.

Night caught him on a mountainside. Only then, as he huddled in his *aba* in the lee of a rock, did he allow himself to dwell on thoughts of Taqla and let the heat rise from his belly to his mind, but once he'd started that he couldn't stop. Perhaps it was the only thing that stopped him freezing to death. He was hurt and furious, and every conversation they'd ever had echoed round and round in his head until his skull ached. Every sharp glance she'd given him, every admonishment, the cracked spite in her voice at the end—they all came back painted in the hues of injustice and pain.

What a fool you were for loving a witch, he told himself bitterly. They weren't like other women. Their hearts were dead, even if they weren't all hewn from stone. Hadn't he seen that from the start? Every overture he'd ever made to her had been repulsed, and she'd never made any secret of her cold contempt for him. Even if she had succumbed briefly to lust, it hadn't changed her fundamental antagonism. After slaking her desire, she had pushed him away once more, despising his protestations of love. Rafiq clenched his fists in his armpits and shivered. How do you thaw a river of ice? How do you touch a heart barricaded behind a mountain of rock? She'd heard his confession but tossed it back in his face. He'd offered her marriage and riches, honor and devotion, and he didn't know what else he could possibly promise her—but it wasn't good enough. Nothing was enough for her. He'd allowed himself to love her, against all his better judgment, and it was like throwing himself against a stone wall. He could beat himself to death on that obdurate surface and she would never let him in.

Scrunched against the bare rock, his feet and hands and rear numb with the mountain chill, Rafiq didn't manage any sleep that night and little in the way of rest, though after a while he was too exhausted to rage anymore and simply fell into a nauseated stupor. It was, he recognized, one of the worst nights of his life, worse even than that one in the Abu Bahr when they'd had to endure the suffocating sandstorm, because at least there he'd had Taqla to hold—

He caught the thought and thrust it aside with an angry grimace. Of course he regretted the loss of her warm, smooth body, he allowed grudgingly. She'd been a more than adequate bedmate. Not skilled, of course, but passionate and fluid and trusting. And serious in a way that he'd found deeply touching. He remembered the feel of her body straining beneath his, the look in her eyes as she'd yielded to him, the cries she'd made as pleasure broke upon her.

For a moment the pain under Rafiq's breastbone robbed him of the ability to breathe.

She'd spurned him. That was all there was to it. He wouldn't think about her again.

In the morning, by the time he'd uncoiled his aching limbs and staggered out to the Horse, Rafiq had taken the fierce coals of his anger and buried them under a mountain of ice.

That day the Horse galloped over snow as well as rock, and passed no human habitation. Rafiq was riding over terrain that no mortal animal could possibly cope with now, unless it was those mountain sheep that he once glimpsed picking their way up a sheer crag. The Horse sprang from rock to rock as lightly as if it were cantering over firm sand, and only the rattle of dislodged stones in deep ravines let Rafiq know how closely he was dancing with death.

He'd been riding for a good many hours when he caught his first glimpse of his goal and brought the Horse to a standstill with a shout. When he jumped down, his boots sank into the snow halfway up his shins. He waded upslope to where an outcrop of icy rock offered dryer footing and a better view, and then just stared.

"In the name of God," he whispered.

There was not the slightest doubt that this was the place he'd been searching for because the drag in his belly was pulling him straight toward it—and because he'd never seen anything like it in his life. He was standing on a boulder that jutted out from the lip of yet another steep valley like so many he'd passed. The bottom of the ravine was the bed of a milky-blue stream, which ran downhill among banks brushed with the faintest fuzz of green toward what looked like the opening to a larger and more verdant valley. Upstream, the valley kinked a little, back and forth, but not enough to hide the construction that had been built there, straddling the cleft and towering high over the two walls. It had the glitter of ice but it was pink, the color of the roses of Dimashq. It was the shape of...well, of something Rafiq had no real words for. A sea anemone perhaps, or a flower of some kind. It had translucent-looking petals certainly, that burst from a tighter clustering centre and crisscrossed and intertwined. It was hard to judge the object's scale, but at the very least it must be hundreds of feet deep and hundreds of feet from side to side, and it bridged the valley like a spider's web strung across a gap between two bricks.

Rafiq's heart sank. Anything that had created this immense glass structure must be powerful beyond the dreams of any human caliph or emperor. For the first time the true hubris of his quest came home to him—but then his jaw tightened. This was what he had come here for. This was his goal, the palace of the djinni. This was his Fate.

His stomach rumbled.

Biting his lip, Rafiq rummaged through his pockets, not entirely able to tear his eyes from the roseate vision before him but distracted by human weakness. He was used to going hungry for days at a time while travelling, but it wasn't precisely enjoyable. He hoped to find a forgotten date or crust in some corner of his numerous pockets, but what his hand actually closed over felt harder than either of those. He brought it out before he remembered what it was—the piece of bone from which he'd carved a face in the Abu Bahr. He looked down at it as it lay in his palm. Grease and dirt had worked into the lines, making the features stand out quite clearly. It was Taqla, of course, and he'd been absent-minded enough to almost let her see it at the time. He'd done a good job of the eyes, he thought. Those fierce, troubled eyes always too serious for a young woman. He'd been less certain about the line of the mouth, out of unfamiliarity, but he'd captured the stubbornness well enough even if he hadn't done justice to the curve of her lips.

Oh, how he'd wanted to unveil that mouth, and to kiss those lips.

Rafiq felt a small stab of pain like a fine knifepoint, one that threatened to cut much deeper and wider. Of course, he'd carved this the day she'd told him about her father being killed by a djinni. That bastard of a father who'd tutored her so well in the cold-hearted ways of sorcerers.

Something shifted inside him. Like ice melting. Or like coals crumbling to ash.

The father, he thought, feeling dizzy and a bit sick, who had in one day taught his small daughter two such important lessons—that though women might betray men, men could destroy women. And that whatever she did in her life, she must *never* let a man have power over her.

"Taqla," he whispered, closing his fingers over the carved face.

Suddenly his mind was made up, without need for debate with himself. He turned on his heel—and there standing in the snow behind him was Ahleme, the Flower of Dimashq.

"Whoa!" he yelped.

She was exquisite. Slender but molded to enticing curves, rather shorter than Taqla, with hair that fell in a waterfall of enchanting curls. He'd actually forgotten how beautiful she was, but right here he was left in no doubt because she was barely clothed, so he had a clear view of that narrow waist and those breasts that defied her otherwise virginal slightness by being full and firm and pouting. Against the dead white of the snow her flawless golden-brown skin—and he could see a great deal of that—seemed to glow with an inner warmth. She wore only a transparent scarf of yellow silk swathed about her hips, and a top of the same material that cupped her breasts but was so sheer that he could see not only the shape but the dark tint of her erect nipples. The roll of her hips, the curve of her thighs—they were designed to drive a man mad, he thought. Her lips were lush and ripe for kissing, and when she smiled her face lit up. "You've come to rescue me."

"Ahleme?" Even as he said it he knew it wasn't her—that it couldn't be. The magical lodestone in his entrails was not pulling toward her, whatever other attraction his body might be feeling. And he doubted very much that the daughter of the Amir of Dimashq had any means of arriving in the middle of a snowfield so swiftly that she made neither warning—nor footprints. "Aren't you...cold?" he said, letting his gaze fall pointedly to her bare feet, which did not even dimple the snowcrust.

"You do remember me?"

"I remember Ahleme," he said softly. "You're not actually her."

She flushed, oddly blue. "No. Of course not. I cannot leave

the Palace of Glass. The djinni has me trapped there! Only—my dreams seek out those whom I remember...with affection."

"I see. I'm flattered."

She stepped onto the rock and looked up into his face, her eyes huge and trusting. "You have come to rescue me, haven't you?"

"I..."

"You mustn't lose heart now! I'm held at the mercy of that evil djinni. You must save me! I cannot bear this slavery!" She put her hand up and caressed his cheek, her fingers quite warm and real, her touch tremulous on his jaw. "Yazid means to force me to bear his child."

"Ahleme," he whispered. "I'm so sorry."

"You don't understand." Her breath was like perfume of roses, the scent of her skin intoxicating. "He wants from me a son with Djinn powers but the authority of a Child of Solomon. He means to free all the Djinn from their bonds so that they're no longer subject to the rule of Mankind. You must not let me bear that child. Take me away swiftly or slay me, but I must not bear such a son."

"What?" This was entirely new to Rafiq and he was furthermore struggling to think past the caress of her fingers on his skin and the heave of her breasts beneath the straining silk.

"A child with the magic of the Djinn and the heart of a Man! Do you think anything will stop such a one laying waste to all the Earth? Do you think that anything living will escape enslavement or death?"

Rafiq grabbed her wrist and pushed it from him. "Ahleme, I can't."

"You can." She pressed up against him bodily, then turned and rubbed like a cat, the curves of her barely veiled behind writhing into his crotch while she looked up and back at him, her eyes pleading, her arm lifting to caress his cheek and to tilt her perfect, quivering breasts. "Yazid is away from home now. You must come and steal me swiftly away. Your reward will be beyond price, my rescuer."

It would have been impossible to have been unmoved by that lithe body, the roll of those slinky hips and the press of her firm skin. Rafiq couldn't help his arousal, but he clenched his teeth and took her by the shoulders and pushed her away. "Ahleme, no," he said, rather more roughly than a man should ever address the daughter of his amir. "I can't. I'm sorry, but I am not the man who will rescue you."

"Why not?" she demanded, tears brimming in her doe eyes.

He swallowed. "Because I love another."

"Another?" She looked incredulous.

"And I will not lose her or leave her. Because I'm going back to her now, God willing. I've made a mistake. My Fate lies with her, not here."

Her mouth twisted. "You presume to decide what Fate is written for you?"

"Yes," he said flatly.

The dream-Ahleme took a deep breath, going pale—not pale like bloodless flesh but pale like snow, then whiter yet, colorless like the very burning heart of a furnace, so bright that Rafiq could hardly look at her and he flinched away, wanting to retreat but having nowhere to go. He could feel the blast of her body heat scorching his eyeballs.

"You're in for a sore disappointment then, Son of Earth," she hissed, and as she spoke, she started to grow. Two, three then four times as tall as a man she grew, still beautiful, still naked, but no longer Ahleme either in color or features. Across her white-hot skin black script danced, indecipherable, and around her head and shoulders flame raged, wilder than any hair. "If Yazid will not abandon her and you will not rescue her, then I will have to kill the little whore myself," she spat. Then she raised one foot and slapped it down on the boulder, and with a crack like a whip turned into a silken scarf that fluttered away into the sky.

Rafiq didn't have any time to watch where she went. He could feel the rock sliding away beneath his feet. He flung himself forward upon the snow but suddenly his boots were scrabbling in empty air. He flailed his arms but the snow slipped and fragmented under his blows, and without warning, he was falling backward down the steep hillside, blinded by white, snow beneath him and above him and in his mouth, choking even his final cry.

When he hit the bottom the white turned to black.

She saw him fall. Circling high overhead, the swallow had watched as he pushed the girl away and the girl became a giant, and then the giant vanished. Now she saw the collapse of the ice and she dropped through the air, blue wings glinting. She didn't have much strength left. She'd flown night and day, always eastward, pursuing a Horse that travelled faster than even she could fly, snatching insects on the wing and ignoring the danger of nocturnal predators as she flew blind under the stars. Her consciousness had narrowed down to a tiny point, such that even the sight of the woman embracing Rafiq hadn't made any impression. But when he fell, the last part of the swallow's mind that was still able to think as Taqla took her down into the narrow valley, scudding though the cloud of hanging ice crystals and flopping onto the lumpy snow.

She changed, bursting from swallow form into a writhing ball of yellow fur, growing with every kick and snarl and roll until she was lion shaped and lion sized, her amber eyes frantic. She shook herself off as she found her unsteady feet and then bounded across the fallen snow, head low, nostrils flaring. She sought the scent of man among the nothingness of ice, the faintest hint of warmth, and when after long long minutes she was almost witless with despair, she found the coppery tang of blood and began to dig. Broad paws scooped and shovelled. He was a foot beneath the surface, a lumpen, huddled shape blanketed in white. She grabbed the folds of his clothes in her great jaws and hauled him out bodily, dragging him beneath her and between her paws until she'd laid him out on the surface. His head sagged limply. The blood was from a gash on his cheek, but it was already freezing.

That was when her lion shape failed and Taqla collapsed on top of Rafiq's chest. She moaned with pain then bit her lip to stifle the noise. Running her hands over his chest, she tried to discern if it was still rising and falling. Snow stuck to the weave of his clothes.

"Rafiq!"

He didn't respond. His eyes were shut, his black hair caked with powdered crystals. Taqla pressed her cheek to his chest, trying to still her own gasps so that she could listen for his heartbeat. Her cheek went wet. She could be sure of nothing.

"Rafiq, please—God is merciful—please hear me! Wake up!"

"Taqla?" His voice was little more than a gasp, but it was a voice.

She flung herself on him then, kissing his cold lips as if she could breathe life into them, wiping the ice and the blood desperately from his face. "You're alive! You're alive!" The pain in her every fibre was forgotten as his lids opened and his dark eyes looked up at her. "Oh, God is great!"

He lifted stiff fingers to touch her cheek, like the hand of winter itself. "You're not the real Taqla either," he said with a weak smile. "She's got a temper like a scorpion and she treats me like dirt."

That was when Taqla realized that she was straddling him, and she sat back hurriedly into the snow, breaking from his grasp. "I'm sorry," she muttered.

Rafiq started to ease himself into a sitting position, wincing as he discovered his bruises, his gaze fixing on her as he drew deeper and surer breaths into his cold chest.

"Are you hurt?" she asked.

"Nothing too bad." He brushed ineffectually at the caked snow on his torso and tried another smile. "You came back to me."

"I came to help you." She could feel the blood rushing to her cheeks. "I thought you might need magical help, that's all. Nothing's changed. We're not... I just don't want you to die."

"Nor me. That was too close." Rafiq managed to roll onto

his knees.

"So why weren't you wearing this, you fool?" she demanded, brandishing her wrist and the scarab necklace looped around it.

"A fool, am I?" He said it wryly, without rancour, and she blushed even more.

"It could have saved your life!"

He shook his head. "What is it?"

"Don't you know? You gave it to me! Where did you get it from?"

"It was a gift from the Pale People."

"Why didn't you tell me?" she gasped. "You could have used it to show me where you lay in the snow! What if I hadn't been able to find you? You could have been buried there forever!" Her voice cracked.

He grinned, crookedly. "So you still love me then?"

"I..." She shut her eyes, trying to block the gaze that seemed to be eating into her soul. "That's not important. We're not going to be together, we're no good for each other. I'm just—" And then her eyes flashed open again because Rafiq had taken hold of her and pulled her to him. With a squeak of protest, she flung up her hand. She was going to push his face away, but he caught her wrist.

"Don't hit me again," he said, his eyes twinkling. "I might get to like it." He was holding her to his chest, his arm snaking round behind her to keep her trapped. Her heart started to hammer painfully.

"Let me go," she said through clenched teeth.

"No." He was still smiling, but his eyes were now serious. "Never. I'm taking you home to Dimashq, Taqla. I'm not going to marry Ahleme or become the grand vizier, I'm going to marry you. You and no one else. And I will love you and you alone until I die, and on the Day of Judgment I will walk through the gate of Paradise at your side. That is my Fate."

Her eyes burned with tears, but she laughed. "Don't be a fool. And don't take me for one."

"Taqla," he said with a shake of his head, "listen to me. I will bow to your wisdom and your whim all my days, but I'll not surrender to your fear. You can't make me run. However you hurt me—and, you know, you do that quite a lot; I'm getting used to it—I will still love you." His lips brushed hers, his face so close that it filled her whole world, his voice dropping to a whisper. "I will still love you."

His kiss closed on her. His lips were cold and chapped and bloody—and they broke her. She opened to him, clinging to him, tears streaming down her face, and he kissed her hard and fierce then sweet and gentle, then wild and hungry and then deep and aching with promise—all the kisses of a lifetime. And in the middle of all those kisses she understood that there were some things that no one, not even a sorceress, could control. Some things that simply had to be trusted. In the shape of a bird she had flown a thousand miles for the sake of this man, and she had done it not by commanding the wind beneath her pinions but by trusting it to bear her up. She wrapped her fingers in his loose, wet hair and kissed him back until they were both burning and dizzy and had to break to draw breath.

"Will you love me then, my sorceress?" Rafiq asked. "Forever?"

She stroked his face, trembling so much she couldn't speak but managing to nod. He laughed and kissed her once again, this time with a joy that bubbled up so uncontrollably that he pulled her over on top of him and they fell into the snow. He rolled her and pinned her and she gasped with laughter.

A thin, high wail cut into their ears. They both froze, and Rafiq lifted his head. Taqla saw the color drain from his face.

"What's that?" she asked.

"I think it's the djinni killing Ahleme," said he.

There was another noise, a roar, like a lion upon a desert horizon. Snow sifted down from the steep walls of the ravine at its note. Then a howl harsher than a falcon's made Taqla's blood curdle. The two, roar and howl, rose together in a cacophony on the pellucid air.

"And that?" she gasped.

"That'll be the other djinni."

"There are *two*?" She struggled from beneath him into a sitting position.

"Apparently so." Rafiq knelt up. "One wanting to sire his children on her, one wanting to stop it." He looked at her somberly. "It's not our problem, Taqla. We're going home and staying alive."

The first thin scream echoed out again.

"We can't just abandon her," Taqla whispered. "Not now."

Rafiq brushed her cheek with his fingers.

"They'll tear her in half." Taqla scrambled to her feet. "Come on. We have to try to save her at least."

He sucked his cheeks but nodded and joined her standing. "How do we get there?"

"Like this," she said, gritting her teeth and stepping away to give herself room. Then she changed shape. Not smaller than her own form this time, but much bigger. It didn't hurt so much as shrinking herself, but it hurt enough to make her cry out. The sound was musical as it left her throat. She shook out her copper-colored feathers and clawed at the snow, a perfect facsimile of the Senmurw bird.

"In the name of God!"

"Get up on my back," she fluted, "and hold tight."

Rafiq shut his sagging jaw and waded forward, climbing up between her wings as she stooped to make it easier. Taqla felt his hands tugging the feathers of her neck uncomfortably, but her Senmurw muscles took his body weight easily enough—at least until she spread her wings for flight. Then she realized what an effort it would be to carry him too, but she launched herself into the air, her wings and chest labouring, and he clung with legs and hands to her feathered body as they gained height in great lurches.

"Taqla—by Iblis's balls—be careful!"

"Just hold on!"

She'd decided on this form, thinking they'd need to spy out the situation from a safe distance, but almost immediately it became clear what they were up against. Boiling out of the air above the insane glass palace came two huge forms, taller than minarets and trailing silken streamers like banners of war—a djinni and a djinniyah. He was as blue as the ocean and she as white as snow, but both were vast, with a multitude of arms, some bearing huge weapons with which they struck at each other, some armed only with savage claws. Their faces were twisted with fury—twisted to the extent that they were no longer human but tusked like boars, their jaws opening to reveal scarlet tongues as forked and sinuous as the tongues of serpents.

Where they took hurt, they bled yellow flame.

Taqla, breasting a rising crest of air and letting it take the strain of flight, stared, almost mesmerised by the two combatants. She couldn't imagine getting involved in that fight. It would be as futile and senseless as coming between two thunderstorms. But Rafiq thrust his head close to her neck and shouted over the roar of the battle, "Down there—on the left of the palace!"

He was right. A figure too insignificant for her to have noticed, human in size and coloring, hung from one of the great glass petals like a dewdrop from a spider's web. And it was screaming, its thin cry audible in a lull during the cacophony of the djinn. Taqla angled toward it, scooping the air with her great wings. Her eyesight in this form was as sharp as any bird of prey's. She saw clearly that the figure was identical to the girl who had accosted Rafiq on the hillside, her bare legs kicking over the frosty void. Lithe and near naked, she was clinging with both hands to a length of yellow silk looped over a great tongue of glass. If she let go she would fall—she was hanging over the snow-filled ravine, but almost certainly the height would be enough to kill her.

"Ahleme!" called Rafiq, though his words were snatched away by the wind of their flight. "Hold on!"

But *almost certainly* was not good enough for the djinniyah, it seemed. Just as Taqla and Rafiq wheeled within hailing distance of the girl, a huge white hand swept down from the sky and scooped the girl up. The djinniyah shrank to less than a third of her previous size, and as the djinni flailed at the thin air she had previously occupied, shot skyward with her prisoner in one fist. There was no way Taqla could keep up, but she swooped between the rose-pink arches and started to spiral, trying to gain height. The blue djinni roared with rage and shrank too, hurtling upward on the pale one's heels. His huge fists caught at her but she dodged, her limbs flickering like flame in and out of sight, and even when he grasped at her, she seemed to melt to shreds in his fingers. Against the cloudless sky they zigzagged back and forth, their blades flashed like lightning, and Ahleme—held in the only limb not engaged in battle—was almost impossible to see as they grabbed and lashed at each other. The two djinn no longer looked human even in form, resembling more closely two twisting multi-limbed centipedes knotted together in a tumbling bicolored tangle.

Then the djinni got the djinniyah by the throat, and this time she didn't slip from his grasp. For a moment they froze, a massive tableaux hanging hundreds of feet up in the air, and then the djinniyah flung her arm out and threw Ahleme away. Her tiny body spun as it fell.

The djinni vanished. One moment he was locked in a grapple with the djinniyah, the next he was beneath Ahleme, reaching out to snatch her from her plunge. He caught her in his right palm and lifted her before his face, unfurling fingers like lapis pillars in order to inspect his prize.

"Ahleme!" he groaned, and the mountain shook.

At that moment the djinniyah fell upon him, her bare feet striking cleanly into the back of his bowed neck. He crumpled and spasmed—letting Ahleme slip from his hand.

Taqla folded her wings and stooped, plummeting toward the mountainside. She had one chance to intercept the girl and that was all. She felt the wind burning her eyes, but she narrowed them and arrowed onward, aiming at a point Ahleme was not at yet. "Catch her!" she screamed, and then the girl's bare limbs flashed into view.

Rafiq caught her. He reached up from Taqla's back and snatched her from midair, and quite suddenly all three of them were falling together. Taqla snapped out her wings and tried to brace them. There was no chance at all that she would be able to fly with that extra weight, but she could try to mitigate their plunge into a glide of sorts. She steered toward the whitest patch of hillside, some detached part of her mind wondering if her bones would splinter before they hit or only after they crashed, and by straining every muscle to the utmost she brought them in at a shallow angle. She couldn't slow, though, because she had no strength to flap. They plowed the snow in a long furrow and then she flipped head over heels, shedding her riders. Taqla blacked out before she came to rest.

She came to in her own form, lifting her head weakly and coughing out the half-melted ice that had crammed her throat. Everything hurt. Every bone in her body was filled with the grinding ache that came as the price of shapeshifting, and for a moment she wished she hadn't regained consciousness. But she hadn't been out long, she realized groggily. Over her shoulder she could see Rafiq climbing to his feet and unsheathing his sword.

The djinniyah landed lightly on the snow, human in shape once more but tall as a citadel wall, and as beautiful and terrible as an avalanche. Her skin was now the color of a winter sky. Her translucent draperies fluttered around her and she drew herself up imperiously, but there was no doubting the punishment she'd taken in the battle. Liquid flame, like lava, oozed down her skin, and one of her eyes was nothing but a whitely burning hole in her face.

"What do you think you're up to?" the giant woman hissed at Rafiq.

"I'll take the girl!" he answered, desperately. "I'll take her away!"

Taqla looked round and saw Ahleme crouched on all fours beyond Rafiq. She must have fallen off first; she looked unscathed. In the distance, the male djinni had collapsed over the spires of the glass palace. He was still twitching.

"Too late, Man of Dirt," the djinniyah boomed, and strode forward to seize the girl. Her hand was as long as Ahleme was. The girl screamed, and Rafiq dived forward and slashed at the huge wrist with his scimitar. The blade flashed in the sunlight, cutting through djinn flesh as if it were smoke—and doing precisely as much damage. She laughed and scooped the girl up. "Try harder, Born of Shit," she sneered, swatting at Rafiq with the most casual of back-handed slaps. It sent him flat, and the djinniyah staggered, coughing. Then she shook herself off and stood, looking down at her captive.

Taqla tried to think of something she could do, but she wasn't sure she had the strength even to stand. Rafiq floundered, trying to regain his feet, and the djinniyah didn't even glance at him.

"Zubaida!" shouted Ahleme. "In the name of God—have mercy!"

"I am being merciful," she answered, her wildly beautiful face drawing to a frown. "On all of us. On the generations to come, both Djinn and Men, that would curse your name."

Taqla braced herself inwardly, expecting the huge woman to crush the smaller one with a squeeze of her hand. But Zubaida glanced upward at the blue sky.

"Yazid!" screamed Ahleme.

Then as Zubaida's bare toes lifted from the unsullied snow, Rafiq lunged forward over and struck at her for a second time, not with his scimitar, which lay sunk in the snow somewhere, but with something much smaller. *The knife*, thought Taqla. The knife that could cut out an immortal heart. Only, Rafiq was incapable of reaching the djinniyah's heart. Even grasping her trailing garments and leaping, he just managed to plunge it into her thigh above the knee.

This time, Zubaida shrieked. Flaming blood squirted across her azure skin, and Rafiq jumped back to stop it splashing on him. But he wasn't fast enough to dodge the sweep of her hand.

She grabbed him bodily and lifted him to her snarling face.

"Son of Shit!" she roared. "I shall hurl you both from the Gates of Paradise itself!"

"In the name of Solomon the Wise," he gasped, "I bind you as my slave."

The Ring of the Djinn ate her. Taqla saw a look of utter horror cross Zubaida's face, and then she shrank to nothing in less than a heartbeat, disappearing completely. Rafiq and Ahleme fell back into the snow, both sinking so deep they vanished from Taqla's sight. She found then that she did have the strength to get up. She staggered over to the hole he had made in the crust and nearly fell over him where he lay.

"Rafiq!"

"I'm all right. I'm all right." He sounded winded and breathless. He held up his arm and she saw the little bronze ring glint on his finger. "Aah— No...I'm all right. I got her, didn't I?"

"Yes." She grasped his wrist and helped him pull himself upright.

"How's the girl?"

Taqla glanced over, just as a shadow fell across the bright day. The mountainside trembled.

"Man of Earth," said a huge voice from behind her, resonant enough to start snowfalls on the higher slopes, "that was my sister that you enslaved. Now you'll die."

Chapter Twenty-One
*In which a sorceress both loses and gains,
and a traveller comes home.*

The djinni Yazid hulked over them, dark blue like a thundercloud. Around his naked feet the snow boiled away to steam. He looked battered, but no less terrifying for that. Flame ran from his nostrils down over his jaw and dripped onto his bare chest.

"Oh," said Taqla in despair. "God is great." There was nothing else to say. They had used their only weapon against the first djinni. The ring could not consume another. This was the end.

Yet Rafiq lurched to his feet. "Do something clever," he muttered as he moved, putting himself between the djinni and her—a futile gesture, she thought, but it touched her.

"I will take you fathoms beneath the earth and leave you to suffocate in darkness," the djinni snarled, stooping. "You will lick the rocks for moisture and die unable to even lift your hands, and you will know what it is to imprison one of the Fire-Born!"

"Do you want me to summon Zubaida from the ring?" Rafiq asked. "One move and I will order her to fight you to the death! Are you ready for more?"

The djinni roared with fury, raising his fists, and rocks slid into the ravine nearby. Taqla felt the ground tremble and wasn't sure that that the whole shoulder of hillside wasn't about to collapse into the valley. Then Ahleme pushed into view, facing the giant.

"Yazid! Please don't! They saved my life!" Her voice was clear, and even dishevelled and gasping, there was a confidence about her that took Taqla aback.

"Zubaida is my sister!"

"She was going to kill me!" Ahleme reached her hands up to him beseechingly. The fact that she was dressed in nothing more than netted pearls did not reduce her appeal. "They saved me! Yazid, please!"

The djinni hesitated, and then diminished in size so that he was only three times as tall as a man and could speak without the air shaking. He levelled a finger at Rafiq. "She has just bought you your life. You will not find me ungrateful. Now release my sister."

"Forgive me, but I don't think so."

"Release her, or I'll change my mind about your continued survival."

"He can't," Taqla said firmly, putting her hand on Rafiq's arm. "The ring binds her for a hundred years. He hasn't any choice."

The djinni's pale eyes widened. "One hundred years of servitude? To...a talking ape?"

"An ape," said Rafiq grimly, "with enough sense not to release someone who was recently trying to slaughter me—and everyone else."

"This is intolerable!"

"Yazid," said Ahleme, cupping her hands between her bare breasts, "please think. If you free her, she'll try to kill me again." With the air of receiving a revelation, she added, "She's already tried it once, in the lake of fire! She hates me, I don't know why. But these people are my friends, they saved my life. I would be dead if they hadn't come for me."

"Your friends? You know them?"

She glanced shyly over her shoulder at Rafiq. "I remember him. He comes from Dimashq."

"Yes," said he. "Her father sent us to find Ahleme. To bring her home." He clenched the hand wearing the Ring of the Djinn. "Father of Storms...it's time to let her go."

Yazid barked derisively at that, spraying fire. "No. She's

mine."

"She's human. She belongs with her family."

"She wishes to stay with me," said the djinni.

Rafiq's eyebrows rose. "Is that true?" he asked, shifting so that he could look Ahleme full in the face, and Taqla thought then that if she hadn't loved him before, she would have loved him for that—that he was asking the girl what she wanted. But Ahleme didn't answer. She folded her arms over her breasts and looked stricken and shamed, catching her lower lip fearfully between her teeth, her lashes lowered. The pearls trembled against her dark skin.

Of course, thought Taqla with a frown, *how could she dare admit to desiring her abductor?* Even if it were true?

"She is mine!" repeated the djinni impatiently. "I found her! I laid claim to her womb so she will bear me a son, a child of power, who'll free all the Djinn from your rings—and your jars—and your dominion."

Ahleme's face crumpled.

"Or enslave you all, forever," Rafiq answered. "Your sister had a point, you know."

"I will be the hero of my people! The father of salvation!"

"Alas, no. She's coming home with us."

"And who are *you* to decide that?"

"I'm the talking ape with the Ring of the Djinn," said Rafiq, quite softly, but his eyes hard.

"You're threatening me?"

"Oh no. I'm simply pointing out that there will have to be some accommodation between us on this matter. We did come a very long way for her."

But Taqla was still watching Ahleme, and she'd seen the look on the girl's face. "You *do* know she's barren?" she asked with a croak.

"What?" The djinni's lancing gaze shifted abruptly to her. She cleared her throat.

"The girl is barren. She won't bear you any child." She ignored both Rafiq and Ahleme and met the djinni's eyes squarely.

"How do you know that?" he roared.

"I'm a sorceress. That's what we do! Reading the fertility of women is the simplest of arts. Besides, use your common sense. Her father was an only son and so was his father. She has no brothers. Her bloodline has dried up. She is almost its last speck."

For a moment a huge silence hung over the mountain slope. Everyone was looking at her. The djinni opened his mouth as if to answer, and Taqla braced herself.

Then the great blue form was gone. There was no warning, no movement, only an absence. He did not so much as leave the snow disturbed.

They were alone.

"Well." Rafiq was the first to speak. "There is no Fate..." he added softly, spreading his hands.

Taqla nodded, her attention elsewhere. Ahleme's full carmine lip was pinched tightly by her perfect teeth, her jaw thrust out, her eyes bright with tears. Her nails bit into the flesh of her upper arms. And her expression—oh, Taqla knew that expression, even if it appeared on the peerlessly beautiful face of a young woman whose lush body looked so warm and smooth that Taqla wanted to warm her cold hands on it. It was the look of a woman who loved but who knew herself unloved in return. Her heart fell. Sighing, the sorceress took off her long-sleeved *aba* robe and went over to wrap it around Ahleme.

"I'm not cold," the girl said in a tiny, tightly controlled voice.

"You're not *dressed*." Taqla turned away, still dizzy with the rush of events, wondering what she should say to the girl—what there was she *could* say. The thin air lapped at her skin like a cold tongue. The sun was so bright that the temperature wasn't unbearable, but her feet in their sandals were painfully cold.

She'd taken no more than a couple of paces before Rafiq came up to her with his own *aba* in his hands and furled the voluminous robe about her, wrapping her in his arms too, and pulling her close to stand on his boot-tops. The garment smelled of him and was warm from his body, and as he kissed her, she felt him flood her senses like a hot tide until the ache in her limbs and the chill of her feet were forgotten. Face-to-face they stood, holding each other, so close that it was easier to taste each other's joy and relief than to see it. Suddenly she wanted him so very much, even there, that her legs felt weak.

"My sorceress," he murmured. He took one of her hands in his, holding it against his chest, and pressed the Ring of the Djinn into her palm. "You do know I've no idea how to use this thing?" he whispered, and she couldn't help giggling. Then, "Your feet must be frozen."

She nodded, slipping the ring back onto her finger.

"Can you command the djinniyah to get us all out safely?"

Taqla winced inwardly. "Not here...and not yet, please. She's going to be...I need to get my strength back." The truth was that she didn't want to summon Zubaida from the Ring before she'd undertaken a great deal more research on the commanding of djinn. Even the most amiable were hard to control, she understood, and this was one who held a personal grudge. It was going to be some time before she dared try.

"Well then." He sat her down in the snow and knelt before her, taking off his headscarf and tearing it lengthways before wrapping her feet and sandals with the strips. "We've got to get off this mountain before nightfall," he said as he worked. "There looks to be a bigger valley down the bottom of this one, a green one. We need to get down out of the snow, or we're in serious trouble."

"Where's my Horse?"

"Well, if it didn't get knocked down the cliff when Zubaida lost her temper the first time, it's still at the top of this face here." He pointed with his chin to his left, along the ridge.

"If we retrieve the Horse, we can all get down into the valley quickly."

"Yes." He lowered his voice and his eyes flicked past her shoulder to where Ahleme stood gazing at the Palace of Glass, motionless. "Is she all right?"

Taqla grimaced, wondering if he knew why the girl was so stricken. But she guessed that in his eyes it was only natural that she be broken with grief. She'd been abducted and ravished and shamed, so a cheery gratitude was hardly to be expected. "After what she's been through?" she asked.

"You should talk to her."

Like I know anything about comforting other women, she thought, aghast. "Yes. Later."

Rafiq nodded and stood, clearing his throat. "Come on then. We need to find the Horse Most Swift. It'll get us all back to Dimashq."

Taqla went over to where Ahleme stood. The girl was blinking back unshed tears and her mouth looked wobbly. *I should hug her*, she thought. *But if we're nice she'll just go to pieces and then Rafiq will have to carry her down this blasted mountain.* "Come on, Ahleme," she said briskly, taking the girl's arm. "We have to walk. We're going home."

Ahleme went where she was pulled. Rafiq cast them both a concerned glance and then led the way, breaking a trail through the unmarked sheet of snow, each footfall creaking. Their shadows stretched out, blue and growing longer. They made slow progress. Ahleme dragged on Taqla's arm and the sorceress was just beginning to think that she would have to change shape into a bird again and fly ahead to the Horse, and was wondering if she had the strength or would simply faint, when Rafiq swore. The two women stopped in their tracks and looked up.

Standing a little way ahead of them was the djinni Yazid. He was only human-sized this time, and much paler—gray marbled with blue—but his fiercely handsome features, set in a stony frown, were unmistakable. His arms were crossed over his bare chest. Taqla noticed abstractly that his wounds seemed to be healing nicely.

Ahleme let out a little whimper.

Rafiq glanced back at Taqla, his eyes wide.

"Ahleme." The djinni's voice was gravelly and stumbling. "I have been thinking. I have decided that even if you cannot bear me a son...though it is grievous to me...yet I do not wish to lose you. I would rather you stayed with me." He lifted his eyes. For someone so big and powerful he seemed to be having a hard time meeting the gaze of a girl. "If you would like that," he added. "If you wish to stay."

Taqla let go of Ahleme's arm. The girl lifted her face to her, eyes wide and questioning.

Taqla shrugged. "Your choice."

"Truly?"

Taqla didn't look to Rafiq for confirmation. "Yes."

With the faintest of smiles just beginning to dawn in her face, Ahleme stepped out toward the djinni. She stopped within a few paces, when she was level with Rafiq, but it was Taqla she turned to address. "Tell my father that I'm well," she said huskily. "And happy. And would love to have his blessing."

"It would sound better from you," Taqla answered. "I'm sure you could find a way to send him a message."

She nodded.

"Hold on," Taqla added, and caught up with them. "Take this," she said in a low voice, slipping the blue scarab on its thong from about her wrist, and wrapping it around Ahleme's instead. "I don't think you'll need it. But...just in case. You only have to hold it between your hands until it warms through, then call for help, and it will fly to seek the person you call upon. I will come find you if you need me."

Rafiq's eyebrows shot up, but he didn't protest.

Ahleme dipped her chin, smiling. Then she turned and ran toward Yazid, and as she ran, she threw off Taqla's robe so that her bare limbs flashed against the snow. Taqla's eyes widened. *Beautiful*, she thought, *but so young. I was never that lovely. Was I ever that young?*

Then Yazid opened his arms and Ahleme threw herself into them, and he swept her up and swung her about and kissed her. Even now that he was mortal sized, she looked tiny against his bulk. He held her in his great grasp for a lingering moment and then with a puff of steam and snow they both vanished.

Taqla put her arm around Rafiq's waist. "You can stop staring now," she said, unable to keep the smirk off her lips.

"I think my eyes have burned out," he said in a small voice. Then he shook himself and turned to her. His eyes looked fine despite his protestations—except that they were haunted by questions. He picked up her hand and slid his finger and thumb around her bare wrist, the one that had worn the scarab. Lifting her hand to his lips, he kissed each cold finger in turn and then folded them in his warm grasp. "That might have been useful to us sometime, you know."

"There's no one out there for me to call on for help."

"There is now." He stroked her straying hair back from her cheek. "Magic or no magic. I promise."

"Let's go," she whispered. She wanted to be somewhere warm enough to allow them to remove at least some clothes.

Rafiq nodded and went to fetch her robe for her, beating out the snow. "So that was it?" he wondered as they turned along the ridge once more. "That was my Fate, I mean? All that way...and we didn't rescue the girl after all."

"The djinniyah would have killed her without us being there. You saved her life."

"So that she could go back to the djinni who'd stolen her?"

"She loves him."

"And who are we to stand in the way of love?" he said, a little wry. "But..."

"Well maybe that's the Fate written for her," said Taqla, "to love a djinni. Maybe that is what God has written, so that they may have this child of power."

"You said she was barren."

"Yes, well..." Taqla pulled an uneasy face. "These things are never certain. There is no Fate but the one given to us by God."

Rafiq shot her a look both shocked and impressed. "You *lied*," he said. "You lied...to a djinni!"

"Is that worse than lying to the Senmurw bird?"

"It might be more dangerous."

Taqla spread her hands. "I thought they both needed to know whether he loved her for her own sake or was using her as a means to his end."

Rafiq rubbed his neck. "What about what Zubaida said, that this son will be a tyrant?"

"Maybe. But any child born may choose a path of evil—should we stop having children because of that? At least this one will be born to parents who love each other. It's a good start."

"Wait... She's actually pregnant, then?"

"Uh-huh. I wasn't lying about the sorceress thing. We're good at that."

He shook his head. "Well, I suppose the djinni will be delighted."

"He'll be in for a shock," she countered. "Their firstborn child, the one who will inherit his power... It's a girl."

Rafiq opened his mouth as if to exclaim, but he never got the chance to say a word. There was a clap like muffled thunder, and the bright sunlit world of the snow-clad mountain vanished. The soft snow under their feet turned to hard earth and they staggered, clutching at each other as they tried to balance. They found they were still on a slope, but a much steeper one, and among trees. It was late afternoon, and they were standing on a hill overlooking a walled city.

"What the...? What? They've moved us!" said Rafiq. Warm air wrapped them like a blanket. A brown veil of smoke and dust hung over the distant rooftops.

"Oh no!" cried Taqla. She whirled round. "My Horse!" she screamed at the slope, the sky, the thinly spaced olive trees with their gray-green leaves and their twisted trunks. "Give me my Horse Most Swift!" But there was no answer, only the noise of starlings flocking overhead. There was no one in sight. She caught her breath and sagged to her knees. Crickets were leaping about in the dry grass. She rammed her fists into the soil and clenched her teeth.

"We're…home."

"What?"

Rafiq sat down rather hard next to her. "That's Dimashq down there—look. See the big mosque? Three minarets—recognize the Tower of the Bride? The Issa Tower? She's sent us home! We're on the Jebel Qassioun, just north of the city."

"My Horse Most Swift," Taqla groaned. "Oh…what am I going to do? I was going to return to the Abu Bahr and bury that temple. How am I going to do that now? How am I supposed to travel anywhere?" She looked around despairingly, but no answer presented itself from the olive grove.

Rafiq held out his hand, saying, "Is this any use to you?" He thumbed off the twist of wire that allowed the wearer to control the Horse Most Swift and offered it to her.

Taqla took the ring but shook her head. She had no idea if she could bring the Horse safely back to her over such an immense distance. She greatly doubted it. When Rafiq put his hand on her shoulder, she shrugged him off angrily. "Don't!" Then her face crumpled. "I'm sorry," she whispered.

She let her shoulders slump and bowed her head, and when he put his arm about her, she leaned into him with a sigh.

It was good to be warm again, she had to admit.

"We should try and get back to the gate before dark," he said after a while. "It's walking distance, anyway."

"A good job," she said, a little grimly.

He ran his fingers over her temple, through the disordered locks of her hair. His touch made her shiver. "You've lost so much on this journey. Your scarab, your Horse, your Bag. And you gave up the Seed of Knowledge. It's a lot for me to make up for. Will you let me try?"

Taqla lifted her head, the line of her mouth softening to a smile. "Every day," she said, and he laughed.

"Come on then." He jumped to his feet and held his hands out to help her up. "We have a judge to find." His eyes twinkled as he added, "Not to mention food. I don't know about you, but

I'm starving."

"I..." she said, and at that moment something rather less than the size of a human head popped out of the air and fell to the ground, rolling against her bandaged feet. It was a ball of silver wire.

"They're not deaf then," said Rafiq, a grin lighting his face.

Taqla picked it up, her eyes welling with tears. "Thank you," she whispered happily. "Ahleme, Yazid—peace be upon you."

If they heard, they made no sign.

"Well?" Rafiq said expectantly.

"We're not riding to the city," she said, stuffing the ball away into a pocket. "We're walking, we have to be discreet." Anxiety seized her. "Oh—what are we going to tell people? About us? About me?"

"That you are Taqla bint-Umar, and that your father hired me to bring you to him from your mother's people, and that at great risk and with many perils that is exactly what I have done. And that now we will marry."

"I will have to live in my own house. In Umar's."

"If you wish." Rafiq was serene. "There's more than enough of my family crammed into mine anyway. I'll explain to them that Umar is an old man and has no other children. It pleases him to have his only child and his son-in-law live with him."

She smiled. "You've always got a good story to tell."

"This," he said, slipping a hand upon her waist, "is better than any of my other stories. Except for the bit where you sent me away." He touched her lips with the tips of his fingers.

"I won't do that again."

"We really do have to stop shouting at each other, you know."

Taqla nodded. "We do. But I doubt that we're going to. It's going to take us a while to rub the rough edges off each other."

Rafiq took her in both arms. "I suspect you're right. How about if, every time we have an argument, I take you to bed and wrestle your clothes off and pin you down—" his teeth grazed her ear, sending shivers down her spine as he murmured, "—and love you until we're both too exhausted to even speak, never mind fight?" He kissed his way back along her cheek and down to her lips, his own communicating a restless hunger that spoke directly to her own need. His arms tightened, drawing her up against him as he tasted her. The strength in his hard frame made her lightheaded. She felt an infinite landscape of desire open up within her, instantly. It almost shocked her how responsive her body was, and how it seemed to know the ways of coupling so well when she was only just starting on her journey into this new realm.

"What do you think?" he whispered, breaking the kiss and leaving her breathless. He smiled, his eyes dancing with wicked promise.

Taqla didn't answer. She just stared, her brows knotted.

"No? Something wrong?" he wondered.

"Nothing. I'm just trying to think of something to start a row about."

His own brows arched speculatively. "What—right now?"

"Yes," she whispered. "Right now."

He started to grin. "Here?"

She slid her hand down his torso and snuggled it between his legs, finding him already spoiling for battle. "Here. Who's to see? Only...it's so pathetic of me—I can't think of anything to complain about at all."

Rafiq pushed her back into the shelter of the olive tree's canopy. His hands sought within and beneath her clothes, searching out the soft, warm skin that thrilled to his touch. Taqla cried out as he found and captured a nipple between his fingers, and arched her back to push her breasts into his hands. "In that case," he said, pressing her to the gnarled bole, kissing her with hot, devouring kisses, "we'll just have to make up now and fight later."

About the Author

Janine Ashbless is a multi-published author of erotic romance and erotica. Her first book was published in 2000. She's always used elements of fantasy, mythology and folklore in her writing, with occasional forays into horror. She particularly enjoys sneaking references to H. P. Lovecraft into completely inappropriate stories.

Janine loves goatee beards, ancient ruins, minotaurs, trees, mummies, having her cake *and* eating it, holidaying in countries with really bad public sewerage, and any movie or TV series featuring men in very few clothes beating hell out of each other. She's a roleplaying geek and can still sometimes be found running round in the woods hitting other geeks with a rubber sword. It is unlikely she will grow up anytime soon.

Janine lives in Yorkshire, England, with her husband and two rescued greyhounds, and is trying hard to overcome her addiction to semicolons. You can catch up with her by visiting her website at www.janineashbless.com and her blog at www.janineashbless.blogspot.com.

Hope dangles by a silken thread.

A Hint of Frost
© *2012 Hailey Edwards*
Araneae Nation, Book 1

When the head of the Araneidae clan is found poisoned in her nest, her eldest daughter, Lourdes, becomes their clan's new maven. If her clan is to survive, she has but one choice: she must marry before her nest is seized. All she needs is a warrior fierce enough to protect her city and safeguard her clansmen. Such a male is Rhys the Cold.

Born the youngest son of an impoverished maven, the only things Rhys has to his name are his sword and his mercenary reputation. His clan is starving, but their fondness for the flesh of fellow Araneaeans makes them unwelcome dinner guests. Torn between loyalty to his clan and fascination with his future bride, Rhys's first taste of Lourdes threatens to melt the cold encasing his heart.

Amid the chaos of battle, Lourdes's sister disappears and is feared captured. Lourdes and Rhys pursue their enemies into the southlands, where they discover an odd plague ravaging southern clans as it travels north, to Erania. Determined to survive, Lourdes will discover whether she's worth her silk or if she's spun the thread by which her clan will hang.

Warning: This book contains one mercenary hero with a biting fetish, one determined heroine who gets nibbled, and an answer to the age-old question, "What does dragon taste like?" Matricide and sibling rivalry are available upon request. The house special is revenge, best served cold.

Available now in ebook from Samhain Publishing.

www.samhainpublishing.com

Green for the planet.
Great for your wallet.

SAMHAIN
PUBLISHING

It's all about the story...

Romance

HORROR

www.samhainpublishing.com

Lightning Source UK Ltd.
Milton Keynes UK
UKOW031652051012

200096UK00001B/54/P